# MEDICAL
## Pulse-racing passion

**Healing The Single Dad Surgeon**
Sue MacKay

**Redel Doctor's Boston Reunion**
Amy Ruttan

MILLS & BOON

HEALING THE SINGLE DAD SURGEON
© 2024 by Sue MacKay
Philippine Copyright 2024
Australian Copyright 2024
New Zealand Copyright 2024

First Published 2024
First Australian Paperback Edition 2024
ISBN 978 1 038 92164 2

REBEL DOCTOR'S BOSTON REUNION
© 2024 by Amy Ruttan
Philippine Copyright 2024
Australian Copyright 2024
New Zealand Copyright 2024

First Published 2024
First Australian Paperback Edition 2024
ISBN 978 1 038 92164 2

This is a work of fiction. Names, characters, places, and incidents are either the
product of the author's imagination or are used fictitiously, and any resemblance to
actual persons, living or dead, business establishments, events, or locales is entirely
coincidental.

MIX
Paper | Supporting
responsible forestry
FSC® C001695

Published by
Harlequin Mills & Boon
An imprint of Harlequin Enterprises (Australia) Pty Limited
(ABN 47 001 180 918), a subsidiary of HarperCollins
Publishers Australia Pty Limited
(ABN 36 009 913 517)
Level 19, 201 Elizabeth Street
SYDNEY NSW 2000 AUSTRALIA

Cover art used by arrangement with Harlequin Books S.A.. All rights reserved.

Printed and bound in Australia by McPherson's Printing Group

# Healing The Single Dad Surgeon

Sue MacKay

MILLS & BOON

**Sue MacKay** lives with her husband in New Zealand's beautiful Marlborough Sounds, with the water on her doorstep and the birds and the trees at her back door. It is the perfect setting to indulge her passions of entertaining friends by cooking them sumptuous meals, drinking fabulous wine, going for hill walks or kayaking around the bay—and, of course, writing stories.

Visit the Author Profile page
at millsandboon.com.au for more titles.

Dear Reader,

When I decided to write a story about Anna giving up her baby for adoption, it was a no-brainer for Eli to have been adopted when he was a baby. The tension between my hero and heroine would be instant and hard to overcome.

Even when romantic sparks fly between them, they both hang back, with the *adoption* word coming between them. But driven by something deep and meaningful that is beyond their control, Eli and Anna have to find a way forward and let love in forever.

I hope you enjoy their story and how they come to accept their pasts and can let those go to have a wonderful future.

*Sue MacKay*

# DEDICATION

This is for my writing group, without whom I'd go crazy at times. Love you all.

# CHAPTER ONE

'ELI, YOU MIGHT want to hand over the final suturing to your sidekick. Your son's had an appendectomy and been taken to Paediatrics.'

'What?' Surgeon Eli Forrester stared at his friend Duncan. 'Why wasn't I told earlier?' Jordan had had surgery and he knew nothing about it? Of course, he didn't have his phone with him in Theatre so his sister Liz could've rung or texted in that time. 'Who did the op?'

'I did. I was between a rock and a hard place knowing you'd want to be with him and that you were in the middle of a very difficult surgical procedure. I couldn't dither though, as the appendix was close to bursting.'

Eli shuddered. His boy had had surgery and he hadn't been there for him. He couldn't blame Duncan for his decision. He'd been doing a three-hour op that had taken all his focus and could not have been interrupted without serious consequences for the patient. But Jordan had been under the knife and he hadn't even known.

It would've been a huge distraction. He knew that and respected his friend's decision. But he was a dad first and foremost. His gut squeezed painfully. 'I'm glad it was you,' he conceded. If he'd had a choice of surgeon, Duncan would've been the man.

'Jordan came through it fine and is recovering as he should. So get out of here, and go be with him.'

Already peeling his gloves off shaky hands, Eli turned to the surgeon who'd been with him throughout the procedure. 'You okay with finishing off?' He had no concerns that the guy wouldn't do a good job.

'Try stopping me. Your son needs you.'

He was already halfway out of the room and answered over his shoulder. 'Thanks.' Why hadn't Liz called him the moment she suspected something? She didn't work Mondays and would've been giving Jordan her undivided attention. When had she noticed Jordan had abdo pain? She'd had him at her place since seven that morning so surely there'd been some indicators? Though with Jordan having Down syndrome it wasn't always easy to understand what he might be carrying on about, or if he even was.

The lift up to the children's ward took for ever. 'Should've taken the stairs.' If Jordie was anything like his usual self he'd be restless and demanding to get out of bed, but hopefully he'd be half asleep from the after-effects of anaesthetic.

'Leanne, how's Jordan?' he asked the nurse sitting at the main desk when he raced into the ward.

'He was grizzly and yelling for you, but Anna's calmed him down so he's happy at the moment. And fighting going to sleep.'

Anna. The nurse everyone adored. Jordan wouldn't be any different. Hell, when she wasn't being sharp with him, he was attracted to her and that was saying something. Sometimes he had to turn his back on her before he came out with something like, 'How about joining me for lunch?' Keeping his head on straight and squashing any random feelings for a woman was imperative to protecting his son—and himself.

'Anna's stayed on after her shift ended to sit with Jordan as we're one nurse down at the moment.'

No wonder she was so popular. Didn't she have a family to go home to? 'What room?'

'Three.'

'I'll be with Jordan from now on.' He spun around and headed to room three. He had to see Jordan, hold him, to reassure him—and himself—that everything was all right, though it sounded as if Anna had beaten him to it. He'd stay the night as his son would likely wake up and panic when he found he wasn't in his own bedroom. Now he really and truly understood the fear his younger patients' parents went through.

Striding into room three, Eli took in the scene before him. Nurse Anna was sitting on the edge of the bed reading a story in a soft, seductive voice, her deep red hair in its usual neat plait lying down the centre of her back. He felt a tingle of something alien. Lust? Attraction? Hardly. Though he'd often felt the same sensation when he'd been too close to this particular nurse while discussing a patient. So far he'd always managed to move on and ignore the way she did that to him, but it was getting harder by the week.

Jordie appeared mesmerised by Anna, taking in every word as though she were handing him his favourite chocolate biscuit. Eli's heart stumbled. This was getting too much. Without knowing it, Anna was pushing too many of his buttons to ignore. But he had to. It was the only way to be safe. Approaching the bed from the opposite side to where Anna sat, he found a smile. 'Hey, Jordie. How's my boy?'

'Daddy,' Jordan shrieked. 'Nurse Anna's reading my favourite story.' The words tumbled out of his mouth in such a hurry Eli wouldn't have understood them if he weren't used to the speech challenges that came with his son's Down's.

'Aren't you lucky?' Hunching down, he carefully wrapped his arm around Jordan's tiny frame and hugged him as close as he dared, mindful of the abdominal wound, while desperate to hold him in tight against his chest. Brushing a light kiss on top of his head, he felt the tension he'd been carrying from the moment Duncan had told him about the op start to fade. 'Thank you for staying on, Anna. It means a lot.' She really didn't have to. 'Jordan can get distraught when confronted with a new situation and this in particular would've been very scary for him.'

'No problem. He was quite wound up and calling for you so I figured I'd see what I could do to help settle him down. Seems he likes stories about puppies.'

'His favourite at the moment.' Eli sat on the bed, arm still around Jordan, trying to ignore Anna's caring smile directed at Jordan and not succeeding. He focused on his boy. 'You probably need to get some sleep now, matey.'

'No. I've been sleeping lots.'

True, but the last thing the staff wanted was Jordan when he got overtired and refused to sit still for even a minute. So far he had the room to himself, another perk of being a surgeon's son. 'I'm going to stretch out here with you.' He'd have to try and sort out some time off tomorrow.

It wouldn't be easy with a full operating schedule but hopefully his colleagues would step up as they usually did for each other.

'He's calmed down a lot and there've been a few yawns he's tried to hide so you might get lucky with the sleep idea.' Anna smiled at him this time, and his stomach knotted tighter.

No wonder she was so popular around here if she smiled at everyone like that. Half the male staff must bend over backwards to get her attention. Was she single? Funny that he hadn't considered that before. No wedding ring in sight, but that didn't mean a thing. Most of the staff didn't wear jewellery on duty. Anyway, she could be in a steady relationship. Why was he even wondering about her status now? He wasn't interested. He had Jordan to think about, and that meant protecting him from any woman he got close to who wouldn't give his son all the support he needed. 'Right. Thanks again. I'm sure you want to get home now.' He spoke brusquely in an attempt to cover what he was really feeling.

Anna gave him a sharp look before standing up. 'Goodnight, Jordan. I'll see you tomorrow, buddy.' Then she strode out of the room without a backward glance.

'Jerk,' Anna muttered as she strode to the main desk. Eli Forrester came with a reputation for being blunt. More like rude in her book. They'd had a few run-ins over his terse manner with the nurses. He was a superb general surgeon, especially with children, but he'd never read the manual on being friendly with staff. He seemed to think everyone should toe the line when he was around. Not that that stopped her from taking second glances at him when he was on the ward. Not only was he drop dead gorgeous, but there was something about his aloofness that caught at her and had her wanting to know more about what made him tick—when he wasn't being rude, that was. Though he did thank her for staying on to be with Jordan. *'It means a lot.'* That was a small step towards being friendly, which was probably a one-off.

A picture of his face as he held Jordan and kissed the top of his head made her blink, and filled her with a softness for him she wouldn't have believed possible before now. He'd been abrupt with her, but when it came to his son he was a marshmallow in hiding. He obviously loved that boy totally. As any parent did, or should.

Another image tapped her mind. Eli looked shattered. His face was drawn and his body unusually slumped. According to Leanne, Eli had been doing a complicated operation when Jordan was admitted so it would've come as a shock to learn his son had had urgent surgery for appendicitis. No wonder he looked beyond exhausted. He'd have been in a hurry to see Jordan and make sure his boy was doing okay so he wouldn't have stopped to grab a coffee or something to eat.

How come Eli was on his own with his son? There had been no mention of a mother coming in to be with the boy. Was Eli a solo dad? She didn't know the guy other than as a general surgeon qualified in paediatric surgery who sent a lot of patients to the paediatric ward. Plus the fact he was super sexy—when he wasn't being remote, which wasn't often.

'Hey, you'd better get out of here while you can.' Leanne looked up from the computer on her desk.

'I'm on my way. Mr Forrester says he's staying the night with Jordan.'

Leanne's eyes twinkled. 'Why did you call him Mr Forrester and not Eli as per normal?'

'Because he annoyed me.' His blunt manner when she'd been taking care of his son had got to her. She wasn't asking herself why when it was nothing out of the ordinary.

'I know that's not unusual but he is pretty upset about Jordan having surgery when he didn't know.'

Anna let out a long sigh. 'Yeah, I get it.' Well,

she would if she were a mother with a young child. Mother to her son. Stop it. The pain from having to give her son up for adoption always hovered just below the surface, raising its head at all sorts of moments to distress her. 'Does Eli drink tea or coffee?' She was going to be nice. It wouldn't hurt and who knew? He might be nice back.

Leanne's eyes widened. 'You're going to get him one?'

'Might as well do the decent thing.' As a reward she'd take another look at that long, sexy shape no doubt now sprawled the length of the bed, then go home and forget all about him. Ha!

'I think the answer's coffee, white with one. While you're at it, can I have a black tea? Pretty please?'

'No problem.' Might as well also heat up the pie she'd brought in for lunch and not got around to eating. Eli probably wouldn't be heading out to grab a meal any time soon, if at all. There was a supermarket handy where he could grab something but she'd save him the bother. She laughed to herself. She was stretching the 'be nice to the jerk' thing, but then she was known for helping people out. Today Dr Eli was no different when it came to needing a helping hand.

Ten minutes later, after she'd given Leanne her tea, she walked into room three carrying a tray.

Eli looked up from the story he was reading to Jordan, who appeared to be two breaths away from sleep. 'Thought you'd be long gone by now.' His voice was barely above a whisper, probably hoping not to wake Jordan. His tired gaze went to the tray. 'What've you got there?'

'Coffee, as well as pie and salad. I figured you probably haven't eaten in a while,' she answered just as quietly, handing over the tray.

'What's in the pie?' He was staring at the plate as though stunned. Maybe he was. Did no one do anything as simple as offering him something to eat?

'Are you allergic to any foods, or is there anything you prefer not to eat?' she asked. It was her version of bacon and egg pie with mushrooms, tomatoes, cheese and parsley thrown in.

'No.'

'Then eat and enjoy. It was my lunch I didn't get time to have.' She got the feeling he didn't want to accept her generous offer. Why had she bothered?

'Anna.' He hesitated, which was so unlike Eli that she had to swallow a smile.

She looked directly at him, her heart tightening at the sight of that gorgeous face. 'Yes?'

'Thank you so much. I do appreciate this. I haven't eaten for hours and since I'm staying here for the night I was going to go without till the morning.' No hint of remoteness now. Instead it had been replaced with something akin to friendliness in his face and steady gaze.

Her heart loosened, letting him a little closer than she liked. 'It's nothing fancy, but it'll fill a gap.'

Eli glanced down at Jordan and then back to her. 'Jordie thinks you're the bee's knees, by the way.'

That was one way to get to her, for sure. She adored children. If only she— *Stop right there.* Nothing could ever change the past, or bring her son back to her. 'He's gorgeous.'

'I think so, but then I am biased,' Eli said with the softest, most caring smile she'd ever witnessed from him.

Blimey, if he smiled like that more often he'd have the whole hospital at his beck and call. He'd certainly have her in the palm of his hand, and she didn't like being at the end of anyone's leash. Working alongside him, she often felt a tingle of longing slide under her skin. He was good-looking in an outdoorsy way, with tanned skin and slightly too long dark hair, and legs that ate up distance in a blink. But then he'd say something in his take-no-prisoners tone and the tingle would disappear in a flash, replaced with annoyance that she'd been aware of him as more than a doctor.

'Aren't all parents?' Stupid thing to say. Hers hadn't been. They'd thought she should do absolutely everything their way when she'd screwed up big time by getting pregnant when she was fifteen. But then they'd always put themselves first. Unfortunately she'd had to do as they'd insisted because there'd been no other option if she wanted her child to have a decent life. One that she couldn't have provided by herself.

A shadow crossed his face. 'Most are, I suppose.'

Ouch. Something, someone, had upset him. Had she put her foot in it? She wasn't asking. That'd only lead to another abrupt comment. 'I'm off. See you both tomorrow.' If Eli was spending the night with Jordan then most likely he'd be here when she started her shift at seven. As for bringing him breakfast, forget it. She'd done her good deed for this man. He could fend for himself tomorrow when he'd be in a better space. Wouldn't he?

'Goodnight, Anna.' Her name sounded like molten chocolate on his tongue, something she could all too easily get used to.

Waving a hand over her shoulder, she left the room without a word. It was enough to have him waking her up more than usual. He was certainly a different man around his son—loving and vulnerable. The vulnerability was a surprise. At least, Eli showing it was. Who knew what else lay behind that intriguing face?

So much for thinking she was immune to a sexy man. Immune, or worn down to the point she'd given up trying to find one to fall in love with and have the family she longed for. It hadn't happened so far and she'd just turned thirty-four. Now, whenever she got close to a man, she started getting nervous about sharing what she'd done with her son because twice she'd told the man in her life and been called a selfish bitch and worse. That made it so much harder to be open about her past and upped her insecurities about being good enough for any man who wanted to have a family with her. She *had* given up her son when he was twenty-four hours old. There'd been no choice. Not that that made her accept what she'd done. If she could go back to that day, she knew she'd do it all over again. For her son's sake, not hers.

It had been the right thing to do. Or so she'd kept telling herself ever since, because how else could she get up every morning to face another day? Barely sixteen years old when he was born and with her parents saying they'd disown her if she kept him, she'd had no choice. She was still at school and even if she'd got a job it wouldn't have paid for accommodation and supporting her son. Her heart had been smashed into so many pieces as the nurse took her baby out of her arms. Not all those pieces had found their way back into place. This was why she got so much from being a paediatric nurse. She could care for children, make them smile, and then let them go home to their families knowing she hadn't let them down. She could never make it up to her son, but she could do her damned best to look out for other children.

With an unusually heavy heart Eli watched Anna go. She got under his skin so effortlessly. No denying it. She'd often had him looking at her twice, or feeling out of sorts around her, but exposing his feelings wasn't possible when he had so much to protect. If his boy's mother could walk out of their lives then how could he trust another woman to stay around for them both? He'd always been able to pull on his neutral face and carry on regardless. Not tonight. He could put it down to exhaustion after a difficult day and Jordan keeping him awake half the night before. But really he'd been shocked to learn Jordan had had surgery. That had knocked him off his feet.

He did like how Nurse Anna had made Jordan happy. Anna, the woman off duty, had worked out he wouldn't take the time to get something to eat because he desperately wanted to be with his son so had brought him food and coffee. He liked her very much for that. But that was where it stopped. He wasn't looking for a life-time partner.

*Not true, Eli.*

It really wasn't. For him, falling in love with a wonderful woman to share everything with seemed impossible. Share being the operative word here. Melissa hadn't known the meaning of it. Her pregnancy had been unplanned as they had both still been studying in their respective careers and Melissa had struggled to cope with being pregnant. She'd found it even harder accepting Jordan had Down syndrome. Just before his second birthday she'd asked for a divorce, saying she needed to go offshore to finish her studies in fashion design and that it wouldn't be fair to expect Eli and Jordan to go with her. In other words, she was bailing on her wedding vows *and* her son. One of the upsides was he'd got full custody of Jordan. The other was he'd learnt to be super careful when it came to falling in love. As in it was not happening again while his boy still lived at home, which would be for many years.

He leaned close to Jordie. He loved the little guy so much it hurt. How Melissa could give up her son was beyond him. How could any mother? Or father, come to that. He knew too well how it felt to be abandoned by the one person who should never be able to sever ties with their child. His mother had handed him over to the welfare system when he was six months old because it took too much effort to keep him happy and she had better things to do. He'd been extremely lucky when Jackie and Kerry adopted him. They loved him as much as their two daughters, his adoptive sisters, who'd taken to him just as quickly. He'd grown up knowing he was loved without any boundaries, and always would be. But it still rankled how his birth mother didn't want anything to do with him even now. It wasn't as though he was asking anything of her except to be accepted as a small part of her life.

'That pie's getting cold.' Leanne stood at the end of the bed. 'You won't want Anna to find out you didn't eat it.'

He glanced up at her. 'I was miles away.'

'I could see that. Why don't you sit in the chair while I check Jordan's temperature and vitals?'

Carefully sliding off the bed so as not to disturb Jordie too much, he did as suggested. Savouring the flavours humming across his tongue, he gave a happy sigh. 'This pie's to die for. Did Anna make it?' He'd questioned what was in it and she'd got annoyed. He owed her an apology.

'Probably. She loves cooking. Shh, Jordan. Lie still for me or I'll tickle your chin.'

Jordie's eyes were open and he was staring around as though he'd forgotten where he was. Putting the tray aside, Eli got up and went to hold his hand while Leanne finished the obs.

'All good. I'll give him some more antibiotics when he's due in an hour.'

'Thanks, Leanne. For everything.'

Her eyes widened as though she was unused to him being quite so friendly which, he admitted, was true. He didn't do becoming buddies with his colleagues other than a couple of surgeons he'd known since specialising. He came to work to help patients and then went home to be with Jordan. There wasn't a lot of energy left for anything else.

She said, 'Just doing my job. If you're staying the night then we'd better get a bed in here for you.'

'I'll be fine in the armchair that's across the hallway. I'll haul it in later.' One thing learned along the way to becoming a doctor was sleeping on any manner of furniture. Though it had been a few years since he'd last done that.

'There's a bed that should be in here that the orderly hasn't returned. I'll get it brought up and you cross your fingers we don't get another unexpected wee patient during the night.'

'Can I finish the pie first? Crossed fingers could make for awkward eating and I don't want to waste a crumb.'

Another surprised look came his way before Leanne laughed. 'As I don't want to be the one Anna blames for you not finishing it, I think you'd better get on with the job.'

He couldn't imagine Anna being cross with anyone—other than him. Experience had taught him how it felt when she took offence to his curt instructions. Settling into place beside Jordie, his legs stretched to the end of the narrow bed, he relaxed and enjoyed his meal while thinking about Anna Passau—because it was too easy. She was gorgeous.

Today she'd got under his skin more than ever with how she'd calmed Jordan down, how she'd got him something to eat. Not to mention those damned smiles. He couldn't afford to lose his heart and yet she was making it difficult to remain aloof. He struggled with being let down again after his birth mother and Melissa had each done their number on him. He owned half the marriage break-up because surely if he'd been a good husband she wouldn't have gone? He shouldn't feel like that when his adoptive family had never once let him down, always gave him all the love and support anyone should get from their family, but it was hard to forget how those other two women hadn't cared enough. They'd undermined his belief in himself.

Anna, with her crazy red hair that made his fingers itch at the thought of running his hands over it and her suck-me-in smile that caused his gut to tighten, was a complete turnaround in women for him. Did she have what it took to be that certain special woman? The fact he was even wondering had his toes twitching. He'd have to get back to his usual remote persona tomorrow. Except that felt wrong now. Anna had been nothing but kind and friendly. Even Leanne had laughed with him. Getting onside with the staff could make for happier days at work. He'd learned to be aloof with everyone he worked with after two nurses had continually pestered him for dates and more when they'd heard Michelle had left him. Neither of them had understood the meaning of no and he'd changed his approach to all staff, especially the females.

Putting aside the tray, he turned to study his little man and his heart expanded as Jordie smiled in his sleep. He was a tough wee fella, took the teasing some kids gave him on the chin. He had some good friends who attended the same preschool. Preschool was his dream come true with lots of games to play, books to read, and other kids to run around with. His teacher aide was exceptional in teaching him basic skills with a pen and paper. With lots of help from his family, Eli worked hard to give Jordan the same loving environment he'd grown up in.

The sound of a bed being wheeled along the corridor diverted him. Something he probably needed about now. All this thinking didn't achieve anything but too many questions he had no answers for. Standing up, he went to help the orderly put the bed in place, even though the guy had done it a thousand times before and he was probably getting in the way. Seemed everyone was stepping up to help him. Especially Anna. A grin spread across his face, stretching his lips further than they were used to. Anna was getting to be a pain in the backside with the number of times she popped into his head.

Quite a gorgeous pain though. One he was happy to put up with for now anyway.

# CHAPTER TWO

'MORNING, EVERYONE.' Anna bounced into the ward before seven the morning after Jordan's operation feeling chipper. She loved this job *and* she'd had a good night's sleep despite the exciting interruptions from her brain bringing up images of Dr Forrester. Make that *Mr* Forrester. He wouldn't be pleased with her for calling him 'doctor'. Some specialists couldn't care less, but she didn't intend to find out how Eli felt about that. The fewer grumps from him the better. 'How was the night?' she asked the nurses crowded around the main desk ready to hightail it out of the place asap after the night shift finished.

'Not too bad considering the afternoon you had yesterday,' Debbie answered for everyone. 'No new patients and apart from the girl in the car crash yesterday morning the rest were relatively quiet. Jordan Forrester did wake a couple of times grizzly as all be it, but his dad quietened him down in no time at all.'

'The father's touch,' Anna said. 'You can't beat it.' Except maybe with a mother's touch. *Stop it, Anna. Jealousy won't get you anywhere.* 'Is Eli still here, or has he gone to get some breakfast?'

'I'm showered and dressed for work, which is a lightened workload thanks to my colleagues pitching in to take over some of my minor cases so I can be with Jordan on and off during the day. I'm about to go to the café along the road for a full breakfast,' answered the man himself as he appeared in front of her. He looked a lot more relaxed this morning. Gone were the lines around his eyes and those shoulders were back in place filling his shirt to perfection.

Her heart did a little skip. 'You obviously slept all right despite where you were. How's Jordan doing this morning?'

'Ready to get up and tear the place apart.' Eli laughed. Laughed, as in really let it out.

Unheard of. By her, at any rate. 'I'll be with him shortly.'

'He's asking where you are, and why can't he go to preschool today.' The laughter faded from Eli's eyes. 'Do you have any answers for that one? It must be a question you hear often in here.'

'I'll come up with something. If I'm working

with him, that is.' She turned to Leanne, who'd just arrived, looking flustered. 'You okay?'

'I'm good. Luca didn't want to go to kindy and we had a bit of a battle when I tried to get him out of the car.' She shook her head. 'I won in the end. Bribery works wonders sometimes, though now I've got to remember to buy a book about policemen at the end of the day.'

'Sometimes there are no other choices when it comes to getting them to do what's necessary,' Eli said.

Crikey, the guy *was* opening up. Could be due to the fact he'd spent a night in the ward with his son and got to see first hand how hard they all worked and the endless care they gave the kids? But he'd know that. It was more likely that he had a kind, soft side that his son brought out too easily. Another side to him that lifted her already happy spirits and made her take another, longer look at him. He really was something else. 'What do you bribe Jordan with?' she asked, fully expecting him to not answer.

'Chocolate fish.' He smiled, then shrugged. 'Hey, it works at those times I've run out of patience and want to get on with preparing dinner or running his bath.'

'I bet it does. I'd probably behave for a choc fish. No, make that a bag of them.'

Another laugh came her way. It was as though

they were the only ones here, but they weren't. Looking around, she drew a breath. Everyone was watching them as though something funny was going on. So she laughed because, damn it, if this wasn't funny then what was? Eli acting relaxed with her was new. Face it, being relaxed with all of the nurses was new.

'Okay, everyone, let's get the day under way.' Leanne had pulled on her sensible hat but there was a cheeky glint in her eyes as though she thought there was more going on between Anna and Eli than was anywhere near close. 'Fill us in on the night and get out of the way. Eli, you're not needed for this. I take it you're up to date with Jordan?'

'I am. He'll be restless now that he's feeling a little better. Just warning you,' he added with a look of worry in those grey eyes that Anna knew never missed a thing.

'We've dealt with similar situations. We'll manage with Jordan,' Anna told him. 'Though his abdomen will be tender for some time to come he'll be fine, promise.'

'I'm sure he will.' Eli didn't look as though he believed himself.

She'd make sure the boy was happy and comfortable in between looking after other wee patients. Moving closer to Leanne, she listened as their patients were assigned to various nurses, and sighed happily when Jordan was given to her. The little guy had tweaked something that had her wanting to spend more time with him. Just like his dad. Careful. That couldn't happen. Any sort of relationship with a surgeon she worked with could only lead to problems as far as she could see.

She'd dated a paediatrician once and when he'd called it quits after learning she'd given a child up for adoption he'd made sure everyone knew that she wasn't good enough for him. Another nurse who'd also had a similar nasty experience with the jerk about something in her past soon made it known who wasn't good enough and it wasn't Anna or her. Anyway, she wasn't going to dive into anything more than a possible friendship with Eli, and even that was unlikely as everything would settle back to normal once Jordan was discharged and Eli wasn't worried about him.

'Anna, Louisa Crane's coming up from ED shortly. I'd like you to take her too. We'll put her in with Jordan as there aren't any other beds available until the specialists have done their rounds so it works quite well for you.'

'No problem.' Louisa had cystic fibrosis and was a regular here. On past experience they knew she'd be quiet until the treatment kicked in to help her breathing and then she'd want to read stories to Jordan. Though that could take a while, depending on how sick she was. 'How bad is she?'

'Lung infection causing strain on her heart.'

So she wouldn't be reading any stories today. Hopefully Jordan wouldn't be too active or they'd have to look at shifting one of them to another room. 'I'll go see Jordan.' Get the day started.

'Nurse Anna, I'm all better,' Jordan shouted when she walked into his room.

'Jordie, stop shouting. You're in hospital and other kids are sick,' Eli said sternly from the other side of the room.

Anna wasn't prepared for the sudden flash of heat in her veins. Looking across to Eli, she was confused. He made her light-headed and still she was wary. What was going on? 'Th-thought you were going to breakfast.'

'On my way. Jordan has been talking to his grandmother on my phone.'

'Granny's coming to see me today.' Jordan bounced up and down on the bed, then cried out. 'Ow, that hurts.' His hand went to the surgical wound on his abdomen.

'You have to stop moving around so fast.' Anna took his hand away and lifted the pyjama top. 'If you don't, you'll hurt yourself some more.'

'I don't like hurting.'

'I bet you don't. I'm going to put a new bandage on here and then you can have some breakfast.'

'What do I get?'

'Let's wait and see. It's a surprise.'

'Careful,' warned Eli. 'He's a picky eater.'

Like his father? she wondered, thinking how he'd asked what was in the pie she gave him last night. 'I'll sort it.'

'By the way, that pie was delicious. Thank you for sharing.'

She hadn't had a mouthful of that particular pie. 'You got the lot.'

'I know.' His mouth twitched. 'What did you have instead?'

She'd been having him on. 'The second pie I made at the same time. No point in only making one.'

'You enjoy cooking?'

'I get a kick out of it. So many different recipes to follow—or not.' Though not having someone to share the results with often made her efforts seem pointless. She was popular around here for the cakes and biscuits she brought in for them to try whenever she had a cooking spree, which was quite often. Luckily her hips didn't seem to mind being loaded with yummy treats.

'I'd better get a move on or there won't be

time to check up on Jordan before I scrub up for surgery.'

Why did that sound sexy? Scrubbing up in preparation for going into Theatre had to be the most tedious process out there, nothing to do with heating blood or super-active heart rates. But still, the thought of Eli doing that was winding her up something terrible. Focusing on her little patient, she waited for her heartbeat to return to normal. 'Let me have a look at your tummy, Jordan.'

He'd pulled his top down. 'No. It hurts.'

'That's why I want to see it.' She didn't think there'd be anything wrong but there was only one way to be certain. Gently extricating the pyjama top from Jordan's fist, she lifted it up and pulled his bottoms down enough to expose the covered wound. 'I'm going to remove this,' she reaffirmed as she tapped the dressing.

'Why?'

'You need a clean one.'

'Why?'

'So you get better faster.'

'How?'

Did this kid ever stop with the questions? 'There's a cut in your tummy. It will be getting back together and we need to help it by keeping the dressing clean.' Glancing around, she saw that Eli had left them. Or left her to the list of questions. He'd probably known they'd been coming. Back to Jordan, she grinned. 'You'll have a little line there to show your friends. They'll be jealous.'

'Yes.' He fist-pumped the air. 'I like that.'

Hopefully she'd talk him into eating his breakfast just as easily.

When he returned from breakfast, Eli found Jordan sitting up in bed looking at a picture book, a wide smile on his face. 'Hey, man, you look happy.'

'Nurse Anna got me this book out of a cupboard. She told me it's the best one about elephants.'

Again Nurse Anna to the fore. 'What else did she tell you to do?'

'I had to eat the cornflakes and peaches first.'

*Good for you, Anna.*

Bribery wasn't off her list any more than his, he thought with a grin. Of course, if she were a parent, she'd be a dab hand at getting the result she wanted. Did she have any kids of her own? 'And you did.' Jordan wouldn't be holding the book otherwise.

'I have to look after my tummy. Dad, did you know I've got a line on my skin? Nurse Anna told me. I'm going to show it to everyone when I get to school.'

The things that made kids happy. 'It's called a scar.' Hopefully a very small one. Though at the moment, Jordan would no doubt be happy if it was large. Nurse Anna had a way of making everything come up smelling of roses when it came to his son. Something to be aware of. He didn't want Jordan to think she was becoming a part of their lives, as he often did with people he liked a lot. Sometimes that caused problems when he realised they weren't going to stay around. With a bit of luck and all going to plan, he'd take Jordan home tonight and then Anna wouldn't feature in Jordan's life any more. Except *he'd* have to accept she'd still be here, working with some of his patients, filling the air with the scent of vanilla and reminding him of the cookies his mother baked for him as a kid.

'Can you read to me?' Jordan asked, hope in his face.

He hated to disappoint him, but he had no choice. 'Sorry, Jordie, but I've got to start work. I'll be back to see you later.' First up was a thyroidectomy, then, because Duncan had taken his next patient, he had a break to be with Jordan before his next scheduled op at eleven.

Jordie's face screwed up with disappointment. 'That's not fair.'

'You know I have to help people get better.' He was always explaining how he had to work and that not all his time could be spent with Jordan, but, like most kids, Jordie always tried to persuade Eli to hang around for a bit longer.

'Like Nurse Anna does?'

Time to get out of here. 'Yes.' Nurse Anna had certainly turned his son's head. He hoped she didn't do the same to him. He hadn't been able to put her out of his mind all night. He only hoped that was because he'd been in here where she worked, and not because of the way she distracted him and heated his body all too quickly with little more than a glance. 'See you later, boyo.' He brushed a kiss on his son's head. He was the luckiest man alive, having Jordan in his life. Thankfully everything had gone well yesterday, and they'd soon be back to normal.

The sound of Anna laughing reached him as he walked to the lift. Certain muscles tightened and his mouth tipped up into a cheerful smile. Her laughter made him light-hearted and it hadn't even been directed his way.

The lift pinged and the door slid open.

Stepping inside, he pressed the floor for Theatre and turned to lean back against the wall.

'Wait.' Anna flew through the closing doors and tapped floor two before spinning around and colliding with him.

Eli grabbed her to keep her on her feet. 'Careful.'

She looked up at him. 'Oh, Eli, sorry.'

'Where are you off to in such a hurry?' He didn't remove his hands from her arms, just absorbed the warmth in his hands and gazed down into those suck-him-in eyes that had followed him into sleep last night.

'Pharmacy.' She sounded surprised, as if she'd forgotten what she was doing. Her eyes widened, but she didn't pull back.

He could feel himself falling into her gaze. 'Anna.' Her name roared through his head. Dropping his hands, he stepped back, bumped up against the wall. Anna was beautiful inside and out. And waking him up fast. Too fast considering it was only yesterday Jordan had his surgery and he hadn't had time to think about what was going on. Yet his body was zinging with lust. It took all his self-control not to reach out and haul her against him, to kiss those sensational—

Ping. The doors began sliding open.

He straightened instantly, and drew a lungful. What the hell had he been thinking? They were at work. Nor were they an item. Anna might be out-of-this-world attractive but hell. He slammed fingers through his hair.

*Get back on track, go see some patients, forget the heat firing you up.*

That easy? Hardly. Worse, now he knew she was even more kind and generous than he'd realised. Remember he had a son to protect, as well as a heart to keep safe.

Anna charged out of the lift without a backward glance.

'See you later,' he said under his breath as she disappeared along the corridor and other people stepped into the space she'd vacated. No one took his breath away as Anna suddenly did. No one. Pulling on his professional face, he leaned against the wall and waited impatiently for the lift to drop another level so he could get on with his day without any distractions of the bewildering, taking-over-his-rationale kind.

*Damn you, Nurse Anna. You're something else, and I'm getting rattled by how easily you're undermining my strength to remain aloof when it comes to women.*

Ping.

Thank goodness for something. He stepped around people who weren't budging and made his way out of the lift and along to Theatre, to work, his go-to place when he couldn't cope with problems.

*Anna's not a problem.*

Too right she was if she could trip him up so easily.

'Morning, slow coach.' Phil, the anaesthetist he was working with, tapped the computer screen when Eli joined him in their theatre unit all scrubbed up. 'Millie Lewis is prepped and ready to go nigh-nigh soon as you're ready.'

'It was hard to leave Jordan.'

'You're fine. Millie was only brought in two minutes ago. Just like winding you up.' Phil was looking at him as if there were a wart growing on his chin. 'How is the wee lad?'

'Bouncing around too much but Anna seems to quieten him down easily enough.'

Phil laughed. 'No surprise there.'

Seemed Anna's reputation as a superb nurse was well known. Time to focus on the operation and forget her. 'I'll talk to Millie now.' The teenager was having a thyroidectomy and was lying on the table a few feet away, no doubt already dozy from the sedative she'd have been given after Phil talked to her. 'Morning, Millie.'

The girl dragged her eyes open. 'Hello, Doctor.'

'Looks like you're ready for this. Any last-minute questions?' Always a tricky one but he liked his patients to feel confident about going under the knife. As much as possible anyway.

'None. Just get it over, will you?'

'Phil, I think that's your call to give Millie something stronger. I'll talk to you later, Millie.' He waited until the anaesthetist gave the nod that she was properly under and then picked up the scalpel. 'Everyone ready?'

Nods all round gave him the go-ahead. 'Right, let's do this.'

\* \* \*

Prescription in hand, Anna took the stairs back to the ward to avoid bumping into Eli again if he decided to check on Jordan before going to Theatre. Knowing her luck he'd be in the same lift if she pressed the button and right this minute he was the last person she needed to see. He'd already pressed her buttons, which was left-field considering how, until now, she'd always managed to keep a lid on the flare of excitement she often felt when he was around. And all the moments when he annoyed the hell out of her with his aloofness.

Yet back in the lift, she'd wanted to lean into him, to touch him, feel that amazing body against her. Talk about losing her mind.

Now what? It wasn't as if she could avoid Eli. She couldn't spend her shifts watching out for him and then hiding in the linen room until he left the floor. So back to ignoring the way he got her in a tizz and carry on as though he didn't interest her one little bit. These sensations he caused meant nothing. Just focus on the fact they were doctor and nurse in the same hospital. Doctor and nurse! Ha. Sounded like a line for a romance novel.

Except her romance couldn't include falling for a man who had a son because of her history of two relationships going pear-shaped when the man involved learned about how she gave up her baby. Neither of them had accepted she'd had no choice. She had no doubt the same would happen if she got close to Eli and told him her story. Losing Eli if they were involved would be bad, but it would be dreadful to hurt innocent little Jordan, who'd have no say in the matter. Of course, she was getting ahead of herself, something she didn't normally do. They weren't in any type of relationship, but this was a big indicator that she was already caught up in his aura. She hadn't had thoughts like this about any man in a long time.

'You look like someone stole your lunch out from under your gaze.' Leanne laughed when she reached the ward.

The problem with best friends was they knew her too well. 'If only it was that simple.' She said that? Once more it showed how much Eli got to her. 'I had to come up the stairs as the lifts were busy.'

'Try again. You take the stairs at least once a day, usually more often.'

Anna said nothing, instead picked up a file and pretended to read it.

'Nothing to do with Dr Delicious by any chance?'

'Why would it be?' she snapped, a dead giveaway if ever there was one.

Leanne laughed again. 'Knew it. You'll have to work harder at keeping a straight face if this is going to continue.'

Dropping onto a chair, Anna huffed out the air stalled in her lungs. 'It's not.' Another give-away. Talk about losing grip on her sanity. All because of a sexy man in boring scrubs with the most intense grey eyes that saw far too much for his own good. Or hers. 'He's too aloof for me.' That intense way he'd looked at her in the lift gave her the shivers. Hot shivers full of need.

'Eli keeps everything close to his chest. We've all commented over time about how he never gives anything away about himself. I reckon it's because we had Jordan in here that he's let go a little,' Leanne commented. 'How good you were with his little boy did get to him and probably helped him relax a bit. It was obvious he liked how you made Jordan feel comfortable. He's been watching out for you ever since.'

She did not need to hear that. It only intensified her thoughts about him. 'I'll have whatever you're on, Leanne, because that sounds like a load of drivel even to me.' But if she was right, then she might be willing to look a bit deeper into what made the man tick. Take a risk? When it could, and most likely would, turn to rubbish and make life very awkward here. Because no matter what happened in her personal life she was not leaving this job. She loved it, loved help-ing other people's children get better, loved mak-ing them laugh when all they wanted to do was cry. It went a little way to atoning for letting her son go.

'He's a great guy.' Leanne was still laughing but there was sympathy in her eyes. 'Why not get to know him better? You deserve a break, Anna. You should have someone to go home to at the end of the day. Someone to share more than work with.'

Another problem with besties was they didn't know when to shut up. 'Stop right there. I'm not ready.' Which was a lie. She was past ready, but hadn't found a man who'd accept her for who she was, and not what she'd done. Throw in that she didn't believe she deserved such happiness when she'd let her son go and a happy ever after was never going to happen. But could it be time to move on? Could she do it? A picture of Eli as he'd gazed at her in the lift filled her head. Why not try? Simple. Getting hurt again wasn't an op-tion. There were only so many times her heart could take a hit, and she'd already done them.

'You're well and truly ready.' Leanne picked up the prescription from where Anna had plonked it. 'Now, let's get back to work.'

Relieved, Anna headed over to see an eleven-year-old girl who'd had a plate attached to a broken ankle yesterday. 'Hey, Jenna, how's things?'

'Sore. The physio made me do exercises and they hurt.'

Back to normal. This she could deal with. Way better than spending minutes in a lift with Dr Sexy. Damn it all. Because she did feel disappointed that nothing could come of these new sensations Eli caused. Nothing. It was too risky.

# CHAPTER THREE

ON FRIDAY A loud bell buzzed indicating an emergency. Eli leapt up from the computer where he was going through patient notes. 'Room four,' he said loudly as he sped down the ward so anyone around might hear and come to help.

Leanne was right beside him. 'We put an eleven-year-old boy in there two hours ago after he came back from Theatre where he had fluid drained off his lung. But there are two other boys in that room too.'

When he entered the room the first thing he saw was Anna desperately holding down a boy fighting to get off the bed. 'What's going on?'

'Adverse reaction to something,' Anna said through gritted teeth. 'He's been fighting me for a few minutes and I had to get one of the other boys to press the call button as I needed both hands here,' she gasped.

He moved to the other side of the bed and placed his hands on the boy's shoulders. 'Here, let me take over.'

'Anthony, can you hear me?' Anna asked, still holding down the boy. 'He won't answer any of my questions. I'm not even sure he *can* hear me.'

Typical for a seizure, which was what this looked like. 'What analgesic was administered after the procedure?' Pain killers didn't usually have this effect but he knew it wasn't always the case. The boy's breathing was shallow and rapid.

Anna told him and added, 'He's also on another medicine for hyperventilation.'

Great. 'Leanne, get the defib just in case.'

'Onto it.'

Anna placed a hand on Anthony's wrist, tried to take his pulse. 'Not easy when he's pulling and shoving. Calm down, Anthony. We're trying to help you.'

'Sweat's pouring off him. Oof.' An elbow slammed into Eli's side, knocking the air out of his lungs.

Anna reached for the boy's arm, grabbed it and held tight. 'He has no idea what's going on, does he?'

'Afraid not. This is severe.'

'I didn't get a proper pulse reading but it's rapid.'

'Exactly as I expected. Damn.'

Anthony had suddenly gone limp. His mouth hung open and his chest was still.

'No pulse,' Anna reported calmly.

Clenching his hands together, Eli placed them on the boy's chest and pressed hard. One, two. 'Where's that defib?' Three, four.

'Coming through the door.' Anna stood ready to breathe into the boy's lungs when he reached the number of compressions required.

'Here we go.' Leanne placed the machine on the stand and handed Anna the leads to place on Anthony's chest.

'Twenty-nine, thirty,' Eli called calmly.

Quickly setting the leads aside, Anna drew a breath and exhaled into Anthony once, then again before straightening up and placing the tabs from the defib on the exposed chest. Nodding at Leanne, she said, 'Ready.'

'Stand back,' Leanne replied.

Eli stopped the compressions and moved back one step, ready to go again if the electrical current didn't start Anthony's heart. 'Ready.'

The boy's body jerked upward, dropped back onto the mattress. The defibrillator showed a green line moving up and down.

Relief poured through Eli. 'That was close.' Having to continue compressions on a kid was awful. Their ribs often cracked under the pressure and instinct said go lightly even when medical training said the opposite. 'Right, let's see where we're at with this guy.'

Anna was already taking his pulse, and there

was a relieved look on her face. She didn't mess around for sure. When she saw him looking at her, she nodded. 'Steady and stronger than it was. Still fast but nothing like before.'

'His chest's steadier too. His skin's hot.' He took the temperature gauge Anna held in her free hand and placed it in Anthony's ear. 'Thirty-eight point three. Who's his specialist?'

'Hillary. She's got appointments at Outpatients now.'

'I'll give her a call.' It wasn't his place to take over treating Anthony now that they had him under control. 'He needs sedating and no more of the drugs he's had.'

Anna's nod was sharp, but he didn't take offence. She'd know all that but accepted it was his place to point it out. 'I'm not leaving his side for a moment. Fingers crossed he doesn't have another seizure.' Her smile was sad. 'The poor kid. That was scary.'

'You all right? He fought hard when you were trying to hold him down. You didn't get a whack too?'

She shook her head, making her ponytail swish across her back.

His fingers tingled as he imagined those red curls spilled over her skin. *Down, boy.*

'No. You were the unlucky one there.'

'It wasn't too hard. I got more of a surprise

really.' There'd probably be a bruise to remind him to be careful around out-of-control patients. 'I'll be back once I've talked to Hillary.' Heading out of the room, he refrained from turning around for another look at Anna. He was at work, and the emergency might be over, but there were still things to be done for Anthony. The kid could have another seizure any time. Though he doubted it would happen, this was the medical world and no one knew exactly what was coming at any moment.

When he returned to room four and saw Anna gently wiping down Anthony to remove the sweat, a flutter of longing caught at him. This was how she'd been with Jordie the other night. So gentle and caring. He wanted a part of that. Pulling up sharply, he smothered a groan and said, 'Hillary's on her way up.'

'Good.' Anna lifted her eyes from Anthony and looked directly at him. 'He's a lucky boy.'

*Because you helped save him.*

'Yes, he is.'

Rubbing her lower back at the end of night shift over a week after she and Eli had worked to save Anthony's life, Anna sighed. 'Glad that's over.' It had been a busy night on the ward with a boy coming from emergency surgery to his abdomen after being in a car accident, followed by another boy being admitted with both his arms badly fractured after falling out of a second-floor window. All a bit much to cope with.

'Get out of here while you can,' Gabrielle said. 'I've read your notes, and don't need any further explanations.'

Anna gave the other nurse a tired smile. Thank goodness for something. Throw in that it was Saturday and she had two days off and things could start looking up. 'Hope your shift's not too stressful.' She'd say break a leg, but was afraid of tempting fate. 'See you. I need some food to shut up my grumbling stomach.' She turned and almost walked into Eli. Jerking backwards, she said, 'Oh, hello.'

'Hi.' He caught her arm to steady her, then drew her away from everyone else. 'Glad to hear you're hungry because I'm here to suggest you join me for breakfast at the café down the road.'

Why would he do that when he'd been all but avoiding her since that awkward moment in the lift last week unless a patient was involved? 'Are you sure?'

His mouth twitched in amusement. 'Wouldn't ask if I wasn't.'

Fair enough. But did she want to spend time with him outside work, or anywhere? Sitting at a table together could be tricky. There again, it might help thaw the chill between them and they could get on with being friendly. So, 'I'd like that. Be warned, a piece of toast won't fix what's upsetting my stomach.'

His laugh was light and sensuous, not what she needed if she was going to eat. 'Nothing like a full breakfast to do the job.'

As they rode the lift down to the ground floor, she aimed for light conversation. 'Why are you here this early?'

'I had a patient in General to check on.'

'You knew I was on nights?'

'That's why I'm here to ask you to join me.'

It was starting to sound like a date, except it wasn't one. Couldn't be. Not after how stilted they'd been around one another recently. 'You don't have my number. But then why would you?'

'No reason except I'd like it now. Who knows when I might get the urge to give you a call?' He looked a little surprised at himself.

She definitely was. She'd never have believed Eli Forrester would say something like that if he hadn't thought it through first. Good sign? Had she rattled him a little? Cool. Because he'd done more than rattle her so it was only fair he should suffer too. 'I'll give it to you over breakfast as long as I get yours in return.' Not that she could imagine calling him without good cause. But who knew what that might be? Could be she just wanted to hear his deep, husky voice. Oh, yes.

He smiled at her. 'Deal.'

Now Anna laughed, freely and happily. She was sharing breakfast with a man she'd never have believed would want a bar of her. He was so polished and kept to himself so she couldn't imagine she'd be his type in any way. She might be exhausted but this was giving her new energy.

'I want to thank you for that dinner you gave me the other night,' Eli told her, dampening her excitement a tad.

'You don't owe me for that.'

'It's an excuse, all right?'

An excuse for what? He didn't need one. But then she didn't exactly put it out there how attracted to him she was. That would be beyond stupid. Back to feeling happy, she said, 'Fair enough.' That wasn't giving anything away about how she truly felt, if she even knew.

'How is Jordan? Back up to speed?'

'Pretty much. He's excited to be going to pre-school today.'

'I bet he is.'

'In here,' Eli indicated the café they were going to.

'Morning, Eli,' the woman behind the counter called as they walked in. 'Grab your usual table while you can. I'll bring the menu over for your friend.'

'Cheers, Margaret.' Eli pulled out a chair at a table for two set by the window. 'Here you go.'

A gentleman too. But then she'd have been surprised if he wasn't. He seemed to look out for people in many ways without giving anything away about himself. Sitting down, she asked, 'So Jordan's back on his feet?' He'd gone home the day after his surgery when Eli had finished work.

'There's been no stopping him since he got home. Almost too energetic at times. It worried Mum he might do some harm to himself but you can't keep a pup down for long.'

'Are you a solo dad?' No mother had turned up to be with Jordan in hospital. Might as well gain what info she could while she had the chance. Unless he changed his mind about sharing breakfast. She shrugged mentally. Too late to be worrying about that.

'I am.' He sat up even straighter. 'Mum and my sister Liz help out a lot. I owe them big time. Dad too.'

*Lucky you.*

'Do they look after him when you're on call?' Would he carry on with this?

'He stays over with Mum or one of my sisters then. Everyone's so helpful, but then they adore Jordie.'

'Nothing like a good family.' If only. Not only had her family not given her any support when she was pregnant, they'd been infuriated when she'd managed to put herself through nursing school without asking for a cent. Working at supermarkets filling shelves when not studying had been hard but a good lesson on life.

'You winced then. Your family not close?'

Guess she deserved to be asked personal questions when she hadn't kept her mouth shut about his, but that didn't stop her speaking sharply. 'Let's just say that my parents haven't always been there for me when I've needed them.'

A menu appeared on the table in front of her.

'Here you go. What would you like to drink?' the woman asked.

Saved from further questions about a tricky subject, she smiled at the woman. 'A pot of tea, thanks.' After quickly scanning the menu she glanced up to find Eli watching her. 'I'll have the full breakfast with eggs scrambled.'

He nodded. 'Way to go. Make that two, Margaret. Plus the usual coffee.'

'Done.'

'It must be difficult at times raising your son on your own.'

'It has its moments but I wouldn't change a

thing. I have full custody of Jordan. My wife left when he was two.' Eli looked away, swallowed hard.

She felt bad for asking now. 'You're a very caring dad. Spending the night with him in hospital to make sure he wasn't frightened whenever he woke and found himself amongst strangers in a strange place was lovely.'

'Thanks.'

'I'll shut up now.'

'Good.' Eli looked at her, and a tiny smile emerged on his sensuous lips. 'I might as well finish the story then your mind can rest. Melissa wanted to move to New York to further her career in fashion design. Though the idea of living in such a huge city didn't appeal I was prepared to back Melissa in her choices, and thought we'd go as a family as people do. Turned out I wasn't wanted. Nor was Jordan.' He didn't sound sad or upset. More relieved, if anything. Not such a great marriage in the first place?

'I'm sorry to hear that.' For his sake. Maybe not hers. *Settle.* They were having breakfast, not on a hot date.

'What about you? Been married?' He'd flipped the conversation back on her.

Damn him. 'I've had two serious relationships.' She could talk about those without giving too much away. 'The first man was Danny.

When we met he was a trainee doctor and I'd been qualified for a year. We were together about two years before we began to drift apart. No argy-bargy, nothing awful.' Apart from the fact he was appalled that she'd given up her son, though he'd tried to accept it for a while. His re-action had made her believe she didn't deserve to have a happy family life after putting her son up for adoption. 'We were spending more and more time apart, doing our own things, and fi-nally went separate ways.'

Their drinks arrived and she took a moment to pour a mug of tea. 'I've seen Danny a couple of times since and have no regrets. He's hap-pily married with two toddlers hanging around his feet.' If only she'd been so lucky. But there was still time. Thirty-four wasn't too old to have babies, or to raise them into something resem-bling decent young adults. 'The second relation-ship was no better.' A lot worse. 'I wasn't good enough and that was that.'

'I'm sorry to hear that.' Eli was regarding her with something like compassion, which didn't please her.

He didn't know the whole story and if she told him there'd only be disgust in those beau-tiful eyes. She'd seen it often enough to know what to expect.

Move on before he asked something she'd refuse to answer. 'Does Jordan's mother keep in touch with him?'

His mouth flattened. 'She phones for his birthday and Christmas, and a few other times. Whenever she returns to New Zealand, which isn't often, she'll drop by for a brief visit.'

*I haven't met her and I don't like her.*

'That's so not fair.' It seemed there were more ways than one to lose a parent. Which was worse? To never have known your birth mother, or to have spent two years with her and still lose her? Tea slopped over the rim as she picked up her mug.

Eli handed her a paper napkin. 'You're right, but then there's no knowing when someone will put themselves before their child.'

More tea sloshed out of her mug. She put it down fast. Eli would definitely be appalled to learn what she'd done. He wouldn't listen to the reasons, would only hear that she'd left her son. 'You're right,' she said, instantly regretting her reply. This man was too astute for her to be saying things like that. He wasn't right though. Her boy had deserved better than she'd been able to give him.

'You okay?'

No, she wanted to run out of here, get away from Eli and his questions. But it was her fault he'd asked since she'd talked about Jordan first.

Anyway, if she was going to start looking for the life she really wanted, she had to stay, face up to whatever came next because if she found a man to love then she'd have to tell him everything. Did she want that? Looking at Eli, she knew she did. Not why, only that it was time to turn her life around. Starting now. 'Sorry, I get upset when I hear about parents doing awful things with their children.'

A frown appeared on that handsome face.

Her reaction had been strong, too strong for what she'd said. Warning—Eli wasn't a pushover. Again she lifted her mug and this time didn't spill a drop—probably because the top half had already splashed onto the table. 'The reason behind that is something I don't want to talk about.' She couldn't be more honest than that. Not yet. He didn't need to know her history until she knew him way better, until he understood more about her so he might accept why she'd done what she did.

Slowly his frown disappeared. 'Fair enough.' He sipped his coffee, looking worried. 'We have opened up pretty quickly.' Then he smiled and she knew everything was all right for now. 'I'm not used to doing that, and I suspect behind that regular smile you're much the same.'

He understood that while she talked a lot, she didn't often say anything about what really held her back from a normal life. Dredging up a smile in return, she admitted, 'True.'

'Relax. I'm not going to push for answers.' He stood up. 'But I am going to get a cloth to wipe away that tea.'

Just then Margaret appeared with two laden plates. 'I'll do that. You sit and enjoy this.'

Anna stared at the plate. 'I'm going to be here half the day.' There was enough food to feed the kids in room one on the ward.

'We do doggy bags.' Margaret laughed.

'I haven't been known to leave anything on my plate,' Eli said as he ground black pepper over his. 'Not even here.'

Where did he put it all? There wasn't any sign of over-indulging on that amazing body. 'Is that a challenge?' Yeah, and she knew where the result would show on her figure.

'Could be,' he said through a grin, looking relaxed again, as if their tense conversation had taken a back seat.

Hopefully it had because she wasn't prepared to tell him about her baby. Very few people knew and that was how she liked to keep it. 'You're on.'

For a while they focused on eating and not talking, which was fine with her. She could talk the tail off a donkey but not when it came to personal subjects.

When Eli placed his cutlery on his empty plate and pushed it aside she knew he had something to get off his chest. He wore a studied look. Something serious was going on behind those grey eyes. For the life of her, she could not think what it was, and her stomach knotted.

Then he pulled an envelope out of his pocket. 'This is for you.'

*Nurs Ana* was written on the front in a young child's wobbly style. 'From Jordan?'

'Yes.'

'That's sweet.' Sliding her finger under the flap, she opened the envelope and withdrew a card. Warmth stole through her. 'An invitation to a party?' Then she remembered something about him starting school soon. 'Jordan's birthday?'

'Yes.'

She opened the card and read her name again, spelt properly this time. The party was on Sunday afternoon. Tomorrow. If she accepted, that meant a shopping trip after she'd grabbed some sleep this morning. Why was she invited? She didn't know the boy other than his time in the ward. He was adorable, but she wasn't part of his life, though it was tempting to accept because she did like the little guy, *and* she'd get to see Eli outside the hospital. As she was doing now. She glanced at him, her heart sinking. The worried look she was receiving said he didn't want her to accept. 'What's the problem?'

Leaning back in his chair, he asked softly, 'Do you want to come?'

Put it back on her, why didn't he? She'd go with honest. 'I'd love to but I'm not sure why I've been invited. Was it your idea, or Jordan's?' She thought she knew the answer but wanted to know for sure.

'Jordan's.'

Got that right at least.

Leaning forward, Eli added, 'I'll be truthful. I tried to talk him out of it but he refused to listen.'

'You don't want him getting too close to me and then me not being around any more. He'll be hurt.'

'Correct.'

'So you want me to turn down the invitation and hurt him anyway.' She did understand. Better now than later when they'd had a bit more time together, but Eli wasn't giving her a chance to show she could be reasonable and keep the barriers up.

'No, I don't.' So Eli could surprise her on more than one thing. 'I'm between a rock and a hard place but then my dad always says I over-think things, that sometimes I should let them unfold as they're meant to and deal with the consequences later, if there are any.'

She stared at him. 'I have no idea where this leaves me. He's a great little guy and I'm thrilled to be asked to come to the party, but I also don't want to be the cause of any problems for either of you.'

Eli sat quietly, as though thinking it through some more. Finally, 'Tick yes on the reply card and I'll give it to him when I get home.' There was a wobbly smile on Eli's face that gave her no clue to what he was really thinking.

'Are you sure?'

'I'm very protective of my son, and don't ever forget that, but yes, I'm sure.'

'Can't say I blame you about looking out for Jordan.' His mother had done a bunk. A few phone calls and rare visits didn't make up for that. 'His heart must've been broken when Melissa left.'

'I don't think he'll ever understand. Why would he? I don't.'

There was a depth behind those words she didn't quite understand. Anger at what his wife had done, sure, but she sensed more to it. The pain over losing the woman he loved too would have something to do with it. Not that she'd be asking. She did know when to keep her mouth shut sometimes. So why was she laying her hand on top of his? 'He's a very lucky boy to have you for a dad.'

Eli's hand turned over and his fingers wrapped around hers, squeezed ever so lightly before he pulled back as though he'd been stung. 'Thank you.'

Despite his withdrawal she liked this man a lot. He was genuine and caring and adorable. Her kind of man, if she had a kind. So far she'd always been wrong about the men she'd had anything to do with romantically and that had made her believe even more that she didn't deserve to be happy. She dug in her bag for a pen. 'I'll answer the invitation now.'

'When's the last time you went to a kid's party?' he asked with a crooked grin.

'Another challenge?'

'Could be.' He laughed, totally relaxed again. This man could go from hot to cold and back again pretty quickly.

'It was two months ago. Leanne's a close friend. She and her husband have two youngsters and I spend quite a bit of time with them.' They were the children she let most into her heart, believing they'd always be in her life in one way or another.

'Damn, I think I've lost that one before we've even started.'

Not quite, Anna thought the next afternoon when she walked around Eli's house with a plate of chocolate-chip cookies she'd baked that morning, following the excited shrieks coming from the back lawn. It wasn't the kids that were giving her butterflies, but meeting Eli's family. They were the unknown, and must wonder why Jordan had invited her. Hopefully they'd accept it for what she presumed it was—a result of spending time with him when he was hurting from his surgery. She'd briefly met Jackie, Eli's mother, when she'd come to visit Jordan in hospital, but as they'd been flat-out busy and her shift had been about to end it had only been a passing hello.

'Nurse Anna, you came.' Jordan charged at her like a bull on steroids.

She braced for the impact, caught him as he banged into her. 'Happy birthday, Jordan. Thank you for asking me to your party.'

'You had to come. I wanted it. Is that for me?' He was reaching for the brightly wrapped parcel in her shoulder bag.

'Steady, Jordan. Remember your manners.' Eli strode towards them. 'Howdy, Anna. Glad you made it.' He looked genuinely pleased as he took the cookies from her hand.

'I wouldn't not come after saying I would.'

'I figured. Now, Jordan, what do you say?'

'Thank you, Anna. Can I open it now?' He was already tearing at the paper.

'Of course you can. It's yours.' She smiled at the excitement on his face. Fingers crossed elephants were still the flavour of the month.

'Yippee,' Jordan shrieked as he stared at his gift with big eyes. 'Look at this, Dad. Grandma, look. I've got a elephant.'

'*An* elephant,' Eli corrected through a smile. 'Thank you, Anna. You've really made his day. Now come and meet the tribe.'

'Glad I got it right,' she admitted. 'Kids change their minds about what they like all the time.'

'Dad, this is Anna Passau. Anna, meet Kerry Forrester, and mum, Jackie, who you've already met.'

'Nurse Anna, lovely to meet you. Jordan hasn't stopped talking about you since he came out of hospital.' Kerry gave her a brief hug. 'You rock, apparently.'

Wow, talk about making her feel comfortable in an instant. 'He's a great wee guy. Nice to meet you, and hello again, Jackie.'

'Hi, Anna. We are thrilled you've joined us for the party.' Another hug came her way.

Thrilled? A bit OTT, surely? But then again, she could get to like the family after a welcome like this. Down, girl. It was only a birthday party for their grandchild, nothing more. 'Glad to be here.' Even when it did seem a little strange being invited to a patient's party, even if his father was a colleague and getting a little closer. As a friend or more? No idea. 'I really am.'

Jackie flicked Eli a smile before saying to her, 'You have to meet the sisters and their better halves. Come on.'

Eli shrugged exaggeratedly. 'I've been made redundant.'

'You get to run pin the tail on the horse,' Jackie said.

'Great. I had Anna down for that. From what I've observed she's good at keeping kids under control.'

'I'd far rather watch you do it,' Anna said.

'You're returning my challenge, aren't you?' His shoulders lifted and he winked. 'Just watch and be warned.'

'Hi, you must be Anna.' A woman dressed in jeans and a black and white striped shirt held out her hand. 'I'm Liz, Eli's big sister.' Nothing big about her, all slim and short.

'Hello, Liz.'

'Bossy sister,' Eli called over his shoulder as he knelt down to sort out the game.

'No, that's my role. Hi, Anna. I'm Karen, the best sister.' Another hand to shake. This time getting a thorough once-over.

Suddenly Anna felt almost shy, which was unheard of. 'Hello, Karen.' Why were these women checking her out so thoroughly? She was here for Jordan's birthday, nothing else. Except she had been looking forward to spending some time with Eli as well, when and if he had any to spare given it was his son's party.

'Feel like a wine?' Liz asked. 'It might be Jordan's party but adults are allowed to relax too. It might help you deal with all of us. We're not known for being aloof.'

*Unlike your brother?*

'I'd love a small one.' She followed Liz to the table set up on the veranda. 'Which are your two?'

Liz looked surprised she knew that. 'Over there by the bouncy castle is Mackenzie. She's six, and Thomas is the boy in a green T-shirt giving his father a hard time about cooking the sausages on the barbecue. He's seven.'

Anna felt a familiar tug at her heart. She'd missed out on so much with her boy, especially the simple things like sharing a barbecue. 'They're lovely.'

'They're hell on legs, is what they are.' Liz laughed. 'But I love hell when it comes packaged as my two. What about you? Any children?'

'Not yet,' she said. It was her standard answer to save having to go through the story that could never be changed. 'But who knows what's around the corner?'

'Always fun taking a peek. Here, Sauv Blanc or Pinot Gris?'

'Pinot Gris, thanks.' When she took the glass Liz handed her, her first instinct was to swallow the lot and get a refill. She needed to calm down, and stop thinking everyone wanted to learn all there was to know about her. This was Eli's family. Of course they were being chatty and asking what for most people were perfectly normal questions. Looking over at Eli, she said, 'I'd better go see what I can do to help.'

'No need. That's not why you're here.'

'Old habit to the fore.' Keeping busy meant staying away from difficult questions.

Eli clapped his hands. 'Okay, kids, over here. We're going to put blindfolds on you and then you have to stick a tail on the horse. The one who gets closest to the right place gets a parcel. Let's do this.' He glanced at Anna. 'Want a turn? Or would you prefer to take a tumble on the bouncy castle?'

He really was different away from work. Because he was with his family and could relax completely as he didn't have anything to hide from these people? There was a thought. But what would a man like Eli need to hide? He was always calm and confident. And aloof. Of course.

*Stop with the questions and get on with enjoying yourself.*

Good idea, Anna admitted. 'Not if you want that castle to stay in one piece. Even pinning the tail on could have dire results. My sense of direction isn't flash, and that's without a blindfold.'

'You're hardly going to get that confused,' he said happily. 'From what I've seen you're always aware of where you are and what you're doing.'

She could take his compliments any time. He'd obviously been taking notice of her at work, which made her feel good. Desperate to be noticed by an attractive man, by any chance? 'Come on, the kids are impatient to get started.'

Eli just laughed. 'What's new about that?'

'True.' She'd dealt with enough kids of all ages through her job to know he was right.

By the time all the children had had a couple of turns sticking the tail on the horse they were eager to know who'd won while demanding food and sodas at the same time. Eli studied the stuffed horse and scratched his chin. 'I think this tail is closest to where it should be. Whose is that one?'

'Mine,' shrieked a little girl.

'Mine's best,' Jordan yelled.

'Hey, buddy, Alice's is closer and it's only fair she wins. You won the dunking doughnut competition.'

Jordan calmed down and took the small parcel from Eli to hand to Alice. 'It's yours.' He gave her a hug.

Aww, he was so cute. Anna blinked once and looked to Eli. 'Dunking doughnuts?'

'Don't ask. It was messy. One of Liz's not so brilliant ideas for a game.'

'Nothing wrong with a bit of stickiness,' Liz retorted. 'You've got to get messy at these parties, Dad.'

Eli just laughed. 'Didn't see that in the rule book.'

Anna took a step back, trying to breathe normally. Eli really was different from the man she'd known prior to today. Couldn't fault either version of him. Though previously at work there'd been plenty of times when she'd wanted to tell him to stop being a jerk, she wouldn't be thinking that today. As her lungs slowly returned to normal she wondered how far she could take this. How far he might be interested in going.

'You know how to handle kids.' Liz appeared beside her. 'I guess that's because you spend so much time nursing them when they're at their most vulnerable.'

'Yes, I do seem to be able to manage children. I've always had an affinity to them,' she added thoughtlessly, then gasped. Eli wasn't the only member of this family who had her talking too much. Must be something in the Forrester genes that made them able to suck her in without realising until it was too late. She hadn't let out anything important but it was a warning to be careful.

'Why wouldn't you? They can push every button you've got and some, but there's something wonderful about children.' Liz grinned. 'I'd better go sort the food problem before someone throws a tantrum because there's no cake on the table.'

Anna watched Liz stroll across to the house and felt a moment of loneliness, which was out of character. Eli's lot were easy to be around, and obviously got on well. Suddenly she wished she and her parents could bury the hatchet. She'd lost more than her son, she'd lost the two people who should've always been there for her, no matter what mistakes she made. While they did sometimes call her on special occasions she was never comfortable. The past hung between them like a fence too high to climb, and probably always would. She'd once tried to breach the gap only to be told she'd wasted her intelligence becoming a nurse.

'You look like you're about to run away,' Eli said quietly behind her.

Spinning around, she stared at him. 'Not likely. I'm having fun.'

One dark eyebrow rose as he locked his gaze with hers. 'You can do better than that, Anna.'

True, she could. 'Your family's lovely.'

'What's wrong with yours?'

'We don't get on at all. I did something many years ago that changed everything.'

'That's tough. Everyone makes mistakes along the way. What did you do? Or would you prefer I didn't ask?'

Tell him and Eli would have her out of here before Jordan cut his birthday cake. Funny thing though, she did want to tell him the truth and get it over and done with so she'd know where she stood. But this wasn't the right time or place. 'I don't mind that you asked, but now's not the time to give you an answer. This is Jordan's day.'

He continued to watch her for a long minute, then finally nodded. 'You're right, but if you ever want to get something off your chest, you only have to nudge me.' Then his gaze dropped to her chest and his eyes widened. Hadn't he noticed she had breasts before?

She had to laugh, because otherwise she was going to leap into his arms and hold on tight. She hadn't known a man quite so refreshing and understanding as Eli. 'I just might do that.' How understanding would he be if he knew the truth? She shivered, already believing she knew the answer.

'Come on, it's feeding time at the zoo.' He took her elbow and led her across to the deck where a laden table was surrounded with excited children and parents trying to make them behave.

'Who made all this food?' Anna asked. Ten kids were never going to eat everything.

'Mum and Liz. What's not eaten today will go to day care with Jordan tomorrow.'

'I thought he'd be starting at school tomorrow.'

'It's mid-term break this coming week so he's starting the following Monday, which gives more time to getting over the op. Not that it's been holding him back much so far. He's been back at preschool since Wednesday, only for half days. They've been very vigilant but there've been no problems. How I'm going to keep him from getting over-excited during the intervening days I have no idea.'

'You'll manage. I saw you calm him when he was frightened in hospital and when he was hurting. You're a great dad.' Hadn't she told him that once before? Nothing but the truth was the way to go.

Eli looked at her again. 'Thanks.' He ran a finger down the side of her face. 'I like you.'

A scream rent the air before she could answer. They both spun around, searching for the child making the racket. Eli raced across the lawn to a girl near the hedge. 'Sarah, what's happened?'

'A bee got me,' she gasped. Her eyes were wide and her breathing was slowing. 'It—' she tried to breathe '—stings.'

'Here, I'm going to take you inside.' Eli had Sarah in his arms and was striding back to the house as a woman rushed up to them.

'What's wrong? Sarah, are you all right?'

'Jane, has Sarah got any allergies?' Eli asked as he laid the crying girl on a couch.

'Not that I know of.'

His mouth tightened before he said, 'She's been stung by a bee and I want to check her over thoroughly.' He said no more but Anna had seen the swelling beginning around Sarah's eyes and noted how her breathing was getting more laboured with every breath she took.

'Want me to call for help?' she asked him quietly.

'Yes, definitely. Jane, we're calling the ambulance. I think Sarah's having a reaction to the sting and it's better to have the medics here.'

'In case something goes wrong? Is that what you're saying?' Jane slumped against Anna, then straightened to reach a hand to her daughter. 'Sarah, you'll be all right. Jordan's daddy's looking after you.'

Anna had her phone pressed to her ear. 'Ambulance,' she told the man who answered her call. Then she explained to the call base operator. 'We have a young child who's been stung by a bee and appears to be having an anaphylactic reaction. No known allergies.' She gave the address, Eli nodding when she got it right. 'Thank you.' Hanging up, she moved closer to Sarah and Eli and watched him counting the breaths. Taking Sarah's wrist, she timed the girl's pulse.

'What's happening?' Kerry asked from the doorway. 'I heard Sarah screaming. Has she hurt herself?'

Looking around, Anna realised the room was filling with anxious-looking parents. 'Sarah's having a reaction to a bee sting. Could someone wait on the footpath for the ambulance and show the medics the way in when they arrive?'

'Can everyone else move back to give us some space while we look after Sarah?' Eli said in his no-nonsense voice Anna knew from hospital.

Liz came to stand by Jane, put an arm around her waist as she stared at her daughter, her teeth biting into her bottom lip. 'She's in good hands.'

'But—' Tears trickled down her cheeks. 'What if—?'

'Don't go there. Be brave for Sarah.'

Anna spoke quietly to Eli. 'Pulse's weak.'

'Fits the picture. She's not reacting to my touch now.'

'How far away is the local ambulance base?' Surely they wouldn't have to wait for one to come from the city centre. No, there was one at Wigram, not far away at all, she recalled.

'Ten minutes max.'

'I'm ready if we have to do CPR.'

'Me too.' His face was grim. Then he drew on a smile and looked up at Jane. 'She's doing well. Has she ever been stung before?'

'Yes, often when she's gone to her grandparents' farm. But this never happened. Are you sure it's anaphylactic?'

No doubt about it. Anna had seen this often enough to know. 'Some people don't react the first time they're stung or eat a food item they're allergic to. It can build up slowly.'

Jane looked at her with a question in her eyes.

'I'm a paediatric nurse.'

A bleak smile touched Jane's face then disappeared. 'Thank you for helping.'

'No problem.' Sarah's wrist was limp in her hand. She glanced at Eli, saw worry reflected back at her.

Ten minutes felt like an hour, but finally the sound of an approaching siren filled the air.

Sarah gasped. Her eyes closed. Her chest stopped moving.

Eli joined his hands and pressed down hard on

the frail chest in front of him. 'One, two, three.' On he went, paused at thirty presses.

Anna breathed into Sarah's lungs.

The little girl coughed, sucked in air, opened her eyes, and cried.

The air shifted and two uniformed men appeared beside them with a large bag and a stretcher. 'Hi there. Is this Sarah?'

'Yes, this is Sarah, and her mum, Jane, is right here too.' Eli stood up and filled the medics in.

Anna got out of their way and went to stand with Jackie and Liz. 'Her breathing's improving a little but the medics will put a mask on to give her oxygen.'

'She looks so little,' Jackie whispered. 'I can't believe this is happening.'

Anna gave her a quick hug. 'She'll be fine now. But it is a huge fright for everyone. How about I go put the kettle on?'

'Good idea,' Liz said. 'I'll do that. I need to be busy.'

Anna understood. 'Fair enough.' Crossing to Eli, she said, 'That was a bit of a shock for Jane.'

His arm went around her shoulder, drew her closer. 'Sure was.'

'Sarah's lucky we were here.'

His arm tightened around her. 'Yes.'

# CHAPTER FOUR

'ONE HELL OF a shock for any parent,' Eli said again a couple of hours later when the party had wrapped up and Jordan was tucked into bed, sound asleep after Anna read him two stories. He was cuddling his new elephant tight, which had to be uncomfortable since it was made out of wood. What a day. Asking Anna to stay on for a wine had only added to the awkwardness. She fitted in too well.

'I can't begin to imagine how Jane felt. I mean, she was terrified but no one expects something like that to happen to their child.'

'At least we were around to help.'

Her smile was brief. 'Sarah's going to have to be vigilant from now on. I bet Jane will be watching over her closely for a long while to come.'

'Hopefully Sarah's old enough to understand it could happen again and that she needs to carry an EpiPen everywhere she goes.'

'Poor kid.'

'Yeah. No child likes to be different from their mates.' Eli looked around the kitchen and dining area, and sighed. Once again his family had come to the rescue by helping clean up after everyone had headed away. 'Where would I be without them?'

'Your family? Busy scraping plates and storing leftovers in the fridge and freezer.' Anna looked a little sad. She'd told him her family weren't on good terms so her feelings on that were probably coming to the fore.

'You did your share too. Thanks, Anna. You got more than you bargained for coming here today.' She did seem to have enjoyed herself. 'Jordan was thrilled with his present, and your presence,' he added. His son thought the world of Nurse Anna. But he was more than a little concerned about how attracted he was to her. She was adorable. And sexy beyond reason. He still couldn't believe how he'd managed not to get too interested before now, but they'd only known each other at work where both of them focused on patients, not each other.

'I suppose I'd better head away,' she said, looking anywhere but at him.

'You haven't finished your wine.' She'd been taking her time over it. 'I can get you a taxi if you don't want to drive. We can also heat up some leftovers if you're hungry. Or I could order something in if that doesn't suit.'

*Slow down. You're sounding desperate.*

Maybe he was. It had been a while since he'd felt so interested in a woman. Since Melissa he'd given women a wide berth other than the occasional one-night fling to ease some of the tension that arose every now and then.

That long curly red hair slid across Anna's shoulders as she shook her head, making his fingers itch. 'Don't go to any trouble. There's heaps of food stacked in containers in your fridge.'

'Does that mean you'll stay a bit longer?' He wasn't sure why her answer was important but his breathing was on hold as he waited.

'Yes, I think I will, thanks.' Her enthusiasm levels weren't overwhelming but her smile seeped into him like a slow-heating oven, getting warmer by the second.

'Good.' Leaning back into his seat, he asked, 'There isn't someone else who could pick you up later?'

'I'm single and live alone in my own town house out in Lincoln.' Sounded as if there was something she needed to get out of the way underlying that.

Did that mean she wanted to spend more time with him? Did he want to see more of Anna outside work? Unfortunately he did. So he shouldn't have invited her to share leftovers because he couldn't afford to get caught up in a relationship that might harm his boy. He dug for a smile. 'I take it no other patient has invited you to their party?'

'Never.' She studied him as she sipped her wine. 'I'm glad I came despite your concerns that Jordan will have expectations about me being around on and off.'

'The thing is, Jordie's been hurt big time by his mother, and I can't bear to watch him go through that again so I'm very cautious about who I let into my life.' That didn't come out well. 'What I mean is I'm single for a reason.' He still got angry about Melissa putting herself before her son. He'd never understood how his birth mother could've given him up, and then he'd married a woman who'd done a similar thing.

Anna looked stunned. 'Me too.'

He wasn't the only one talking about things best kept to himself. 'Which is?' Never let an opportunity go by.

Putting her glass aside, she began to stand up. 'I'd better go now.'

Leaping to his feet, Eli put his hand out to stop her. 'Anna, no, please stay. I promise not to ask any more personal questions.'

Her eyes were full of sadness as she looked at him. 'I enjoy your company, Eli. I really do, but I'm not prepared to talk about my past. Not yet,' she added so quietly he wasn't sure he'd heard right.

'Then I won't mention it again. Let's see what we'd like to eat, and get it warming up.' And forget this moment. For now anyway. Without thinking, he reached for her hand and was surprised when her fingers tightened around his. Talk about mixed messages. Was she as insecure as him when it came to relationships? Guess he wasn't about to find out any time soon since he'd keep his word. 'I can still order in something more exciting than party leftovers.'

Stepping away from him, she laughed softly. 'I'm sure you can but I'm more than happy with some of those yummy whitebait patties and a bit of salad.'

'Shouldn't have invited you. Whitebait's one of my favourites.'

'Tough. Hope there's plenty left or you'll have to go without.'

So she could tease him. He kind of liked that. It meant she wasn't tiptoeing around him as some women he'd dated off and on had. He knew he was a bit remote at work, but he also didn't want women fawning over him to get his attention. Anna didn't, which was refreshing. 'I'm in luck. There're quite a few left. The kids didn't touch them and even the adults didn't get stuck in.'

'Let's do this. I'm starving.'

Within minutes they were sitting at the counter, enjoying their patties and other leftovers. Eli had brought their drinks across and he lifted his glass to tap against Anna's. 'Here's to the end of a rowdy day.'

'To a fun afternoon.' She tapped back and took a small sip.

'I'm still happy to get a taxi for you if you're worried about finishing your wine.'

'It's all right. I haven't had much so a few sips won't hurt.' Looking around the room, she grinned. 'I love the artwork.'

Jordan's paintings were on the fridge door and the wall by the table. 'He gets a kick out of using a paintbrush.'

'He must be shattered after today but he still managed to keep his eyes open while I read stories.'

'He's got preschool in the morning too so any hour spent asleep has to be a bonus for everyone.'

'Is he a good sleeper?'

'On and off. Sometimes he wakes nearly every hour, then there'll be nights when he doesn't wake until dawn.'

'That must make it hard for you some days.'

'All part of being a solo parent. Probably not a lot different for couples with kids. There'll always be sleepless nights for one reason or another.'

'Imagine his first date. What's he doing? Is he safe? Behaving?' Anna chuckled.

Warmth stole through him. He liked that she didn't talk about Jordan as though he was different. 'Even though they're some time away I am not looking forward to those years. Yep.' He laughed when she glanced over at him. 'I'm already worried.'

Her eye roll was cute. 'Why am I not surprised?'

'Because you already know I like being in charge.'

'At work, yes. I'm only beginning to find out how you do things in your private life.'

It stung that she thought he liked being in charge at work, even though he'd said it in the first place. Had he been looking for a compliment instead? 'It's not so much about being in charge as making sure what's necessary for a patient gets done properly.'

Anna blanched. 'I understand that.' She shoved her empty plate away and picked up her glass. 'The only problem with that is we all know what we're doing and do it well.'

'You'll get no argument from me there. It's just

that I am a perfectionist, which goes against the theory of medicine because there's no such thing as being perfect when every person's symptoms vary according to their physical details.' Enough of being serious and defending himself. It was a tad boring. 'You never wanted to be a doctor?'

'Not at all. Too many years' study required for that.' Her hair swung over her shoulders. Dang, he loved that intense red shade that reminded him of the Christmas roses his mother grew. 'I couldn't wait to leave school and get out in the real world. Except I didn't do that. I'd always dreamed of becoming a nurse so I stuck with it to get my leaving certificate before enrolling for nursing school.'

He wasn't surprised. Anna came across as dedicated to whatever she believed in, whether it was looking after young patients or turning up to have fun at a kid's party. He had no doubt she'd be the same in a relationship. Except she wasn't in one and didn't want to talk about her past so he presumed something had gone more badly wrong for her than she'd said. 'Nursing is more hands on, isn't it?'

'I love that intensity, getting to know a patient a little bit and trying to help them by talking or not, whichever they want.'

If only she'd talk to him about what had happened to her. But was he ready to tell her about the woman who gave birth to him and then gave him away? How he'd been angry with her for many years? How, despite all that, he'd grown up in the best family possible. Too soon by far. If there'd ever be a right time, now wasn't it. As he turned around on his stool his knee bumped up against Anna's. Stayed there. 'I was going to be a fireman, then a policeman, and a horti-culturist.'

Her eyebrows rose at that last one.

He relaxed some more. 'Finally medicine called. I loved science at school, especially bi-ology, and here I am. A no-brainer, really.'

'Isn't it a great feeling when you realise you've got it right for yourself? I used to think I wanted to be a nurse because my grandma had been, but the dream never left, and when I walked into the nursing school for the first time I knew I'd made the right call.'

Did she know she'd moved her hand to lie on his knee? Placing his over hers, he waited to see if she withdrew. When she didn't he lifted it and brushed his lips over her knuckles. 'I've enjoyed having you here today. I know I was hesitant about you accepting Jordie's invitation but I am glad you did.'

'So am I.' Heat crept up her cheeks.

It was as though she was shy when she wasn't being Nurse Anna. Not so confident in other aspects of her life? There was so much to learn about this wonderful woman, and he wanted to know it all. Now. Impatience was another of his characteristics, though one he kept on a tight rein. Leaning closer to her tempting mouth that was curved into a small smile, he kissed her lips lightly. At least it was a soft kiss until Anna pushed closer and her mouth covered his and then it was intense, filling him with a longing he hadn't known in years. Not only for a physical release but for a depth he'd spent most of his adult life looking for. A depth that could lead to understanding—and eventually love.

Standing, he pulled Anna onto her feet and into his arms, and went back to kissing her blind. Or was it him who was going blind with passion? It certainly felt like it as he gave in to all the hot sensations filling him.

Anna's hands were on his back, rubbing softly, hard, then soft again. Her mouth was warm as he tasted her. Her scent teased him, wrapped around him, drew him in deeper than ever.

Suddenly Anna jerked back. 'Oops. Think we'd better stop.'

'Why?' he croaked through the desire filling his throat.

'Daddy? Where are you?' Jordan called from his bedroom.

Dragging his fingers through his hair, he

pulled his other hand away from Anna's waist, and tried hard not to be cross with his son for interrupting the most amazing few minutes he'd had in a long time.

'Daddy!'

'Coming,' he called back.

Anna was already picking up her handbag.

'Anna, I'm sorry.' He probably should be thanking Jordan for interrupting them before it got too far out of hand. He wasn't ready to take this any further. Too much to consider, like the wee man down the hall demanding his attention.

'Not a problem.'

Her wry smile nearly undid any thoughts of not grabbing her and dashing to his bedroom after he'd seen to Jordan. *Jordan*. He came first. 'See you at work.'

'Sure.' Now she sounded annoyed, as if he'd said the wrong thing.

Tough. He was looking out for his own.

And then Anna was gone, taking the heat out of the room but leaving desire swirling through his overwrought body and tightening him with longing.

Anna got into her car and slammed shut the door. Leaning her head back, she closed her eyes and breathed deep, then deeper. What had she nearly done? That kiss was a start-up button for sure.

If they hadn't been interrupted, she felt certain they'd have made their way to Eli's bedroom. Unless he'd woken up to the fact his son was in the house and then she knew he'd have poured cold water on the desire filling her. And him. His erection had been hard as it pressed against her thigh.

'That kiss finished far too soon.' Opening her eyes, she sat forward and started the car. Eli knew how to push all her buttons and some she hadn't known were there. Just the feel of his back under her hands was a turn-on. As for his kiss—she'd easily lose her mind over more of those. He was something else. He'd often had her looking twice when he was on the ward, but then he'd be abrupt and she'd immediately get over the mild attraction. Only to feel it all over again next time he turned up to see a patient.

A quick glance at the house and she pulled away. Time to go home and have a cold shower. She was roasting hot with need for Eli. She hadn't really realised until these past weeks since Jordan was admitted to the ward and she'd seen another side to Eli that attracted her in ways that she didn't usually feel with the men she sporad-ically dated nowadays. There was a lot to him she hadn't noticed before. Not in an open and finite way.

He had a big heart. Seeing him with his son

made it so obvious, but it didn't go away when around his family or friends. Since Jordan had spent a night on the ward and Eli had been a patient's parent, not the doctor on the case, he'd opened his mind to the staff and seen them in a different light. He'd also been wonderful to her at times when normally he'd have treated her with some aloofness.

'Where to from here?' she asked the darkness in the car. What did she want from Eli? A fling? Friendship with benefits? Or something deep and meaningful, long term and permanent? That idea felt good. But did she deserve him? So far she hadn't been successful in finding the ideal man to spend the rest of her life with. She didn't deserve to since she'd given her son away to be adopted at birth. What right did she have to be utterly happy when she'd done that?

At first Danny had made her believe she might get a second chance. They'd lived together, talked about getting married, and had been happily in love. So she'd believed—until he'd changed his mind. As for Jock, he'd gone ballistic, calling her all sorts of names, and told everyone she was a bitch. The only thing she'd been grateful about was he'd never mentioned her baby to anyone. She had no idea why when it would've played into his ego.

Despite Danny and Jock, she still wanted to

find that passion she'd always hoped was out there.

*Like you felt when Eli kissed you?*

Exactly like that. Legless. Hot. Tender. Loving. Heady. How to work with him, day after day, and ignore those sensations? It wasn't going to be a picnic. Not now that they'd kissed, and she'd felt his need for her as much as hers for him. But she would not quit her job to put space between them. That would be the craziest thing she could do.

Ahead, red and blue lights were flashing. A police car had pulled up behind a ute and the cop was standing at the driver's window. A timely reminder to focus on driving and not Eli.

She managed not to think about him too much for the rest of the drive home, but he was fully back in her head the moment she slid between the sheets and turned out the bedside light.

Minutes later her phone pinged. Eli. Really? Yep.

His message read: Wow.

She stared at the screen, certain she was seeing things. But no, she wasn't. It was for real.

*Wow?* Yeah, it had been that all right.

Never in a million nights would she have believed Eli Forrester would send a message like that. Another warning to tread carefully.

'Afraid so,' she admitted before tapping her phone and replying to his wow.

Goodnight.

Eli knew he shouldn't have sent that message to Anna the moment he touched send. It spoke volumes about how screwed up he was. Hopefully she would think it was normal for him.

Sitting in his lounge with a bottle of icy water in hand, he laughed at himself.

*Dream on, man. Anna ain't stupid.*

If anyone was, that would be him. Pouring water down his throat wasn't doing anything to cool him down either. Anna had been gone forty-five minutes and he was still hot for her. As in on fire. Not even Jordan's tears over being told he had to stay in bed and go to sleep so he wouldn't be tired for school had dampened anything going on inside his head and body.

Anna Passau hadn't just tweaked his interest; she'd grabbed him around the throat and wasn't letting go. Not even when he knew he had to put Jordan first.

So he wasn't allowed a life that included a sexy woman and maybe one day love? As long as none of that hurt Jordan, then yes, he was. But how could he guarantee Jordan wouldn't get let down badly if Anna left his father after they'd become more deeply involved? He couldn't. His family kept saying he had to let go the past and make a life for himself and Jordan would be as happy as ever. They were right. But when Melissa had walked away from her son as his mother had him, not quite the same circumstances but close enough, he'd got angry for Jordan. With his history of being given up by his birth mother he'd have thought he'd have seen Melissa for who she really was before they married and had Jordan.

None of this meant Anna was anything like her, but he couldn't trust himself not to make the same mistake. But there was only one way to learn to trust and that was get out there and start taking some risks. Slurping down more water, he swallowed hard when his phone beeped. He smiled, heated right back up.

Anna had come back.

Goodnight.

His smile dipped. Not wow. And here he was, acting crazy all over a kiss. A couple of kisses. Not enough. He wanted more. Lots more. Followed by something deeper and sexier—if that was possible because Anna's lips were to die for. She seemed to be pulling back. That alone should quieten his racing pulse, but not at all.

Holding the water bottle over his shirt-covered chest, he squeezed it empty in an attempt to cool off. Didn't work.

Pacing around the house did nothing to help either. Jordan was out for the count. His own bed looked empty and lonely. He could hardly mow the lawns at this time of night and remain on good terms with the neighbours. What was a man supposed to do when his mind was out of control?

Think of somewhere to take Anna on a date. A date? As in pick her up from her place and go for a meal or the pub and take her home again? What else did people do on dates? Kiss Anna again. That was his pick. She hadn't come back with a happy text, just goodnight.

*So show her you're more than a kiss or sex.*

Grabbing his phone, he found the ad for a rock concert at a vineyard in Waipara next Saturday Phil had been talking about in Theatre during the week. He'd ask Anna if she'd like to go. Or he could buy the tickets now and talk to her about it later on. He could also arrange a picnic with wine and roses—no, forget the roses. They suggested more interest than even he was willing to admit. But great food would be in the basket. If Anna declined the invitation he'd give the tickets to one of his sisters. And pretend not to care.

\* \* \*

On Monday Eli came onto the ward as Anna was getting up to speed with patients for the three to eleven shift. 'Hi, Anna. What'd you get up to this morning?'

Warmth spread through her. His friendly approach was continuing despite the abrupt end to last night. Would he continue to be friendly to everyone here or only her? Surely not that. He wasn't stupid and wouldn't want staff noticing his attention was only on her if it was. Then again, she was probably looking for something that didn't exist. After his kiss and text? The warmth was turning hot.

*Thought you were pulling back?*

'Digging part of my veggie patch to plant more chillies and capsicums for a later crop. Hopefully this fine weather will help out.'

'What else have you planted?' The surprise in his question made her smile.

'It's a long list. Nothing like fresh vegetables from my own garden.'

'She brings half the crop in here for us,' Leanne piped up from her desk. 'A person can only eat so much lettuce in one sitting.'

Anna ignored the look in her friend's eye that suggested she knew darned well she'd seen Eli over the weekend. 'That's not what you say when I give you a couple at a time.'

'Put my name on the list, will you?' Eli said as he reached past Anna to pick up a file. 'I've seen Andy, Leanne. You're right. There is an infection in his abdominal wound, which seems internal as well. I'll fill out a prescription for stronger antibiotics.'

'Talk to Anna about Andy. She's taking over. I'm off to pick up my kids and take them to swimming lessons.' Leanne nudged Anna none too gently as she stepped around her. 'We missed you yesterday.' Her grin was more than cheeky.

'I was busy.'

'I figured. See ya tomorrow.'

'How long have you two been mates?' Eli asked.

'We went through nursing school together. Now, is there anything I need to know about Andy? I've seen the case notes.'

Hopefully getting down to business would settle her racing heart. Who'd have thought she couldn't even stand near Eli any more without getting in a pickle? All because she'd gone to a kid's party.

*Try again, Anna. All because he's kissed you and smiles like the devil.*

'He presented in ED this morning with severe gastric pain caused by a bowel infection. I've gone in and removed the source, cleaned up the site as best as possible, but infection was a given.' He'd know he was repeating what she'd read but then he did like to be careful. 'Septicaemia is of concern. I'm watching closely. I want bloods taken every two hours for a CBC.'

Anna had the file back up on screen. 'Right. That'll be done. Anyone else in here who's your patient?'

'Not at the moment. I'm doing a tonsillectomy on an eight-year-old girl in the morning, which should be straightforward.'

'Careful.' Anna grinned without thought.

'True. Tempting fate is not usually my thing.' He turned for the door. 'See you later maybe.'

She gave up trying to stay focused only on work. 'I'm not going anywhere till eleven.'

Eli waved over his shoulder and left without another word.

Not that she could think of any answer to her comment—other than 'Come visit me when you leave here. We can pick up where we left off last night.' If only. The chances of that happening were zero with Jordan at home. The man was super protective of his boy and she couldn't see him being happy if Jordan were to find him in bed with a woman. Then again, this was only supposition, going on what little she knew about Eli. She could be totally wrong.

The next time Anna saw Eli he'd returned to check on his patient. 'Andy's slept a lot,' she told him. 'He was given antibiotics and light pain relief earlier because apparently he said it was hurting a lot. Otherwise all good.'

'Just as I expect,' Eli answered as he read the printout from the monitor, looking pleased with the result.

'Then I'll get back to my desk.' The ward was quiet other than the sound of chatter and laughter as parents boosted their sick children's moods. It would be dinner time soon and that would change as kids either gobbled down their meal or grizzled that they didn't like it.

'Got time for a coffee?'

'I have.' When they reached the staff kitchen dining room she was happy to see it was empty. Sharing Eli wasn't her idea of a good time together, even at work when either of them was likely to be called for at any moment. She held up the coffee plunger that was full and hot. 'Someone's beaten us to it.'

Eli placed a hand on her arm and turned her to face him. 'I'm sorry we were interrupted last night.'

'Me too.' She watched his mouth coming closer to hers and caught her breath. He was going to kiss her. There was singing in her veins. So much for staying in control of herself.

Eli's mouth covered hers. His tongue slipped inside and touched hers. Her knees softened. She grabbed his shirt to stay upright as she returned the kiss with all the pent-up frustration that had been knocking at her since she'd driven away from his house last night.

'Eli,' she murmured against his mouth.

His mouth pressed harder, driving her insane with desire. Then he stepped back, shoved his hands in his pockets and looked around as a nurse walked in. 'Hey, Gabrielle, did you make the coffee?'

He sounded so in control it bothered Anna.

Was he having her on? Was this not a real deal for him?

'Hope you don't mind sharing,' Eli said to Gabrielle, before turning and mouthing 'Phew' to Anna.

Had he heard the other nurse coming? She wouldn't have heard a bomb blast, she'd been so engrossed in kissing Eli. 'I agree,' she said quietly.

'There's enough for all of us. I'm taking mine back to the desk as I've got some notes to enter about the kid who's just been brought up from Theatre,' Gabrielle told them.

Anna had to shake her head to remember she was talking about coffee. 'Thanks for that. I'll join you shortly.' Grabbing her mug, she sank onto a chair. Work had never been so entertaining. But then she didn't usually take a lot of notice of the males who worked here. Nothing like how Eli had her attention. 'That was close,' she said to him when Gabrielle was well gone. 'Have you got extrasensory hearing or something?'

'Just a sixth sense that someone was coming.' He stirred sugar into his coffee and joined her at the table.

'Glad it worked.' She sipped her coffee thoughtfully. It would've been awkward to have been caught out. That particular nurse wasn't known for keeping quiet about just about anything.

'Relax, Anna. We got away with it.' Eli looked ridiculously comfortable, as though he couldn't care two tosses if someone had interrupted their kiss.

'Something you're used to?' she asked before putting her brain in gear. Then again, so what if she spoke her mind? Only way to know what was going on.

His mug banged on the table. 'No, Anna, it is not. As you have pointed out, I haven't been known for getting friendly with the staff in any way.'

Guilt made her grimace. 'I'm really sorry. I am a worry wort about these things.'

'You don't like people knowing you're having fun?'

'I don't want the nurses I work with giving me

a hard time about you. It wouldn't feel right. Not that I'm spending time with you but— Oh, hell, I don't know what I'm trying to say.' She stared at Eli, resisting the urge to throw herself into his arms and never let go. Which wasn't how she acted any time with anyone. She'd learned eighteen years ago it didn't get her anywhere other than mess with her relationships.

Eli turned his hand over to encase hers and stood up. 'Come here. Believe it or not, I understand what you're trying to say. You seem as cautious about getting close as I am so let's enjoy each other's company and see what happens.'

What a man. She could love him already if she were open to the idea. Which she wasn't sure she'd ever be after trying to let love in before and having it fail. She did want to fall in love with the right man and the scary thing here was Eli felt as though he could be that—if she allowed him in. If he allowed her in. But first she needed to know what held him back other than his ex and Jordan. Or was that more than enough? 'Done. Now I'd better take my coffee back to my desk before someone comes looking for me.'

'Not before we finish that kiss.'

Before Anna had time to think she was in Eli's arms and his mouth was covering hers, cranking up her hormones all over again.

Then he was walking out of the door as though he'd just had the perfect cup of coffee. Then he turned around and came back. 'I meant to ask if you're free on Saturday night to go to the rock concert out at a vineyard in Waipara. We'd take a picnic dinner and get some wine there.'

He was asking her on a date. A real date. 'I'd love to go with you.'

'Thank goodness or I'd have to decide which sister to give the tickets to.' His grin was mischievous. 'Talk later about details.' This time he did leave the ward.

Her eyes followed him, as did her heart. No doubt about it, Eli was special. She skipped back to the desk and sat down, only to realise her coffee was still on the table back in the kitchen.

# CHAPTER FIVE

ANNA LOOKED BEAUTIFUL in her butt-hugging jeans and low-cut emerald-green blouse. Her hair was free of any ties and fell over her shoulders to her breasts, accentuating their wondrous curves. Eli was beyond happy as he returned from the wine stall and stopped to watch her surveying the crowd. Hard to believe she'd always tickled his interest but only recently had she tripped him up with her sexuality and looks. And delightful personality.

Getting in a bit deep, he thought, and shrugged. He was here to have fun with Anna and that was what he'd do. He'd let reality back in tomorrow. A guy was allowed to have some fun.

'I see you've got the glasses out ready.' He laughed as he uncapped the bottle. Laughing came easy around Anna. 'They're doing a big trade in the wine tent.'

'Hardly surprising considering whose wine it is. Plus the fact we weren't allowed to bring our own.'

Sitting in the outdoor chair beside her, Eli filled the glasses and handed Anna one. 'Here's to a great night.' Who knew how it would unfold? All he could think was that he was with a lovely lady, and feeling so relaxed he had to keep pinching himself to make sure this wasn't a dream.

Rock music split the air as the first band for the night started up, silencing the audience all around them. Anna's fingers began tapping the rhythm on her thigh. 'Cool.'

At least that was what Eli thought she said. It was impossible to hear himself think, let alone whatever Anna said. Taking her hand in his, he settled back to enjoy the music, and the company, which couldn't be better. To think Anna had been there, right in his daily life at the hospital, and until recently he hadn't taken a lot of notice of her. Not quite true, but he'd deliberately ignored the flare of interest and the spark of heat she'd often provoked with little more than a glance or a shrug. 'Seems I can't ignore this any longer.'

Anna leaned closer. 'Ignore what?' Her hearing had to be sharp if she'd heard him.

He hadn't realised he'd spoken out loud. Seemed to do too much of that around Anna. 'The hamper full of food?'

'Try again.' She wasn't buying it.

Being so close to her brought that vanilla scent to his nose. 'Having fun on a date with a woman I am coming to like more every day.'

Jerking away, she stared at him, surprise lightening the green of her eyes so they looked like emeralds in the sun. She shook her head. 'I must be hearing things.'

*I wish you were.*

He'd shocked himself by being so open. Showed how out of practice he was when it came to dating. Tugging her close, he said, 'It's true.' Might as well stick with honesty. It wasn't as though he'd told her he'd fallen in love with her so he didn't need to retract his words and spend the rest of the night hoping the bands would pack up and go back to their hotels early.

'You never stop surprising me,' Anna told him.

'Until Jordan's op you'd only known me as a surgeon, nothing else. There's more to me than scalpels and vinyl gloves.'

'I guess.'

'You guess? I can't be doing a good job at showing you who I am.'

'So tell me more.'

'Later when I'm not competing with the band.'

*And have had time to think where I'm going with this. With Anna.*

She unfurled from her chair and took his hand. 'Come on. Let's boogie.'

'Me? Boogie?' Now she'd get one answer to learning more about him. He couldn't dance or boogie to save himself. Looking around at the crowd now on their feet, he shrugged happily. Nor could half the people here and no one seemed to care less. 'You're on.'

An hour later the band members hung up their gear and headed off stage, making way for the next band.

Anna sagged against Eli. 'I need water and food, in that order.'

'Me, too.' They hadn't stopped moving since they'd stood up. He wouldn't call either of their moves by any dance name, but it had been fun. Anna had been as sexy as all get out. But then he suspected she could be swimming in mud and he'd find her hot. 'Our wine didn't survive the moves.' The glasses lay empty on the grass between their chairs.

'What a waste. That's a tasty wine.'

'We can have some more with our food.' He opened the hamper. 'But first you wanted water.' He handed her a bottle and then unpacked the appetisers.

'These look delicious.' Anna picked up one and bit into it.

He tightened as he watched. So fast, so easy

with this woman. Something to be wary about. If she could upend his world biting into a pastry then she could cause a lot of damage with a kiss or sex. Right now he was ready to ignore the signs and have a fabulous time. Tomorrow he might regret everything, but tonight he'd enjoy being with Anna.

'Do you want to come in?' Anna asked Eli when he pulled into her drive hours later. She was putting herself out there with Eli, taking a chance that they'd continue the wonderful time they'd been having without him pulling back and leaving her wondering what he really wanted. The thing was, she wanted him. Badly. Not only in bed but in her life. So far they'd got along a lot better than she'd have believed not so long ago. She wanted that to continue.

'I'd love to.'

That was easy. 'Great.' Was he the man for her future? She had no idea. There was only one way to find out and that meant spending more time with him. The odds on him dumping her sooner than later were high. He'd said he'd do anything to protect his son. Because she didn't deserve happiness she always managed to cool off with any guy she dated, but Eli was different. Walking away wouldn't be easy. His caring side touched her deeply along with his sense of fun, his loyalty to Jordan and his family. But more than that, it was how he understood her, or, when he didn't, how he tried to. Of course he had no idea what she'd done, and if he did would probably move on from her. He made no bones about his feelings towards his ex over how she'd abandoned Jordan. He'd think the same if not worse about her giving her baby up for adoption.

'You seem to be deep in thought,' Eli said as he followed her up to her front door.

Shaking away the errant thoughts, she spun around to kiss him. 'I'm right here with you.'

Eli's mouth took over hers, kissing, tasting, turning her into a puddle of desire. Hot, wet need. Falling into him, she held him tight and gave back as good as she got.

'Anna,' he groaned against her. 'Open the door, will you?'

It took three attempts to get the key to work but finally they fell through the gap and she slammed the door shut again with her hip as she placed her hands on Eli's cheeks and stretched up to continue kissing him.

He was hard, pressing into her abdomen as his hands moulded around her butt. Damn it, but he was sexy, and turned her on without a blink. 'I want you.'

'Patience, Anna. We've got all night.'

'Patience, my ass. I won't be able to wait five minutes, let alone all night.'

He growled out a laugh. Then swung her up in those strong arms. 'Which way?'

'Straight ahead,' she said before pressing her mouth to his neck and licking up a storm. He tasted divine. Smelt even better. His skin was smooth and hot.

'Anna, slow down or I won't last the distance.'

She was already well on the way to combusting. 'Me either. In here.'

The moon lit up her bedroom like a hundred-watt bulb. Eli laid her on the bed and she held onto him, pulling him down on top of her quaking body.

'Clothes.'

Always something to get in the way. She tugged at his shirt, but it was stuck between them.

Eli was slipping her jeans down over her hips as he lay against her.

Pushing her hand between them, she found his erection and took it in her grasp.

'Anna… Wait.'

'Can't.'

'Have to.' He sat up, dug into his pocket for a packet and then shoved out of his trousers and pulled his shirt over his head. 'Condom.'

'I'm on the pill.'

Pulling a packet from his pocket, he said, 'I

always make sure I'm covered.' He began undoing her blouse one agonising button at a time. Slowing them down while the urgency grew and grew.

'Better safe than sorry?'

'Absolutely.'

She couldn't blame him for that. No one wanted to find they were unexpectedly going to be a parent, especially when they were having a fling, not a full-time relationship. Taking him in her hand again, she slid her hand up and down, up and down.

'Stop.' Eli took her hand away, then covered her nipple with his mouth, running his tongue over and around it, sending her into another world, full of sensations that wound her up tighter than ever, bringing her to a climax without touching her sex.

Grabbing his hand, she placed it on the hot spot between her legs, and cried out when his fingers moved over her. Her body bucked against him, again and again. Then she exploded with heat and desire, with need for this amazing man.

Eli knelt between her legs and lifted her up. His throbbing sex slid into her slowly, gently, and pulled back.

She cried out. 'Eli, please, more.'

He obliged. In, out, the tempo increasing with

each move until she thought she was going to fall apart. 'Eli, now.'

He drove into her, hard and fast, and called out as he came. 'Anna, oh, Anna.'

Her name on his tongue was sensual, sexy, alluring. As he fell away he took her with him, held her close, wrapped in those arms she was coming to adore. His chest rose and fell rapidly. Like hers as she struggled to regain composure. 'Eli, that was beyond wonderful.'

His arms held her tighter.

Snuggling against his chest, she let her eyes fall shut. Every other sense was wide awake. It felt as though they were in a little world of their own. Tuned into each other, not needing to say a word, their bodies touching was enough. Wow. She'd been waiting for ever to feel like this. Hadn't known it was even possible, yet now Eli had set a benchmark there'd be no ignoring.

'Anna,' he whispered. 'I don't know what to say other than I'm more than happy.'

'That's enough. To try adding to it will only undo the wonder you've just given me.'

His lips brushed her forehead. 'You're amazing.'

'Takes two to tango.'

'I think we did way better here than with our dancing.' His laughter was low and light. And as sexy as it was possible to be.

When Eli began tracing circles on her thigh

she knew they were going to make love again. This time they took their time discovering each other's body from top to toe and back to the centre where they both throbbed with need. After Eli made her pause so he could put on a condom Anna rode him hard, gazing down into his adorable face as they came together.

Snuggling up close afterwards, she slipped into sleep, her heart full of wonder at what had gone down between them. She woke as Eli was getting out of bed. 'Eli?'

'I'm heading home. Liz is bringing Jordie home first thing as she's got to be somewhere. Thanks for a wonderful night.' He leaned down and kissed her gently. 'I have seriously enjoyed our date.'

'Me, too.'

'We'll have to do it again.'

Try stopping her. 'You're on.'

Eli looked stunned, as though he hadn't meant to say that.

Anna ran a hand over his chin. 'No rush.'

'You're right there.' He was withdrawing. Pulling on his clothes fast.

Within moments of getting out of her bed. 'Thanks, Eli. You certainly know how to kill the moment.'

He hesitated. 'Anna, I didn't intend that. I've had a wonderful night with you. An amazing time.'

'But?'

'Reality's kicking in. I can't spend lots of time with you. I have other commitments that come before anything else.'

'You think I don't understand that? Stop treating me as though I expect you to put me first all the time. We're not even seeing that much of each other.' So much for a wonderful night. It was going up in smoke fast.

'Fair enough. I'd better get going. See you at work.'

Anna stared at her empty doorway until she heard the front door close, then she got up to make sure it was locked since there wasn't a hope in hell Eli would come back tonight. He was on a mission that didn't involve her.

Thank goodness she was on nights for the first three days where chances of bumping into him were remote. Her heart was heavy. So much for getting to know him better. The biggest message she got was he didn't want to allow her into his life if it meant Jordan could be upset. Fine, except it seemed that boy ruled his father completely. Or was Eli hiding behind him? Now there was something to think about.

Night shift worked. Anna didn't see Eli at all for the first half of the week, though she couldn't stop herself from looking out for him. She had it bad. After making love, she felt she'd found someone so special that she was willing to risk everything to be with him. Apparently she hadn't affected him half as much, which highlighted the fact she didn't deserve to find true love.

On Thursday she was on morning shift with Leanne.

'Feel like checking out the sales for some summer clothes when we're finished here?'

Not really. What was the point? Come on. Don't let Eli wreck everything. 'I could do with a spruce up,' she said half-heartedly.

Her friend laughed. 'Nothing to do with a certain surgeon by any chance?'

Not at the moment. 'Whatever makes you think that?'

'The fact you're always keeping an eye out for him between patients.'

'We're not seeing eye to eye just now.'

'So I gathered, which is why shopping is a good idea.' Leanne glanced at the computer screen. 'You'd better grab a bite to eat while it's quiet.'

Standing up, Anna stretched her back. 'I'll be in the canteen if you need me.'

Leanne looked past her and grinned. 'I'll try not to call you.'

Instantly Anna felt Eli's presence. He'd got to her so much she always seemed to know whenever he was around, but not this time. 'I'm off. Hi, Eli. Have you come to see Laurie? She's doing well today. No more pain, and the infection's abating.'

'I've just seen her. She's improved a lot since yesterday.' Eli had his serious doctor face on.

'Problem?'

'No. Mind if I join you for a coffee in the canteen?' Still serious.

Why would there be a problem? 'Of course not.' She headed for the lift, not waiting to see what he'd do. When the door opened and he stepped in beside her she sighed with relief. He had her stirred with worry over a simple question, and that demeanour that had been absent lately. 'Everything okay?'

'Yes.'

Sounded more like no to her. 'Any plans for the weekend?' He hadn't mentioned them going on another date. Had she got it all wrong and he'd only been there for one night's pleasure. If that was the case she'd toughen up and get over it. Better to find out now and not weeks down the track when chances were she'd be right into him. *Aren't you already?* Pretty much, she admitted silently.

'Jordan's got another party to go to. His best friend's turning five and will start at the same school on Monday.'

'How's Jordan enjoying school so far?'

'Loves it.' Eli's mouth flattened. 'It's one of my concerns that he'll get teased for being different.'

'He comes across as quite tough.'

'You haven't seen him when he's been bullied by kids who think they're perfect.'

No, she hadn't, but she could imagine Jordan's little face screwed up with tears pouring down his cheeks as he tried to work out why kids teased him. 'Hard for you both.'

'Are you working this weekend?'

Was he going to ask her to join him at some point? 'I'm rostered for Sunday night, otherwise I'm free.'

'I'm sure you'll be busy with something.'

The hope lifting her heart fell away. So they weren't getting together. Stepping out of the lift, she headed for the canteen. Not that she was hungry any more but she'd do her best to eat something so he didn't see how hurt she felt. 'I'll get you a coffee.'

'Thanks. I'll grab a table.'

Something definitely wasn't right. He hadn't called her since Saturday. Not that she'd tried to get in touch either. Yet here he was, wanting to talk to her. Nothing added up. When she sat down with her lunch and two coffees he gave her a warm smile, confusing her even more.

'Cheers, Anna. Jordan was asking after you last night. In fact he does just about every night.'

Light-bulb moment. 'Is that a problem?'

'I hope not.'

Another punch to her heart. 'I can't see how it would be.' Unless he didn't want his son to have another woman in his life.

'After what Melissa did I am probably over-protective but I do not want him hurt again. I still struggle to understand how she could walk like she did. How any mother can leave their child for that matter.' He raised his hands in a futile gesture. 'How does a woman give up her baby for adoption after carrying him, nurturing him, for nine months? It's beyond me.'

Anna's stomach lurched. There was the answer she'd been dreading all along. They were over before they'd started, if that had been on the cards. No need to explain that she'd given up her son, and why, and that it wasn't as easy as he seemed to think to keep a baby when you were sixteen and no one was there for you. Because she got the sense that she was included in that general statement about women because he didn't trust any female who might get close to him.

'You think I might hurt your son? Well, Eli, if we were to get any closer—' obviously they weren't but she couldn't let this go '—it would be both of us involved and we would talk about Jordan and how to keep everything shipshape for him.'

He leant back in his chair, looking baffled, as if he didn't know how to deal with her. 'You know what I like about you? You don't hold back. You're not into trying to get on my best side by saying what you think I want to hear, you just get on with speaking your mind.'

That was a surprise. Very honest. Hope he liked how she made love to him too, though right now that would be the last thing on his mind. 'Only way to go.' Though there were things she had no intention of telling him now unless they progressed further. He'd find every fault with what she'd done and wouldn't understand she'd had no choice if her son was to have a good life. He'd return to being aloof Mr Forrester, which would hurt almost more than anything else.

'Yes, it is. Anna, I don't want to stop seeing you.'

Then she'd better tell him. Get it over with. At least she'd know where she stood. She already did though. Seeing his reaction, hearing what he'd have to say, would only underscore what Danny and Jock had said and she didn't need to hear that again. Except she wasn't going to be a coward. Big breath. 'Eli, I—'

'I hate that Jordan's so vulnerable. It's one

thing for me to worry about where I'm going with our future but it's quite another to think he could get close to someone I bring into the family and then be hurt badly.' He paused, drumming his fingers on the table. 'Anna, I need to take things slowly. If that doesn't work for you then I guess we remain solely friends.'

Doubt that would be the case when he heard what she had to say. 'I hear you but first—'

His pager interrupted.

Was she ever going to be able to finish a sentence? Though relief was taking over. It wouldn't be pleasant telling him about her past. Besides, doing that here in the cafeteria, surrounded by people, wasn't the wisest idea.

He stood up. 'Got to go. A patient in ED requires my attention.'

'Catch up some other time.' That sounded as if she was going with the go-slow option, and maybe she would give it a try, even if it meant her heart might take a hard knock in the end. As she watched him walk away her head spun. Eli really had got to her and she couldn't imagine not getting along with him as more than friends.

'Hello. Are you Anna Passau?' A young man stood beside the table, watching her warily.

'I am.' She stared at him, not knowing who he was yet feeling as though she should. 'Do I know you?'

'I'm Charlie.'

Her mouth fell open. She *had* to be hearing things. 'Who?'

'Your son.'

'They named you Charlie?' The name she'd chosen even when knowing she had no say in what her boy was called or that she'd likely ever see him again.

'Mum and Dad did it for you. And for me.'

She was still staring at him, drinking in the sight of her son. Her son. Charlie. No. Couldn't be. What was he doing here? How had he found her? What was going on? 'Charlie.'

'Can I sit down?'

'Yes,' she all but shouted.

*Don't go anywhere.*

'I don't know what to say. I mean, I'm stunned, surprised, happy, scared. Every emotion possible is racing through me. I can't believe this is you. Why are you here? I mean, why at the hospital and not at my house? Or don't you know where that is?'

*Slow down, Anna. Give the kid a chance to speak.*

Pulling out a chair and sitting down, he blushed. Her heart swelled.

'Um…it's like this. When my brother, adopted like me, approached his birth mother the first time it was at her house where her husband and other kids lived. She screamed and yelled, saying he had no right turning up in her life. I didn't want that and kind of figured you'd be quieter if there were lots of people around.'

She closed her eyes, counted to ten, opened them. 'I'd never say that. I've wanted to see you ever since you were taken—' Her mouth dried. Reaching for her mug, she swallowed cold coffee and tried again. 'Since the day you were born. I am thrilled you're here.' More than thrilled, but she couldn't find another word to describe the feelings rolling through her.

'Did you ever try to find me?'

'I had nothing to go on. The adoption papers included a no visit edict.'

'You signed that.' He wasn't giving anything away.

'I had no choice.'

'You could've kept me.'

'Again, I had no choice.' Again, she closed her eyes and drew a long steadying breath. Locking eyes with Charlie, she tried to explain. 'I turned sixteen two weeks before you were born. I was still at school. I would've left and got a job, two jobs, to support you but I wouldn't have earned enough to put a roof over your head, let alone feed and clothe you.'

'You lived with your parents. Mum and Dad told me,' he snapped.

'They said they'd kick me out if I kept you. I'd have dealt with that if I could've managed on my own.' Hesitantly she reached for his hand, felt a stab of love when he didn't pull away. 'I really would have. I wanted you. I did not want to adopt you out. You are my son. No way did I want strangers raising you.' He felt warm, but he was shaking. Or was that her? 'It was the most difficult time of my life. All I could hope was that one day you'd understand I put you first. You had to have a good life. That was the most important thing.'

He jerked his hand away. 'You don't think growing up with my birth mother would be more important?'

'Yes, I did. I do. At least I think I do but I'm not in your position so I could be wrong.' Clenching her hands in a knot in her lap, she stared at this young man who'd approached her. She had no doubts he was her son. None whatsoever. Even if he didn't have the same green eyes she saw every morning in her mirror she'd know. He was tall, unlike her. His hair was fair, not red. But there was something in the way he sat, back straight, mouth firm, that spoke of her at times when she was stressed or worried.

'I have always dreamed of meeting you, of telling you that you did me a favour because

I did not want to have anything to do with a woman who could give me away.'

Pain sliced into her. Hot and hard, and deadly. She slumped in her seat. 'I can't explain how sorry I am, but I believed I was doing the right thing for you.' He'd never understand, or believe her if the angry look in his eyes was anything to go by.

For a moment Charlie was silent and Anna wondered if he'd walk away, never to see her again. She waited, swallowing the words that threatened to spill across her lips. There was so much she wanted, needed, to know, and was afraid to ask for fear he would disappear out of her life again.

Then he stunned her once more. 'In some ways you did. Mum and Dad have been the best parents I could've wished for. They love me so much, as I do them. They've given me a fabulous life, supported me through everything, including trying to make me see you had to do what you did.'

'I didn't ask for that clause that said I'd never get in touch to be included.'

'They told me your parents did that.'

'Yes.' She'd never forgiven them, which probably got in the way of at least having a family-friendly relationship.

'You're a nurse.' He'd changed the subject fast.

'I am.'

'I'm in my first year training to become one.' For the first time there was a glimmer of a smile coming her way.

Not a big one, but, hell, did she feel so, so much better. 'We have something in common,' she told her son, hoping that wouldn't send him running out of the room.

'That's what I thought when I found out.'

'Where are you training?'

The smile switched off. 'In Wellington where I've been all my life.'

'Wellington? I had no idea that's where you grew up.'

'No, of course not.' The anger had returned.

'How did you find me?'

'I didn't.' He was watching her with wariness. 'Mum did. She won't tell me how, only that she knew your family lived in Christchurch at the time, and she went from there. I think she knew your father was in business of some sort and started asking around.' His shrug was tight. 'She understood I needed to know who you are, and that I also didn't want to know.'

Again pain slammed into her. Yet she thought she understood where Charlie was coming from. It still hurt. From the moment he'd been taken out of her arms she'd hoped for this day. Now he'd turned up she wasn't going to wish him away. No way could she. He was her son whatever he felt. 'You'll never know how glad I am you decided to see me.'

'I've often been angry at you, while still wanting to find out about you.' He stood up. 'Time I got going. I've been in Christchurch at a general practice doing some training and I've got a flight back home at five.'

Leaping to her feet, she cried, 'Charlie. Don't go. Not yet. Please.'

'I have to.' He hesitated. 'Can I have your phone number?'

'Absolutely.'

He pulled a phone from his pocket. 'What is it?'

So he wasn't ready to give her his. 'Can I have yours?'

'No.' Then he muttered, 'Not yet.'

'Fair enough,' she supposed aloud, but what if he never got in touch again? She'd be heartbroken for ever. But she had finally seen him, knew what he looked like, how his voice sounded. It wasn't anywhere near enough. She gave him her number. It was better than nothing.

What name did he use for her number? It wouldn't be Mum.

Charlie glanced up from his phone, suddenly looking like a little boy who'd lost something monumental, instead of having found it. Had she failed him? What had he expected?

'Charlie?'

'I'll see you around,' he said and walked away. No hug, no last look over his shoulder. Nothing.

Anna stared at his retreating back until he left the cafeteria, and then she stared some more but he didn't come back. Sinking back onto the seat, she put her head in her hands and cried.

# CHAPTER SIX

'HERE, GET THIS into you.' Leanne placed a fresh mug of coffee on the table in front of Anna and pulled up a chair to sit beside her.

Anna raised her head slowly, feeling utterly ravaged. Her cheeks felt puffy from crying and tears were still pouring down them. 'I doubt I can swallow a thing.' Leanne had come looking for her when she hadn't returned to the ward, and when she'd told her Charlie had turned up, her friend had sat down beside her, ordered more coffee and held her hand.

'Give it a go. It'll perk you up.'

Coffee splashed over the table when Anna tried to lift the mug. Banging it back down, she stared at it as if it were a monster. 'I can't believe it. All Charlie's life I've waited and hoped I'd get to meet him and now it's happened.' Tears splashed on the backs of her shaking hands.

Leanne's smile was understanding. 'You've wanted this for so long. It's going to take time to absorb it all. You'd better sign off for the rest of the day. You're in no shape to go back to work.'

Staring at her hands, she whispered, 'I am so glad he found me, so amazed, yet I feel all over the place, like there's another bombshell to come.'

'Of course you do. It's only natural.'

'Thanks, Leanne. Where would I be without you?'

'You'd manage. You're tougher than you think.' Leanne hugged her. 'I'd better get back to the ward. We'll talk tonight. Be patient with your-self, girlfriend.'

'Me?'

'Yeah, you. Ring me later.'

'Will do. Think I'll go for a walk in the park. I need to get my head around this.' If it was even possible. Charlie had walked back into her life. Charlie.

Anna wandered around Hagley Park for endless hours, not taking a lot of notice of where she was going, just walking and thinking, and thinking and thinking.

Charlie. Her boy. Impossible to believe he'd come to find her. But there was no denying the vision of him standing beside the canteen table looking at her as though she was an apparition. He was for real. Charlie. Her boy. Not her boy. Yes, her son.

Her heart was all over the place. Happy, bewildered, sad, full of love for the young man she'd brought into the world eighteen years ago. There'd been moments when he'd looked ecstatic to see her, and others when doubt would darken his face and he'd looked disappointed. That was to be expected. He must've grown up wondering why she'd left him, and no doubt would've hated her at times for that. Did he regret finding her? Did she measure up to his expectations? What were those? He wouldn't understand how hard it had been for her too, and that if only she'd known where he was she'd have sent him birthday cards and presents. Would've banged down the door to his home to see him and hold him in her arms.

Now he was here. And she still hadn't held him. No, he'd gone. Back to Wellington and his parents. Mum and Dad. That hurt. Sure, it shouldn't. She had no right to keep him here, to demand he spend time with her. She wouldn't do that to him. It would be unfair and would only lead Charlie to believe he was better off not being a part of her life.

Now that he'd come to her, she could not let him walk away again. She had to be more patient than she'd ever been, let him make the decisions about what he wanted and when. And hope like crazy that included her. She wasn't asking to become part of his life twenty-four-seven. No, just to have some phone calls, visits, talk about what he was up to, all the general goings-on of a family life—part removed.

Family life. Eli.

Anna tripped, straightened, continued walking. Eli. She'd come close to telling him about her son. Charlie. Her son, Charlie. His adoptive parents had given him her chosen name. That said a lot about the couple, said he'd been very lucky getting them for parents. They cared, not only about him but about her.

What would Eli think now that she could add to her story that her son had found her? Would he still walk away because of what she'd done? Or would he stop and think it through, realise she'd only done what couldn't be avoided, and that Charlie had been fine?

She had to stop tormenting herself. There was already too much going on in her mind about Charlie to get wound up about Eli right now. Nor could she let him go completely.

As she turned for the car park there was a light spring in her step, as if a huge rock had fallen away to leave her filled with hope. Maybe she wasn't so undeserving of love as she'd believed.

'Hey, my man, how's things?' Eli swung Jordie up in his arms and hugged him tight.

Jordan wriggled to get down. 'I learned to write your name, Dad. The teacher said I'm good at writing words. Want to see?'

'Of course I do.' This was one reason why he loved being a dad. He got to share all Jordan's excitement over small things like learning to spell. Though it wasn't so small for Jordie.

'Here.'

Eli unfolded the piece of paper he'd been handed and saw his name in lower case and erratic capitals and his heart squeezed with love. Bending down, he kissed the top of his son's head. 'That's awesome. I'm going to put it in a picture frame and have it by my bed so I know my name when I wake up in the mornings.'

Jordan laughed. 'Silly Dad. You know your name.'

Scratching his chin, Eli asked, 'What is it?'

'Eli Forrester. Like my name. Jordan Forrester.'

'Have you written your name on a piece of paper? Because then I could put them both in the picture frame.'

'You know my name too.'

Sometimes his kid wasn't as slow as people thought. 'You're right, I do.'

'How do I write Anna?'

*Crunch.* Eli's mouth dried. This was what

he'd been dreading. Jordan getting too involved with her.

'Dad, tell me.'

There'd be no avoiding this. Don't show him how to spell Anna and Jordan would throw a paddy. On the other hand, show him and he'd have more to worry about. Right now he did not need a tantrum. Giving in too easily? Giving into Jordan or the lift of his heart that usually came when he was with Anna? Though he had managed to put a dampener on that over the past few days, there were cracks appearing in his façade. He did want more to do with her, despite holding out about Jordan. It could work out if he let go of his caution and put everything he had into a relationship with Anna. 'Here, give me your pen and paper and I'll show you.'

As soon as Jordan had finished copying Anna's name he said, 'I'm hungry.'

It was hard to keep up sometimes. 'Let's see what Grandma's made us for dinner.'

Where would he be without his mother? She provided so many meals it got embarrassing, but whenever he suggested she take a break she'd look sad and say she loved being able to help out. She'd always been there for him and his sisters, helping wherever needed and loving doing so. A big-hearted woman who knew no bounds when it came to her family. He'd been incredibly lucky to be adopted by her and Dad.

'I want beans on toast.' Jordie leapt up and down in front of him, Anna forgotten for now. 'I don't like shepherd's pie.'

'You loved it last week.' Eli flicked the oven on and slid the pie inside to warm through. 'You had two helpings.'

'Did not.'

One of these nights, just when he didn't need it. Eli sighed. Did any parent ever need them? Loud shouting came from the TV where the home side was playing the Aussies in a cricket one-day match. 'Go, Barker.' A fielder had caught the ball and Aussie was down another wicket. The run rate was ten an over. The Aussies needed to lose a few more wickets.

'I want beans.' Jordie banged a tin on the bench.

Eli didn't have the energy to argue. Today had been hectic and seeing Anna had tightened those places he couldn't control around her even when their conversation had been stilted. When he'd explained why he didn't want to rush things he'd sensed she was holding back on something important. He needed to know what it was and, being him, wouldn't be able to let it go until he did.

They'd been talking about keeping their budding relationship—his word, not hers—moving slowly because of Jordan. He'd also said he didn't understand Melissa leaving her son and that was when Anna had pulled back. It didn't make sense, when he'd been honest about how he felt.

Anna, Anna, Anna. She was dominating his thoughts too much.

He'd slept with her. That had been beyond amazing. She was wonderful and had woken him up to all sorts of possibilities, along with increasing his wariness. So wary that he'd walked away without a backward glance, without hugging and kissing her goodnight and promising more to come.

Was he afraid to give in to these feelings she engendered in him?

Was he using Jordan as an excuse to protect his heart?

The ward was busy when Anna arrived at six forty-five the next morning after lying awake thinking about Charlie—and Eli—all night. 'Wow, what happened?'

'A three-year-old with appendicitis was admitted from surgery at four this morning. Then there's a seven-year-old girl with fractures and severe bruising who came in late last night,'

Jacob told her. 'She'd been beaten but of course no one knows when or by who.'

Anna shivered. Some people didn't deserve children. 'That's hideous.'

'It certainly is. Jossy is being kept under sedation. She was beyond distressed when she was brought in.'

'Who's her surgeon?' Eli? She wasn't sure she wanted to see him this morning. His comment about women giving up their babies still hurt despite Charlie turning up in her life and making her happy. While Charlie appeared to have had the good upbringing she'd hoped for, she wasn't ready to explain everything to Eli and hear how wrong she'd been in the first place. This might mean that once more she was alone, single. Harder to swallow than before Eli came along. But she did have a son who'd made contact. Not everything was bad.

'Duncan saw her during the night but I don't know if he's following up today or Eli will take over.'

The way things went, Anna figured she already knew the answer. Sitting down at the computer, she updated herself on patients who'd been admitted since she'd left yesterday. Getting back to work would help settle her overactive mind and get her back on track. It was amazing that Charlie had approached her and she would wait to see what came next, feeling confident that he would get in touch again. As for Eli, she was worried, and had spent time thinking about him during the night when Charlie hadn't been ruling her mind. Did that make her a bad person? Depended who she asked.

Eli said they needed to go slow. That she got, but Jordan couldn't rule the relationship if there was any chance of continuing once she did pluck up the courage to tell him everything.

*So you still want him in your life despite what he said?*

If he listened to her and accepted how it had been for her, then yes. If not, then no.

First she needed to know they were still on good terms. They'd got on so well. Hopefully they still did and she was exaggerating everything.

Two hours later, when she was dressing a wound on a boy's leg where he'd fallen onto a garden stake, she felt a thrill of anticipation run up her spine. Totally out of place.

'Morning, Anna.' Eli stood at the end of the boy's bed, watching her closely.

'Have I got jam on my chin?'

'No, shadows under your eyes.'

'Not enough make-up obviously.' She couldn't make him out. Not overly friendly but neither was he being aloof Mr Forrester. 'Are you taking over Jossy's case?'

'For today anyway. Duncan rang me earlier about her. It doesn't sound good. I've read the notes and am on my way to see her now.'

So he'd stopped in here to say hello. All was not lost. She had been getting in a stew over nothing. 'I'll be there as soon as I've finished this dressing.'

'It's all right. Leanne's already there.' Leanne. Without her, Anna wouldn't know where to turn. They'd talked for an hour on the phone last night and Leanne had said she shouldn't be so quick to judge Eli. He might be venting about his past, and not really serious about what he'd said. Anna wasn't so sure, but she was already smitten with him and didn't want to walk away too quickly. Honestly? Yes.

Eli headed out of the room without a backward glance.

She didn't cover all the cases, and not even all the new ones, but that felt like a deliberate snub. Couldn't be when he'd dropped by to see her. She was still looking for trouble. She was falling for Eli, was what she was really doing.

Ten minutes later Eli was back. 'Anna, I've ordered a prescription for different antibiotics for Jossy. The ones she's been having aren't doing a lot of good for that wound in her chest.'

Glancing up at him, she nodded. 'I'll see that it's collected.'

'She also needs bloods done.'

'Okay.' The request would've been emailed to the lab downstairs and a phlebotomist would come to the ward on her rounds, unless Eli had marked it urgent. 'What are you checking?'

'CBC, liver function, non-fasting glucose, CRP.' Run of the mill tests.

'Her grandmother will be here soon to sit with her.' Not her mother. But then no one knew what or who was behind the beating Jossy had received. 'I hate these cases.' They brought tears to her eyes and wound up her anger levels. Why were some people so cruel as to hit a child? It was beyond comprehension. She'd be grateful for ever that Charlie obviously hadn't had any abuse growing up. It would've been in the back of his eyes, behind the few things he'd told her. She'd have known. Wouldn't she?

'Don't we all?' Eli muttered before heading away again.

Nothing about seeing her for a coffee or lunch. Nothing personal at all. The fact they were at work had nothing to do with it. He'd moved on from being reticent when it came to spending a few minutes with her here. Watching that straight back and those long legs eating up the distance to the lift filled Anna with sadness. They were back to square one.

The lift opened and an orderly pushed a bed out and along towards the desk. 'Molly Hebberd to see you,' he joked.

'Hello, Molly. I'm Anna, one of the nurses who's going to be looking after you.' Molly had had pins inserted in her right tibia, which was fractured in two places.

'Hello, Anna.'

'Room three,' she nodded to the orderly and led the way. 'You've got two roommates, Molly. Both are your age.' Fourteen going on twenty judging by the chatter and giggles coming from the room when she'd arrived on the ward earlier.

'Cool. How long am I here for?'

'I'll have to ask your specialist. Didn't he tell you?'

'Dr Duncan said I'd have to wait and see how soon I get used to crutches.'

'There you go. We've got a physio coming to see you this afternoon. She'll be starting you on easy moves.'

'Anna, can I see you for a moment?' Eli was back.

For a second, hope flickered, but one look at his serious face and she knew whatever he needed it had nothing to do with them. 'I'll be right back, Molly.' As she followed Eli out into the corridor, Anna's heart was tight. How she wanted to wind her arms around his waist and hold him close, breathe in his scent, feel his warmth under that plain blue shirt. Instead she slipped her hands into her pockets and asked, 'What's up?'

'I want to ask that you keep a close eye on Jossy and any visitors she might get. Her grandmother has talked to me and implied that not all the family should be allowed anywhere near Jossy.'

It was good the girl was in a room on her own. The last thing anyone wanted was trouble in front of other sick children.

'Has anyone contacted Social Welfare?'

'That was done as soon as she was brought in. They'll be here soon.'

'Thanks for the heads up. The problem being we won't have a clue as to who should be allowed to visit and who shouldn't.'

'I'll speak to Security but there's not a lot we can do. The grandmother wasn't very forthcoming with names, only that Jossy would be distressed if certain people visited. It's not what any of us want a patient to have to face. Keep me posted if anyone causes trouble.' Eli was on his way again, not a smile in sight.

'Of course,' she replied to his back. She was glad she had two days ahead where she wouldn't be bumping into him and wishing for more than a medical discussion about one of his patients. What was his problem anyway? He hadn't been there when Charlie turned up. Had he decided going slow meant going nowhere and hadn't got around to mentioning it? They might be at work but five minutes in the staffroom would suffice. It was busy around here though. She shrugged. She had no idea what was going on with Eli, or herself. Focusing on patients was the only answer for now.

The weekend wasn't going to be a barrel of laughs. She had no plans other than the usual routine of housework, shopping and maybe catching up with friends on Sunday for lunch. And probably cooking meals to put in the freezer for night shifts as that was always a go-to when she needed a distraction. Being creative in the kitchen was a balm to her soul and filled in lots of hours, and the deep freeze. Funny how that had never bothered her until Eli came into her life. Now she wished they could get together and have fun, whether it was taking Jordan somewhere or getting between the sheets for some hot sex, and enjoying her cooking.

This playing cautious was driving him nuts. Eli's hand tightened on the steering wheel. Waiting till he'd figured out whether he wanted to pursue the relationship they'd begun was all very well—if it was a relationship at this point—but it was damned hard to keep on with doing it. One kid's party, one date with unbelievable sex. Did that add up to a relationship? Add in coffees and lunches and chit-chat on the ward, and it sounded a little better.

The fact was, Anna was special. He wanted more time with her. Wanted to get to know everything about her. To enjoy her company regularly. Unfortunately he had said they needed to go slowly, something he struggled with. It would be easier to stop altogether because then he wasn't building on the level of happiness she made him feel. He did care for her a lot, to the point it wouldn't take much to fall totally in love with her and that was downright scary. The fact she'd held back on something the other day suggested she could hurt him. He couldn't abide being kept in the dark by someone important to him. He'd suffered the consequences of that before. Yet his heart wanted to open up and be free.

Jordan already thought Nurse Anna was the bee's knees, always asking when he could see her again. That Anna could let him down frightened the daylights out of his father. He didn't want Jordan growing up thinking all women were selfish when it came to children.

*Anna's not selfish.*

She was big-hearted and generous with her time and self. He couldn't see her putting herself first over anyone in her life. But he had to look out for Jordan because if Melissa could do what she did, then anyone could.

Was he being unfair? Possibly, but he knew what it was like to be put aside by a parent. When he'd tracked down his birth mother only to be told she really didn't care if she saw him again or not, he'd felt as though a spear had been slammed into his heart. That was behind his feelings about any woman who gave up their child, no matter why. Call him narrow-minded, but he'd grown up longing to meet his birth mother only to be rejected. While struggling to forget that, he also acknowledged how lucky he'd been with his real family. His birth mother hadn't wanted him. When Melissa had left him he'd known more pain, but when she'd said Jordan wasn't going to be a part of her life in New York his anger had exploded and he'd said a lot of things that could never be taken back, and nor had he wanted to. He'd meant every single word. Still would if Melissa ever changed her mind about raising Jordan. Chances of that happening were remote, and legally she'd have a battle on her hands given how he was raising their son perfectly well with the help of his family.

Pulling into the school car park, he switched

off the motor and leaned his head back. Anna was awesome. Within a short time she'd sneaked under his caution radar and made him start thinking about the future. A future with a woman he loved and a brother or sister for Jordan. Possibly one of each. He grinned. As if he'd get a choice. He hadn't thought too much about finding another woman to share his life with, then along had come Anna. Wrong. Anna had already been there. He'd refused to take notice of her other than as an excellent nurse. Oh, and a woman who made his skin tighten and his toes curl. Now he knew better. There was a lot to her. She had a big heart, cared plenty for others, never complained about anything, gave as good as she got in bed. At least he hoped she got as good from him, because he'd certainly had an amazing experience.

The screen on his phone lit up.

You going to sit there all afternoon?

Followed by a grinning emoji. Typical. His sister Karen always gave him cheek, and had done pretty much most of his life.

He headed for the gate and the school playground where Jordie was trying to throw a basketball through a low hoop. 'Hey, man, how're you going?'

'The stupid ball won't go in.'

'Here, stand like this.' Eli stood with one leg back, and held his arms above his head. 'With the ball in both hands.'

Jordie tried to copy him, then threw the ball and missed. 'Stupid, stupid ball.'

'Try again. You've got to watch the hoop, not the ball. Look where you want it to go.'

The ball banged on the side of the hoop. 'Yes!' Jordie fist-pumped the air. 'I want to do more, Dad.'

'Just a few. I've got to get back to work soon.' He'd take Jordan home to his mother's and have a few minutes with him over orange juice and cake.

'He's had a good day.' Karen stood beside Eli. 'He mentioned Nurse Anna a couple of times when I saw him at lunch time. Says he hasn't seen her for ages.'

Eli tried for nonchalance. 'She's not a regular visitor.'

'And you're not happy about that.'

So much for thinking he could fool his sister. 'It's my choice, not hers.'

'Aah, so Anna would be happy to pop by occasionally. Or even more often.'

He wasn't so sure about that. They weren't exactly best buddies at the moment. He missed her though. It wasn't the same seeing her on the ward. That didn't give him the warmth he got whenever they were alone. And he wasn't thinking about sex. Just being with her, talking and laughing, was more than enough to make him happy. 'Jordie, come on. Time to hit the road.'

'You like her a lot, don't you?' Once Karen started there was no stopping her until she'd got whatever was on her mind out there.

Might as well be blunt. 'Yes.'

'So what's the problem?'

'You know I'm waiting until Jordan's a lot older before I get into a serious relationship.'

'What I know is you're avoiding one because you're afraid you'll get hurt. It's not all about how Jordan copes if a relationship doesn't work out. He'll cope, as he's done before. He's a tough little guy. Like his dad. That's all I've got to say.'

'Which was too much anyway.' Eli laughed, because there was never any dodging the bullets his sisters fired when they thought he needed putting in his place. 'I hear you, but you're not going to change my mind.'

'No, but Anna might.'

The problem with that, Eli thought, was Karen might be right. Which was one reason he'd been a bit remote with Anna at work this week. He was trying to be sensible. 'Don't you have work to do, headmistress?'

'It's not as much fun as ribbing my brother.'

'Come on, Dad. I'm hungry.'

He ruffled his son's hair. 'When aren't you?'

He'd missed Anna so much over the past days, and it was all his fault. He'd been the one withdrawing, not Anna. The resignation that had filled her face when he'd spoken to her as he used to before they'd become friendly made him sad. Also guilty, but not guilty enough to do something about it. It was very apparent there was something bothering her. He should talk to her, ask if he could help her with anything, not avoid involvement.

*It's not too late.*

Or was it? Only one way to find out.

'There you go, Lucy. You're all set to go home as soon as Dr Eli says so.' Anna finished taping the bandage in place around the ten-year-old's thigh where she'd had surgery to remove an embedded metal stake.

'Yippee.'

Yippee. Yes, exactly how she felt too, after talking on the phone for an hour with Charlie last night. He'd rung as she was about to go for a walk. At first he'd sounded nervous, but slowly he'd relaxed and they'd chatted about themselves and a whole load of ordinary everyday stuff. As a mother and son would normally do, except it wasn't normal and Anna felt it was going to take a lot more talking before it was for either of them. She could understand Charlie had trust issues, and all she could do was wait and give him the time he needed to get to know her.

'What do you say?' said Lucy's mother.

'Thank you, Nurse Anna.'

'No problem. You've been a great patient.' No complaints at all. She grinned. 'I'll go and fill in your paperwork. It's the last thing to do other than wait for the doctor.' Hopefully Eli turned up sooner rather than later as Lucy was more than ready to be on her way. 'Any sign of Eli?' she asked Leanne at the desk.

'No.' Her friend looked up at her. 'Mr Forrester is back. Eli seems to have fallen off the planet.'

Anna couldn't argue with that. In the days since he'd walked out of the cafeteria before Charlie turned up in her life, he'd become remote again. He always said hello and asked how she was, but there was no real warmth in his smile when he did. 'You're right. Everything's gone back to the way it was.' The rest of the staff were also paying for something that had nothing to do with them.

'Hello, ladies.' Eli spoke from behind them.

Anna slowly turned around. 'Hi. Lucy's impatient to go home.'

Eli was watching her, looking a little taken

aback. He must've overheard her and Leanne talking. 'I'll deal with her in a moment.' He stepped closer. 'My apologies to everyone for being subdued lately. Rest assured, I'll stop being so quiet from now on.'

Why now? What did that mean for her? Anna wondered. Was he going to start talking again as though nothing were off balance between them?

Leanne looked at her, and when she didn't say anything turned to Eli and said, 'Good, because it's so much easier working with you when you're being cheerful and friendly.'

Go, girl. That was her friend sticking up for her, as well as the rest of the staff. Giving her a knowing smile, Anna said to Eli, 'I'll be with Lucy when you're ready.' Then she walked down the corridor with a bounce in her step. Nothing Eli could say or do right now could dampen her happiness over hearing from Charlie.

'Anna,' Eli called. 'Wait.'

She slowed, but didn't stop. 'Lucy's fairly pain free, but will need some analgesics to take home.'

'Anna, wait, please.'

She did as asked, leaning against the wall and glancing around to make sure no one was in sight. 'I owe you an apology, Anna. I shouldn't have closed down on you like I did.'

'You're dead right there. I know you worry

about Jordan, but that doesn't give you the right to judge me without getting to know me properly first.'

'You're right. I am sorry.'

Lucy appeared in the doorway of her room. 'There you are, Dr Eli. I can't wait to get out of here.'

End of that particular conversation. For the first time ever Anna wished the ward were much longer and that Lucy's room were furthest away. But it wasn't, and now she had to focus on work, not the man playing with her heart. 'Don't think you can play tennis for a while yet, missy.'

Lucy giggled. 'You're like my mum. Don't do this, don't do that. Bet you tell your kids not to jump off the deck too.'

If only she had kids to tell off. 'Not saying.'

'Lucy, Nurse Anna tells me your pain is light but I still want you taking painkillers every four hours for another two days.' Eli used his doctor-to-patient voice, calm, kind and not to be messed with.

'Why?'

'Because they build up in your system and if you stop now they'll wear off and then you will be in real pain.'

'Okay.'

'I'll see she does what's necessary,' her mother reassured Eli.

'Good, then I'll go and sign a prescription to take with you. You'll get a follow-up appointment in about two weeks' time.' He didn't rush away to do the prescription, as if he was waiting for something. Someone? Her?

Anna shrugged mentally and helped Lucy onto her feet. 'Look after yourself, young lady.'

Back at the desk, she tried to appear busy but it was impossible with Eli taking up space and air at the computer next to her. 'I'll go and check on Rosie.' The tiny tot had had a hernia removed that morning and they were keeping her heavily sedated for a few hours.

'Isn't Kay with her?' Eli asked as he pressed the print button. Of course he'd know that. He'd done the surgery and would've popped in to see the child before coming to the main desk.

'Yes, but I still like to keep tabs on everything.' It was her job after all.

'Feel like a coffee?' He swished his signature across the bottom of the script.

'That depends.'

'I'll be nice, promise.' No cheesy smile with that. He must be serious.

'Go on,' Leanne piped up from the office next door. 'I'll check on Rosie. You're due a break.'

*Thanks, friend. You're making it too easy for Eli.*

'Fine.' She stood up and went to her locker

to get the muffin she'd brought from home and hadn't had time to eat. 'Want half?' she asked Eli when they sat down in the cafeteria with coffees.

'No, thanks.'

'Good, because I'm starving.'

'You're looking tired again. Something causing you problems? Someone?'

The muffin tasted gluggy. This was not the place to open up about Charlie. Or them. 'I'm fine. A few restless nights, that's all.' Not an answer, but she was looking out for herself here.

'I'm here for you, Anna, if you want to talk about whatever's bothering you.'

Anna had to grip her hands together to prevent herself from reaching across and grabbing his. It would be so easy to let go what was holding her back, but again, wrong place, wrong time. If there ever was a right time with Eli. 'I will say I think you're overreacting about me and Jordan. It's as though you've got more to protect than you're letting on.' Like her.

Surprised grey eyes locked on her. 'You read me too well sometimes, Anna. I'm not sure if I like that or not. You're just like my sisters in that respect, though somehow it feels different coming from you.'

She stared at this man, being so open and honest as he was prone to do when she least expected it. What had come over him? 'How?'

'I guess because you're not a sister. You haven't known me since I was swathed in nappies and crying all night to be fed.' Now he gave her a full-blown grin. 'Apparently I wasn't an easy baby. I think when Jordan was born, Mum was hoping he'd give me a hard time, but he was an angel. At first, anyway. Now he's a troublesome but gorgeous boy.'

Unable to stop herself any longer, she reached for his hand. She had to feel his warmth, his skin against hers. 'Eli, he's lovely.' *So are you.* 'He's lucky to have you, too.'

He held her hand lightly. 'Like I said, you're different. But that's not why I suggested coffee.' He took a mouthful of his drink. 'I have let you down. I suggested we go slow, then backed off totally.' When she went to answer, he held his hand up. 'Hear me out. Obviously I have a lot of issues with people who won't share with me what's bothering them. Those I care about anyway. You're doing that at the moment.'

Pulling her hand free, Anna sank back in her chair, and picked up her coffee in shaky hands. Where was this going? Was there a massive but coming?

'I might not always see things your way but, like I've said before, you won't always see it my way either.'

'So why the cold shoulder since Thursday?'

'I'm trying to get my head around some things bothering me.'

'That doesn't explain why you withdrew from all the staff as well.' Did it matter? He'd given her an answer to her question she couldn't refute.

'I don't know. It seemed easier to fall back into the old mode of not talking to everyone about anything but patients.'

'I don't understand why you do that. You're so different outside the hospital it's like you're two different men.' But she also knew he wasn't the only doctor who did that. It was often a way of coping with very ill patients and not letting the nurses see their emotions. She shrugged as she drained her coffee. 'I'd better be getting back or Leanne will send the squad out to find me.' As if, but she couldn't sit here all afternoon talking to Eli. 'As for you being there if I need someone to download on, that's great.' About Charlie? Not so sure, but it had to be done, and the sooner the better.

He stood up, too. 'Who knows? You might be good for me, too.'

She had no answer for that. 'See you tomorrow.'

'Actually, Anna, how about we go out for a meal tonight?'

'What about Jordan?' He didn't like asking his family to babysit any more often than necessary.

'I can twist Karen's arm. She'll grizzle and growl and do it anyway.'

She answered without overthinking it. 'Then I'd like to go out with you.' She was going on a proper date. The second one with Eli.

'I'll pick you up at six, if that suits. Put your glad rags on.' There was a bounce in his step as he left the cafeteria. Surprised she'd said yes? So was she. Did she regret it? No.

# CHAPTER SEVEN

ELI SMILED NON-STOP. It had felt so good when Anna said yes to coming out to dinner, especially as there'd been some hesitancy about her throughout their conversation. He was buzzing. It had been a long time since any woman made him feel so full of anticipation. A date with her was a good, exciting thing to be doing.

Anna was gorgeous. He took her elbow as they strolled into the top-end restaurant he'd chosen because if he was going to date Anna then he wanted to give her the best possible night out.

'Mr Forrester,' the waiter said. 'We've reserved your favourite table for you.'

Anna glanced up at him with a comical look on her face. 'Your favourite table? Blimey, I am being honoured.'

Cheeky wench. He laughed. 'Only the best will do for you.'

She blinked, and looked away.

He'd gone too far, but that was what she did to him. He lost control of his emotions whenever he was with her. Forgot he needed to be extra careful because, no matter how he felt about her, he was not ready for a full-on relationship, though it was getting harder by the day to believe in his reasons for holding back. 'I rarely come here. I know the waiter from when he had surgery on his shoulder after a rugby accident and I'd say he was being cheeky. Come on. Over here.' He led her to a table by the window overlooking the Avon River.

Anna sat down and stared out at the green river banks and tall trees. 'Wow. That's pretty.'

Eli stared at the beautiful woman opposite him. Her short, thin-strapped emerald-green dress highlighted her stunning body and creamy skin to perfection. Her make-up was light and becoming, and that satiny hair fell over her shoulders in shiny waves. His heart began pounding. Easy, man. The night was only beginning.

'Have I got egg on my face?'

'On your chin,' he replied and reached over to run a finger over her skin.

'Glad you noticed.'

Sitting back, he struggled to get back on track. Touching her chin with his fingertip sent his hormones into overdrive. If he wanted to back off he'd made a big mistake by asking her out when he knew she'd do this to him. Was she even aware of how she wound him up? 'Would you like a glass of wine?'

'I'd love one. Pinot Gris if that's all right with you?'

Why wouldn't it be? 'You can have whatever you prefer.' He turned to the waiter and ordered two glasses of the same wine. 'Likewise with the menu.' In case she was thinking she had to be careful about what she chose, though why she would he couldn't understand.

'I was thinking that if you didn't like Pinot Gris and were going to order a bottle of wine it would be a waste.'

'I'd have taken it home for you.' This wasn't going quite how he'd hoped. 'Anna, let's start again. We're having dinner together and nothing else matters.'

She blushed. Cute and unexpected. 'I'm not usually so obliging about menus and drinks.'

'Why with me?'

Her forefinger drew circles on the table. 'I'm not sure what you expect of me, I guess.'

That stung. 'To be yourself is all I ask.'

'I have been, but there might be a few surprises along the way you aren't comfortable with.'

'True. Isn't that the case whenever we start seeing someone?'

'Of course it is.' Her stunning eyes locked

on him, sucking him in as if he were about to dive deep into the unknown, something he might even like.

Leaning back in his chair, he tried to gather his wits, and did okay. 'Let's decide what we want for dinner.'

Once their orders had been placed and the wine brought to them, Eli picked up his glass and held it out to tap Anna's. 'Here's to getting along and having fun.'

'I agree.' She tapped back.

Relief soared. He hadn't realised how worried he was she'd ignore his gesture. Incredible how much Anna had got to him so fast. He hadn't been looking for another partner, but it seemed he mightn't have as much say about his feelings as he'd thought. 'Where did you do your training?'

'Here in Christchurch. I've lived here all my life.'

There was a seriousness behind that he couldn't quite put his finger on. He dug a little deeper. 'Not interested in moving around to other cities or small towns?'

Her finger was doing that circle thing she often used when she was thinking. 'I've never had any desire to dash off around the world like so many do. This is home and I'm comfortable here.'

So she hadn't gone anywhere else. There was more to this than she was letting on but he'd wait until she was ready to tell him. That was something he'd decided to do—wait, not push Anna and risk everything.

'It's odd that we didn't bump into each other a long time back. I've spent most of my time as a doctor here, apart from one year in London specialising in paediatric surgery.'

'I did work in ICU at St Clair's for a while. You were doing surgery there then.'

The private hospital in the city. 'Five years ago. I was married then.' Wouldn't have been taking a lot of notice of other women. When he'd loved Melissa so much.

The waiter arrived, bearing plates of delicious-smelling food.

'Thank you, Sebastian. That looks wonderful.'

'Enjoy.' He smiled widely and left them to themselves.

They talked about work and friends as they ate, relaxed, comfortable with each other. Just how Eli liked it, and how he'd wanted it from the moment he'd invited her to dinner. Thanks to Karen looking after Jordan, he'd been able to bring Anna somewhere special. So much for always being organised. He didn't do making sudden plans, liked to be in control of everything so there was less chance of something going wrong.

Yet he'd hoped Anna would say yes without any forewarning. And she had. 'Thank you.'

She frowned. 'What for?'

'Coming out tonight. I'm enjoying this.'

'I can't imagine you being turned down often.' Her wink was cheeky.

He grinned. 'No comment.' The fact was he didn't ask many women out these days. They always wanted more than he was prepared to offer, and the ones who were happy with a one-night stand weren't his type. He was hard to please. Except when it came to Anna, and even with her he had some problems. 'How come you're single?'

Her back straightened and she placed her knife and fork down on her plate. No cheeky winks in sight now. In fact she wasn't even looking at him. Not like Anna at all. 'It's how I choose to be.'

'I don't believe you.'

Looking around the restaurant, she appeared to be gathering her thoughts.

He could be patient when necessary.

Finally she looked at him. 'I told you I'd had two serious relationships and that they went wrong. I ended up believing maybe I don't have staying power.' She shrugged. 'Who knows?'

*Be warned, Eli.*

That was exactly why he hadn't got into deep

and meaningful relationships since Melissa. He couldn't bear to be left again.

Anna obviously didn't like the silence that hung between them because she continued. 'I haven't been hiding in the cupboard ever since. There've been a few brief flings but that's it.'

'Sounds lonely.' He understood how that felt.

'It has been.' She picked up her glass and took a mouthful of wine. 'Have you been with anyone since your marriage finished?' She obviously wasn't ready to tell him any more, might never be.

'No. Like you, the occasional fling, nothing more serious.' Was that what this was? It didn't feel like it. Anna had him thinking beyond the next week to considering what might be out there for them if he could get past his concerns that dominated everything.

Understanding filled her eyes. 'A lot easier that way.'

'You're making me feel bad. As though I treat women as objects. I assure you I don't. It's only that I don't want to get too involved.'

Her mouth flattened. 'That was not what I was thinking at all. When we're getting along you're kind, caring and considerate, to mention a few things. I understand how you mightn't want to get involved with anyone yet, but I don't see that lasting for ever. You have too much to give.'

Knock him down. He hadn't seen that coming. He picked up her hand and kissed her palm. 'Thank you.'

She shrugged. 'Just saying it how I see it.' There was a worried expression crossing her face.

'Anna.' He still held her hand. 'I want to keep seeing you, going on dates and having some fun. I can't promise any more than that for now.'

Her fingers wound around his hand as the worry slowly disappeared. 'I like your honesty.'

He waited, because this was Anna and he'd learned she didn't leap in to say things she might later regret.

'I'd also like to spend more time with you whenever possible.' Finally a beautiful curving of those sumptuous lips he remembered all too well tracking kisses all over his body.

'You're on.'

The way her blood kept pounding through her body, Anna thought she might have to see her GP for some blood-pressure pills to slow it down. Or she could just let go and have a hot session with Eli. She wasn't thinking about the days when he'd barely talked to her, wasn't even going to consider how he'd feel about her when she told him about Charlie. This was about them, and how he turned her on so easily. This was now, and the rest could wait for later.

He pulled up outside her house and switched off the motor.

'Coming in?' she asked, the pounding getting louder in her ears.

'I was hoping you'd ask.' He was out and striding around to her side before she took another breath. Feeling as wound up as she was?

She hoped so or she was going to look stupid. Once out of the car, she took his hand and almost ran to her front door.

Eli was laughing as he swooped her up into his arms the moment they were inside. 'I'll take you out to dinner every night if this is the result.'

'You're on.' His neck was right by her mouth, and she had to kiss his skin, taste him as he headed for her bedroom.

Within moments they were naked and touching, kissing and feeling each other everywhere. Desire shot through her. She reached for him, held him and rubbed up and down.

Eli pushed her back. 'Wait.'

'I don't want to. I'm ready.'

'Thank goodness because I can't last either.'

Then they were on the bed, together in the most intimate way, moving in unison, crying out as they came.

'Anna.'

'Eli.'

Then she was free falling, taking Eli with her, not wanting to let him go ever again.

If only, was her first thought as she came to, curled up against Eli, his arm around her waist. He was amazing. Certainly knew how to tick her boxes when he made love to her.

'Hey, you,' he whispered against her neck.

Rolling over, she kissed him lightly. 'No messing around, was there?'

'No, straight down to it.' He grinned. 'You're incredible.'

'Thanks.' She'd take all the compliments she could get. It wasn't often she got this close to a man. Sex was one thing, but with Eli it felt like making love. Love. There was that word again. It was occurring more and more whenever she spent time with him. Even when she hadn't over the past week she'd felt something for him and tried to deny it. It could be a one-way ride to hell if it didn't work out but she wanted to try and make it happen. Yes, she was beginning to accept she might deserve some happiness in the love department. 'You're not so bad yourself.'

He gave a mock groan. 'Seems I need more practice.' He rolled over and covered her with his sexy body. 'How's this?' He touched her nipple with his tongue. 'And this?' The other nipple tightened. 'What about this?'

Intense desire spread throughout her, following every touch Eli made, setting her alight again. So fast, so soon after the first time. Unreal. Incredible. Sliding her hand over his backside, she made to find his sex.

'No, Anna. This is my time to give you pleasure.'

Keep this up and she wouldn't have the strength to return the compliment when he'd finished. 'Together?' she croaked through the heat in her throat.

He raised his head from her breast briefly. 'Nope.'

She lay back and absorbed every sensation, every touch, kiss and more. Way more. This time she was free falling without a parachute.

And when she finally landed and caught her breath, she straddled Eli and gave to him what he'd given her—touches, kisses, and lots more.

Less than ten minutes after Eli had left Anna's phone rang. Her heart bumped hard. Charlie's name was on the screen.

'Hello, Charlie.' It was quite late to be phoning, wasn't it? Was he ringing to tell her he wanted nothing more to do with her?

'Hi, Anna.'

That was it? 'How's things?'

'Good. I'm back at polytech at the moment.

My next secondment is a month at Wellington Hospital in Theatre.'

The tightness around her chest eased off. He hadn't gone silent on her. 'How do you think you'll cope with that?' She'd fainted at the first operation she'd been assigned to observe. All that blood.

'Not sure, but we've been told it only gets better after the first day.'

'True, it does.' It was pretty cool how they'd both chosen nursing as a career. 'Did you always want to be a nurse?'

'Not really. It was only when my granddad got hit by a bus and spent two months in hospital that I began to think I'd like to be one. Everyone was so amazing to him.'

Granddad. That should've been her father's role. Would've been if her parents hadn't been so determined she get rid of her baby. 'My grandmother was one too. Seems it runs in the family.' Anna winced. Charlie mightn't like that comment.

But, 'That's kind of neat.' Then there was another silence.

This time Anna waited it out.

'Um…is it okay if I come down and see you again in a couple of weeks?'

Her heart swelled. 'Of course it is. Any time.' *Stop. Don't overdo it or he might back off.*

'Um…good. Um…what about if Mum and Dad come too?'

'They want to meet me?'

'Yes.'

Wow. That had to be good, didn't it? 'Then tell them yes, I'd like to meet them too.' Would she? Of course she would. These were the people who'd raised her son to be a great young man. And a nurse. She smiled to herself. 'When you know when you're coming, I can pick you up.' She presumed they'd fly down.

'Dad's going to hire a car. We'll only come for a day, depending on your shifts.'

They weren't planning on spending too long with her. Guess that made sense. It was a strange situation for everyone. 'I'll text my roster to you.' Charlie's number had been in her phone from the first time he'd called her. 'I can meet up with you anywhere it suits.'

'Thanks, Anna. Bye.' He didn't mess around making small talk, then.

Staring at her phone, Anna felt a bubble of excitement expanding in her chest. Her son was bringing his parents to meet her. Strange as it was, it was also beyond what she'd hoped for so soon. Yippee.

At work on Friday, Anna saw Eli enter the ward and look around until he spied her.

Smiling, he came across. 'Afternoon, Anna. How's things?'

'All good.' Great was the real answer, but she downplayed it at work. Other staff members had exceptional hearing at the most inconvenient moments, especially Leanne. Her date with Eli had been nothing short of magic and she was constantly recalling every moment of it. 'Which patient are you here to see?'

'Benjamin. How's his wound?'

'It's clearing now that the antibiotics are kicking in.' The teenager had had a splenectomy after a cycling accident where the handlebar rammed into his abdomen. The infection was a result of pathogens on his skin from another medical problem he had.

'That's good.' He looked around, saw they were alone. 'Would you like to join me in taking Jordan to swimming lessons tomorrow morning? It's Saturday, I thought we could go to the beach afterwards, take a picnic with us.'

'I'd love to.' Eli was seriously asking her to go with him *and* Jordan? That was progress. He was normally very protective when it came to his boy. 'Let me sort the picnic. Anything Jordan doesn't like?'

'Easier to tell you what he does like.' Eli grinned. 'He's a picky little blighter.'

One of the other nurses was heading their way.

'Let's go see Benjamin. His dad's with him at the moment.'

Eli nodded. 'Right. I'll be there at nine-thirty,' he added quietly.

She presumed he meant her place as she didn't have a clue where the lessons were held. 'Everything will be ready.' Especially herself. She was already thinking about the new bikini she'd bought a few weeks back. Sky blue with splashes of white, it fitted her perfectly. Her feet were all but skipping as she entered the room where Benjamin was sprawled over the bed, talking to his father. 'Hey, Benjamin. Dr Eli's here to give you the once-over.'

'You already did that.'

'Yeah, but nothing like the real deal from the doc.'

'Anna will have done exactly what I'm about to do, and I totally trust her observations, but I'm a bit of a control freak and like to take my own notes.' Eli was still grinning.

As her feet were dancing? Were they becoming an item without realising it? Without setting out to do so? Whichever, she was happier than she'd been in ages. Happier in a different way. She had met a man who touched her in so many ways. She laughed. Touched her? Fingers and hands on her overheated skin. Funny how since Charlie had turned up out of the blue, she felt more worthy of a love life. What if this time she could follow through and fall so deeply in love that she wouldn't walk away from it—from him? Something chilly ripped down her back. It wasn't possible. She hadn't been lucky so far and she was thirty-four, so why would it happen now that she'd met Eli?

She had no idea whether Charlie had forgiven her but he was staying in touch so far, which had to be a good sign. During their phone conversations he hadn't come out and said she was a terrible person for giving him up, but there were moments when she thought she heard anger in his voice. Hopefully that was because he was coming to terms with everything she'd told him about why she'd done what she had. But she did feel more at ease now that her son had found her and hadn't fled to the hills afterwards. That ease seemed to be flowing into other aspects of her life, such as her starting to let Eli into her heart.

'Anna, can you put a new dressing on this?' Eli interrupted her musings. 'There's been some seepage.' There was a question in his eyes when he glanced at her.

'I'll get the tray.' He really had disrupted her usually orderly mind if she was thinking all that while standing at a patient's bedside with a surgeon.

When she returned with the required equipment Eli and Benjamin's father were animatedly discussing cricket, a game that bored her silly. 'Here we go, Benjamin. You're not into cricket either?'

The boy was on his iPad. 'Rather watch paint dry.'

She laughed. 'Know what you mean. Okay, lift your top up and lower your pants. I'll get this sorted as fast as possible.'

'Hang on, not so quick,' Eli interrupted. 'I want to have another look at the wound.'

Hadn't he already done that before requesting her to change the dressing? She stepped back to allow him room to move without bumping into her. Not that she didn't mind the odd nudge but not here with patients and parents.

'Change the dressing every hour, Anna. Apply cream to the other infected sites each time too. The sooner we knock this on the head, the better.' Eli straightened and looked right at her. 'That's it.' There was a slight twist to his lips as though he'd read her mind earlier and was having a good old laugh at her.

But she knew she was safe. He had no idea what she'd been thinking other than maybe something about him. It wouldn't do for him to know she was contemplating getting closer to him. His guarded manner would step in and put the brakes on her faster than it took him to make her orgasm the other night. 'All under control,' she said, tongue in cheek.

Benjamin didn't wince when she cleaned his wound and pressed the new dressing on. Nor did he move when she cleaned and creamed the other messy sites on his body. 'You're a toughie,' she told him as she finished up.

'Nah, you don't hurt like the last nurse did.'

She'd take the compliment and carry on as usual. 'There, all done. You can get back to that game you're trying to win. You might like to click on the bottom left-hand picture and I bet you'll get a great score.' She recognised the game that many teens who came into the ward enjoyed playing.

Benjamin stared at the screen for a moment, then grinned. 'You're right.'

'Of course I am.'

'How did you know that?' Eli asked on the way back to the desk.

'I spent a whole eight-hour shift with a girl who played it non-stop in an attempt to ignore the pain in both her fractured legs. Seemed to work too as she became zoomed out.' The things she did as a nurse weren't all about bandages, injections and blood pressures. 'Does Jordan have apps for games?'

'Unfortunately, yes. I try to keep him off his tablet as much as possible but it's hard when nearly every kid has one these days. There are time limits though, which I insist on, and they often lead to tantrums, which lead to more time off the tablet.'

'The joys of parenthood, eh?' What she wouldn't have given to experience them.

'I'll see Ollie now and then head to the clinic.' Eli peeled off into the next room and Anna followed. 'How's that tummy?' he asked his patient, who'd had a splenectomy that morning.

'Sore.'

'Ollie's last analgesic was less than two hours ago,' she told Eli.

'Give him another dose at the four-hour mark.' Eli was examining Ollie's sutures. 'Everything looks all right.'

'A placebo might be a good idea,' she told him on the side. She doubted Ollie, who was only nine, knew what a placebo was, but kids these days were quick to look up on the internet to find out anything, so she'd best not let him hear what she'd suggested.

Eli's eyes widened in acknowledgement. 'I'll write up a prescription.' Not necessary, there were some in the drug cabinet, but Eli was onto it in that he was acting as though Ollie were getting a different painkiller.

'I'll make sure we give him the tablets soon.' Ollie was complaining non-stop about his pain and discomfort. He'd had his mother demanding more drugs last night and from the moment she'd arrived to see her son that morning. She'd gone off to get something for Ollie's lunch, hospital food not being good enough for her son.

'Ollie, your wound is looking good. It will start healing soon.'

'But it hurts.'

'Any surgery hurts a little bit. Best thing you can do is not to get too active for a day or two. I'll see you again tomorrow.' Eli headed for the door.

Anna tucked Ollie's pyjama top down and pulled the blanket up. 'I'll be back with some pills soon.'

'I want them now.'

Eli came back into the room. 'You'll have them when it's the right time, and not before, otherwise you'll get sleepy and that's not good for your recovery. Understand?'

'Yes, Doctor.' The boy looked more annoyed than repentant.

Anna knew she was in for some attitude later on, but she had broad shoulders. 'Thanks, Eli,' she said as they left the room.

'I probably was a little harsh on him. It would've been a shock having an operation today.'

'You're right but it doesn't help when his mother fuels his ego.' She glanced around, saw no one close, and said quietly, 'You weren't too tough on him. Sounded to me more like a dad trying to do his best.'

Eli laughed. 'Yeah, right. Might need to re-think how I deal with my patients.'

'No. Keep on doing what you do best, being kind, considerate and good at surgery.' With that, she went into the nearest room to see any patient that could distract her from Eli. She said too much to him these days. Almost as though she was stroking *his* ego, and probably giving him the wrong idea about what she thought of him. Not that she'd said anything she didn't mean, but she didn't want to appear as a simpering fe-male who'd do or say anything to get his undi-vided attention.

'Anna,' he called from the doorway.

So much for getting away from him. 'Yes?'

'Nine-thirty, tomorrow. Your place.' Then he was gone.

She'd be ready and waiting, most likely at eight-thirty. She wouldn't want to be late for her date. Grinning widely, she crossed over to Jessica. 'How you doing, sport? Your hand feel-ing any better today?' One thing for sure, Anna thought, *her* heart was feeling lighter than it had for a while.

# CHAPTER EIGHT

'DID YOU HAVE to wear that bikini?' Eli groaned as he watched Anna slather her fair skin with sunscreen. The bikini left nothing to his imagination, but then his imagination needed no help. His mind knew her body very well. A tightening in his groin suggested he should go take a dive in the sea right now.

'I could go naked.'

'That wouldn't be much different.' Taking the tube of sunscreen lotion from her, he rubbed cream on her shoulders and over her back, swallowing hard as another part of him hardened.

She laughed. 'Jordan, come here and let me put some more screen on your face. You're going pink.'

'Pink's a girlie colour.'

'Exactly.' Anna rubbed some cream on his skin.

Eli moved to hide his reaction to Anna's smooth skin, thankful Jordie was engrossed in whatever Anna was telling him. His heart was

expanding with love for his boy, and for Anna.
No, he wasn't in love with her, but he was letting
go of the things holding him back and letting her
in. She was so special it hurt to think he might
not follow up on these new feelings. Glancing at
Jordan, he felt a moment of panic. Jordie thought
Nurse Anna was the best. Which was good. It
was also a worry. They hadn't established a relationship, were only dating occasionally. Yeah,
so, wasn't that a relationship of sorts?

Jordie laughed at something Anna said.

Eli couldn't help thinking that was lovely too.
His boy did deserve a mother figure in his life.
But was Anna the one? Only way to find out was
to keep seeing her and go with his gut instinct.

'You've gone awfully quiet.' Anna nudged
him. 'Something not right?'

'Not at all.' Not entirely true, but near enough.
'Let's go get wet.' He stood up and grabbed Jordie, tucked him under his arm and began jogging
down the beach to the water. He didn't look to
see if Anna followed them, just ploughed into
the water with Jordan squealing in his ear and
jiggling fit to bust as the water crept up their
bodies.

A slim body in a blue and white bikini went
splashing past, tightening him some more. Anna
stopped and rolled onto her back. 'This is good.'

'Anna, watch me.' Jordan began dog-paddling towards her. 'I'm fast.'

Paddling beside him, Eli held back a laugh. Fast as a snail. 'You're doing great, Jordie.'

'Come on, you're getting closer,' Anna encouraged.

Jordan disappeared under the water, popped back up coughing and spluttering. 'Yuk. That tastes horrid.'

'You're not supposed to drink sea water.' Anna laughed. 'Not frightened, is he?'

Eli wanted to grab him and hold him close, but that would be OTT. He had to give Jordan space to be a boy, no matter what the ramifications—up to a point. 'Unfortunately not.'

'Come on, Dad. He's happy, and we're right here.' Anna was laughing at him, but there was also understanding in those beautiful eyes.

'I know.'

'But.'

'Always plenty of buts. No wonder people go grey. It's all about raising children.'

'Remind me to check how many grey hairs you've got later.'

Later? When he took her back to her place with Jordan in the car? Not happening. Jordan was not going to get used to sleeping at Anna's house. That was getting too close to being like a family unit for comfort. 'One hundred and twenty-three,' he told her.

'You've missed some at the back of your head.' She flipped onto her back. 'Come on, Jordan. Race you to the beach and then we can have our picnic.'

Jordan tried to swim on his back but all he managed to do was sink.

'Try paddling,' Eli suggested. He could see Anna was going as slow as possible so Jordie would pass her. 'Hey, I'll hold you around the waist and you start running. Once your feet touch the sand you do it for real.'

'I'm gonna beat Anna, Dad.'

'You bet.'

When he did, he fell about laughing, before asking, 'Are you coming to my swimming next week, Anna?'

'I'll have to see if I'm working first.'

'Say you can't.'

'If only it were that easy.' She grinned.

The picnic was great, something for all of them to enjoy, and more points for Anna from Jordan when he found chocolate fish in the chilly bin.

'What treat do I get?' Eli asked her.

'You'll have to wait and see.' There was a sexy twinkle going on in her eyes.

'We're not staying the night at your place,' he

warned. Disappointment struck. He wanted to be intimate with her again. To hell with it. 'But you could come back to my house for the evening.'

'That was the plan,' she admitted. Then her face dropped a little. 'I'm not being too presumptuous, am I?'

So unlike the Anna he knew that again he wondered if she wasn't as strong as she made out to be. 'Not at all.'

'Sorry.' She fidgeted with the edge of the towel she'd wrapped around her waist when they returned from the water. 'It's only that I'm not really sure where we're at. I know you don't want me getting too close to a certain little man, but then we have an explosive time together and that takes over my thinking.'

She was trying to fit in with his requirements when it came to their relationship—yes, it was one even if he'd been denying it—which meant not letting Jordan take her presence for granted. He could love her for that alone. But he didn't, wouldn't. Not yet. If only he could drop the worries and be free to do as he wished. It was so tempting, and yet so hard. His ex really had done a right number on him by taking his love for granted until she no longer wanted it. Add in his birth mother turning him away when he found her, and it was very difficult to give his heart to anyone else. On the other hand, Mum and Dad and his sisters had never let him down, and that was how he was with them and Jordan. Could he do it with Anna? Did he want to?

Short answer? Yes. Longer, sensible one? Still yes if he could be absolutely certain she wouldn't let him down. No one got that card. It was a wait and see situation.

'Ahh, hello, Eli? Is this where I get up and go find a taxi to take me home?'

*Gees, man, get a grip. Stop this procrastinating and make the most of your time with Anna.*

'I was off in doo-doo land. I know what you mean about not knowing where we're at. How about we carry on as we are and see where it goes from there? I'm not one for rushing into anything, especially relationships.' Funny how he was so upfront with Anna at times. He didn't have it in him to hide everything he felt or thought from her. Just some things. Nor was it funny; it was disturbing and said a lot more about where he was at with her. He wanted more, lots more, and the only way for that to happen was to trust her not to let him down and give as much of himself as he was comfortable with.

'When we're finished here you can drop me off at my place and I'll shower and change, and drive over to yours afterwards.' Her uncertainty made that sound like a question.

'I—I'd like that.' Gulp. He'd nearly said he

loved the idea. What would be wrong with that? It was a normal thing to say. Yeah, but he was afraid of the love word at the moment. It had a lot of meanings, and therefore repercussions. 'Really like it.'

Later that evening, after they'd made love— the love word again—Eli sat up in his bed and reached to hold Anna against his chest. She was warm and soft, and limp after falling apart under him when she climaxed. Intimacy with Anna was something else. Unbelievable. Of course there hadn't been a lot of sex going on in his life lately but he was sure that making out with Anna would always be mind-blowing. The sensations she caused in him had him feeling as though he'd found something magical. Something he didn't want to let go ever again. 'You're amazing,' he said as he brushed a kiss on her cheek.

She snuggled closer, sliding her arms around him. 'I quite like you, too,' she murmured through a laugh.

He heard a cough coming from Jordan's room and swore. 'Sorry, but I think Jordan's waking up.' Coughing was a common start to him coming up out of a dream. 'That means we have to get out of bed. The last thing I want is for him to find us together in this state.'

Her smile disappeared as she sat up and put

her feet on the floor, ready to get up. 'Seriously, Eli, I got the message the very first time you told me how worried you get about Jordan being hurt.'

The look on her face suggested it didn't make her happy either. Well, she'd have to accept it or they were over. He leapt out of bed. 'Jordan's too young to understand what we were doing. Plus I'm not ready for him to see you in my bedroom. That's suggesting you're going to be here a lot.'

'Eli, give it a break. I'm not stupid. I get what you're saying. I was thoroughly enjoying being held by you and didn't want to move away. That's all.'

Tugging on some shorts, he leaned over to cover her mouth with his. 'Thank you.' He hadn't apologised to any one half as much as he seemed to with Anna.

'I'll head home now.'

'Fair enough.' Not that he wanted her to, but it was the best option with Jordan waking up.

'Daddy, where are you?'

'This is always the result of a bad dream.'

'Does he have many?' Anna shoved into her T-shirt, apparently not worried about her bra and more concerned about Jordan walking in.

Thankfully he'd remembered to close the door when they'd made their mad dash down to his bedroom. 'Not really. He'll settle down again after I've heard what he was dreaming about.'

After zipping up her denim shorts, she grabbed her bra and opened the door. 'Right. Time I was out of here. See you on Monday, unless you're going in to check up on a patient tomorrow.'

'You're on tomorrow?'

'Yep. Nights for the next four shifts.'

There went any idea of getting together soon. Might be a good thing as there was a bit going on in his head that needed sorting before they went too far. Another kiss and he opened the front door for her. 'It's been a great day, Anna.'

'It has. Thanks for everything.' And she was gone, no lingering looks or glancing over her shoulder. Leaving him bereft when he had no right to feel that way.

Thank goodness for night shifts or she'd be beating down Eli's door to be allowed in to make love, Anna thought. She reached for some pills from the drug cabinet for a young patient with nausea after surgery for three fractured ribs that had pierced the lung. There was no such thing as too much sex. Not with Eli. The man was incredible. He seemed to read her like a book with a size twenty font. He knew what she wanted and when.

She hadn't seen him since Saturday as he was gone by the time she signed on at eleven in the evening, and she was home tucked up in bed by the time he was turning up on the ward. Bed. That word had taken on a whole load more meaning lately. He had phoned every night before she'd started her shift to see how her day had been and what she'd been up to. She liked talking to him and felt they were getting more relaxed with each other about everyday issues and learning more about each other as time went by. There was still the problem about Jordan. Where she didn't mind having to step back for his son, Eli was still overprotective at times, and she believed he felt she was getting too close to the boy.

That made her cross. No way would she ever intentionally hurt Jordan. Of course, if she and Eli did get into a full-time relationship there was always the chance it would sour and then Jordan might be upset, but that was a risk Eli had to decide was worth taking or not. At the moment, she suspected he wasn't ready to commit to much more than they already had, and yet he mightn't be ready to back off entirely either if the way he kept asking her out or phoning her meant anything.

There was also the other elephant between them. Charlie.

In her pocket her phone vibrated. Pulling it out, she sighed. Eli.

Goodnight. xxx

Okay, that was a move in the right direction. She replied.

Sleep tight. xxx

The simple things made her happy, and loving. In love a little. Or was that getting to be a lot? Who knew? Not her, and she was over trying to work it out. It was early days and for now she'd run with the flow and make the most of the good times.

But on Saturday when she got a call from Eli saying he'd catch up with her later in the day after Jordan's swimming class, her happiness deflated a little. It stung a bit that he hadn't asked her along, but then she couldn't really expect him to ask her along every weekend. They weren't that close yet. 'How about you come here? Leanne and her husband and kids are coming round for a barbecue on the back lawn at about four. Bring Jordan,' she added carefully. 'He can play with Leanne's youngest, who's five.' Going on twelve some days, but she wouldn't mention that.

'You don't mind if Leanne knows we're seeing each other?' Surprise lifted his voice.

'She's one of my best friends and has known for a while that we're spending a bit of time together. If it bothers you, then rest assured she doesn't gossip. You'd have known by now if she did.'

'What can I bring?'

*Guess that's a 'Yes, we'd love to come' then.*

'I've got it covered, but if there's anything you think you want feel free to bring it along.'

'See you later, then.'

With or without Jordan? Anna shrugged. Men. Sometimes they could be difficult, but worth putting up with for the good times. Eli was anyway.

Jordan was happy as a kid in a candy shop playing with Leanne's son, Luca, Eli thought as he watched the boys chasing each other around the lawn, laughing their heads off and shouting like crazy. 'Your neighbours will be calling in the noise control at this rate,' he said to Anna.

Craig, Leanne's husband, just laughed. 'They're used to it. There's another young lad along the road who often comes along to play with Luca when we're visiting.'

Anna added, 'Can't have too many friends at their age.'

It was getting too easy to fit in with Anna. Jordan was happy. *He* was happy. Her friends accepted him, especially Leanne. But then why wouldn't she? It turned out Craig was a GP and he'd met Leanne when he was doing his training in Dunedin. Doctors and nurses falling in love everywhere. A pathologist once said to him, if a doctor qualified without finding the love of his life in the medical world then there was something wrong with him or her because there were so many wonderful people working in the system to choose from. Maybe the pathologist was right. He should've gone for another medic. They'd at least understand the long hours required, something that Melissa had constantly complained about.

'Time we hit the road.' Craig stood up. 'These kids have got sports day tomorrow.'

Eli glanced at his watch. Seven o'clock. Where had the time gone? 'Guess I'd better make tracks too. Jordan should be tucked up by now.' He could blame Anna for sidetracking his usually controlled mind, but for once he would just go along with the fact he'd been having a wonderful time and forget about worrying about running late getting his boy home. But first, 'Want a hand clearing up, Anna?'

'Where have you been? Leanne and I did that a while ago.' She looked amused. Pleased that he'd been so at ease with everyone?

'Guess I got that wrong.'

'I bet Craig was keeping you occupied talking so he could pretend he didn't know what we were doing,' Leanne retorted as she gathered up her kids' gear. 'He's allergic to doing dishes.'

'Best allergy to have if you're going to have one,' replied Craig. 'Thanks for a great afternoon, Anna.' He planted a friendly kiss on her cheek. 'Always good to get out of the house.'

She laughed. 'You're never in it. If not at work, you're digging the garden.'

'True. Keeps me out of mischief.'

'Oh, come on.' Leanne laughed. 'Glad you joined us, Eli. We'll have to get together again soon. At our place next time.'

'I'm glad Anna invited us along. Jordan's had a blast with Luca.' Another friend to talk about. Where was he anyway? Looking around, he couldn't see him anywhere. 'Jordie?'

'He's curled up on my bed with a book,' Anna informed him. 'He asked if he could go in there and I couldn't see why not.'

'Not a problem.' That meant they might stay a few more minutes, and he could briefly have Anna to himself.

'See you both tomorrow,' Leanne called from the door before closing it behind her family.

'Want a coffee before you go home?' Anna asked.

'Love one. I'll just check on Jordan, make sure he's not getting into mischief.'

Not a chance. Jordan was sound asleep, hugging one of Anna's pillows to his face, looking completely at ease. Something his dad should take note of and try harder to become so relaxed, thought Eli when he returned to the kitchen. 'He's out for the count.' When Anna started to smile wickedly, he held up his hand. 'Be warned, he can wake up just as quickly as he went to sleep.'

'Then I'd better kiss you while the coffee's brewing.' Her arms were around his neck and she was pulling his face down to meet hers. Her mouth tasted of fruit and heated him instantly.

He groaned as he returned the kiss, deep, tightening him, as she always did with little effort. She really was so damned sexy and attractive that he couldn't remain calm around her. 'Is there a lock on your bedroom door?' he joked.

'If only.' She went to pour the coffee. 'Let's sit in the lounge. We can share the sofa.' Her wink was saucy. 'Who knows? We might get lucky.'

'Daddy. Where are you? Come here.'

'There goes that idea.' Eli said. He placed his hand on Anna's cheek. 'All part of being a parent.'

'Not a problem,' she replied. 'I didn't really

believe we'd have a chance of getting too close tonight.'

He couldn't help asking, 'You're not disappointed?'

'Duh. Of course I am, but I totally understand that when Jordan's with us things are different.'

He should be glad she wasn't causing trouble or demanding time alone with him, instead of overthinking what she said. Her mouth beckoned, and it was hard to resist so he stepped away. 'I'd better get Jordan before the trouble starts. As in I keep kissing you and forget what I'm supposed to be doing.'

'I can't see you doing that.'

But then she had no idea how much she tipped his world upside down. Best she didn't find out either. Not yet, anyway. He had a way to go before getting fully involved. He went to Anna's bedroom and lifted a sleepy Jordan into his arms to carry him out to the car.

Anna picked up Jordan's bag and Eli's chilly bin that he'd brought beer and nibbles in and followed him outside. At the car, she leaned over and kissed Jordan's cheek. 'Goodnight, little one. See you again soon.'

'Nigh, nigh, Anna. Love you.'

Eli jerked back, pulling Jordan away from Anna, shocked. That was not meant to happen.

His heart was thumping. How had he got to this point? Now Jordan really could be hurt.

Anna placed her hand on his back. 'It's what kids say all the time. Don't take it too seriously.'

*Damn it, Anna. I thought you understood my concern?*

'Jordan doesn't, and even if he did, it worries me that he's looking for something that's not there.'

'Thanks a lot, Eli. I know you're very protective of your son, but I don't deserve to be shoved aside willy-nilly when something happens that you're uncomfortable with. A few minutes ago you wanted to get into bed with me. Don't say you didn't,' she snapped when he stared at her. 'If you're not going to be open-minded about how your son and I get along then I suggest we stop seeing each other as of now.'

The problem was he didn't want to. He was halfway in love with Anna and wanted to find the other half. Wanted to give it a chance. Most of the time that was. There were all the questions he kept putting to himself, but deep down where it mattered he cared for her a lot. A hell of a lot. 'Please be patient with me. This is new for me and obviously I'm not doing a good job of getting it right.'

She stared at him. 'You'd let me spend time with him?' She nodded at Jordan who was nod-

ding off again, unaware of his role in this uncomfortable conversation.

'I'd better put him in his seat.' His bundle was
getting heavier as they stood beside the car.

'That's hardly an answer, Eli.'

He waited until he'd clipped the seat belt in
place around Jordan and closed the door before
answering. 'You're right. It's not. You have no
idea how much I want this to work out for all of
us.' There, he'd put his heart on the line. 'I'm not
saying you'd deliberately let him down but if we
get more involved then decide it's not working
he is going to be hurt.'

*So am I,* he thought, but he'd keep that to himself. He was nowhere near ready to tell Anna
how he felt about her.

Her sigh rippled through the warm air between them. 'Low blow, Eli. You'd better get
going. I'll see you at work tomorrow.' With that,
Anna turned around and strode up her drive to
the front door where she went in and closed it
behind her without a backward glance.

He stood by his car, staring after her, feeling
ill as sadness engulfed him. Had she just pulled
the plug on their burgeoning relationship? Or
did she need time to think about how to come
back from what they'd both said? Because she
wasn't happy with him. Not at all. An enjoyable
few hours had gone belly-up in a matter of min-

utes. Minutes he'd do almost anything to retract. Anything but set Jordan up for a fall. Or was he protecting himself here? Using Jordan as an excuse? Hardly. Jordan came first.

But if he listened to his sisters, and his parents, he was wrong. They all said if he found happiness then Jordan would be a happy boy and would have a normal life. And if it went wrong, he'd survive because he had a loving dad and a great family.

# CHAPTER NINE

'THAT WAS DANDY,' Anna muttered to herself as she leant back against her front door and listened for him to drive away. 'As if I want to upset Jordan in any way.' Surely Eli was being oversensitive? He was a good dad, but this was getting out of hand.

Damn him. It was like taking two steps forward, one, sometimes two, back. On again, off again. He'd kissed her as if there were no tomorrow, then gone all weird on her. Did she wind him up that much he lost control of his serious side?

She laughed bitterly. Good. Because that was what he did to her when she was with him. She didn't want to be alone when it came to feeling hot and horny. So was she willing to spend more time with him? Sex-starved brain says yes. Serious brain? Same answer because she believed there was something very special developing between them. She had to accept she'd fallen for him, but there was more to it. When they were getting along they jelled well, understood each other, sometimes read each other's mind without a word being spoken. They liked doing similar things and eating the same foods. Neither of them spent all their spare time rushing around trying to look busy when all they wanted to do was relax.

But there was a huge monkey in the room and she had to deal with it.

Finally she heard the car drive off. What took him so long? Thinking about coming back to give her some more grief? Or to apologise? No, he didn't seem in the right frame of mind to do that. Was he expecting the same from her? Should she be sorry for speaking her mind? She had been blunt, but that was her. Take it or leave it.

*He's left*.

But he did have a child to get to bed. They'd see each other tomorrow on the ward and then she'd see where things lay. 'Goodnight, Eli.'

Next morning Eli strolled onto the ward as though nothing had gone wrong between them. 'Morning, Anna. Sleep okay?'

Hardly, when she'd been thinking about his sexy body and what they might've got up to if Jordan hadn't been there. 'Like a log.' She'd got over her funk by the time she'd switched her bedside lamp off, and had started imagining Eli lying beside her. She had it bad. She could no longer put off having that talk with him. 'Did Jordan go back to sleep when you got home?'

'He was up and down every hour. Wanted a drink of water when there was already one by his bed, a story, which he didn't get, then to climb into bed with me. Again, that didn't happen. Then something to eat. He got a banana.'

'No wonder there're shadows under your eyes.' Eli looked even more tired than she felt.

'Yeah, it was a long night.' He looked at the screen she had up with notes on one of his patients. 'No change in Hayley's readings, I see.'

'There was a spike in her temperature around midnight but it's dropped a little since. The wounds on her thigh are still inflamed, and she's feeling some pain despite the drugs we're administering.' The girl had been knocked down by an angry ram on her father's farm two days ago and suffered external and internal injuries from the animal's horns.

'No surprise there. If only I could sedate her for longer but it's not a healthy thing to do. She's coping very well for a nine-year-old, though. A tough wee thing.'

'Her mother's struggling this morning. She needs a good night's sleep, too.'

'I'll see if she wants something to help with

that.' Eli sat down at the computer next to her. 'How about Mason? Did he manage to eat anything this morning?'

'Guzzled down porridge and stewed peaches like he hadn't eaten for a week. He says his throat's still sore but a lot better.'

'A normal result for a tonsillectomy, then.' Eli looked relieved.

'Do you worry about every patient?'

'It's hard not to when they're children.'

'Fair enough.' She stood up. 'I'll be with Hayley unless you need me for anything else.'

'I'll be right behind you.'

*Not watching my backside in the horrible scrubs, I hope.*

'I think Leanne has a patient she wants to talk to you about.'

'Where is she?'

'Grabbing a coffee while she can.' It had been hectic so far. Anna walked away feeling happier about Eli than when he'd left her place last night. He didn't seem to have any problems he wanted to deal with this morning, but that was also annoying because it was as if he believed he didn't have to explain anything else. Did she need to? Definitely. He had to learn about Charlie. However, they were at work, not the place for that conversation. But she'd been expecting Eli to have returned to his aloof manner, not be so friendly as he'd done before. No doubt about it, he was good at confusing her.

'Anna, up for a coffee when I'm done here?'

Like she said, confusing. Was he about to talk over things he'd refused to last night? This was the last place she wanted a personal conversation, even if they were the only ones using the staffroom. 'Sure.'

'I only have one muffin again,' she told Eli when they were sitting at the tiny table with coffees in hand.

'I'm not hungry as I had a big breakfast.'

Good, because she was starving. Having slept through her alarm, she'd had to dash to work to get here for the start of shift, forgoing breakfast apart from the banana she'd grabbed on the way out of the house. Drinking her coffee, she waited for Eli to say what was on his mind. If there was something bothering him, that was. He seemed serious enough for there to be some issue.

Eli rinsed his mug in the sink, and took hers to do the same. 'Can I drop by later when you're at home?'

The look in his eyes said this wasn't about lovemaking. Well, the time had come for her to say her piece and tonight would be it. 'Of course.'

'I'll come round after I'm done here. Jordan's at Mum's for dinner tonight.'

'I'll look out for you.' So he wasn't taking a hike yet. She'd stop by the supermarket to get some cheese and crackers to eat while they sat on her deck with a wine or beer. Or she could heat the zucchini pie that she'd made yesterday. Somehow she doubted she'd be able to swallow anything but she had to try.

In the meantime she had a wee patient to nurse and take her mind off Mr Forrester, who knew how to wind her up fast and confuse her big time. Was she so out of practice when it came to dating that she didn't know what was happening? The few guys she'd dated over the past couple of years hadn't intrigued her half as much as Eli did so it was possible she was looking for too much, and not accepting what was on offer because she couldn't see it for the mess in her head.

One thing she was certain about was that tonight she had to do what she should've done weeks ago. And most likely lose Eli for ever because of it.

Eli grabbed the bottle of wine he'd bought on the way and strode up Anna's pathway. He couldn't stay away from her. Yes, he was here to find some answers to what she wanted from them but he had to spend more time with her for his own sake. If that wasn't falling in love then he had no idea how to explain his actions.

'Hi there,' Anna called from the vegetable garden against the side fence where she was getting a sprinkler sorted to water the plants. She looked as confused as he was, though he didn't know if the same reason was behind that.

Holding up the bottle, he asked, 'Where do I find some glasses?' He hadn't needed to look for any last night as Anna had had everything required on a table handy to the barbecue. And he hadn't helped with the dishes afterwards.

'Cupboard above the fridge. I'm nearly done here.'

'Don't rush. I'll bring the wine over.' Her gardens were in good condition with early cauliflowers and broccoli coming on. A zucchini plant was still producing at one end, with another coming up to speed. His mother always said those were like weeds, but weeds he loved when she made chocolate zucchini cake.

'There're some nibbles on a plate in the fridge if you can grab them.'

'Onto it.' Anna made him feel quite at home despite how he'd been towards her last night. Another reason to wake up to the potential he was trying to ignore. They did get on well when he wasn't looking for reasons not to. He found her already sitting on a deck chair when he went outside with their glasses and the platter, and laughed to himself. She obviously didn't feel the need to check to see if he'd found his way around her kitchen. He liked that. There wasn't much he didn't like. 'Here you go.' Placing one glass on the small table between the two deck chairs, he sat down and looked at her. 'This is a good space. Open and light, and your gardens enhance the yard.'

'Even the roses have done well this year, if I may say so.'

'It's a lot quieter tonight than it was yesterday.' He laughed. 'The kids know how to make a racket, don't they?'

'It's what they're good at. I love it when they're here. They don't hold back at all. Jordan fitted right in.'

'He was talking non-stop this morning on the way to school. Luca this... Luca that.' He'd wanted to know when he could come back to Anna's again.

'Leanne's kids are here quite often so if Jordan's free he can always come by.' The wariness in her voice told him she was questioning whether he was prepared to allow his son to visit again.

'He'll be rapt. Making friends is big with him at the moment. I think he still misses those from his preschool and is afraid he won't make enough at the new school.'

'That's understandable.'

'Would you like to have children one day?' He had no idea why he asked, but now that the question was out there, he was eager to hear what she had to say.

'I'd love to. The biological clock is starting to tick quietly. I know I'm only thirty-four, but I can't help thinking about the women I met when working on the gynaecology ward who hadn't been able to get pregnant in their late thirties.'

'You've got time, though I see where you're coming from.'

'I'm not going to leap into a relationship just so I can have a baby. It's got to be all or nothing.'

'You're looking out for yourself. It's the right way to go.' Which he was doing when it came to getting close to Anna, looking out for himself. Except he was beginning to see that it might be the wrong thing to do. He was falling deeper in love with her by the day. Time for a change of subject. Except he couldn't think of one to distract him from those long, tanned legs stretched out in front of him. Damn, but she was sexy. Heating him up faster than he'd once have believed possible. Not even a gulp of chilled wine did a thing towards cooling him down. Talk about being all over the place with Anna. Last night he'd been cross with her, and now he wanted to carry her inside and make wild passionate love to her, instead of discussing serious things.

She was looking out over her tidy lawn, seemingly far away from where his mind was going. But then she turned to face him and he knew she wanted him here. 'I'm tired of looking out for myself. I'd just like to let go and have some fun, to hell with the consequences. Except I know it doesn't work like that. Things tend to come back and bite me on the butt if I don't keep control on my emotions.'

'Seeing you out of control isn't new. Not when we're between the sheets.' There was fire in his veins. Anna did that to him too easily. It was her way and it was his to fall into the blaze and try to make her feel the same. If she didn't already.

A rare blush turned her face pink. 'How long before you have to go?'

He placed his glass on the table and stood up. 'Long enough.' Once again he'd gone off track, and once again he couldn't wait to get into bed with her.

'You haven't stopped smiling all week,' Leanne said as she sat down beside Anna at the desk. 'He's that good?'

'Nope.' Anna grinned to herself. 'Better.' Eli had woken her up in ways she'd not believed possible. In bed, that was. When he'd asked if she wanted children the other night, she'd known what she had to tell him, but then he'd looked at her with such heat in his eyes that everything had gone out of her head except getting down and dirty. Her grin faded. She couldn't hold that against him.

'Afternoon, Anna, Leanne.' The man himself strode into the office. 'How's things?'

'All good. None of your patients are causing problems,' Anna replied as she breathed in the sight of that gorgeous body she now knew very well.

'Good, because it's been a long day in Theatre and I have one more patient to operate on when she's been prepped.' Eli dug into his pocket and pulled out his phone. 'Sorry, got to take this. Hi, Mum, what's up?'

Anna shut down the files she'd been looking at. Nearly time to head off and go to the supermarket to deal with the long list of groceries she'd made that morning.

'Don't worry, Mum. I'll sort something out.' Eli dropped his phone back in his pocket, a worried frown forming.

'Got a problem?' she asked.

'Mum's stuck in a traffic jam due to a truck and trailer unit rolling just this side of Kaikoura and won't make it back to pick up Jordan from school.'

'And you've got surgery to deal with.' Anna shrugged. The groceries could wait. 'I'm out of here shortly. I can pick him up and take him to my place. Or yours, if that's what you'd prefer.'

'I'd get Karen to look after him in her office but she's got parent-teacher meetings this afternoon.' Eli looked around, then returned his gaze to her. 'Okay, thanks. That would solve the problem.'

'Your place or mine? If mine, I can make dinner for all of us to have when you're done here.'

'I'd prefer mine. Jordan has a routine after school that I like him to stick to.'

'All right.' She wouldn't admit he'd hurt her a little. What harm could it do for Jordan to spend a couple of hours at her house? But then Eli was always over-careful when it came to his boy. 'How do I get in?'

He rattled off the security code for the keypad. 'I'll try to get home as soon as possible.' He turned to go.

'Hang on, Eli,' Leanne called. 'What about the school? They're not going to let Anna take Jordan away without your permission.'

He shoved a hand through his hair. 'It's not a problem with my sister being the headmistress, but you're right, I'd better phone and tell her what's going on.'

Anna tuned out as he explained to Karen she'd

be picking up Jordan. Time with him would be fun. He was such a busy wee guy and they got along fine.

'Sorted,' Eli said from behind her. 'Ask for Heather Brown, Jordan's teacher, Anna. She'll take you to his room.'

'Go now,' Leanne told her. 'It's nearly three and the next shift's starting to arrive.'

'I will. It'll take some time to get to the school at this hour. Does Jordan know I'm collecting him?'

Eli was watching her. 'Karen's gone to tell him.' Then he surprised her by stepping close and touching her shoulder. 'I really appreciate it.'

'No problem.'

*Just don't overthink it,* she begged silently.

'It's no big deal.'

Wrong thing to say, if the way his hand on her back tightened was anything to go by.

She added hurriedly, 'I had nothing else on.' Nothing important anyway. Her pantry wasn't bare. Except she realised she'd probably made matters worse because it sounded as though she wouldn't have offered if she did have something else to do. 'I mean, I'm happy to do this. I'd better get going or Jordan will think I've forgotten him.'

Eli's smile went a way to lifting her spirits. 'You're right about that.'

It took longer to get to the school than Anna had expected with traffic banked up all over the town. When she parked outside she sighed with relief. Mums did this all the time. Talk about stressful. Out of the car, she spied Jordan kicking a ball around with another boy. 'Hey, Jordan, I'm here.'

He raced across and threw his arms around her. 'Hello, Nurse Anna. You're taking me home.'

'Yes, I am as soon as I see your teacher.'

'Here I am,' said an older woman behind her. 'No need to ask who you are. Jordan's reaction is all the proof I need, though for legal purposes I need to see some ID.'

'No problem.' Anna tugged her phone from her pocket and found her driver's licence.

'You're good to go, Jordan. See you on Monday.'

'Okay, Mrs Brown. Anna, can I have an ice cream on the way home? A big one in a cone. Chocolate with sauce.'

She rolled her eyes. 'You're setting me up to get in trouble, young man.'

'Dad always buys me one when he picks me up.' The impish look on Jordan's face suggested otherwise.

But she might give him a treat. It wasn't as if she'd done this with Jordan before and once couldn't hurt. Could it? Would Eli see that as trying to win him over? Too bad if he did. It was what she did with Leanne's kids. There was no difference as far as she was concerned.

Her phone played a tune. 'Hi, Eli. Thought you'd be operating by now.'

'There's been a hold-up as the previous operation went beyond expected time. How's Jordan?'

'He's good. Want to talk to him?'

'Sure.'

'Jordan, Dad wants to say hi.'

'Dad, Nurse Anna's going to get me a ice cream. Okay, *an* ice cream. Yes, she is. She told me.'

Um…that wasn't quite how it had gone, but still.

She took the phone back. 'Hope that's all right?'

'Make it a small one or he won't eat dinner. Right, got to go. We're on.' And he was gone.

An hour later when she was playing hopscotch with Jordan on Eli's back lawn, Eli rang again. 'Just checking everything's all right.'

'Of course. Why shouldn't it be?'

'You might've forgotten the code to get into the house.'

'I didn't need it as Jordan spouted it off numerous times when I turned into your drive.'

'He knows it? I didn't have a clue.'

'He's not silly. Want to talk to him again?' To

make sure she hadn't beaten him or tied him to the bed?

*Calm down, Anna. Eli's a caring dad.*

Of course he'd ring to check all was okay.

'Not at the moment. My patient's coming round and I'm needed in Recovery.' Gone.

This was starting to become annoying. Two calls to check up on Jordan when he'd often said that she was good with children. Bet he didn't phone his mother or Liz to check on how they were doing all the time. 'Bye, Eli,' she muttered as she banged the phone down.

'Was that Daddy?'

'Yes, he's still working.'

'That's okay. I've got you to play with.'

Therein might lie a problem, if Eli's wariness had anything to do with it. In the meantime she'd get on with keeping his son happy and if he didn't get home soon, she'd make Jordan some dinner. The kid was hungry despite the ice cream he'd gorged on earlier.

When Eli called again at six o'clock she snatched the phone up and growled, 'Jordan's fine. He's had a bath and I'm about to feed him. Anything else bothering you?'

Silence. Then, 'I was calling to see if you'd like pizza for dinner.'

The air left her lungs in a rush. Closing her

eyes, she counted to ten in her head. 'Sorry, Eli. Really sorry.'

*That's enough. You don't have to grovel.*

'If that's still on offer, then I'd love one. Seafood if possible.' She was going to stay after that? Sit and eat pizza as if nothing were wrong? Actually, it was a good idea. She'd have it out with him and finally learn where she stood.

'See you soon.' Gone—again.

Why had she reacted so fast and not given Eli time to say why he'd rung?

*Because I'm afraid he'll find me wanting, that I'm not good enough to look after his son. Not good enough for Eli to love me.*

Just when she was feeling she might be able to move on she went and blew it. The doubts that had haunted her for eighteen years were still there. But then, were they ever likely to disappear? Maybe after forty years in a stable relationship?

'Seafood pizza as requested.' Eli placed a box on the table in front of Anna, noting the stress in her face. They'd talk shortly. He swung Jordan up in his arms and hugged him. 'I see you've been having stories read to you.'

'Yes, Daddy. Nurse Anna reads all my favourites.'

'Cool. Now it's time to clean your teeth and

go to bed. It's already past your bedtime.' He glanced at Anna. 'That's not a dig at you. I knew he'd insist on staying up until I got home.'

'I have no idea what time he usually goes to bed, and wasn't asking.'

'Good thinking. He'd have said ten o'clock.'

A small smile lifted her face, but whether it was for him or his son he didn't know. 'That's what I figured.'

'Give me ten? And pour us each a glass of the wine that's in the fridge?' The situation was awkward enough so he'd try to be relaxed and casual.

Without waiting for an answer, he carried Jordan to the bathroom and supervised the teeth cleaning and the other requirements before getting into bed. After a few minutes listening to how his day at school had gone, Eli kissed him goodnight and went out to face Anna.

She was twisting her glass back and forth in her hands, looking thoughtful and not happy.

'Thank you for looking after Jordan. It's much appreciated.'

'I enjoyed it.' She sipped her wine and put the glass down. 'You thank me and yet you kept ringing up as though you expected something to go wrong.'

He put plates and serviettes on the table,

opened both pizza boxes, and sat down. 'Call me paranoid.'

'Distrustful, more like.' She picked up a piece of pizza and took a large bite.

'That, too.'

She flinched. 'Great.'

The wine didn't taste so wonderful tonight, but he swallowed a large mouthful anyway. 'It's not you personally that I have trouble with. In fact I've got further with you than any other woman since Melissa.'

A puzzled expression came his way. 'I'm not sure how to take that.'

'Damn it, Anna. This is ridiculous. We get on so well, and yet here we are arguing like kids.' Another gulp of wine and he pushed the glass aside. Wine wasn't going to solve a thing. 'You know why I worry.'

Her eye roll was exaggerated. 'You tell me so often I wonder if this isn't more about you not trusting me not to hurt *you*.' She locked formidable eyes on him. 'Actually, forget Jordan. This *is* about us. You and me.' Her finger tapped the table with each word. 'You're afraid of being let down again. I get that because I have fears about being let down too.'

That was a slap around the head. It had never occurred to him she'd think that with him. 'What's behind those fears?' Would whatever was worrying her explain those days when he'd believed she was hiding something?

A solitary tear rolled down her cheek.

His heart was breaking for her, but he remained where he was. It was for Anna to make the next move.

The piece of pizza she held hit the bottom of the box. 'Easy said. The thing is, I'm not even certain I can be trusted to stay in a relationship. I've got a bad track record. Even with family. So I don't have a lot to offer in the way of guarantees.'

That concurred with all his worries. 'Then we're in a deeper quagmire than I'd thought.'

'Want to keep trying to sort this out, or is it time to bail before it gets too difficult?' More tears filled Anna's eyes.

His heart dropped—hard. She was hurting. He was hurting. He wanted to leap up and haul her into his arms and never let her go. But if he did, it was a commitment he wasn't ready to make until he knew what was behind those tears. She might not want to be there for him for ever. She was right in that this was as much, if not more, about his feelings as Jordan's. If he committed it had to be for ever and he wasn't sure she could reciprocate.

Her glass was going round and round in her hands. 'When I was fifteen I got pregnant.'

He hadn't seen that coming. Everything in him stopped as he waited for Anna to continue.

'I turned sixteen two weeks before my son was born.'

What did that have to do with anything? She'd had a baby. Where was he now?

'My parents refused to help or support me.' Imploring eyes lifted to look at him. 'I was still at school. If I kept the baby they'd have kicked me out on the street and I wouldn't have been able to support him.'

'There are social services that'd do that.' Bile soured his mouth. Why hadn't she told him before? It made all the difference to his decisions to stay with her.

Her head moved slowly from side to side. 'I talked to them. Was offered accommodation in a home with other girls in similar situations but I was sixteen and totally out of my mind about what had happened. Friends talked about drugs and other things that terrified me. I couldn't see how I'd ever be able to give Charlie everything he needed.'

The bile got stronger. 'So you gave him up for adoption.'

'I had no choice. It was the best I could do for him.'

He could not believe what he was hearing. Anna was so good with kids. All the pain from his own mother's abandonment filled him, making it difficult to breathe, let alone think straight. Yet she was also very good with Jordan. Jordan. Deep breath. Thank goodness they hadn't got too deeply involved. This was the end of anything between them.

'But not for me. I have lived with guilt and sorrow every day since they took him away out of my arms.' Her face glistened with tears.

He went to get a box of tissues. 'Here.' Sinking onto his chair, he shook his head. 'I don't know what to say, Anna. You've shocked me.'

Her head shot up and there was anger in her glare. 'You don't have any right to judge me, Eli. I didn't walk away from my boy because I had better things to do. I gave him up for his own good.'

'Yeah, well, maybe, but you don't know what he will have gone through in the intervening years wondering about you and who you are and why you did what you did.'

'And you do?'

'Yes, I damned well do. Mum and Dad are my adoptive parents.'

Her mouth fell open. Her eyes widened. All colour drained from her face. 'I see.'

'No, you don't. I was six months old and my birth mother didn't want me any more. She had better things to do than raise me.' He stood up and paced around the lounge. 'She told me that when I tracked her down six years ago.'

'Charlie found me. Last week.'

'Last week?' That explained a lot. 'You didn't think to talk to me about him then?' They were never going to get close and involved. She'd kept this huge piece of information from him.

'I wanted to. I tried.'

'I offered an ear when I thought you were worried about something. That's not how it works in a good relationship.'

'The thing is, I wasn't sure if we had one of those, or were even starting out on one.' She was getting stronger by the minute. 'I knew once I told you there'd be no chance of you wanting to have anything more to do with me.'

'Are you saying you intended to hide it from me for ever?'

'Never.' She swallowed hard. 'I—' Another swallow. 'I have a lot of feelings for you. I stalled. I know that was wrong, but I couldn't lose you so soon. I kept fooling myself that you might fall for me and understand why I did what I did. Of course, I didn't know about your adoption.'

'Anna, I'm sorry, but I've taken two hits in the heart. I can't take another.'

Her face crumpled. Then she said so softly he had to strain to hear the words. 'Charlie and I are talking. He's beginning to understand why I gave him up and that I've always loved him.'

What could he say? It hadn't worked out like that for him, but he was pleased for Charlie. Anna had such a big heart. The young man deserved no less.

Anna stood up slowly, as if hoping he'd stop her before it was too late. He couldn't. When he didn't, she shook her head sadly. 'Goodbye, Eli.'

His heart was already aching. There'd be more of that to come. Tomorrow he'd be back to being Mr Forrester. He'd bet his next salary payment on that. 'Goodnight, Anna.'

# CHAPTER TEN

'I'VE FILLED OUT a prescription for Tobias.' Eli stood up from the desk and moved away as Anna came into the office. 'See that he starts the antibiotics immediately.'

'Onto it,' she said, nurse's head firmly in place as she dropped into the chair he'd vacated.

'Thanks.'

Anna watched him stride away as though he hadn't a worry in the world. If she hadn't seen the sadness in his eyes she'd believe that to be true. It had been the week from hell. They'd dodged each other as best as possible, and when they couldn't they had exchanged only the bare minimum of words. He was never going to forgive her for not telling him about her son right from the start of their relationship. She might not forgive him for being so cold about it all either. He hadn't shown any compassion, probably too busy protecting his own feelings. 'Thank goodness for Fridays.' She had the whole weekend to bury her head under her pillow and wait for her heart to get over itself.

Make that most of the weekend. Charlie and his parents were flying down to see her tomorrow afternoon. It would be exciting if she didn't feel so wound up about how the meeting would go. Charlie had tried to reassure her his mum and dad were happy he'd met her and only wanted to get to know her a little. But she'd lived with the idea of this moment for so long she couldn't relax. Dealing with the bust-up with Eli as well didn't help. It was too hard. If only he were around for her to curl up against and talk about her fears. But that was never going to happen.

'What's going on?' Leanne asked after looking around to make sure they were alone.

She hadn't told Leanne what had happened. It would make it even more real. 'Nothing's going on. We're done and dusted.' Except she doubted she'd get over Eli in a hurry, if at all. She hadn't loved a man as she loved him. It had really come home to her during the night as she tossed and turned while trying to accept they were through. He hadn't made any attempt to stop her leaving, had sat there watching her walk away, while her heart was crumbling, filling her with pain unlike anything she'd known except for the day they'd taken Charlie away from her.

'I don't believe you, Anna.' Leanne had turned to look at her, worry covering her face. 'You were getting on brilliantly.'

'Were being the operative word.'

'You're going to give up that easily?'

'Nothing easy about it.' Her sigh was filled with pain. 'I love him, Leanne.'

'I know you do. It's been obvious from the get-go. You've been more you: happier, bubblier, laughing more if that was possible.'

How was she going to cope? Her heart was shattered. The phone rang and she grabbed it for the distraction. 'Paediatric ward. Anna speaking.'

'Pete from the pharmacy. I've got an urgent prescription for one of your patients ready.'

'On my way.' She stood up. 'Don't say any more, Leanne. I have to think about what comes next.' All she knew was that whatever she came up with, it wouldn't include the man of her dreams.

'I'm your buddy. You don't get away with that. But it will have to wait until later tonight when you come round for dinner with the tribe.'

Thank goodness for besties. 'I'll bring chocolates for the kids.' There was no way she wanted to go home to her empty house. Funny how she'd never had anyone else living with her and the house had never felt empty. It didn't feel like home any more. Home would be wherever her heart was, and that was with Eli now.

'Do that and you'll have a bed to use if required.'

'I might do that and all.'

In the end Anna didn't stay with Leanne and Craig, instead drove home around midnight and crawled into her own bed to pull the pillow around her neck and try to go to sleep. But all she could think of was Eli and how he was back to being aloof. She hated that. She deserved better now that they'd been intimate and had enjoyed being together. Especially now he knew about her past. She did deserve better. She did. Charlie had muttered he could see why she gave him up. Why couldn't Eli understand her reasons? His mother hadn't wanted him. But she had wanted her son and she'd told Eli so.

Throwing her pillow at the wall, she cried, 'I love you, Eli.'

She was ready to commit for ever? Not to back off after time? Yes, she was more than ready, but Eli wasn't. He never would be. Not with her.

She'd pulled away from her parents after they'd put the pressure on her over Charlie. She'd let Danny go when she should've grabbed him and marched down the aisle on his arm so she could prove she wouldn't let him down. There were other men she'd let slip through her hands all too easily because she hadn't believed she deserved to be happy.

Then along came Eli. The one man who'd got past her barriers, had made her realise she was capable of love and ready for the whole she-bang, and now she wanted it more than any-thing. With Eli.

Why had she walked out of his house with-out putting up a fight? Was that a habit? Or was fear the reason *he* didn't reciprocate her love? And that he'd never get past what she'd done to Charlie?

She had no idea how he felt about her. Appar-ently she'd been a breath of fresh air for him, and he'd liked how she talked openly about most things, but he didn't trust her not to leave him. Forget Jordan. He was one of Eli's concerns, but she'd swear nowhere near as big as his own fear of being let down. That she could understand, feeling much the same.

Since she couldn't promise to be there for him for ever, he had probably done the right thing by not asking her to stay any longer. Throwing a second pillow after the first did nothing to calm her distress. 'I love you so much it's painful, Eli. Do you even love me a little bit?'

Eli groaned as he rolled over in bed when Jor-dan bounced under the sheet. No such thing as a sleep-in these days. 'Hey, little man, go easy on my old bones.'

'Wake up, Dad. I want to do something.'

Like what? He'd learned not to ask. 'Starting with breakfast.'

'Can we see Anna today?'

His heart crunched. 'Afraid not, Jordie.' If only they could bowl around to her place and sit on the deck.

*Why don't I? Just go, do it.*

He should ignore all the noise in his head and listen to his heart. Talk to her about her son, and really listen to her as she talked about him. If Charlie could accept what had happened, then why couldn't he? Anna was nothing like his birth mother. Not at all. She loved her boy.

Could it be that easy to move past this? Was he making it harder than necessary? He knew what his family would say. Which didn't make it any easier. They weren't the ones who had to front up to his gremlins. 'Come on, let's get up and ready for swimming class.' Something to keep him busy for a couple of hours at least and then he'd think of something else to do with Jordan.

It was a long tedious day that brought only more questions and no answers. Despite what she'd told him, he missed Anna like he couldn't believe, yet they'd never spent a whole weekend together. This felt final. They weren't going to work through it and start over. Nor would they carry on with what they'd already had. Everything was different now.

*What are you doing today, Anna?* he asked silently again and again. *Missing me? Cursing me for being stubborn?*

Finally he gave up trying to fill in the hours until sunset and packed Jordan into the car and headed around to Liz's where Jordan would have someone to be busy with.

The first thing he said when he walked into her house was, 'Don't say a word.'

She studied him for a moment and nodded. 'Fine. Beer's in the back fridge and Gary's in the garden picking peas. Take him one, too.'

He gave her a hug. 'Thanks.'

After roast lamb and vegetables, and an apple tart with cream that Eli barely tasted, Jordan crawled into the spare bed in his cousin's room and fell asleep.

'Guess that means you're staying the night,' Liz said.

'Might as well,' he agreed and reached for the wine Gary had poured them after dinner.

He didn't sleep any better than the night before at home, tossing and turning until finally at around five o'clock he got up and went for a walk through the quiet streets, Anna with him all the way. He couldn't let her go, didn't want to let her go.

He loved her. Yeah, he could admit that to himself. He was head over heels in love with Anna Passau. Which left him with little choice. He had to follow up, to expose his heart and tell Anna how he felt about her, and then ask her to believe in him. He needed to accept her history so they could go forward *together*. It shouldn't be hard to do.

It was a huge weight holding him down, preventing him from opening up. 'Why?' he asked the sun peeking over the horizon. 'Why can't I do this?'

Because of Jordan.

Not true. Eli tripped. Stared around, barely seeing where he was, the realisation in his head blinding him to everything else.

He *was* hiding behind his son. Using his son as an excuse to protect his heart. He didn't want to be hurt again. He knew that, had always known that, but he hadn't realised how deep his need to do it had become. He needed to be shaken awake so he could focus on reality and drop the what-ifs. There was only one way to live and that was to be open about his feelings with other people. Most of all, with Anna. As he always was with his family.

Turning back the way he'd come, he thought about where to go from here.

Placing the baguettes in the oven, Anna turned to the fridge to get some zucchinis to make fritters. Nothing like zucchini and parmesan together, she thought as she began grating the vegetable.

After the Zoom call with Charlie and his parents she'd hit the kitchen. It had been another disappointment to get over when Charlie had phoned to say the weather in Wellington was so bad most flights had been cancelled and could they have an online meeting instead.

The meeting had gone better than she'd expected. She even found herself liking Charlie's parents and at the end they'd all agreed to get together some other time. Charlie had given her a cheeky smile that had really lifted her spirits.

Until she closed down her laptop and Eli flooded back into her head, taking over all thoughts.

The oven timer beeped. Removing a cake and placing it on the wire rack, she groaned at herself. 'Who's going to eat all this?' Her appetite had disappeared along with any chance Eli might decide they should be together. Looking around the benches where a lasagne and two bacon and egg pies sat cooling, she shrugged. She'd find someone to give it all to. Leanne and Craig were always happy to receive her cooking.

She'd been filling in hours here in the kitchen, trying her damnedest not to think about Eli. And failing completely. He was there with every egg she broke into the bowl, every piece of pasta she placed in the pot, every punch of the dough that was now baking and filling the air with a delicious fragrance. Face it, Eli was in her heart and head and wasn't going anywhere else any time soon.

She loved him. He didn't know that. She hadn't told him.

Would it have made a difference to how he'd let her walk away if she had? Would he have leapt up and hauled her against that strong chest, never to let her go? Not likely. He'd more likely have shaken his head and told her to get a life.

Only one way to find out. Which meant laying her heart out for him to see. Was she brave enough? Could she afford not to be? People said nothing ventured, nothing gained. They didn't say what happened if it failed. She had to know. Though after seeing his shock when she talked about Charlie, she knew he would never let her in his front door.

To hell with the bread. She flipped the oven off as she untied her apron. Same for the fritters. She shoved the bowl of batter into the fridge.

She had to do this. Had to. If Eli never knew she loved him, then she had only herself to blame for whatever came next.

Knock, knock.

Someone was at her back door. 'Bad timing, because I'm outta here.' Pulling the door open, she gasped. 'Eli?' Who else did she know who was so good-looking and sexy and kind and caring and—? She slumped against the doorframe. 'I was just coming to see you.'

He took her hands, held them tight. 'Anna.' His eyes looked haunted, and his face was so sad it brought tears to her eyes. 'I—' He swallowed, hard.

Noise from the street made her straighten up. 'Come inside.' She forced her lungs to breathe, and, still holding one of his hands, pulled him in and closed the door on the rest of the world.

'Anna, it's been a long weekend and it's nowhere near over. We need to talk.'

She kept moving, not wanting to have this conversation in the entranceway.

Eli moved with her, as though he never wanted to let her go again. That had to be good, didn't it? But 'we have to talk' sounded quite the opposite. They sat at the table, watching each other warily. After a laden minute, Anna bit down on the words her heart wanted to put out there, and said, 'Go on.'

'I'll be blunt. I love you, Anna. I've fallen hard and deep and I never want to let you out of my life.'

'You what?' Her heart was pounding, her head spinning. Never had she expected that. If anything she'd thought Eli would've given her a hundred reasons why he was reticent about telling her his feelings, not come straight out with the words.

'I love you,' he repeated, looking relieved. As if getting the words out had lifted a huge weight off him.

Standing up, she moved around beside him and took his stubbly face in her hands. 'What about my past? What about Charlie?' She didn't want to spend time with Eli only for him to decide again he couldn't deal with it.

'I've done a lot of soul-searching, and I talked to Mum and Dad about this. I hope you understand I had to hear their perspective as adoptive parents. Anna, I haven't been in your shoes. I can't criticise you for what you did. Bottom line, you didn't have a choice if you wanted your son to have a good life. I admire you for that.'

Her heart cracked wide open. Not once had she expected Eli to tell her that. 'Thank you. It means everything to me to hear you say that.'

His smile was tentative. 'I mean it with all my heart, Anna.'

The last knots around her heart broke away. She was free at last. 'Eli, I love you with all I've got. I have for a while now.'

She didn't get any further as he pulled her down onto his knees and placed his mouth over hers. His kiss was gentle and loving and told her more than his words had. Eli Forrester loved her. Her heart was safe. She kissed him with all she had, and more.

When they finally pulled apart and regained their breaths, Eli smiled. 'I've been fighting with myself for a while about how to approach this. Do I tell you? Don't I tell you? Until in the end it was a no-brainer. I had no choice if I wasn't going to go mad. I'm sorry I visited my fears about Jordan on you, Anna. You didn't deserve that.' He paused, then drew a deep breath. 'But I'm even more sorry that I used my concerns over Jordan being hurt to hide behind. You were right. I was, still am a little, afraid to commit my heart. But I'm doing it. I can't not when you mean so much to me.'

Tears began streaming down her cheeks. 'Neither of us is perfect. I always believed I didn't deserve love because of what I did, and then I met you and thought I might be able to change that. Charlie turning up when he did helped me see I could be totally happy, but really it all comes down to you. I've been waiting for you to come into my life. When you did, you chipped away at my fears bit by bit without me understanding what was going on until I was in so deep there was nothing else to do but tell you I love you. That's what I was coming to do when you knocked on the door.'

'Mum and Dad support you one hundred per cent, by the way.' Brushing her cheeks with his fingers, he kissed her again, a loving, heart-sharing kiss that spoke of their future together, for ever. Then they sat holding each other tight, not saying anything, absorbing the love that bonded them together.

Anna in his arms was the best feeling in the world, Eli thought as he brushed a kiss on the top of her head. She loved him. He was still getting his head around that. He believed her, of course he did, but it was hard accepting that he'd found a woman who meant so much to him and seemed to think the same of him. It was the most wonderful thing to happen in a long time.

Looking over at the kitchen benches, he chuckled. Typical Anna. 'I take it you've been cooking up a storm as a way to shove me out of your head?'

'That's only this morning's efforts. I baked some cakes late last night too.'

'What are you going to do with it all?'

Green eyes met his grey ones. 'Give it all away, I guess.' Then she blinked and smiled. 'Or, we could ring your lot and tell them to get their butts around here for lunch so we can share our news. Along with Leanne and Craig.' She got up and switched the oven back on before returning to Eli.

His heart swelled even further when he didn't believe it was possible. 'Why not?' Then he asked, 'What are we saying? That we're in love?'

'Isn't that enough for now?'

'There'll be endless questions about what we're going to do about it.' He had to warn her, though she probably already knew.

'Leanne will be no different. They'll all have to wait and see.' Anna grinned, then grew serious. 'What are we going to do?'

'Spend as much time together as possible. Make plans for our for ever future together.'

'Plans that include Jordan.' She smiled.

'Yeah, and maybe add to the tribe?' Eli knew Anna wanted to become a mother again, this time to go the distance, and who better for his son to have as a stepmum? Anna would never let his boy down. Never.

'Did I say I love you, Eli Forrester?'

'Once or twice.' Damn, his heart felt good. Full and happy and ready for anything.

# EPILOGUE

*Twelve months later, at the beach*

'MUM ANNA, I want a juice.' Jordan flopped down on the beach towel beside her.

'Help yourself.' Sometimes she still had to blink away the tears that his name for her brought on.

The moment Eli had explained that she was moving into their house to live with them, and that Dad loved Anna, Jordan had leapt into her arms shouting, 'Mum Anna, I love you too.' Her heart had imploded with love for the little guy.

Glancing across at the other Forrester male who did unbelievable things to her heart, she sighed with happiness. Life couldn't get any better. Her hand sat on the baby bump under her singlet top. She was too big for a bikini at the moment.

'Mum Anna, I want a beer.' Eli sat down on the blanket she'd spread on the sand and gave her one of his heart-stopping smiles.

She could never get enough of those. And his kisses. And their lovemaking. 'Help yourself. I'll have a water while you're at it.' The only downside to being pregnant was not being able to share the occasional wine with her man. It wasn't a biggie. Their baby was far more important. She could barely wait for Rose to pop out so they could all get to know her. But she'd have to. Ten weeks to go.

'How's Rose this afternoon?' Eli handed her a bottle of sparkling water.

'She was snoozing since I went for a swim.' Made a nice change from all the energetic kicks that had been going on earlier. Leaning back in her beach chair, she watched the man she loved so much. How lucky she'd been to find him. 'I could almost thank Jordan for getting appendicitis.'

'It was the tipping point for us, wasn't it?'

Her eyes dropped to the emerald ring on her finger. The colour to match her eyes, Eli had said when he'd held it out after proposing. His favourite colour, he'd added. 'Yes, it was. When I called you a jerk that night, I'd never have believed that I'd fall in love with you, even though I was already feeling the heat whenever you were around.'

'Little hot blasts that made my toes tight,' Eli

said with a sideways glance at Jordan. 'If you know what I mean.'

'Not at all.'

He grinned. 'Bet you didn't expect to be having *my* baby and getting married once she's here.'

'Never crossed my mind.' Though she had hoped for something like that once she'd accepted she'd fallen for him. 'Nor did I know how much effort goes into planning a wedding.' But now the venue had been booked, the caterers lined up, and a dress was being made with allowances for a change in her figure after Rose was born. The invitations had gone out a week ago and already most people had answered. Including her parents. They were coming. It had been tense the day she'd taken Eli to meet them, but he had been at ease with them and soon they had all been talking. It had almost been like old times for Anna. Since then they'd made an effort to see more of her and had met Charlie too.

Which reminded her. 'Charlie's got a partner for the wedding.'

'I'm surprised he didn't already have one. He's such a cool dude.'

'He's choosy.' He was also adorable. They got on really well nowadays, and he and Eli seemed to have a natural bond together.

Eli. The love of her life. Reaching across for

his hand, she gripped him tight. 'Have I told you lately that I love you?'

'Over breakfast this morning.' He lifted her off the chair and onto his thighs. 'I love you too, soon-to-be Mrs Forrester.'

'As in aloof like Mr Forrester? I don't think so.' She chuckled.

'Okay, then, soon-to-be Mrs Anna Passau-Forrester.' He grinned, kissed her.

'Yuk. I'm going for a swim,' Jordan shouted, and charged down the beach to the water, bringing their kiss to an end as they kept an eye on him.

* * * * *

# Rebel Doctor's Boston Reunion

Amy Ruttan

# MILLS & BOON

Born and raised just outside Toronto, Ontario, **Amy Ruttan** fled the big city to settle down with the country boy of her dreams. After the birth of her second child, Amy was lucky enough to realise her lifelong dream of becoming a romance author. When she's not furiously typing away at her computer, she's mom to three wonderful children, who use her as a personal taxi and chef.

Dear Reader,

Thank you for picking up a copy of Madison and Tony's story, *Rebel Doctor's Boston Reunion*.

I love reunion romances. I also wanted to write about doctors who work to save the lives of those affected by cancer. I've lost too many people I love to that dreaded disease. This is my love letter to those who fight, who have fought and those who have moved on.

Madison is determined to be the oncologist who cures cancer since she lost her mother at a tender age. She's willing to try the latest to give her patients a chance. She has dreams and she's not one to settle for long.

Tony is a brilliant surgeon. His childhood was one of upheaval, and risks are not something he's comfortable with. He longs for roots and a family, but his heart still belongs to the one who broke it— Madison.

Now they're working together. The only thing that's constant is their burning passion, which is reignited in the cancer ward.

I hope you enjoy Madison and Tony's story!

I love hearing from readers, so please drop by my website, www.amyruttan.com.

With warmest wishes,

*Amy Ruttan*

## DEDICATION

For all those who fight...Dad, Gramma Marg, Sharon

For those who won...Theresa, Jennifer, Helen

And those still in my heart...Nanny, Mum, Barb, Dawn, Grampie, Aunt Dorothy

# CHAPTER ONE

*IT'S SO SHINY!*

Which was probably not the correct thing to think silently, but Madison was ecstatic. She was squealing inside and it was hard to contain her giddiness and remain professional in front of her new colleague. The lab she had been given for the next year was bigger than anything she had ever worked in. All the equipment was brand-new and state-of-the-art.

It even had that fresh, unused smell. Like a new car.

Only better.

The best thing? Her name, Dr. Madison Sullivan, was listed as the lead doctor on the outside of the lab. The last lab she'd worked in she hadn't been the lead researcher. Now she had a sparkling new lab and was an oncologist at a great research hospital.

It was a dream come true.

"What do you think?" asked Dr. Frank Crespo, head of the board of directors, following her discreetly. He was not a medical doctor, but he believed so much in her research that he had reached out and offered her this position at Green Hill Hospital in Boston.

"It's amazing," Madison gushed. "When can I start?"

Dr. Crespo chuckled. "Now, but I want to take you to the oncology wing so that you can meet the rest of the staff and of course, our department head, Dr. Antonio Rodriguez."

"Right." Madison hoped that Dr. Crespo didn't hear the hesitation in her voice, because she was very familiar with Dr. Antonio Rodriguez.

Very.

Familiar.

She and Tony, as he'd liked to be called, had been residents together out in California years ago. They'd constantly butted heads and just didn't see eye to eye on how things should be done. However, when they did agree, things were explosively good.

Hot.

Electric.

The sex had been phenomenal. No one ever had come close to the absolute magnetic pull that Tony seemed to have on her.

If they weren't arguing about something, they were in bed together.

The times they did get along, they worked like an unstoppable team. The problem was Tony was too rigid and took too long to take a chance. He was always questioning her. It felt like he didn't believe in her. He didn't trust her judgment and it hurt.

Too much. And that's why she'd ended it when their residency was over. How could she think of settling down with someone who didn't believe in her abilities?

Not that he ever asked her or talked about a future. And she hadn't asked him about his plans either. Tony had always been so closed off with his emotions.

Just like her father.

It had hurt to let Tony go. In the end it was for the best. Career came before love, marriage or the baby carriage as the old song went. She'd accepted a job in Minnesota and he went back to his home in Boston.

She was a bit worried that she would be working with Tony again and that he'd be her boss. Tony was head of oncology, but she was hopeful that enough time had passed that they could work together. Green Hills Hospital, or GHH, was one of the best on the Eastern Seaboard for cancer and research. This was about saving people's lives by working to cure cancer.

She couldn't save her mother, but she could save someone else's loved one. A brief stab of sadness moved through her as her mind wandered to the memory of her mom. Her mother was her whole reason to pursue this medical field.

This new job at GHH was the next step in her journey. She just needed a good place to work, to research and to publish some more papers on her research into CRISPR-Cas9, an exciting new genome editing technology. When she got some more articles published, she was going to apply to work at one of the most world-renowned cancer research facilities in Europe and hopefully with her idol, Dr. Mathieu LeBret, a Nobel laureate and brilliant physician. He rarely took others under his wing, but she was hoping to be the next one. The research facility and Dr. LeBret had made it clear that she needed more credentials. At GHH she'd get what she needed.

She was so close to that reality and she wasn't going to let a decade-old heartache get in the way of that.

Not at all.

Nothing tied her down and nothing would stop her from making her dreams become reality.

"Well, I'll take you down to the oncology wing. It's just down the hall, not far from your lab." Dr. Crespo opened the door and extended his arm. "Dr. Rodriguez will be eager to meet you."

*Sure.*

The Tony she had once known barely showed any emotion. She seriously doubted the inflexible Tony had changed that much.

Madison reluctantly left her bright, shiny new lab. Dr. Crespo shut the door and they walked side by side down the winding hall that led out into a beautiful atrium which had a gorgeous garden in full bloom.

"This is our cancer garden. Patients, caregivers and even staff can find respite here. We also have memory plants and trees," Dr. Crespo pointed out.

"How lovely."

And it was. It gave a sense of peace in the sterility of the hospital, a place for those hurting to find solace.

He nodded. "Ah, there is the man in question. Dr. Rodriguez!"

Madison's heart skipped a beat and her stomach dropped to the soles of her expensive heels as Tony turned around from where he'd been standing in the atrium. It was like time had stood still for him, save for a few grays in the midst of his ebony hair at his temples. There were an extra couple of lines on his face, but he was exactly the same as she remembered. Stoic expression, muscular physique which seemed to be perpetually held stiff as a board. No smile on his face. He was just so serious.

His dark eyes fixed on her and a jolt of electricity coursed through her.

Her body was reacting the exact same way it always did when she saw him.

And she could recall, vividly, how his hands

had felt on her body, the taste of his kisses, every sensation he aroused in her. His broody exterior barely expressed any emotion, but he showed her through every soft touch, every tender caress how he wanted her. She melted for him every time. It was all flooding back to her in that moment as she stood there staring at him.

Dr. Crespo was blissfully unaware, and for that she was glad. She was annoyed that even after a decade she was still like a moth to Tony's flame.

Tony ripped away his gaze and smiled half-heartedly to Dr. Crespo.

"Dr. Rodriguez, I would like to introduce you to Dr. Madison Sullivan. Dr. Sullivan, this is our chief of oncology, Dr. Antonio Rodriguez."

Tony's eyes narrowed and the fake smile grew wider, but there was no warmth in his gaze. She wasn't surprised he was being polite, but it shocked her how it bit at her. This was the way he was. Nothing had changed, so it shouldn't smart like it did. She was over him.

*Are you?*

He held out his hand, as if it were perfunctory. "It's a pleasure to see you again, Dr. Sullivan."

Her hand slipped into his and she was hoping that she wasn't trembling. "Indeed, Dr. Rodriguez. A pleasure."

Tony pulled his hand back quickly and she nervously tucked back a strand of hair behind her ear.

She was suddenly very hot and she could feel her cheeks burning.

She always flushed when she was angry or sad or happy. Whatever emotion she felt showed up in her cheeks. It was frustratingly hard to keep a poker face.

"You two know each other?" Dr. Crespo aske, in amazement.

"I did mention that," Tony replied stiffly. "We were residents together. We learned under Dr. Pammi out in California."

"I must've forgotten. Dr. Pammi is an excellent oncologist. Well, this is great then," Dr. Crespo exclaimed, clapping his hands together.

Madison swallowed the lump in her throat. "Yes. Great. It is nice having a professional acquaintance in a new place."

Tony didn't say anything but just nodded.

Curtly.

*Big surprise. Not.*

"I'm going to continue to show Dr. Sullivan around. Perhaps after lunch you can show her the oncology wing?" Dr. Crespo asked.

Tony's eyes widened briefly. "Sure."

Honestly, she thought he was going to say no.

*He's a professional.*

And that she remembered all too well. He did take risks, but only those that were well thought out. Tony liked to play it safe and he was a rule follower. Never made a scene, but defended himself when he was sure he was right. Whereas she'd always been a bit of an emotional, exuberant student. She and Tony had clashed so much. And if she made a mistake he'd point it out, which annoyed her.

Greatly.

She went on a path toward oncology research, and he threw his life into the surgical side of cancer treatment. They both attacked the dreaded disease using different approaches.

She'd been foolish to fall in love with him, but being with him had been such a rush. At the time, he made her feel alive and not so alone. It was refreshing after spending a very lonely adolescence taking care of herself and her grieving father.

She was a fool to have those little inklings of romantic feelings for him still. They weren't good together. Leaving him had been agonizing, but it was the right thing to do at the time.

She thought back to one of their characteristic interactions in residency.

*"Why did you say that to Dr. Pammi? What were you thinking?"* Tony lambasted her.

*"Uh, I was thinking about all the research that I did! And how I was right in the end. It worked."*

*"It was risky,"* Tony grumbled, crossing his arms.

*"And it worked,"* she stated, staring up at him. *"Is this why you dragged me into an on-call room? To yell at me for getting something right?"*

Tony sighed. "You just have to be careful. This is a highly competitive program."

"So?" she asked, shrugging. "I'm here to play and win. Don't worry about me. I'm strong."

Tony smiled at her gently and then ran his fingers over her face. "I know, but you're hard-headed too. You didn't have to call Blair a butthole."

Madison sniggered and slipped her hand over his. "But Blair is a butthole."

Tony rolled his eyes and then pulled her into his arms. "You drive me crazy sometimes. You know that?"

"Ditto."

She snuggled into him.

She felt safe with him. Especially in those few scattered moments he let his guard down. This was the Tony she loved.

"Could you meet me at the main desk in oncology in two hours, Dr. Sullivan?" Tony asked, interrupting the memory that came rushing back.

"Sure," she said, nervously. "Two hours. Yes."

"Good. Well, enjoy the rest of your tour at GHH." Tony nodded at Dr. Crespo and quickly walked away in the opposite direction.

Madison watched him striding down the hall, his hands in the pockets of his white lab coat, his back ramrod straight and other people getting out of his way as he moved down the hall like he owned the place.

That hadn't changed.

Tony always had that air of confidence. It's what she was first drawn to. It was clear he still affected her the same way.

Working with him again was going to be harder than she thought.

Tony had been completely off track all day and he knew the reason. It was because Madison was starting today. When he first saw the memo come through from the board of directors he thought about saying something, anything, to keep her from coming here, but that wasn't very big of him.It was petty he prided himself on being professional.

Madison was a talented oncologist and researcher; it would be completely foolish to deny GHH that expertise and talent because he still had feelings for her after ten years. Try as he might, no one had ever held a candle to her.

And he had tried to move on after she left him. Only, he couldn't.

He wanted to marry, settle down and have a normal life, something he'd never had growing up. Tony wanted roots. Except he fell in love with Madison, a wanderer.

Part of him hoped he could change her, but he'd been wrong and she'd left. For so long he'd wondered what had happened. He was sure it was him. He was too set in his ways. He had a path in his mind and nothing was going to deter him from that.

And nothing had.

The number-one complaint he always got from his exes was that he worked too much. It was true. Work never let him down.

Except that one time…

He'd forgotten that Madison was going to be starting today of all days. It was the anniversary of the day he lost his best friend. The one life he couldn't save. The one time he decided to take a risk, act like Madison always did, and it hadn't paid off.

Jordan died.

Even though it wasn't Tony's fault, it still ate away at him. He was reminded of Jordan every time he went to see his godson—Jordan's son, Miguel—who wasn't so young anymore. On the anniversary of Jordan's death, he always went to the garden and spent some time there thinking about his friend and replaying what he should've done over and over.

Not that it did any good, but it was a habit. He'd just plain forgotten Madison was starting and that he would have to show her around. Today was the day that she was walking back into his life.

*Not back into your life. Remember?*

And he had to keep reminding himself of that.

When they had been together, it hadn't been good for either one of them. It led to too much heartache, for both of them, and he knew first-hand what heartache looked like.

He'd seen the devastation in Jordan's widow's eyes and then he'd seen that absolutely soul-crushing and heart-shattering pain when his father eventually left his mother. His father had gambled away her future and then left them in ruin.

Trust was hard for Tony. That was also part of his problem. He just didn't fully trust Madison. She'd left him before and she was so willing to try anything. She was a wandering soul and he wasn't. He was settled here and he wasn't going to put himself through a tumultuous relationship with someone who was going to leave him again.

So no, she wasn't walking back into his life. And today was not a good day. He was struggling to compartmentalize everything, but he was a professional so he just had to suck it up and make it work. He wasn't going to be, as Madison used to call difficult people, a butthole in front of the board of directors.

A smile tugged at the corner of his lips as he thought of her calling many obnoxious fellow residents buttholes. Usually under her breath, but he always heard it. Except himshe never called him that.

When he saw her there with Dr. Crespo, it made his heart stand still, because it was as if time hadn't touched her. It was like the last time he saw her.

The only difference was, there were no tears of anguish and anger in her gray eyes. Her pink lips were as luscious as he remembered. Her blond hair was tied back in a ponytail, the same way it always was, with that tiny wavy strand that would always escape and frame her face. Her cheeks were flushed with a subtle pink and he had no doubt that her skin felt smooth and silky.

He briefly wondered if she used the same coconut shampoo. She always smelled like summer. She exuded sunshine and warmth, especially during the hardest times of their residency. She always cheered everyone up. And she always looked so darn cute in her light blue scrubs and neon sneakers.

Except she wasn't in her resident scrubs and trainers. She was professionally dressed in a white blouse and a tight pencil skirt with black heels that showed off her shapely legs. He recalled the way her legs would wrap around his hips. With aching clarity, he could still feel her skin under his hands.

How soft she was.

How good it felt to be buried inside her.

His blood heated and he scrubbed a hand over his face. He had to stop thinking about her like that. She was not his. Not anymore. It was going to take a lot of strength, but he could make this work. He had to make this work.

# CHAPTER TWO

Tony had done his rounds and tried to put at the back of his mind all those memories and old feelings that Madison was stirring up in him. He focused completely on his post-op patients, making sure they were resting comfortably and managing their recovery well. There were a couple of patients that he was able to discharge and leave in the hands of the oncologist who would administer chemotherapy and or radiation.

After he did that, he made his way to the chemotherapy treatment room and checked on his patients there who'd recently had surgery. The room was always cold, so it helped him to wake up and shake off the ghosts of his past that were pestering him today.

It usually completely cleared his mind.

Except now. It was frustrating. In their short interaction, Madison had gotten under his skin just like she did when they first met.

It didn't matter what kind of wall he put up; she

got through. He could keep others at bay, but she always weaseled her way through.

It was infuriating.

*I can't think about her.*

And he couldn't. Things changed since they were together. He was a different person.

*Are you?*

He had work to focus on. That was what he needed.

When he finished checking on patients, he spent some time in his office going over files and preparing to meet patients tomorrow, which was his clinic dayThere was a huge wait list to see him and he wanted to get to everyone he could. There was a reason people requested him and came to GHH; he was one of the best cancer surgeons.

*You weren't good enough to save Jordan though.*

Tony shook that niggling thought out of his mind as he closed his last file and made his way to the main desk to meet up with Madison.

There was part of him that wished he could put this off, but how would that look? It would be totally unprofessional of him to avoid her. At least if he got this over and done with now, she could go off and do her own work and he could continue with his.

They'd operate in the same realm, but not work side by side all the time. They weren't residents anymore. He spent most of his day in the operating room and he knew she had a lab to do research. Sure, they'd see each other for consults, but they would be working in different spheres at GHH.

If he put off their meeting, it would just eat away at him. It was best to rip the bandage off and do his job as head of oncology.

When he got to the main desk, she wasn't there.

*Typical.*

Madison had always been running late when they were residents.

*"Dr. Sullivan?" Dr. Pammi called out, not looking up from her clipboard.*

"Here!"

*Tony looked back to see Madison dashing up the hall, her lab coat fluttering behind her like a cape. He just shook his head as she skittered to a stop beside him, out of breath and tying back her blond hair.*

*Dr. Pammi didn't even looked flustered as she continued to take attendance.*

*"You're always late. That looks bad,"* he groused out of the corner of his mouth.

*"Thanks for the warning, Grandpa,"* she muttered, rolling her eyes.

*Tony leaned over and whispered, "You weren't calling me Grandpa last night."*

*Madison's mouth dropped open and then she slugged him in the arm.*

*"Dr. Sullivan and Dr. Rodriguez, is there a problem?" Dr. Pammi asked.*

*"No," Madison responded quickly. "There was a fly on his arm."*

*Dr. Pammi cocked her eyebrow, her lips pursed together. "You two are on scut."*

Tony smiled at that memory. He'd been super annoyed at the time, especially to be assigned scut duty with her, but they had made it work. They always bickered, but they had so many good times too. Until the end.

Time healed all wounds, or so the saying went, but with her unwillingness to settle down they just weren't good for each other. It was for the best when it ended and he had to keep telling himself that.

Tony's stomach knotted and he tried to lock away all those memories. This wasn't the time or place to reminisce. Only, he couldn't help it. She was haunting him today.

Dr. Crespo was walking with Madison toward the main desk. Well, at least that explained why Madison was late.

"Sorry for keeping her, Dr. Rodriguez. We got a bit waylaid with the board of directors. They're very excited about the research that Dr. Sullivan is going to be doing here," Dr. Crespo explained.

"Oh?" Tony asked, intrigued. "What research is that?" He was curious. He knew that she had come to GHH for research, but didn't know what she was actually studying.

"CRISPR-Cas9," Madison responded. "I have some testing I would like to explore. Clinical trials and the like."

Tony swallowed a lump in his throat. "That's... ambitious."

CRISPR-Cas9 was fairly new and there was a lot they didn't know about the groundbreaking technology. It was a hot topic in the medical world. What Tony knew of it made him wary. There was a lot of risk involved, and when she said that she was going to test it, he immediately resisted because it reminded him she hadn't changed.

Not really. She was still taking risks.

When she was a resident she was so gung-ho about clinical trials and always eager to join them. Most times it would blow up in her face and she'd be devastated.

Clinical trials were important but she never took the time to really think of the implications.

*I'm sure it's different now.*

"Ah," he responded, because he wasn't sure what was left to say. The logical part of his brain was telling him that she was making a mistake and that CRISPR-Cas9 wasn't safe for his patients, but if his patients wanted to sign up for medical trials, he couldn't stop them.

Even if he wanted to.

*"This time it'll work, Maria. I swear," his father lamented.*

*Tony had crept downstairs because his parents were fighting again. His dad had obviously come back, but when his dad did come home, it always made his mom upset and he never stayed around for long.*

*"We're saving that money, Carlo," his mother sobbed.*

*"It'll pay off. You have to trust me."*

*"I don't though," his mother said softly.*

*Tony was relieved she said it, because his father couldn't be trusted. He gambled everything away.*

*"You love me though, Maria. Don't you?"*

*Tony's fist clenched. He was annoyed his father was once again using love to manipulate his mom.*

*"I do," his mother sighed. "Take it."*

*"Ah, Maria. I promise it'll be better this time. I'll make so much that I can buy you that house and we can put Tony into a better school."*

*"Sure..."*

"Dr. Rodriguez?" said Dr. Crespo.

Tony shook the memory away, banishing the agony of his past because there was no place for it here. "Sorry," he apologized.

Madison's lips pressed together in a thin line, her gray eyes going positively flinty as she narrowed her gaze at him.

"I have to get back to the board of directors

and I'll leave Dr. Sullivan in your capable hands, Dr. Rodriguez." Dr. Crespo turned to Madison. "Great to have you on board. I am so excited to read your research as you publish it."

"Thank you, Dr. Crespo. You've been too kind," Madison responded tactfully.

Dr. Crespo walked away and she turned to look back at Tony, crossing her arms.

"You're a butthole. You know that, right?"

"What?" Tony asked as he tried to hold back the smile of amusement.

She'd called him a butthole. It was kind of endearing she was still using the same insult.

"Don't patronize me, Dr. Rodriguez. I saw that look on your face when I said what I was doing research. Surprise, surprise—you have misgivings. Well, I can tell you that this is the future of cancer treatments. The ability write cancer out of DNA. I don't care how you feel about it. We're not residents. All we have to do is work together and be civil."

"I totally agree," he responded.

"Then why are you smirking?" she asked hotly.

"Butthole?" He chuckled. "Really?"

Madison tried not to laugh, because she was still annoyed with him. When she mentioned what she was researching and that she was going to be offering medical and surgical trials based on her research to patients here, she saw that Tony instantly became protective. And she knew why.

CRISPR-Cas9 was newish, and there were a lot of unknowns surrounding it, and Tony wasn't a risk taker. That much hadn't changed, but it irked her. He deserved the title of butthole, because she knew what she was doing.

She had learned from her mistakes over the years. To excel at something always involved a learning curve. Each misstep hurt and she worked hard to improve. She carried those scars with her, which was why she was so good at her job.

Tony always was more cautious. It took him a long time to decide. She got that; he was a surgeon. She respected it. But she didn't make her decisions willy-nilly like he assumed.

Everything was so thought out. This was solid research. If it wasn't, she wouldn't have been here. She wouldn't be making huge strides in the treatment and the eventual cure for cancer. This is what she had been working toward her entire career.

If she was successful here at GHH and published, then she would finally be able to make her dream come true and work with Dr. LeBret in France. Dr. LeBret was her hero and he was willing to try new things and to take risks. If she got his attention and could work with him, benefactors could potentially offer her way more funding than she could get here. Ultimately, she could save more lives.

It annoyed her that Tony had misgivings. Even after all this time.

Tony was being stubborn, but seeing his eyes twinkle at being called that special name she used brought back all those memories where he had teased her about it in the past. It had been a private joke between them, and Tony was not a whimsical, lighthearted person with just anyone.

*He was with me. Sometimes.*

"I stand by my decision," she replied, haughtily crossing her arms. "I know what I'm doing and I don't need your approval."

"Good," Tony said. "Because you're not going to get it. I have my practice and you'll have your practice. We just have to be professional. That's it."

"That's all I want. I can assure you of that."

Which was true, but his finality still stung her a little bit and she didn't know why. She was not here to rekindle anything with him. That was the last thing on her mind.

Except it also wasn't.

Right now, in this moment, she could recall every touch, every heated glance and every kiss just as vividly as she could recall the way her heart had broken into a million pieces when it ended.

"Paging Dr. Rodriguez to treatment room three.

Dr. Rodriguez to treatment room three," the PA sounded.

Tony frowned. "It's pediatric oncology."

"I'll come with you," Madison suggested. "You were going to show me around the department anyways."

Tony hesitated for a moment and then nodded. "Let's go then. Try to keep up in those heels."

Madison snorted and fell into step beside him as they quickly made their way through the halls. "You don't have to worry about me. I can keep up. In fact, I'm going to run the Boston Marathon in my heels."

Tony rolled his eyes. "Why do you do that?"

"Do what?"

"Make light of things," he groused.

"Because you're too damn serious sometimes. Butthole." She grinned at him and he groaned under his breath, but there was a slight smile playing on the corners of his lips. It gave Madison a brief sense of hope that this could actually work. That they could just leave the past in the past and work together. Maybe even be friends. Which was what she wanted. They were older and wiser.

It wasn't too long a walk to treatment room three. As they put on masks and surgical gowns, a pit formed deep in her stomach. She'd dealt with sick kids before during her residency and at previous hospitals, but she never got used to the idea that cancer would wreak havoc on a child's body, that cancer altered little lives.

*This is why you do what you do,* the voice in her head reminded her as she girded her loins to take that first, tenuous step into the treatment room.

She had to keep reminding herself of that when she saw five small bodies buried under blankets and hooked up to IVs, but it was the faces of the parents that always got to her.

The parents were trying to be so brave, but she could see the anguish that was lurking behind those eyes. Even though she wasn't a parent, she felt that to her core. She had seen that look on her father's face every day that her mother had treatment, and she was pretty sure that it had been reflected back to him in her own eyes.

*You've got this. Remember why you're here.*

She still felt the keen pain of watching her mother fade away slowly and then her father. He shut himself away from the rest of the world and she was alone.

Always alone.

*Focus.*

Madison nodded to herself, steeling herself and compartmentalizing all those feelings. She followed Tony past patients to the very corner of the room where there was an Isolette. She kind of skidded to stop when she saw a tiny baby in the incubator.

The mother was standing off to the side in a

gown, looking terrified as Tony spoke to the nurse quietly.

Madison made her way over to the chart and smiled at the mother. "I'm Dr. Sullivan. May I look at your child's chart?"

"Of course," the mother's voice quavered. "Her name is Gracie. She's six months old."

"She's beautiful."

Gracie's mom smiled from behind her mask. "Thank you."

Madison flipped open the chart to read about Gracie's diagnosis. A neuroblastoma had developed in the adrenal gland. The tumor had been removed and the previous oncologist had ordered a high dose of chemotherapy, along with treatment to increase stem cell reproduction so he could harvest it for transplants. The transplants would help fight the disease.

It was a common cancer among infants, even though cancer in infants was rare. This was the reason Madison was so invested in her research. Neuroblastomas developed in the fetal cells at the embryo stage. If she was successful with her research, then one day they could eradicate this type of cancer in children before the child was born. Then there would be no need for heartbroken parents, hurting children or shattered souls.

Tony came over to the Isolette with gloves. He didn't acknowledge the mother, beyond a curt nod. Madison groaned inwardly. He was a great doctor, but his bedside manner still sucked.

*Definitely a butthole.*

She glanced down as Tony gently examined the baby. He was so gentle with his patient, who didn't stir much as he touched her. And then he gently caressed Gracie's head. It surprised Madison and her heart melted seeing him so tender with the littlest of patients.

"How is she, Dr. Rodriguez?" the mother asked, with trepidation in her voice.

"Her blood cell counts are down and we want to get them up so we can harvest stem cells to continue treatment. I'm going to order some platelets and that should alleviate the problem," Tony responded brusquely. "I'm going to monitor Gracie closely, but I have no doubt this treatment will work. She's been strong and responding well every step of the way. As you know, Dr. Santos has left GHH, but Dr. Sullivan is our newest oncologist. She'll be monitoring Gracie's chemo and radiation."

The mother looked over at her. "And what do you think, Dr. Sullivan?"

Madison was a bit stunned she was being asked for her opinion. She hadn't even had a chance to go over the file properly yet. She glanced over at Tony, whose eyes narrowed for a moment. She knew she had to be careful. If she wanted their work relationship to go well, she couldn't step on his toes the first day, especially when she wasn't familiar with the patient. But she was a doctor too. A damn good one and one with opinions. She did agree with the previous oncologist's treatment though.

"Stem cell harvesting and high-dose chemo is a well-known treatment for this type of aggressive neuroblastoma. I agree with Dr. Rodriguez and Dr. Santos."

The mother's face relaxed. "Thank you both."

"Have me paged if anything changes." Tony pulled off his gloves and began to walk away.

Madison set the chart down and followed quickly behind him.

They left the treatment room and disposed of their gowns and masks.

"Thanks for backing me up in there," he said. "I thought you might start spouting off on some new research thing. Dr. Santos and I consulted closely before I did the surgery."

She cocked an eyebrow. "Well, stem cell treatments are cutting-edge. You and Dr. Santos are doing the right thing. I'm not here to get in your way, Tony. I'm here to work."

And she meant it. She just wanted him to leave her alone so she could do what she needed to do in order to advance her career.

Tony nodded. "Good."

"You could be a little bit warmer though," she

suggested, dumping her surgical gown in the linen basket.

"Warmer?" he asked. "I'm warm."

Madison snorted. "You can be. I do know that, but you were very businesslike with your patient's family. It's a bit...standoffish."

"I'm fighting for their lives. Trust me, when I win over cancer, I'm right there celebrating with them. And I win a lot."

"I know. I've followed your career a bit."

"Have you?" he asked, surprised.

"Of course. You're good at what you do and so am I."

Tony worried his bottom lip. "Maybe we should go grab a drink after work and talk about the parameters of our working relationship and what people around here should and shouldn't know. I've worked very hard on my reputation here."

"No doubt."

"So we should clear the air," he stated. "Maybe meet at Flanagan's at seven?"

Madison wanted to say no, but they needed to talk about the rules and how to navigate working together again.

"Sure. Send me the address."

He nodded. "Let's finish this tour then so you can get back to your lab and you can get caught up on all of Dr. Santos's patients. Or rather, your patients now."

Madison nodded and followed him, shocked by

what had just happened. Maybe this was a mistake. But it would be smart to lay it all out. Maybe then they wouldn't butt heads so much.

She could handle a drink with him.

Right?

# CHAPTER THREE

Tony had whizzed through the rest of the tour with Madison after they arranged to meet for a drink down the street at Flanagan's, where everyone from GHH met. He didn't know what had come over him asking her out like that, but after she had gone back to her lab and he got back to his work, he decided that it was a good idea.

It was better to be out in a public place to hash things out. He had nothing to hide, even though he was a pretty private person. He'd heard that from partners in other failed relationships that he was too aloof, too focused, introverted.

Cold.

Thankfully, none of his patients called him that. Although Madison was right; his bedside manner was a bit brusque.

Sure, he was professional, but he did care about his patients. He was so devoted to them. It was why so many people came to see him at GHH. The survival rates for his patients were higher than for any of his colleagues patients.

*Except Jordan.*

He'd lost other patients. He was a surgeon; it happened. Each one stung, but when it was his best friend? That had destroyed him.

Tony shook that thought away as he glanced at the picture on his desk. It was a picture of him and Jordan when they had been kids. Their arms were around each other, and they were laughing at Jordan's twelfth birthday party.

He smiled and he picked up the photo. He missed him so much.

At least there was Miguel, his godson. In Miguel, Tony could still see his best friend. He loved spending time with him, though it was getting less and less as Jordan's widow had found love again and was planning to remarry. Miguel adored his new soon-to-be stepdad, who was a decent guy.

Tony was happy for them, but he missed Jordan.

He was lonely.

*And whose fault is that?*

It was his. It was easier to push people away. It always had been.

Tony groaned. For one brief second he thought about canceling the drink with Madison, but he wanted to make sure that it was strictly business they were attending to when they interacted. He didn't want all those old feelings that had been muddling around in his head today to resurface. Or rumors to spread.

Madison was his past. GHH and his career were his future. That hadn't changed.

*Kind of lonely, don't you think?*

He scrubbed a hand over his face and finished with his paperwork. After doing a quick round on his patients, he packed up his stuff to head for home so he could change and then meet Madison at the bar for seven.

Thankfully, he didn't live too far from GHH.

It was summer and the sun was still up. June was his favorite month. As much as he loved Boston, he really hated the cold and dark of winter. Not that he did anything during the summer, other than spend a night or two in Martha's Vineyard, where he now owned his late grandparents' cottage. But he'd only bought it last fall and he just never found the time to visit. Work was his life.

*Maybe you need to take a trip out there?*

It was a thought. He'd put some distance between him and Madison.

*Uh, isn't that running away?*

He couldn't do his work from his home in Martha's Vineyard. There were no virtual surgeries like in science fiction.

He was a grown man and this was getting silly. He just had to face this whole thing head on.

He unlocked the front door of the redbrick condominium in Beacon Hill, overlooking Boston

Common. He greeted the doorman with a wave and made his way to the elevator, swiping his card for his penthouse two-bedroom condo.

Not that he needed two bedrooms, but he had bought it years ago when the building was new and the prices weren't so astronomical.

The elevator doors opened and he made his way into his condo, which was sparsely decorated with modern furniture. The space was cold and sterile like him, or so he'd been told. He just found it functional. He learned from a young age not to get attached to things. Especially to possessions that could be pawned off.

He dropped his satchel and coat before making his way to the shower. He undressed and as he stepped up the spray of hot water he closed his eyes, bracing his arms on the wall in front of him, trying to relax.

Instead he saw her.

Madison.

He remembered the time they shared a shower in the locker room at the hospital, late at night. Her body slick as he held her. Her legs wrapped around his waist and her back pressed against the tile wall.

*Dude. Stop.*

Tony groaned. He had to pull himself together. He quickly cleaned up, got dressed and then headed to the pub where he'd be meeting Madison. En route to Flanagan's he couldn't help but wonder where she was staying in Boston. Or for how long. And that was the kicker. She had nothing tying her down and he knew that for a fact.

Madison had said that she was keeping tabs on him over the years, but he had been keeping tabs on her too. Tony knew exactly how much she had moved from facility to facility around the country, and he didn't have high hopes that she would stay at GHH long term.

He had a hard time trusting someone who didn't have any roots. Especially since his father had had that wandering foot. He recalled the pain when his father abandoned them. He had no interest in someone who was always looking for the next new thing. Someone who couldn't settle.

Though he hadn't understood at the time his relationship with Madison had ended, now he knew it was for the best.

*Was it?*

When he got to the pub, Madison was nowhere to be found, which didn't surprise him at all. She didn't have Dr. Crespo to blame for her tardiness this time. He took a seat in a corner booth and ordered a pint of the featured IPA on tap.

As he settled back into the seat, he saw a pair of shapely legs through the window that was open to the stairwell that led down to the bar. The memory of those legs from the shower flooded his mind as he admired her through the window. He recognized those heels immediately. She was still dressed in her work clothes.

Tight white blouse, tight pencil skirt, black stiletto heels. It all accentuated her womanly curves. Curves he was all too familiar with. His blood heated and he curled his fist around his beer to keep himself from reaching out to touch her like he wanted to do.

*Focus on the task at hand, Tony.*

Madison breezed into the bar and saw him. She made her way over and then slid into the booth across from him.

"Sorry, I had some trouble logging into my GHH account. I had to wait for the IT guy to come and fix it for me. Hard to do research when you can't even access the online library database," she said quickly.

"I'm sure," he agreed, swallowing a lump in his throat.

"What?" she asked, looking at him curiously.

He shrugged. "I didn't say anything."

"I thought you were going to give me heck about being late. You always did."

"Don't put words in my mouth," he replied.

"Then don't have those words written all over your face," she teased.

Tony rolled his eyes. "You drive me around the bend. Seriously."

"Aww…" she replied sardonically. "I'm glad things haven't changed too much. Lighten up,

Tony. We can be friends and friends tease each other."

"Not my friends," he muttered.

"Oh, come on. Jordan does."

His heart skipped a beat.

*She doesn't know today is the day Jordan died. She doesn't know he's gone.*

And he didn't want to tell her. Tony cleared his throat. "You're right."

He didn't want to talk about Jordan tonight.

Madison didn't seem to notice his reaction. She was too busy looking at the menu. When the waiter came back, she ordered a glass of white wine and then folded her hands neatly on the table.

She sighed deeply. "You wanted this drink to talk. Let's talk."

He nodded. "Right. I did. I wanted to discuss our working relationship and how we can manage together without…without…"

"The fighting we used to do?" There was a twinkle in her eyes.

He nodded again. "Exactly. I'm the head of oncology and it's my department. I hope you'll respect my wishes. You can't call me a butthole in front of people."

"I won't and I didn't. Look, I've changed, Tony. I'm professional and you have to trust me."

"I would like that." Only he wasn't so sure that he could fully put his faith in her.

She'd left him. She'd broken him.

"You have to meet me halfway, Tony. I'm going to work here at GHH."

"For how long?" he asked, finally getting to the point. It shouldn't matter to him how long she planned to stay. He shouldn't care. Except he did.

He wanted to remind himself why, and maybe if she told him the time frame he could get her out of his mind.

Her gray eyes widened. "What?"

"How long?"

Madison didn't know how to respond to that. Part of her wanted to say however long it took to get more work published and noticed by Dr. LeBret, but she didn't want to share that with him.

Sure, they had been residents together, lovers even, but that was over a decade ago. Even though she had known him intimately then, now he was just an acquaintance and she didn't trust him either. It was hard to depend on someone who didn't put their faith in you. It was hard to be with someone who never fully let you in.

"I don't know my exact time frame, but I'm here for now," she replied and hoped that was a good enough answer for him.

"Okay." Although, he didn't really seem to like that response either.

The one thing that had always driven her nuts about Tony was the inability to read his emotions, which ran hot and cold. He worked so hard to shut everyone out and he never told anyone why. It wasn't her business any longer. They weren't together. And she had to keep reminding herself of that.

All she wanted was a simple working relationship with him. That was it.

It was completely frustrating to her that she'd been thinking about him every second since she returned to her lab. Heck, she'd been thinking about him since she signed the damn contract to come to GHH. She'd convinced herself it would be fine but, so far she wasn't living up to her own promise.

Right now, she kind of felt like that meme of a dog sitting at a table, surrounded by flames, drinking his coffee and saying that everything was fine. This was fine.

*Was it?*

"Well, Dr. Crespo knows we previously worked together. Do you think he'll tell anyone else?" she asked, trying not to think about Tony or how he was making her feel in this moment. She had to maintain this professionality. That's what she wanted.

"People will know, but it shouldn't amount to much."

"And if it does?" she asked.

"How so?"

"We have a past. What if rumors fly?"

"Let them."

Madison was a bit surprised at how unbothered he was by that. "Wow."

"What?"

"You're so nonchalant about it." The waiter set down her glass of wine and she took a sip of it. "Especially when you seemed so concerned earlier."

Tony shrugged. "We don't need to explain ourselves. As long as it doesn't affect our work. We have to be professional. No arguing in public like we used to do."

"I can be professional. I assure you."

"Good," he responded quietly.

"Can I get the same promise from you?" she asked.

Tony cocked an eyebrow. "What do you mean?"

She was a bit taken aback by his feigned innocence. She knew exactly how he felt about her research; it had been written all over his face. He didn't trust it. He didn't trust her.

"I stand by my research," she responded firmly.

"I'm sure you do."

"Are you?" she questioned.

"Well, you did jump around. Your name was attached to some failed trials…"

"That was ten years ago, Tony. Those were mistakes. I admit that."

He frowned. "I just don't want to play cleanup."

Her spine straightened. "I don't need you to do

that for me. I told you before and I'll say it again, I stand by my research. It's sound and I don't have to prove it to you."

"Very well," he acquiesced.

"Are you going to stand in my way during clinical trials?"

"No."

"You don't say that with much confidence."

"I will protect my patients," he replied firmly.

"And you think I won't?" she asked hotly.

"Just be careful. Risks are… They don't always pay off. If I don't think it's worthwhile for them, I'll let them know."

"I'm sure you will," she responded sardonically.

"What's that supposed to mean?" he asked.

"Risks need to be taken, Tony, or medical advancements won't happen."

He opened his mouth to say more when his phone went off and glanced down. "It's Gracie. She's not responding well to the platelet transfusion. She might have a post-op infection."

"Maybe I can help?"

Tony cocked that eyebrow again. She could tell that he wasn't sure. From his expression he wanted to tell her no, but she was replacing Dr. Santos.

"Fine." He pulled out some money and placed it on the table. "Let's go."

Madison nodded.

She was frustrated that they hadn't finished

their conversation, but right now that didn't matter. A patient needed them and he wasn't keeping her out of the loop. They were her patients now too. He wasn't shutting her out.

Small progress was still progress, and a little life was in their hands.

# CHAPTER FOUR

WHEN THEY GOT back to GHH nurses had moved Gracie's Isolette into a private room, which was standard practice. Gracie could be fighting an infection, and there were a lot of other children in the treatment room who could also be susceptible to fevers and viruses. They couldn't put their other patients at risk.

Madison followed Tony as they put on disposable gowns, gloves and masks. Tony was the surgeon and if it was a post-op infection then he would have to take point on it, but she could suggest medicine that wouldn't counteract the chemotherapy they were using to help fight it off.

Gracie's mom was standing off to the side. Her eyes were wide behind her mask and she was wringing her hands. Madison understood that desperation and helplessness. She had seen it time and time again, but she felt it on a deep level too.

She'd seen the same desperation in her father's face as her mother died, and then he shut down, leaving her not physically but emotionally alone. She'd had to grow up fast then. So Madison wanted to comfort Gracie's mom, but there wasn't much that she could say to her right now. Not until they knew more about what was going on.

Tony opened the Isolette and was gently examining the baby. He was so matter-of-fact with patients, but watching him handle that delicate sick baby took her breath away. Madison stepped closer to him.

"Post-op infection?" she asked in a hushed tone.

"Indeed," Tony responded. "She'll need a dose of antibiotics, but we have to find out the strain of staph infection that's wreaking havoc with her."

"I'll draw some blood and get it off to the lab." The nurse in the ICU pod handed her what she needed to do a complete blood panel, but Madison also wanted to check Gracie's neutrophils level, because she had a hunch.

It wasn't uncommon for patients getting high doses of chemotherapy and radiation to have neutropenia. Neutropenia was often the cause of why people fighting cancer would get infections. It also made it harder to heal especially after surgery.

"Her wound is red and leaking," Tony remarked under his breath.

Madison collected her specimens and sent them off with the nurse. She then carefully palpated Gracie's abdomen right over her spleen to see if it was swollen, because a spleen could sometimes be a culprit in neutropenia.

Tony watched her. "Well?"

"It's enlarged. I'm going to have her blood tested for neutrophil levels as well. If she has neutropenia I want to start her on injections of G-CSF."

G-CSF, or granulocyte colony-stimulating factor, helped the bone marrow make more of the neutrophils that could be lacking in Gracie's blood. The platelet transfusion wasn't working. The baby already had an infection and they needed to get her through her chemo before they could harvest stem cells.

"Are you suggesting another stem cell harvest? Dr. Santos has done that."

"I'm aware."

"Should I remove her spleen?" Tony asked quietly.

"No. Not yet," Madison said. "I wouldn't mind getting a tiny sample of bone marrow. For now, let's get her infection under control. She can't take too much strain."

"Agreed."

Madison turned to the nurse. "Start her on a course of general broad antibiotics until the lab confirms what infection we're dealing with. Keep me posted."

"Yes, Dr. Sullivan," the nurse said.

Madison walked over to Gracie's mother, who

was standing there terrified. Tony was removing the bandage and redressing the surgical wound.

"Is my daughter okay?" Gracie's mom asked.

"She has an infection. We're going to start her on some antibiotics and stop the chemotherapy until we get that infection under control."

Gracie's mom nodded. "Okay."

"It's common," Madison assured her gently. "Chemotherapy kills off cancer, but it can kill off the good things too."

She wanted to tell Gracie's mom that her baby would be fine, that there was no reason to worry, but Madison couldn't do that. She had learned that she couldn't deal in absolutes when it came to cancer. All the things she wanted to say, words that she herself had wanted to hear when her mother was fighting her own battle, she couldn't utter to Gracie's mom.

She hoped the little bit she told her was enough to calm her down and give her hope, because hope was all you could cling to in moments like this. Although, those words had done little to help her father...

*"Daddy?" Madison asked, creeping forward. "I have dinner."*

*"Not hungry," her father muttered, not moving from the bed.*

*"You've got to eat." Madison set the tray down. Her father rolled over. His expression blank. "Thanks, Madison, but not now."*

She swallowed the painful memory away, not letting it in to affect her as she smiled gently at Gracie's Mom.

"It's common," she stated again.

Gracie's mom nodded, but she was still wringing her hands. "Okay, Dr. Sullivan. I understand."

Madison reached out and squeezed her shoulder. "I'll keep you updated every step of the way."

"Thank you," Gracie's mom said, choking back her emotions.

Tony motioned with a nod to follow him out of the room so they could discuss things further. Once they were out of the ICU, they disposed of their gowns and gloves. They found a small meeting room outside of the pediatric intensive care unit and Tony shut the door.

"Exciting first day," Tony said, dryly breaking the silence.

"Indeed. I wouldn't have minded a dull day," she replied softly.

"I understand." Tony then pulled out a chair for her. It was a small act, sort of chivalrous.

She sat down, her back brushing against his fingers. The simple brush, the heat she could feel coming from him, sent a shiver of anticipation through her. Madison remembered the way his hand would fit in the small of her back. How he would tenderly touch her secretly as they did rounds, so no one else would know. It had thrilled her, sharing those private moments with him.

*And it led to heartbreak, remember?*

They may have had those tender moments together, but outwardly around the other residents he was closed off. She never knew the real him.

*Did he know the real you?*

Madison cleared her throat and leaned forward, breaking the momentary connection. Tony removed his hand and made his way to the other side of the table, sitting down in one of the chairs. Obviously, he was putting distance between them, which was good.

"You mentioned a bone marrow sample?" Tony asked, getting straight back down to business.

"I would like to do one, but I also don't want to put too much strain on Gracie. I've ordered a CBC so we'll see what her neutrophil counts are before I order a bone marrow. Although, I'd like her to be over her infection. For now, I don't want her on the high-dose chemo. Not until this infection clears up. It's too taxing on her."

"Agreed."

"I had a chance to look over Gracie's file. Actually, I'm surprised that Dr. Santos didn't do chemotherapy before the neuroblastoma was removed."

Tony's lips pursed together in a thin line. "The growth was small. It was an optimal time to remove it. Dr. Santos consulted me and I felt it was a good time to do the surgical removal."

"I know that you're planning a stem cell transplant. What about a tandem SCT?"

"Is this why you were suggesting G-CSF injections?"

"It is. If she takes well to it, it might mean less chemo after the fact."

Tony frowned. "That would most definitely take a toll on Gracie. I don't think she can handle it."

"The tandem stem cell transplant is hard, but I think she can benefit from it. Once she's over the infection we could do the first transplant from the harvest Dr. Santos has done. I have no doubt that her bone marrow has been killed off, which is why she's in neutropenia."

"One stem cell transplant is hard enough, but a tandem? Why should she be put through that again?" Tony argued.

"Are you confident that you got all of the cancer?" Madison questioned as she got a little heated.

This was where the problem always lay when it came to them. Why did it have to be so black-and-white with him? Why couldn't he see that you didn't always have to cut out the cancer? Why couldn't he see other courses of treatment?

It was obvious that sometimes he did see them. She read the file and Dr. Santos's notes. But why, when it came to her, did he question it? Why couldn't he trust her? Even after all this time and her own reputation, why didn't he believe her?

Stem cell transplants, or SCTs, were common. And it wasn't even a huge risky she was taking. She'd successfully done SCTs on infants as young as Gracie before.

Surgery was great to get rid of cancers. But it didn't always solve the problem and took its own toll on patients.

Like her mom. The surgeon hadn't thought before they cut and it had been detrimental, pointless and just prolonged the agony.

"Why are you questioning my surgical abilities?" he asked.

"I could ask the same about you questioning my treatment. I'm not some greenhorn, Tony. We're not residents. We've both been battling this disease for ten years. We're both well established."

Tony took a deep breath. "You're right."

"I know." She smiled briefly. "I'm not going to do anything to Gracie until I have the CBC back and she's overcome this infection. SCT is hard on a child and I won't put any more strain on her than I have to."

Tony nodded slowly. "Very well."

"Good. Thank you." She leaned back in the chair. "I want our professional relationship to work."

"I do too. I don't want our past to muddy the waters."

"I agree with that." That was exactly what she wanted. She had always liked working with him. She'd missed collaborating with him. Not the arguments, but real work.

But seeing him and working with him was already stirring up so much emotion that she had long thought was buried and locked away tight. She just hadn't realized that one simple consult on a case would stir up all these memories and all these feelings.

She'd known this was going to be hard and she wasn't wrong.

"How about we get some dinner, a late dinner, since our drink was interrupted?" he asked.

Her heart skittered to a stop for a moment and she tried to control her surprise. Sure, colleagues had dinners together. But as much as Madison wanted to, she knew that she couldn't say yes to him.

Not if she wanted to keep this professional relationship as the status quo for her time here at GHH. She wanted to ask Tony if he thought that was wise, given their past, but she didn't because she didn't want to talk about their past failings.

It was over.

It was done with.

*Was it?*

"Thank you for the offer, but I think I'm going to stick around here and wait for the lab results.

Once I have all the information, I can formulate my plan of attack to help Gracie."

"Of…of course," Tony stammered.

What had he been thinking? First he invited her out for a drink and now he was asking her out to a late meal? What was wrong with him?

There was a part of him that was disappointed, but mostly he was relieved because he hadn't been thinking straight. She was so calm with Gracie's mother, so kind. He always did admire her bedside manner. She was gentle and such a lovely person.

Her consult with him was sound and he was mad at himself for letting his usual mistrust, the one that ran so deep toward anyone who was willing to jump headlong into the fray, creep in. He'd snapped. Especially after their talk about Gracie's treatment escalated and he got his hackles up. He didn't just think that cutting out the cancer would solve the problem. Why would she assume that?

When he was a resident, yes, he worshipped surgery a bit. He'd thought it was natural to cut out the problem, because he knew that medicine could take its toll. He was cockier when he was a student, but he learned—as that same surgical resident and then under the tutelage of Dr. Pammi and her team—that sometimes the best thing to do in cancer treatments was not to cut but rather to step away.

There were times he had to argue for this fact with his patients, who thought the solution was to have the surgery, but if the cancer spread, surgery would be pointless and harmful. And then there were times when the patients would ignore the advice...

"It won't work," Jordan insisted.

"It can," Tony said gently.

"I don't want chemo."

"Chemotherapy works. It will help and then when get you on the right medicines..."

Jordan grimaced. "I watched my own father go through that. It ate away at him."

"It won't be easy."

"I don't want that."

"Jordan..."

"No, Tony. There's this new treatment."

He balked. "New treatment?"

"It's more natural. It's a clinical trial..."

"And if I don't think it's in your best interest?"

Jordan sighed. "I'll go to someone who can get me in on it. Come on, Tony. You know all the risks, you know the odds. I trust you, but this is what I want. Please, get me in on this trial and support me."

"Tony?" Madison said, breaking through his thoughts.

He shook his head, dispelling the memories of Jordan. "Pardon?"

"Are you okay? You completely zoned out."

"Fine." Tony stood up. "It's been a long day."

"It has," she replied.

"You'll keep me posted about Gracie?"

She smiled sweetly. "Of course."

He nodded. "Thank you, Madison."

There was more he wanted to say to her. He wanted to apologize to her because he did want this working relationship to go smoothly. Only he couldn't get the words out.

He left the meeting room then to put some distance between him and Madison. He had to get control of all these emotions that were threatening to spill out of him. Baring too much could be a sign of weakness. His mother had been soft on his father like that, and his father totally took advantage of her. It was why he locked it all away, so no one could hurt him.

*Madison won't take advantage of me.*

But it was hard to rely on someone who never seemed to agree with him. Someone who had wounded him by ending things, someone who couldn't stand still and someone he continued to care for deeply.

Tony couldn't put his heart at risk again. He wouldn't let his guard down and be tormented over and over like his mother had done. His father was shiftless, never staying one place, and Madison couldn't seem to root herself anywhere.

He couldn't fall for her again. And he couldn't

let another slipup, like inviting her to dinner, happen again either.

They worked together.

Nothing more.

# CHAPTER FIVE

*A week later*

"TONY!"

Tony groaned inwardly as he heard Dr. Crespo call him from across the atrium. He knew exactly what Frank wanted, which was why he had been steering clear of him. He'd also been avoiding Madison, but that was for completely different reasons.

It had been a week since he'd let his own guard down and foolishly invited her out for dinner. Although he had been partly relieved she had turned him down, there was a part of him that was stung she didn't accept. Even after all this time, he still liked being around her.

He was falling into the trap again. It was hard when he kept reacting to her, thinking about her, like no time had passed at all.

On the plus side, she seemed to be keeping away from him too. Other than talking about patients and business, they didn't seek each other out. Which was good. It was easier to maintain professionality that way.

Dr. Crespo, on the other hand, was looking for someone to help with the annual summer fundraiser, which wasn't a surprise. He did it every year. It was for a good cause. There were several free clinics that the GHH supported, and this silent auction raised a lot of funds to help continue programs that provided first-rate cancer treatment to those who couldn't afford it. Tony tried to volunteer time at the clinics when he could, and he approved of the gala. He just didn't want any part of organizing or attending it. Socializing and making small talk with strangers was the worst thing in the world.

He also had a sneaking suspicion Dr. Crespo wanted him to donate something. A weekend at his home on Martha's Vineyard would be a perfect thing to auction off. He had no problem with it, but he hadn't spent a lot of time out there since he purchased his late grandparents' home. He wasn't sure that it could be cleaned up and ready in time.

"Frank," Tony acknowledged as he stopped and waited for Dr. Crespo to catch up to him.

"Just the man I wanted to see," Dr. Crespo said, out of breath.

"It's about my place and the silent auction, isn't it?" Tony asked, cutting to the chase.

Dr. Crespo's eyes widened. "You know?"

Tony snorted. "Frank, I know you've been thinking about it since I bought the place last fall."

Dr. Crespo grinned. "So? What do you think?"

"I haven't had much time to spend out there and get it presentable. I've been busy."

"Well, the auction is in two weeks. You have time."

*Dr. Crespo is too damn optimistic.*

Tony chuckled. "Do I?"

"Come on, Tony. You know it's for a good cause. You're always at the free clinics and you know the need is great."

Tony sighed. "You're right. I'll have it all set for a weekend at the end of the summer."

"Good. You can talk to Dr. Sullivan about it."

Tony's stomach knotted. "Why would I talk to Dr. Sullivan about this?"

"She's collecting the items for the silent auction and volunteered to be our auctioneer."

*Of course she did.*

Tony kept that sardonic thought to himself. Madison did like to throw herself in and help out. It was endearing, but when she moved on, it left a lot of people in the lurch. He was all too familiar with being let down. Not only by his father, but by Madison and by himself.

He'd left himself down by not fighting Jordan harder on taking the traditional route of treatment. He'd helped him get on that clinical trial, took a risk and lost his best friend.

"Okay," Tony agreed, because there wasn't much to say. Madison was in charge.

"Perfect! Thank you, Tony." Dr. Crespo continued on his way, most likely to track down other doctors about donations or spread the word about his place in Martha's Vineyard. Tony sighed because he didn't want to talk to Madison.

*It won't be that bad. Think of this as an extension of work.*

And that's what he had to keep telling himself. This was all business, he reminded himself as he made his way over to where she'd be. He knew that it wasn't her clinic day to see any new patients, so she'd be working on her research.

He actually hadn't been over to her lab yet. It was in a new part of the hospital and hers was the first one in that new wing. He grinned when he saw her name on the door and all her accreditation after it.

Dr. Madison Sullivan.

This was what she'd always wanted.

*"What are your goals when we're done?"* he asked, holding her in his arms and staring up at the ceiling of the on-call room.

*"Goals?"* she murmured.

*"What do you want to do? Where do you want to work?"*

*She propped herself up on an elbow, her eyes twinkling in the dark. "Cure cancer, of course."*

*He smiled. "I'm serious. I have surgery and..."*

*"I am serious. I'm going to research every avenue. I want my own lab one day. That's a big goal of mine."*

*They hadn't usually had in-depth conversations.*

*They'd never really known each other.*

*Not really.*

He knocked, peering in through the small window in the door. She looked up from where she was hunched over a computer and then waved him in.

"Hi," he said, suddenly awkward as he walked in the room.

"Hi back," she said pleasantly in that way that always invited people in. Her warmth had first attracted him, and even after all this time he was drawn to her, to her smile and the kindness in her eyes.

*Focus, Tony. For the love of God. Focus.*

"Sorry for interrupting you."

She stretched. "You're not. Just catching up on some reading. I swung by the pediatric unit and checked on Gracie, and her infection is almost cleared up. I was going to come and find you and talk to you about doing an extraction of her bone marrow. Maybe discuss SCT again."

"Right. Yes. We do have to talk about that."

"Isn't that why you're here?" she asked.

"No. I mean, yes." He ran his hand through his

hair, trying to get the words out. "I do want to talk about that, but I ran into Frank in the hall... Dr. Crespo."

Her eyes widened. "Oh. I see."

"You're in charge of the silent auction."

Madison crossed her arms. "I am. I don't know why I volunteered, but I thought it might be a good way to get to know people at GHH."

"You mean get to know the board of directors," he responded dryly.

She cocked an eyebrow. "What's with the tone?"

"I didn't have tone."

"You so did."

Tony let out huff. "I don't want to argue with you."

"I don't want to either, but you haven't told me yet why you're here."

*Because you won't let me talk!* He kept that frustration to himself.

"I'm offering up my place at Martha's Vineyard. For the silent auction. A weekend." Why couldn't he form a coherent sentence around her? What was going on with him? It was highly annoying.

Her eyes widened. "You have a place in Martha's Vineyard?"

"Yes. I mean... I haven't spent much time there since I bought it."

"Then why do you have it?"

Fair question.

He didn't want to talk about his grandparents now, because that would inevitably lead into his tumultuous childhood.

Those were secrets and hurts he kept to himself. He'd never shared it with her. It was all just work and sex a decade ago. Those damn walls he built for himself to keep everyone out.

"I do want to spend time there. Work takes all my time and I haven't been there since I bought it," he replied hesitantly. It was so hard to talk about, which was ridiculous.

Madison leaned back in her chair. "I don't know if I can include it in the auction."

"Why not?" he asked through clenched teeth.

There was a smile tweaking at the corner of her lips, a sparkle in those gorgeous gray eyes, and he realized she was teasing him.

"I'm kidding around, but I wouldn't mind getting some pictures. Do you think you can take me out there? I can snap some shots and see what you're offering."

*Say no. Say no.*

Only he couldn't because it made absolute sense.

"Sure."

*What're you doing?*

"Great." She beamed brightly, seemingly unbothered by them spending time alone together outside of work.

It was for the hospital. All for the hospital. So, it was like work. Right?

"Good." He just stood there, still kind of in shock over agreeing to take her to his place in light of the fact that he had been avoiding her all week. "Well, I'll send you a text about a good time when we can go out there and check the place out."

"I'm free this weekend," she offered. "How about Saturday?"

Tony couldn't think of a reason to say no. He was completely blanking. "Sure. I mean you didn't want to have dinner last week, but a day away to my place…"

"That was different. I was waiting on test results and this is for the silent auction. It's business."

She had another point. "Okay, we'll arrange something for this Saturday. Do you need to speak with me about anything else?"

Madison smiled kindly. "You came to talk to me. I didn't summon you."

He groaned. He was getting so flummoxed around her. What was it about her? "Right. Well, I'll talk to you later then."

"You know, there *is* something else I need to talk to you about. I was going to book a meeting, but since you're here…" Madison motioned for him to take a seat on the other side of the work top.

Although he wanted to leave and not put his foot in his mouth again, he couldn't. He was the department head. He pulled out a chair and sat down.

"What do you need to discuss?" he asked.

"I have a new patient. Pretty sure she's got ovarian cancer."

"Pretty sure?" he asked querulously.

"The scans at the free clinic point to a large mass on her ovary. It hasn't metastasized to any organs. She's young, a mother of two young children."

"So she needs surgery?"

"Yes, but there's a problem. She doesn't want surgery. She doesn't want to lose her only viable ovary. I've gone through a lot of the pros and cons with her and I said there is an option to do an egg retrieval, because she's not losing her womb. She just wants to do chemo. That's it. She thinks it'll shrink the tumor and chemo will work, but if she has the surgery to remove the ovary, then she might not need chemotherapy at all. The cancer could be taken care of with one procedure. It just seems like a no-brainer."

"It does."

"I'm hoping you can talk to her. She was reluctant, but she seemed open to having an appointment with us both."

Tony scrubbed a hand over his face. "Did she give any reasons why she didn't want surgery?"

"Other than her fertility, she's terrified of surgery. She's also the kind that does her own research."

Tony grumbled inwardly. Just like Jordan had done. That damn clinical trial and Jordan's refusal of chemo. Tony had taken a gamble and went against his better judgment—and reluctantly agreed. He'd stepped completely out of his comfort zone for his best friend, and Jordan had died. If Jordan had just gone with the tried and true methodchemotherapy and radiation——he might be here.

*No. He wouldn't. His cancer was too far gone. It wasn't my fault.*

"If she's willing to talk to the both of us, then I can give her some facts," Tony responded.

Madison nodded. "Good. If anyone can convince her, you can."

"I try," he said softly. He was good at talking to his patients and helping them make informed decisions about their treatment, except Jordan. It still stung. He stood up. "I better get back to what I was doing."

"Thanks for the silent auction donation and for agreeing to meet my patient."

Tony nodded. "Of course."

Madison turned back to her work and he slipped out of her lab. He had managed to avoid Madison for a week and so far they were cordial. Maybe working with her wouldn't be such a bad thing.

\* \* \*

Madison tried to put Tony out of her mind, but it was hard to do. She was slightly kicking herself for not going to have dinner with him, and she couldn't figure out why. She didn't want to strike up a relationship with him again, no matter how good the sex had been in the past.

Amazing sex was not something to build a relationship on. Which was too bad, because when Tony and her got together it was toe-curlingly good. That she did remember vividly. No one else had held a candle to the sheer electricity and the sparks between her and Tony. But marriage was based on trust and loyalty. Her parents had that and more. Still, it didn't mean anything in the end. Her mother died and her father was left alone and heartbroken.

It was vivid in her mind. As fresh as when it first happened. Her father's pain. It terrified her then. It still did.

There had been no time to grieve when you had to keep it all together for your remaining parent. If there had been a cure back then, her mother would be alive and her father wouldn't have shut the world out.

She wouldn't have been so alone.

Which was why she need to be focused on her work and on nothing else.

Things just had to be kept professional. She was doing so well, keeping to her lab in between her patients. Then she got it into her head to help Dr. Crespo out with the silent auction, not only because the free clinics were beneficial to her for finding people for medical trials, but also because she just wanted to give the chance to fight back to those who couldn't normally afford top-level treatment.

Her parents couldn't afford the best when her mother had been battling cancer. Part of her always wondered if her mom had had better care, would she still be here?

These clinics were good. She wanted to help others in financial situations similar to what she'd grown up in.

That's how she met this young mom. When she saw that mass, she knew it was a surgical case and she had to ask Tony to help convince the patient that it was the right thing to do.

Children needed their mom. Madison knew, because even at almost forty, she needed her mom too. It had been far too long since she had her. A lump formed in her throat and she wiped her eyes quickly before shutting her laptop.

Great. Now she was crying.

It was hard sometimes to do the work that she did, to face cancer and remember her mother, but she also wouldn't trade it for anything. It was what kept driving her, kept her working and focused.

"You okay?"

Madison looked up and saw Tony was back, standing in the door. He had changed into his street clothes and she looked around, realizing that he had left a while ago. She had been so stuck in her work the time had slipped by.

"Fine," she said, her voice wavering.

Tony slipped in the room and shut the door. "I don't think you are."

Madison brushed a tear from her face. "Just thinking about my mother."

And she couldn't remember if she ever talked to Tony about her. It was something she was so used to holding back. How could she grieve her mother in front of her father? She was so used to expressing her sadness alone.

Tony's expression softened. "Come on. We're going to get a bite to eat and I won't take no for an answer this time. There's a little café not far from here. We can walk through the Common. It's a gorgeous summer evening."

As much as she wanted to tell him no again, she couldn't because dinner sounded great and she didn't want to be alone right now.

*He's a friend.*

"Okay." She packed up her laptop and grabbed her purse.

Tony opened the door for her and closed it behind them. She locked it quickly and then his hand slipped into hers. It took her off guard, but she didn't pull away because she liked the way his fingers felt against hers.

It was comforting.

It had been a long time since she had that feeling of comfort. Even though they argued, there were so many times she was sure Tony was the one. Except, he obviously didn't think the same of her, which had broken her heart. It was hard to spend a life with someone who shut you out.

*You did the same too.*

It had been hard to let him go, but it was for the best.

*Was it?*

"Uh, Tony?" she said, softly.

Tony looked down and his eyes widened when he realized what he'd done. "Sorry."

She squeezed his hand and then released it. "It's okay. Old habits."

"Yes." His expression was soft and there was a sparkle in his eyes.

Just like old times.

They walked in silence out of the hospital, but she was missing the feeling of his hand in hers. Every moment she spent with Tony, the more she realized that this working with him wasn't going to be as straightforward as she originally thought.

As she'd said, old habits. They were easy to slip back into.

# CHAPTER SIX

THE LITTLE CAFÉ was just a short walk from the hospital through Boston Common. Tony was right; it was a beautiful summer night. It wasn't too hot and a warm breeze whispered through the trees. It was just the humidity that got to her. It was so different from California and her home state of Utah.

She had only ever passed through Boston via connecting flights, so she never got to spend much time here. It was nice just walking in silence with Tony so that she could take in all the sights. She was used to Tony's broody aloofness. He wasn't much of a conversationalist. He always seemed to keep things close to his chest.

He was definitely guarded and always had been. It just solidified the fact he didn't trust her with his emotions, his life. It cut to the quick. How could you have a life or a future with someone like that?

You couldn't.

She spent some lonely years, needing comfort

and someone to talk to as a young woman. She couldn't let herself fall for someone like Tony, someone like her dad. If she ever married, she wanted to share a life with her spouse, not have to guess how they felt or tiptoe around them.

There was a burst of laughter from children who were enjoying an old carousel in the Common. Its top was painted a bright blue with white stripes and it played boisterous organ grinder music. She grinned when she saw it and thought of the old merry-go-round that her mother would take her on, before she got sick.

Madison would climb on the tallest and pinkest horse she could find, her mother would stand behind her, holding her, and they would both scream and laugh. Especially when she threw her hands up in the air. She had this sudden urge to run over there and take a ride.

"Look at that," she gasped.

"What?"

Madison pointed. "The carousel."

"Do you want to take a spin?" Tony asked casually.

"Why would you think that?"

"Because you pointed it out and you can't take your eyes off of it." He smiled. "So, would you like to take a ride?"

It was out of the ordinary for Tony to offer something like this. Past Tony would've rolled his eyes.

She nodded. "I think I would."

"Let's go check it out."

The carousel was just finishing a ride and Madison bought two tickets. She turned and handed Tony one.

"What?" he asked, shocked, staring at the pass in her hand like she handed him a bucket of spiders or something.

"It's for you," she offered, pushing the ticket at him.

"I'm not getting on a carousel," he scoffed.

"You suggested we check it out."

"You seemed interested. Not me."

Madison cocked an eyebrow and then forced the ticket in his hand. "If I'm riding the carousel you are too."

Tony sighed. "Fine."

"You're dragging your feet. Come on, you old curmudgeon."

Tony rolled his eyes, but there was a hint of a smile on his face as they climbed onto the carousel. Madison worked her way around until she found a big white horse with a blue saddle. It wasn't pink, but it would do. She mounted it and Tony reluctantly climbed on the brown horse next to hers.

"This is ridiculous," he muttered. His grumpy expression made her laugh softly to herself.

"Have you never been on a carousel before?"

"When I was a kid."

"You're such a—"

"Don't say it!" he said quickly.

Madison laughed. "I wasn't going to say that, but I was going to say you're too uptight. You always have been. You have to live a little sometimes."

Tony pursed his lips, but didn't look convinced. He was gripping the pole, his knuckles white as the carousel's music amped up and it slowly began its rotation. The lively pipe organ music blared and the lights flashed as the horses went up and down and around.

Madison released her hold and raised her hands in the air to let out a whoop of glee. Tony couldn't help but smile at her then, relaxing slightly. There had been so many times when they were together when she would try to get him to do something fun, but he would always complain or refuse to participate at first.

Then, when he would break down and try something a little outside of his comfort zone, he would have a blast. Tony was always just so afraid of something new, something different, and she could never figure out why, because he never liked to talk about things or get too deep. Madison was different. She'd learned from an early age to rely on herself, but she also knew how to have a good time.

The spinning slowed and then the carousel

came to a stop. She let out a happy sigh, because it was exactly what she needed.

Tony clumsily slipped off the horse and cussed under his breath. She stifled a laugh.

"I'm too old to ride a merry-go-round," he mumbled.

"That's a shame." She slipped off the saddle, but her foot didn't hit the floor sure and she toppled forward out of her heels. Tony reached out and caught her, but her face smashed against his chest.

*Great. Just great.*

"Whoa," he said, gently righting her.

She stood barefoot pressed close against him. She forgot how much taller he was than her. His hands held her shoulders and she could drink in his scent of the clean musk he always wore. There were times she'd steal his scrub shirt and curl up with it in an on-call room, like a Tony-sized security blanket. Her heart was racing a mile a minute as she just stood there, being held by him, staring up at the man she had loved so much. A man she thought she had known back then, but didn't. Still, she'd fallen for him.

His eyes locked on to hers and her mouth went dry. Her body reacted, hoping for a kiss. It felt like time was standing still or it had no meaning, and all those years gone by seemed to mean nothing.

He reached out and gently touched her face, causing a ripple of goose bumps to break across her sensitized skin. Her heart was hammering and she closed her eyes, leaning in and melting for him as he captured her lips with the lightest kiss. Instinctively her arms wrapped around him, drawing him closer and not wanting to let go.

"You need to buy another ticket, lovebirds?" someone shouted.

Madison stepped away quickly. Embarrassed.

"We better get off," Tony said, taking a step back.

"Right," she mumbled. She bent down and grabbed her heels and dashed off the carousel onto the pavement. She made her way around to find a place where she could slip back on her shoes. She held on to a metal post for balance and to ground herself after that kiss.

What had she been thinking?

Her body was longing for more, remembering Tony and his touch well. It was like she was waking up out of a deep hibernation and her body was hungry for more.

"Let me help," Tony insisted. He took her shoes from her and got down on one knee, taking her foot in his strong hand as he slipped on her heels like she was a princess. A shiver of anticipation ran up her spine as she gripped the post tighter. The cold metal dug into her palm.

"Thanks," she muttered breathlessly.

"Well, what did I say about those ridiculous heels?" He got up.

Madison rolled her eyes. "You're impossible."

He smirked. "So you've said. Shall we grab that bite now?"

"Please."

A perfectly romantic moment, or what she thought was a romantic moment, was ruined by Tony's pragmatism. That was another reason why they weren't together. They were too opposite in so many ways, but then again they were the same in others. It was obvious they weren't going to talk about it.

Maybe that was for the best. Just ignore it and sweep it under the rug.

*Sure. When has that ever worked?*

They crossed the Common and headed out on Beacon Street.

"It's not far," Tony commented, breaking the silence.

"I'm not complaining. I told you, I can run a marathon in these heels," she teased, then spotted the bar made famous by *Cheers*. "Oh, hey, look! It's the place where everybody knows your name!"

Tony gave her a serious side-eye. "You would sing that, wouldn't you?"

"I don't understand why you wouldn't. It's catchy."

Tony sighed. "You're always the life of the party."

"And you're like a grandpa, but that's kind of

insulting to grandpas who aren't so set in their ways."

Tony chuckled to himself. "Not much has changed in a decade, has it?"

"Not really."

They stopped in front a small Italian café and Tony held open the door for her. It was a charming place tucked away past the corner of Brimmer and Beacon. Madison loved all the redbrick and the colonial vibe in this part of Boston.

Tony quickly spoke with the maître d' and they were shown to a private corner booth in the back. They both slid in and she accidentally bumped her hip against him when they met in the middle. Her pulse began to race at being close to him again.

"Sorry." She scooted over, trying to give him some space.

The maître d' left them a couple of menus before disappearing back to the front.

"This is…cozy," Madison remarked, hoping Tony didn't sense the trepidation in her voice. She couldn't seem so nervous. It was just dinner out with a colleague.

*Yeah, one I've seen naked and I just kissed him.*

She shook that thought away and tried to concentrate on the menu in front of her, but all the words suddenly just looked like gobbledygook because all she could think about was how close she was to him, how he was affecting her again after all this time.

*Holy mackerel. It's just dinner.*

"I like this place," Tony said, offhandedly. "Good caprese salad."

"Maybe that's what I'll have."

"The chicken parm is excellent too."

Madison shut the menu. "You grew up in Boston, if I remember correctly. Since you know this place, you order for me."

Tony cocked an eyebrow. "You're letting me have control? You never trusted my menu suggestions in the past."

"I am now." She set the menu down. "We're friends, I hope, and I have to be able to depend on my friend."

She was trying to show him that she trusted him and that maybe, just maybe he could finally learn to do the same for her.

"Okay," he agreed.

"Okay we're friends or okay on dinner?"

"Both," he stated. "You're right. We have a past, we're colleagues and I think there's a mutual respect. I would like us to be friends."

"Good."

Tony didn't exactly say that he had confidence in her, but being friends was a start. The waiter returned and Tony ordered some wine to accompany their meal of caprese salad and chicken parmesan. It was a lot of cheese for one meal, but she didn't often indulge in Italian.

"I'm sorry about the kiss," Tony finally said. "I forgot myself."

"It's okay," she replied. She was trying to be nonchalant about it, to casually brush it off, and failing miserably.

"No. It's not. I shouldn't have done that."

"And I should've stopped you." Only she didn't want to stop it when he pulled her into his arms.

It was just like it was the first time all over again. And that's the way it always had been. She couldn't fall into that trap.

*Unless he's changed...*

Though she doubted it.

"I'm sorry I kissed you," he repeated. "I don't know what came over me."

"We both got carried away. It won't happen again." If she said it out loud it meant it was true. In theory.

"You're right. Let's talk about something else."

"Sure. What do you want to talk about?" she asked.

At this point she was willing to talk about anything but them and the feelings he was stirring up in her.

"What brings you to GHH?" he asked.

"Is this that conversation about how long I'm planning on staying?" she asked.

He cocked his head to one side. "In a way."

"I see," she replied stiffly.

"All we ever talked about during our time together was my goal of being a surgeon and your dream of research and finding a cure."

"Is that so bad?" she asked.

"No," he said. "I mean, it does explain all your hopping around from one clinical trial to another."

Madison frowned. "We're not going to bring that up again, are we?"

"No, but I'd like to know your goals. Friend to friend."

Madison sighed. "I need to have more published. My end goal, besides the cure…is I want to work with Dr. Mathieu LeBret at his research hospital in France."

She couldn't believe she was sharing that out loud with someone. She didn't have time for many friends and she didn't like people knowing too much about her aspirations. Her field was a competitive one.

"Wow. Dr. LeBret is a Nobel laureate. Those are lofty goals."

"And what about you?" she asked, hoping he'd open up and share something with her.

Tony shrugged. "I achieved what I wanted. I'm a surgeon, head of oncology. It's safe."

"Safe?" she asked, querulously.

He nodded. "Secure."

"Security is important."

"It's the most important," he replied fiercely.

Madison understood that, but she made her own sense of security in the world. She had to.

"What was the draw with the carousel?" Tony asked, changing the subject.

"My mother, actually." She smiled, softly twirling her finger around the stem of the wineglass. "She used to take me on carousel rides when I was young. I've been thinking about her a lot today, and just seeing that carousel in the park made me think of her."

"Your mother died of cancer, didn't she?" Tony asked.

She nodded. "When I was fourteen."

"What made you think of her today?" he asked softly.

Madison sighed. "That patient of mine. She just reminded me of her. Only, my mother didn't have the best team of doctors because we couldn't afford it."

"I'm sorry," he said, quietly. "It's one of the reasons why I really do support our hospital and the work in the free clinics. I try to donate as much of my time there as I possibly can between work and Miguel."

"Miguel? Who is Miguel?"

First the kiss and now talking about their goals and dreams. At least he had confirmation that GHH wasn't a permanent stop for her.

Whereas it was for him.

Then she opened up about her mother and it just slipped out about Miguel. Tony didn't want to bring up his godson, because he didn't want to have to talk about Jordan or his death. Madison had met Jordan when he'd visited Tony out on the West Coast. Everyone who met Jordan liked him, and in a lot of ways Madison was very free spirited like Jordan. What they both saw in Tony was still a bit of a mystery. Still, they all had a blast those couple of days that Jordan visited.

When Tony returned to Boston without Madison, Jordan lamented to Tony that he had let go of a good one. It was a point of contention between him and his best friend, because Tony regretted the end of their relationship.

Now he was annoyed that he let it slip about Miguel. Now he'd have to talk about Jordan. And it was hard to talk about it all.

As he looked into her eyes, he knew he had to tell her.

*I might as well rip the bandage off.*

"Miguel is my godson. Jordan's son," he stated, hoping his voice didn't break with all the emotion swirling around inside of him.

Her eyes lit up. "Oh! I forgot about Jordan and that he lived out here. We should arrange a dinner—"

"Jordan passed away five years ago from cancer." Just getting the words out was difficult. It was hard to even process it at all, and he was still angry that he took the risk and approved Jordan to take that experimental treatment. He went against the tried and true. He should've fought harder to get Jordan to see his side. That was the reason he was always so cautious now. So skeptical.

"Tony, I'm so sorry." Madison reached across the table and slipped her hand into his. Her hand was so smooth and delicate. He'd always liked holding it. It was why he'd grabbed it earlier out of habit. She squeezed his fingers and he held on tight. He'd forgotten how small her hand was in his.

He didn't want to let go or break the connection.

In fact, there was a part of him that wanted to continue holding on to her for as long as he could, even though he knew he shouldn't.

*Treading a dangerous path.*

Feelings like these, this sentimentality and recalling her and their time together, had made him kiss her. And that had been a complete mistake.

Why was it so easy to forget the walls he planned to put up to keep her out when he was with her?

*Because I loved her.*

It had broken him so much when she ended it. Even though it was perfectly clear they were ill suited to each other. He had what he wanted in life and she had no plans to stay in Boston permanently. Her time here at GHH was limited.

"Caprese salads," the waiter announced, returning to the table.

Madison snatched her hand away and folded both hands neatly on the table in front of her.

"Thank you," Tony said quickly to the waiter, trying to regain composure.

"Well," Madison said, brightly. "This looks great."

"It is. Believe me."

Her eyes narrowed as he said that and she grinned, but it wasn't a warm smile. It was almost forced.

"I do have faith in you, Tony."

A little pang of guilt ate away at him. How could she trust him so easily? He had such a hard time with that, yet she gave it so freely. But it was hard to put that faith in people who constantly disappointed you.

His father, who could never be relied on, had squandered his mother's money and broken her heart and his time and time again. There were so many times he helped his mother out financially, only for her to turn around and send it to his father.

And then there was Madison, who couldn't stay still, who took so many risks that he was too scared to pursue her, to believe that she wouldn't just hurt him again. That she wouldn't leave for something better, just like his father always did. It was clear to him all those years ago that she had the same kind of wandering soul. She was always looking for a new opportunity, whereas he stayed rooted in Boston. He made his own connections and chances without taking a risk.

*Maybe I've grown stagnant here too...*

Tony shook that ridiculous thought away.

There was just no way that he could ever put his heart on the line for her again, especially with an end in sight. It was only a matter of time before Dr. LeBret saw her talent and snatched her up. And he couldn't blame him, because sitting with her now, all of that worry melted away and he couldn't help but wonder why he was so adamant about locking her out of his life for good.

# CHAPTER SEVEN

*DAMN. HE'S NOT WRONG.*

That was Madison's first thought as she took a bite into the dinner that she'd let Tony order for them. She wasn't too keen on letting other people do that. Actually, she didn't know what possessed her in that moment to allow him, but she was glad that she had because it was the most delicious caprese salad and chicken parmesan that she'd ever had.

Maybe that was because she spent so much time doing research that her dinners usually consisted of a cup of instant ramen noodles or a sandwich. She was all about convenience and a lot of times she forgot to eat. This dinner was like her taste buds waking up after a really long nap and saying, *Yes! Now, this is what we're talking about!*

Tony had a half smile dancing on his lips as he watched her. "You look like you've never had Italian before."

"Not this level of Italian."

Tony chuckled. "You can't exist on sandwiches forever."

"You know me so well," she teased. Except he didn't.

"Not so well. I didn't know you could run a marathon in heels," he joked. "Especially, when you can't even dismount from a wooden horse without falling over."

Madison rolled her eyes. "You really don't like these shoes, do you?"

"I never said that," he replied. "Just if you're going to come to Martha's Vineyard this weekend to check out my beach house, then you'll want to wear sneakers or sandals. It's a bit of a walk."

"How long of a drive is it?" she asked. "If I have to rent a car…"

"You're not renting a car. I'll drive us."

A shiver of anticipation ran down her spine. She was kind of hoping that he would offer to take her there, but she didn't want to assume anything. She was so used to handling things on her own because she couldn't rely on anyone to do it for her. She took care of herself and a lot of the time if she wanted something done it was up to her. It was nice Tony was offering to drive. It would also mean spending more time with him outside of work. They'd agreed not to let the kiss happen again, but when she was around him, she forgot herself.

"You don't have to."

"It's fine. Friends, remember?"

She nodded. "Right. Friends."

They could do this. They had to work together and they couldn't let any pent-up attraction from the past come between them. Even if she secretly wouldn't mind that.

"And to answer your other question, it's a three-hour drive."

"Three hours?" she asked, stunned.

"It's a weekend escape."

"It'll be a long day," she lamented.

"You trying to get away from me?" he teased. There was a sparkle in his eyes again. He was relaxing and the tension she had been holding in dissolved. This was the Tony she fell for, but it was also the Tony he rarely let out.

She rolled her eyes and chuckled. "No. I just have work."

"We all do."

"Fine."

He nodded. "I'll be picking you up on Saturday early. Like six."

Madison groaned. "So much for sleeping in."

"You'll have to tell me where you're staying. I don't even know where you're living."

"I'm in a condo building, right across from the hospital."

Tony's eyes widened. "The Commonview?"

A knot formed in the pit of her stomach. "Yes. Why?"

"I live in the Commonview."

Of course he did.

Madison was subletting a place from another physician she was an acquaintance with who was working abroad for the next couple of years. Her lease was for a year and it was a perfect situation because the condo was furnished. Since she never settled in a place for long, she really didn't have that many items. She was minimalistic and liked to travel light.

"Do you?" she asked, choking back a piece of chicken.

"Are you subletting? It's a private condo building."

"I am. Do you know Dr. Ackerman? She's currently in Germany for the next two years. She heard I was coming to GHH and we worked out an agreement."

"I do know Sophie Ackerman. She's a brilliant cardiothoracic surgeon."

Madison nodded. "I worked with her a few years ago when I was in Minnesota."

"We're neighbors. Legitimately, because I live down the hall from her."

Of course he did.

She hadn't seen him in the halls, but then again she rarely went back to the rental. If she did, it was always odd hours, which would explain why she probably hadn't run into Tony.

Yet.

This was just getting weirder and weirder. What was fate trying to pull? Maybe it wasn't fate; maybe it was karma?

"Well then, that should make it easy on Saturday to leave at the ungodly hour in the morning."

"You wanted pictures." He grinne, deviously and winked. "This is what you get for agreeing to help out Frank for the silent auction."

"It's for a good cause," she stated. "Free clinics are vital."

"I don't disagree."

"I've already had some people sign up for my clinical trials."

Tony's expression changed, his back straightened and his eyes narrowed. "Clinical trials. Right."

"Yes?" she asked cautiously. "What do you have against clinical trials? A lot of our advancements in modern medicine are because of clinical trials and testing."

"We also don't want to play with people's lives," he said carefully without looking at her.

"Is this about all the clinical trials I joined as a researcher in our resident days? I seem to recall you had issues with it back then."

He softened. "No, it's not that."

"Okay then, what is it? I'm not playing Dr. Frankenstein here, Tony. I'm not trying to create life out of cadavers and electricity. I'm talking about an advancement in cancer research so that we can find a cure. I'm trying to put myself out of a job."

Tony sighed. "I get that. I'm just more careful."

*That's an understatement.*

She kept that snarky comment to herself.

"I know. You always have been."

"What's that supposed to mean?"

"Nothing," she said quickly. "I don't want to have this fight with you again. The same fight that we had when we were residents. I'm not going to put people's lives in jeopardy. I pride myself on my research, and these people are taking a chance on something when they don't have much to look forward to. When their options are limited."

"I understand that, but sometimes the tried-and-true methods are what works, not newfangled naturopathic things."

She was confused. "When did I mention naturopathic?"

"You didn't. It just reminded me of a patient. Sorry."

"You had a patient who joined a naturopathic clinical trial?" she questioned.

"Yes," he responded tightly. "I signed him up for it. It looked good on the surface, so I took a chance because my patient wanted it."

Since when did Tony let a patient sway him? And then it hit her who the patient was.

She cocked her head to the side. "What happened with Jordan?"

\* \* \*

Tony knew that the conversation would loop back to Jordan, but he didn't want to discuss it. He didn't want to talk about it over and over again. Not that he ever really talked about it to anyone. He'd failed his best friend by not being able to convince him that the clinical trial was too big of a risk. He had his reservations about clinical trials in general, but Madison knew what she was doing. She may not stay settled in one place, but her research was solid. He'd read her papers and she was right; *some* trials gave patients who couldn't always afford health care a fighting chance. But he'd leave that to her, and stick with what he knew and what worked.

After all was said and done, though, he wasn't exactly sure that his preferred method would have worked, that the cancer would've been eradicated. That was one of the problems with being surgeon in oncology: cancer didn't deal in certainties.

"He died of cancer," he answered.

"I'm sorry to hear that," she said gently. "And he was the patient who convinced you to try the naturopathic path?"

Tony took a deep breath. "Yes."

"Not all clinical trials are risky."

"I know," Tony responded. "Look, I don't want to argue. I hate that we are. I promised that I wouldn't step on your toes here and I won't."

He was evading the question so he wouldn't have to talk about it.

Madison didn't look convinced as she poked at the rest of her chicken. "Okay."

"We can focus on Saturday and the trip to Martha's Vineyard. For what it's worth, I'm looking forward to it."

She smiled wanly. "Me too. I haven't spent much time on the East Coast. This will all be a first."

"You'll love it. You loved the beach in San Diego. You'll love the beaches on the East Coast too."

"I'm sure. Tell me one thing I have to do, apart from taking pictures of your place, one thing to try or see when we're there."

"Well, besides the ferry ride, I know a little place that has the best clam chowder."

Madison blinked. "Ferry ride?"

"It's on an island," he remarked. "Didn't you study geography in school?"

He was teasing and trying to relieve the tension. He knew he gave her grief about every clinical trial she'd leaped into in the past, but that was over. He wanted to trust her. He wanted to be friends for however long she planned to stay.

She rolled her eyes at his good-humored jab. "Yes. Do you really think this is a day trip?"

"Sure," he answered with confidence. "We'll probably get home late."

"That's fine. I'm not going to lie—I'm kind of excited about the prospect of clam chowder!"

He chuckled. "I know we had some good clam chowder in San Francisco that one time."

Madison cocked her head to the side and then grinned. "Right! I remember that now. In the sourdough."

"It won't be served in sourdough this weekend."

"Why were we in San Francisco again?" she asked.

"Dr. Pammi chose a couple of us to go to that medical conference where she was speaking."

"Right! Then we spent our free time down at the pier. Remember the chocolate? Heaven." She took a sip of chianti and Tony couldn't help but smile at her. There were so many good times they shared, in between the fighting.

It ached when it was over, but it had been for the best. He understood that now. He couldn't see it back then, but their dreams and goals were so different, which was something else they never really talked about. How could it have been love back then when they really didn't know each other?

Yet when he looked at her, his heart was lost.


They finished their meal and then split the bill. It was dark out, but the Common was lit up with those old-time streetlamps. You could hear the music and see the lights of the carousel, which was running. As they passed it he thought of her in his arms. She was so close. He had loved holding her in that moment. He could still taste her kiss on his lips.

He glanced down at her and caught her gaze. Her lips parted and there was a brief flush of pink in her cheeks. How did he put his heart in her hands, a woman he barely knew? It had been a risk for him, but he did remember how he loved being around her.

He'd had fun with her, however fleeting.

As they walked back to their shared building, there wasn't much to say. He was just enjoying himself spending time with her. It was just as magical as he remembered and he didn't want it to end. It felt like home, in a way.

He hadn't realized how lonely his life had become recently. There had been other women in his life, but it was so fleeting and scattered. Nothing had felt the same as this had. He fought the urge to reach down and take her hand in his again, but jammed them in his coat pockets so he wouldn't be tempted. They were all feelings of nostalgia she was stirring up in him.

There was a time limit to her life in Boston. This wasn't her endgame, but it was his.

They walked into the building together and rode the elevator up, both getting off at the same floor.

Madison lingered in the hall. "Thanks for taking me out to dinner tonight. I wasn't sure that it was a smart decision, but I'm glad that I went and that you extended the invite."

"I'm happy you agreed. Friends, remember?"

She nodded and tucked back a strand of her blond hair. "Right. Friends."

"So I'll see you tomorrow? We have that appointment with your patient, right?"

"Yes. She's coming at ten. I sent you the file."

"I got it. I looked it over and I'll look it over again tomorrow."

"Thank you." There was another pink flush in her cheeks and she was standing so close to him. All he wanted to do was reach out and stroke her cheek. He wanted to pull her in his arms and kiss her. Drown himself in her sweet lips.

*Don't do it.*

Friends didn't kiss and that's all she could be—a friend.

Tony took a step back. "Good night, Madison."

She grinned sweetly. "Good night, Tony."

He watched as she walked down the hall to her apartment and waited until she unlocked her door and was inside.

It was one thing keeping his distance from her in the hospital, but it was another when she was right down the hall. So close, yet still so far away.

Tony had a hard time falling asleep that night, especially knowing that Madison was so close to him. He kept thinking about her sleeping in her bed. There had been so many nights that he would spend watching her sleep. She always had this thing about curling up on her side, with her hands tucked under her head. If he remembered correctly, she also had a penchant for kicking him if he spooned her too close. There were several times she got in a good blow to his groin. The simple solution was not to pull her close when she was in a REM cycle, but he couldn't help himself.

The chance of pain was worth it for him, because he loved holding her close. So many things in his life were taken from him that pulling her tight made him feel like he could hold on to her.

Except, it hadn't worked.

*Sure. I take chances on ball-kicks, but not anything else.*

Tony gave up tossing and turning. He got up and went over the patient's records that Madison had sent him.

By the time he got to GHH in the morning he was exhausted, but coffee was certainly helping him function.

Thankfully, it was a clinic day for him and he didn't have any surgeries on the docket. All he had to do was see Madison's stubborn ovarian cancer patient, a few of his own patients, then do a round of post-op checkups. Tomorrow would involve some procedures. Then the day after that he and Madison would head down to Martha's

Vineyard so she could get the photographs for the auction. He didn't have to complicate this. It was simple.

Nothing had to happen.

*I'm way too optimistic about this.*

He laughed to himself softly and downed the rest of his coffee before collecting the files he needed and headed to the small conference room where they would be meeting this patient from the free clinic.

When he walked into the room, Madison was standing with her back to him, in those high heels that showed off the shape of her calves. His gaze lingered and then slowly traveled up her body. He vividly recalled how she looked, and he remembered how soft she was, how she responded when he touched her.

His blood heated.

She was wearing a tight pencil skirt again that left little to the imagination. Her white lab coat was off and her silk turquoise shirt was sleeveless and he admired her toned arms. Her blond hair was pinned up and he recalled keenly how he used to kiss her long neck.

*Focus.*

Tony cleared his throat and she spun around.

"You look like hell," she remarked.

He frowned. "Thanks for the compliment."

"Did you sleep last night?" She picked up her lab coat and slipped it on.

"Not well."

"It shows. Do you think you'll be okay for this meeting?"

"I'll be fine." He tore his gaze away and grabbed a seat, setting down his files. "You're in a very critical mood this morning."

"Well, I'm worried about this patient," she replied quickly. "Sorry for being so condemning of the dark rings under your eyes."

Tony stifled a yawn. "I'll be fine."

"Have another coffee," she teased.

Tony rolled his eyes and the phone in the meeting room buzzed. Madison answered it and he heard her tell someone to send her patient in before hanging up. She went to the door and opened it as a very young woman shook her hand. Behind her was a young man that Tony could only presume was the patient's husband.

He could see the worry etched on the man's face.

"Jessica and Mark, this is my colleague and the head of oncology, Dr. Antonio Rodriguez."

"You can call me Tony." Tony stood up and came over to greet them with a quick handshake. "Pleasure."

"Why don't you have a seat?" Madison offered.

"Okay," Jessica responded quietly.

Tony pulled out the chair for her and the woman smiled up at him and perched on the edge. He got the sense the patient was on the verge of running and he wasn't a stranger to that. Cancer was a very scary thing—he understood that all too well.

*"I'm scared,"* Jordan uttered. *"You have to look out for Miguel. Promise me."*

Tony sat down next to his bedside. *"I promise."*

Jordan looked up at him weakly. *"You're mad because I didn't listen to you."*

*"I'm not mad."* Although Tony was, a little, at that moment. He was watching his friend, lying in a palliative care bed, wasting away. *"It was your choice. I just... I tried to advocate for you the best I could."*

*"Yes. You are mad. But Tony, nothing would've changed in the end. You know it. It gave me a small percentage. Just like this treatment."*

*"This treatment you took is too new. Chemo is..."*

Jordan held up his hand. *"I would've wasted away with that too. Don't be mad at me, Tony."*

*"I'm not mad."*

*"Just look out for Miguel. Please."*

Tony nodded, fighting back the tears. *"I promise."*

Jordan closed his eyes and then slowly opened them again. *"If you ever get a second chance at something...take it."*

The words hit today as he glanced over at Madison, who was pulling out scans and talking to Jessica and her husband. Tony shook away the memories and tried to focus on the meeting, because he was here to convince Jessica to get the surgery.

"What stage am I?" Jessica asked. "I've been thinking a lot about this…"

"We've been talking and maybe the naturopathic method won't work," Mark piped up.

Tony's gut clenched as he heard them talk about considering alternative medicines. He tried not to react as he leaned forward to talk to them.

"To properly stage your cancer we would have to remove your ovary. It doesn't appear to have spread from your last scan, which is good. However, I can't give you a stage until we can do a biopsy." Tony didn't want to be harsh, but it was the truth. Scans only showed so much.

"An invasive surgery just for a biopsy?" Jessica's voice shook as she said it.

"Well, if we find cancer, we remove it then and there, and I can examine and see if it's spread anywhere else."

Jessica's eyes filled with tears. "We want to have more kids. Only one of my ovaries works and that's the one with the mass."

"Which is why I'm recommending an egg retrieval," Madison said gently.

Tony nodded. "It's a good option."

Mark looked worried. "I don't know if my HMO will cover that."

"I will make sure that it is covered," Tony stated.

"I've already talked to our fertility team here at GHH and they're willing to help out. There are clinical trials of different fertility drugs they could put you on. It will offset the cost," Madison interjected.

Jessica brightened up. "If I don't get the surgery...?"

"The cancer will spread and it will kill you." Tony was blunt, but he wanted to get the point across. He glanced over at Madison, who was frowning at him.

"What will happen?" Mark asked. "If the biopsy shows cancer?"

"We'll do a surgery and remove the ovary that has appeared on the CT scan. I will see if it has spread and then you'll have to go through chemotherapy. I may have to remove your other ovary, which is why we're suggesting egg retrieval, but there is a likelihood that I will have to remove your uterus."

Madison sat up straighter. "We can also do a round of hyperthermic intraperitoneal chemotherapy if it hasn't spread. It's a longer surgery, but delivering warmed-up chemotherapy straight into your abdomen will help."

This time Tony shot her an inscrutable look. He hadn't done many HIPEC surgeries before. Dr. Santos never mentioned it and he knew that it was a fairly new but innovative treatment that was done for abdominal cancers.

It was also expensive.

He wasn't too sure how the board of directors would feel about a HIPEC pro bono surgery. He was annoyed Madison had suggested it without consulting with him about what they could offer this couple, but on the flip side he had no problems with offering this to them if it was approved. He just didn't want to get their hopes up without cause.

"I would like to preserve what I can. If I don't have my uterus, then my egg retrieval will be useless," Jessica said. "I would like to hear more about HIPEC."

"It's a longer surgery. Bigger incision," Tony stated.

"I've worked with surgeons and done HIPEC on some of my tougher cancer patients. It can be expensive, yes, but there is a new dosage of chemotherapy we can try. I can get you on a clinical trial for that," Madison offered.

Tony was fuming inside. A new drug? Without board approval? Madison was just her same old rebellious self, jumping in without looking at all the facts. It was risky. All he could think about in that moment was how his father always leaped before he looked.

It always cost them.

Always.

"We have a lot to discuss, but I would like to do the egg retrieval as soon as possible so that we can get the surgery scheduled," Jessica stated. "I do want to fight this."

Madison beamed. "I'm so glad. I'll get you an appointment this week to see our fertility doctors, and if you're interested in HIPEC I'll get you on my clinical trial."

They all stood then as Madison shook Jessica's and Mark's hands. Tony did too, but didn't say anything else as Madison escorted them from the meeting room. He just waited until she came back in. She was all smiles, but Tony didn't feel like smiling.

Sure, he was glad that the patient was seeing sense about their surgery, but Madison had spoken out of turn. First the HIPEC, and now this new chemotherapy medicine she was researching? Was she going to get the patient to agree to egg donation so she could edit out the cancer gene through the use of CRISPR? It was all too much, too risky for his liking.

What if they couldn't even get approved for of this? They could've just given a patient false hope. He keenly remembered having hope like that dashed away by broken promises.

Madison spun around, arms crossed.

"What?" she asked, obviously sensing his mood.

"HIPEC?"

She cocked an eyebrow. "Haven't you done HIPEC before?"

"Actually, no. Dr. Santos would've had to be the one that worked in tandem with me and he never mentioned it."

"I've done it," she said.

"It's risky."

"It has great outcomes."

He frowned. "A new chemo drug?"

"Yes," she said, firmly. "Not *new* new. Not to me. I know my job."

"I didn't say you didn't."

Her eyes narrowed. "And this is where we butt heads. All the time."

"I'm very well aware."

Madison sighed. "If you don't want to do the HIPEC surgery, I will ask another surgeon. That's if she agrees to it."

"I'm the one donating my time to help minimize costs." He ran a hand through his hair. "I'm sorry."

Her mouth dropped open and then she took a deep breath. "I am too. I should've consulted you about the HIPEC. I guess I'm on edge because…"

"I questioned you and I had no right to do it."

She nodded. "I want you to be the surgeon on this, but we need to trust each other and work together." She had a point, but it was hard for him to trust her. He had to put it behind him. It would be unprofessional to do any less.

"Agreed. It won't happen again," he replied tightly.

"Thank you and I will consult you beforehand. I'm glad I can count on you."

He swallowed a lump in his throat. At least he was the reliable one, always there to pick up the pieces. "You can. I'll be the one doing the first step of the surgery. I'll be there with you."

"Good. I will take care of the medicinal part, because that's what I specialize in."

In that she wasn't wrong, but a part of him was struggling on how he could trust her judgment. What if she was rushing things again?

*You're the surgeon. This is her patient.*

And he had to keep that thought at the forefront of his mind while working with her.

He nodded. "At least she's open to surgery."

Madison's face relaxed and she smiled again. "Exactly. Her scans show that we probably caught it early. She can go through a fertility cycle—it'll take about a month—and then as soon as retrieval is done we can wheel her into surgery. It's going to take that long anyway to get her on the clinical trial and all the necessary financial approvals."

Tony nodded, resigned. He said he was going to trust Madison with this and he was. He was going to support her like a good head of oncology would. "Hopefully, it hasn't spread to her uterus."

"I hope not, but I try to look at the positive. It's all a risk."

The moment she said that, his spine straightened. How could she be so nonchalant about a risk? He just didn't understand that. The one time he gave in to the possibility of risk, Jordan had died. It wasn't his fault, but he was still blaming himself because he could've pushed him harder.

He could've made Jordan see that chemo might've given him a chance. He didn't listen to his own instincts and gambled on something he shouldn't have.

He had to remind himself that this was different. At least Jessica was open to surgery. There was nothing at risk here but the outcome for the patient. Not Tony's reputation or his heart. And they both would make sure Jessica understood what the surgery was about so she could make an informed decision. He just hoped this whole thing worked out.

"Well," he said, quickly. "I've got other patients to see. Keep me posted."

Madison nodded. "I will. And Tony, thanks."

He didn't respond. He just left the meeting room, trying to put some distance between her, his feelings and all the memories of Jordan and his father that were bombarding him today, because it was still hard to let go of the fear.

It was hard to put his faith in something that he didn't understand. Something unpredictable. Something that might cause pain. He'd had enough of that in his life. He didn't need any more.

It was hard to put his faith in Madison. But he

was going to try. He could do this for her. She might only be here for a short time, but he wanted to make this professional relationship work. He wanted her as a friend.

Truth be told, there was a part of him that also wanted her to stay, but he knew that wouldn't happen, so he kept that to himself.

# CHAPTER EIGHT

SOMETHING WEIRD HAD happened after she and Tony met with Jessica and Mark. Madison had pretty much figured it had to do with the fact she was signing Jessica up for clinical trials, but when she talked about the HIPEC procedure and the new chemotherapy, Tony had just become different. A wall went up and she had an inkling, once again, he didn't trust her.

That's when her guard went back up too, because she was falling into the same pattern they had followed time and time again. It had led them both down a path of heartache, and lots of arguing. She wasn't going to feel that pain again.

It took her a long time to get over Tony. It was hard for her to open her heart to anyone else.

*Maybe because I didn't want to.*

Madison had tossed and turned all that night. Sure, Tony had ruined her for a lot of other relationships. That was the easy explanation for why she wasn't married or had a family—and for why her work came first.

That focus on work was something she and Tony had in common, but at least he had some friends and family here in Boston. Madison's dad lived in Salt Lake and she tried to fly out Salt Lake to see him from time to time, but it was hard. She didn't fully forgive him for shutting her out for so many years after her mom died. Their relationship had never really recovered.

At least he wasn't alone. He'd found someone else when she moved away to college. He'd tried to reconnect, but she was always too busy with school and work. Madison had spent the last ten years moving around, getting closer to her goal in her cancer research and her dream of working with Dr. LeBret.

It was hard to make connection, friends, or even date when you were constantly on the move.

*Yeah. That's the reason.*

She had been so pleasantly surprised that what would've been a blowout argument in the past didn't turn out that way. They'd talked, apologized and agreed to move forward as professionals.

It thrilled her to see this change. This is what she was hoping for when she came to GHH, but there was a part of her that continued to be skeptical.

She had no time to dwell. Today was the day she was going to be in the pediatric procedure room while they extracted a sample of Gracie's bone marrow to determine if the neutropenia had killed off her marrow. If so, then they would have to do a bone marrow transplant.

Hopefully, Tony would agree with her that Gracie was a candidate for the tandem stem cell transplant, because Madison had seen this a few times in her various jobs as an oncologist and she was confident that it would work here too.

At least Tony hadn't been totally against that.

*He's not against the HIPEC or the new chemo either.*

It was nice to be able to collaborate with Tony, to have him trust her.

Madison took another deep calming breath as she pulled on her mask and headed into the procedure room. Tony was there already and Gracie was sedated and prepped. He looked over as she came in.

"We're just about to get started, Dr. Sullivan," he said over his shoulder.

"Great. Dr. Santos did a stem cell extraction before her neuroblastoma surgery. Have you given any more thought to the tandem?"

"I have," Tony said. "I think it's a good idea. It does mean going through the chemo process again and potentially risking neutropenia."

"I'm aware, but at least she'll have a chance to recuperate. The high-dose chemo did do its job." Madison stood over Gracie's little body and looked down on her wistfully. She was so cute, so small, so sick. She was vulnerable.

When Madison helped little ones like this, it made her think of her longing for a family of her own, but the idea of her child getting sick and going through cancer, possibly dying, terrified her. She remembered the pain of losing a loved one all too keenly.

"Scalpel," Tony said to a scrub nurse.

All Madison could do was stand back and watch the procedure. Tony was so calm and gentle with the incision he made. He was so confident in everything he did, it was like he belonged in the operating room, but then she had always thought that.

There were times when he'd be in surgery with an attending and she would watch him from the observation room. Tony had no hesitation during surgery. It was a gift, almost like he was born to take control.

And she knew he studied meticulously, working endless hours in the simulations labs to hone his craft. He was so sure of everything.

Except her.

He was always so scared of the unknown, but she was scared too. Scared of spending her life with someone else who shut her out emotionally.

*Don't think about that now.*

She tried to steer her thoughts back to the procedure. She watched every step that he took as he extracted the sample of bone marrow. It was like witnessing poetry in motion.

"There," Tony announced. "All done. Dr. Syme, please close Gracie up."

Dr. Syme, a young surgical resident, stepped forward and Madison followed Tony out of the procedure room into the scrub room. They peeled off their masks and protective gear to wash up.

"I'd forgotten," Madison remarked as she stepped on the pedal for the stream of water to start.

"Forgotten what?" Tony asked.

"How good you really are at surgery."

He smiled at her softly. "I like being in the operating room. I swear it's not a morbid thing, but I feel in control somehow. Other times…things are out of my control."

"Surgery can be risky," she replied. "I don't mean it as a slight. Medicine can be just as problematic too."

"I know you didn't. I think we can learn a lot from each other."

Her heart skipped a beat. "I do too."

She wanted to reach out and touch him, but resisted. When his arms had wrapped around her at the carousel, she'd felt so safe.

So secure.

She couldn't recall the last time she felt that way.

He just continued to scrub out. "So we're still on for Martha's Vineyard tomorrow, right?"

"Yes. I would like to get the pictures squared away for the auction in a couple of weeks. I hope you'll be attending?" She grabbed some paper towel and dried her hands.

"I suppose," he groused.

"You suppose?"

"It's a good cause. I just don't like the schmoozing. I'm not exactly charming."

"Oh, I wouldn't say that." Her cheeks flushed hotly.

*Great. Just great.*

This is the last thing she needed to talk about.

"Maybe you can give me some insider trading about what will be on offer." There was a twinkle in his eyes as he teased her.

*Nice change of subject, Dr. Rodriguez.*

"No way, pal. It's all secret."

"Figures."

They left the scrub room together and walked back to the main oncology wing. She had some more patients to see later in the day and she was aware that Tony had a couple of other procedures and some post-op patients to check on. She wasn't sure why she was hanging around him. Maybe it was the change. Maybe it was the prospect of having a friend again. She didn't make friends easily.

*I've missed him.*

"Have you heard from Jessica, the ovarian cancer patient?" Tony asked, breaking the silence that had fallen between them.

"I have. She set up an appointment with the fertility doctor, Dr. Page, for Monday. Dr. Page invited me to attend and I think I will."

"Keep me posted on that."

"Oh, I will. Have you thought more about the HIPEC?" she asked. "I can send you some information."

"I think I would like that. I haven't done really any, but I want to learn."

"And I appreciate that." Without thinking she reached out and took his hand, squeezing it slightly.

He glanced down and she realized what she'd done. She let go of his hand quickly.

He paused. "Well, I have some post-ops to check on before my next procedure."

Madison nodded. "I have some patients to see myself. I may head down to the free clinic if I get done with my work."

"Good. I'll be knocking on your door bright and early tomorrow. Try and get some sleep."

"Okay," she said softly. "See you later."

Tony nodded and hurried off to the postoperative wing.

Madison took another deep breath. Maybe it wasn't such a good idea to go with him to Martha's Vineyard tomorrow. Maybe she was just asking for trouble. She hadn't been thinking when she took his hand—it just felt natural.

The problem was she couldn't back out now.

She had to go and get the pictures for the silent auction. She was caught between a rock, an island and Tony.

It was definitely a hard place to be stuck in.

True to his word, Tony was prompt and was knocking on her door at six o'clock in the morning.

Sharp.

Good thing she was also ready for him, because she was used to his promptness. He hated when she—or anyone, for that matter—ran late; it was one of his pet peeves. She was sorely tempted to be a minute or two late, just to drive him a bit squirrelly, but she wanted to get this day over with because it would mean less temptation. The sooner she got the pictures of his place, the better.

"Good morning," she said brightly as she flung open the door.

Tony's eyebrows raised. "You're actually up?"

"Why are you so shocked? Have I been late once at GHH? I don't think I have."

"Well, you were late for the tour on your first day."

She frowned. "That was Frank's fault and you know it."

Tony was smirking, his eyes twinkling. "I know. I'm teasing. Come on, I booked a spot on the ferry and I want to make it to our boarding time."

"Sounds good." She reached back and grabbed a light jacket and a bag which had her camera and an umbrella. She locked her door and Tony looked at her gear.

"An umbrella?" he asked, touching the handle that stuck up out of the bag.

"It's supposed to rain. Haven't you looked at the forecast?"

He made a face. "It'll be fine. Besides, I'm not making you walk anywhere."

"It's better to be safe than sorry," she quipped. "Don't make fun of my extra baggage."

Tony chuckled at her little pun. "Fine. I won't."

They took the elevator down to the parking garage, and this was Madison's first time seeing Tony's sporty sedan. It was black with tinted windows, clean and shiny. It looked like it was fresh out of the dealership.

"You don't drive around much, do you?" she asked as he unlocked the doors.

"I used to do more driving. I took Miguel to a lot of activities, but Jordan's widow is about to get remarried and…his stepdad is a great guy." There was a moment of hesitation and he opened up the door for her as she slipped into the passenger seat.

Jordan had been a good guy. She could understand why his death was affecting Tony so much. She knew how close they had been—she'd seen it herself when they were out in California. Tony slipped into the driver's seat. They made their way out of the parking garage and onto the streets of Boston.

It was Saturday, early in the morning, so there wasn't much traffic on the roads. It was a bit overcast and a few drops of rain splattered on the windshield.

"I guess living across from GHH means you don't need to drive as much," Madison remarked, trying to quell the tension that had dropped between them when Tony had mentioned Jordan and his godson.

"Not really, but if I'm going to utilize the vacation house, then yes, I'll be getting more use out of the car."

"You should use the house. I mean, you must've bought it for a reason."

Tony shrugged as he navigated the streets to head out onto the highway. "It was a good deal. I have some happy memories on the island."

Madison was intrigued now. Tony never talked much about his childhood, his parents or anything from his past. He was a closed book. It was like he didn't trust anyone with his secrets.

"Oh? Your parents have a place out there?"

"My mother's parents lived there. I would go spend time with them when I was young. They died before I hit puberty and after that… Well, I was out on the island last fall and feeling a bit nostalgic when I found that their house was back up for sale."

Her eyes widened. "It's your grandparents' home?"

Tony smiled and nodded. "My great-great-grandfather built it. It started out as one of those gingerbread cottages that Martha's Vineyard is so famous for, and it expanded. You'll see. The previous owners did update the inside to make it a bit more modern, but it's still wonderful."

"I'm surprised you're not out there every week-end," Madison remarked.

Tony sighed. "Work and… It's a family home really. I don't have a family."

There was sadness in his voice, a longing, and she understood that keen pang of craving some-thing more too. She wanted to ask him why he didn't get married; she was actually surprised he was still single. He was so adamant about roots. What had held him back?

*Maybe me?*

It was a stupid glimmer of hope that came out of nowhere, and she was mad at herself for think-ing that. They had their chance, and it had ended.

She'd ended it.

They didn't work as a couple. Then again, she and Tony had never talked like this before. He never gave an inkling of ever wanting more and if he did, how could she lay her heart on the line for someone who never opened up to her, some-one who never fully trusted her?

The answer had been simple back then: she couldn't.

Except now, the wall was coming down and she didn't know what to make of it because she didn't believe it was down for good.

She'd been burned by this before.

Still, he was willing to work. They were arguing less. It was nice to really partner with him. Maybe things had changed?

# CHAPTER NINE

TONY DIDN'T KNOW what had come over him when he started talking to her about the house. He didn't like to talk about his family, about how his mother had grown up well-off, but then ran away with a poor man his grandfather didn't really approve of.

His mother was cut off, but that didn't stop Tony's father from slowly bleeding her dry. His grandparents and his mother disagreed and became estranged.

However, the rockiness of that relationship didn't creep down to him. His grandparents took him for a week or two every summer, until they both passed away tragically in a car accident. That's when his mother had sold their family's home and his father had spent every last dime of that money. Even the money his mother set aside for his education.

It's why Tony had worked so hard to get into medical school and then to help provide for his mother, until she passed. His dad had tried to come back into his life before he moved to California to work with Dr. Pammi, but Tony had shut him out.

It was a longing for happier times that had brought him back to Martha's Vineyard last fall. Then he saw his mother's family home was back on the market. He had to buy it, but when he walked through the house after he bought it, it was so hard. It hurt so much.

A part of him worried that by coming back here, he'd be too vulnerable in front of Madison. He was never unguarded with anyone.

He was stunned that he had been talking about it at all with her. It also felt freeing to let it all out. She didn't need to know all the sordid details about his family's past, the embarrassment of his swindler father—that was his cross to bear. But he could share happy memories of his time here. It felt good to share and talk with someone.

He changed the subject to things about the island, the progress with the auction and patients. They made it to their ferry crossing time. They had to leave the car and head up on the deck before the vessel could depart from Woods Hole on the way to Oak Bluffs.

His place was just outside of Oak Bluffs, overlooking Nantucket Sound. He hadn't told Madison about one of the best things waiting at the end of this ferry crossing. The Flying Horses Carousel was the oldest operating merry-go-round in America. Tony had never thought much of it, but since the other night in the Common and witnessing how excited Madison was to see that carousel, he couldn't wait to show her the one on the island.

An image of her looking up at him on the Common carousel filled his mind. He adored that light of excitement in her eyes. And with that image came the memory of the sweet taste of her kiss, of all the kisses from their past. He could drown himself in her lips.

*Don't. Get it out of your head.*

They wandered around on the top deck. Madison was leaning over the rail with her camera out and taking photographs. It was windy and the water was a bit choppy for Tony's liking, but it didn't seem to bother her. She was smiling, her blond hair coming loose out of her braid and swirling around her delicate face.

It made his heart race a bit as he watched her longingly. All he wanted to do was take her in his arms again. She was the family he always longed for, but he just didn't trust someone who flew by the seat of their pants. He was too afraid to reach out and make anything happen. Which was why he was alone.

Sure, it was easy to blame work and the workload, but really who was at fault for that?

He was.

Madison turned and looked at him, smiling brightly, her cheeks ruddy from the wind. "It's gorgeous."

Tony nodded, beaming at her as he made his way over to the railing. "Sorry it's not sunnier."

"You can't control the weather. Or can you?" she teased, cocking an eyebrow.

"I wish. If I did, you'd have the perfect sunny day."

He braced his arms on either side of her, her back to his chest as the waves sent mist into the air. The sound was a bit tumultuous today, but he didn't mind in the least since Madison wasn't moving away from him. She just continued to snap pictures.

"I like the sea sort of stormy. I always have," she remarked.

"I remember," he replied.

And it was true. He did remember. She was from Utah, the land of mountains and snow, tall timber, but also farmland in the valley and red desert rocks to the south. There were lakes there, but he'd been with her the first time she'd walked the beaches in San Diego and seen the sea.

It had been a dreary day, but a group of them had time off from studying and working nonstop under Dr. Pammi and went down for a beach picnic to take a break. The endless shifts of rounding and charting and such had taken their toll. The look of pure joy on Madison's face as she stripped off her sandals and ran out into the surf was something that he'd forgotten about until now.

Maybe he'd locked it away because that was

a moment where he started to fall for her. Others had joined her with reckless abandon, but he had held back, just watching her splash happily in the surf.

Madison had joy. She knew how to live life.

It actually surprised him that Madison was still single. He thought she would've been married by now, but then on the other hand she moved around so much. Maybe she didn't want a husband or family.

It was something they never talked about before. Of course, there wasn't much time discuss any of that when they were studying, butting heads or falling into bed with each other.

When he was around her, all that worry he always carried since he was a kid seemed to melt away. It felt so right with her. But he couldn't have her, and he wouldn't hold her back.

She leaned back against him. "You afraid I'm going to topple over the side?"

"Well, you are from the mountains," he teased.

He stepped back and she slipped her camera back in her bag.

She shrugged. "I love something everywhere I've been."

"Really?" he asked.

"Sure. There's always something positive to look out for."

Tony had forgotten what a sunny kind of person she could be, just willing to jump in, both feet first, into any given situation. It was scary, because that was something he had never been comfortable with.

He'd never been able to just live in the moment. Most of the time, he would have to plan things out meticulously.

It could tend to be a bit tedious.

*Just relax.*

And that's what he planned on doing today—just relaxing and enjoying some time in one of his favorite places.

Madison was leaning over the railing again. "There's a lighthouse!"

He leaned over beside her. "East Chop Lighthouse. We're not far from the ferry terminal."

"How far is it to your place?"

"Not far at all. Just outside Oak Bluffs close to Jaws Bridge."

Her eyes widened. "Jaws…what?"

Tony chuckled. "You know, the shark movie. It was filmed there. That bridge is a great place for jumping off and swimming."

Madison shuddered. "No. Thanks."

"You've swum in the ocean before."

"I've waded out in the ocean. I didn't do surfing or snorkeling or anything like that. I don't like sharks." Madison shuddered again for effect. "I love the ocean, but I don't particularly like the idea of what lurks beneath."

"And here I thought you could find something positive about any place."

"Not sharks!" She shook her head. "No way."

He chuckled to himself. She was so endearing sometimes.

"I'll protect you from sharks. I promise we won't jump off the bridge, but we can take a walk over it so you can get some good shots of Joseph Sylvia State Beach. Beautiful white sand."

"That sounds like a plan."

The ferry pulled into the Oak Bluffs terminal. They went back down to his car and waited their turn to disembark. There was a bit of rain and it was sort of overcast, but it wasn't cold out. In fact, it was warm, even with the breeze.

As soon as they disembarked from the ferry, he drove over to parking.

"We're here?" she asked. "That's a short trip."

"I'm going to show you something you'll like. Especially since you went gaga over the Frog Pond Carousel."

Madison's eyes sparkled. "Seriously?"

"The oldest carousel in America that's still operating."

"Let's go!" She grabbed his arm and shook it.

They walked over to the Flying Horses Carousel. Madison practically squealed when she saw it. The Frog Pond carousel was cute, but this was the epitome of a merry-go-round. It had gilt and lights. The horses shone brightly under the lighting. There was painted scenery from 1879 and brass rings which, if you could grab one, would give you a free ride.

"It's beautiful!" Madison whispered. "I've never seen anything like it."

"It was originally in Coney Island and steam powered."

"We have to go for a ride." Madison was jumping up and down, clapping.

Tony laughed softly. "I figured as much."

They both bought a ticket and then got in the line to wait for the next ride. Tony decided this time, he wasn't going to even attempt to get on a horse; he would just stand next to Madison. She found a golden horse and climbed up.

"Worried about your hip, old man?" she teased.

"Yes." He winked. "I'm good standing here."

The operator shut the gate and the carousel started up, playing its joyous music as it went around and around and up and down. It had been thirty years since he rode this. His grandfather had brought him here once when he was ten, but he didn't enjoy it as much as Madison seemed to. Her eyes were closed and she had her arms outstretched.

At least today she was wearing sneakers and not heels, but he was slightly disappointed that she might not fall into his arms again. Instead, she wobbled slightly in her seat and gripped the pole.

"It's okay," he whispered in her ear, drinking in her scent. "I won't let you fall."

Then he held her steady, his arms wrapped around her waist. She looked back at him over her shoulder. Pink stained her cheeks as the flush crept up her neck and he could feel her trembling. Their gaze locked and his own pulse was thundering between his ears.

*Kiss her.*

Only he resisted.

He promised her it wouldn't happen again and he meant it. Although, right now in this moment, he wished he could take it all back.

The carousel ended and he stepped back, taking her hand and helping her down off the horse. They didn't say much to each other, but his pulse was racing, his blood heating, and he didn't let go of her hand as they exited the carousel. At least this time they didn't get scolded for lingering.

"How was that?" he finally asked, breaking the silence.

"It was wonderful," she said. "Truly. Thank you for bringing me here."

"You're welcome. Well, let's get to my place and get those pictures in. The last ferry leaves at nine thirty p.m., but I reserved our tickets for seven thirty."

"That sounds great. I'm eager to see your family home."

They got into his sedan and the tension was

still there—that sexual energy that always crackled between them. If this had been ten years ago, they would've been in bed by now.

But this wasn't ten years ago. They were no longer those carefree students of Dr. Pammi.

Their feelings were different.

*Were they?*

Madison wanted to say something, anything to Tony. She just couldn't think of a word to say. They had promised after that first kiss to keep things platonic between them, to be colleagues and friends, and they'd been doing a good job. They were working well together.

At least, that's what she kept telling herself.

She was completely deluding herself.

When he leaned against her on the ship and then held her on the carousel, she had melted inside. His touch had a way of making her feel totally secure. She didn't want to push him away, even though she knew she should.

*Friends, remember. We're just friends.*

Instead of saying something and possibly making it all worse, she focused on the scenery outside as Tony drove them away from the town of Oak Bluffs and down along a stretch of coast. She could see the appeal of Martha's Vineyard, even on a rainy, gloomy day.

There were green fields, trees everywhere and

white beaches. The cottage homes were cute and quaint at first, but the farther they drove from the town the more lavish, large homes started to dot the countryside.

Modern style, barn style and farmhouse. She couldn't believe it. It was as cute as a button.

"There's the bridge," Tony pointed out and nodded.

She glanced over and saw the infamous bridge. No one was out jumping off it today.

Tony made a turn up a driveway that wound up a small hill.

"Here we go." He parked in front of a gate, rolled down his window and then punched in a code. The gate swung open. There were trees all around a circular gravel drive and she let out a small gasp as the white coastal cottage came into view.

"It's gorgeous," she exclaimed.

She was glad it wasn't one of those modern square houses. This house felt it belonged.

The gate automatically closed behind them, and Tony parked the car. She got out and followed him to the front door. He unlocked it and then punched in another security code.

Inside, it was a bit stuffy, and the few pieces of furniture Madison could see were covered in sheets.

"Did it come turnkey?" she inquired, looking around, her voice echoing in the empty house.

Tony flicked on a light. "No, this was some of my mother's stuff that she kept in storage. Pieces she saved after her parents died. I brought it all back when I bought it."

"So you've been back here more than once?"

Tony dropped his head and then grinned. "Okay, twice. I do have a maintenance company come and check on it and periodically clean."

"Well, we can't take pictures of it with all the sheets covering up the furniture. It looks like a haunted house." Which was a bit of an exaggeration. Whoever had owned it last had completely updated it, but they hadn't destroyed the beautiful woodwork. Wood trim moved through the house like a lifeline; it looked like it had been planed from driftwood and then stained a red cherry color...

Madison glanced up to see exposed beams and a beautiful banister that disappeared up a set of stairs.

She made her way into the kitchen, which was all modern with wood flooring, granite countertops, stainless steel and white cupboards. There was an old woodstove in the corner, possibly part of the original kitchen, polished and raised up on gleaming red bricks.

The back wall of the kitchen was all window and it led out onto a terrace that overlooked Nantucket Sound from on top of the hill.

There was a small pool and a hot tub. The backyard was open, save for a hedgerow which marked its boundaries.

Tony followed her silently. "Do you think this will work for the silent auction?"

"Oh. I think so."

"Great. We should get some pictures then."

"Yes, but first we clean and remove the sheets. And fair warning—we may have to find a knick-knack store."

Tony's brow furrowed and he frowned. "Why?"

"You have no decorations, and we want this place to scream cozy romantic retreat at the auction."

Tony frowned. "Do I have a say in this?"

She grinned back at him devilishly. "Not at all."

# CHAPTER TEN

MADISON REALIZED QUITE QUICKLY, without a doubt, that Tony was not having the time of his life going through little thrift stores in the village. She could tell by the sour look on his face, his exaggerated sighs, his groans and the way he dragged his feet, but he didn't try to stop her. It was kind of comical. Honestly, that made it even more fun for her. His grandparents' home was beautiful, but it definitely needed some added sparkle.

They had spent the morning cleaning and taking off all the sheets. She checked over the hot tub and the pool, which were both solid. Thankfully, the maintenance company Tony hired to clean and look after the place took care of those items. She had no doubt that in addition to the view, the pool and hot tub would be a big draw in the auction.

After that, she dragged him from store to store and gave him some helpful advice on items to buy, including towels for the bathrooms and better quality sheets—*not* bought at the thrift store.

Now Madison was getting a kick out of him

grumbling behind her as she went through little knickknacks to bring some decorative beachy touches to his place.

"How about this?" she asked, picking a large wooden seagull off the shelf. It looked like someone had hand-painted it thirty years ago, back when folk painting and stenciling was the height of interior decorating, just like salmon-colored walls and teal carpeting.

He shot her an inscrutable look. "Do I have a choice?"

"Ye-es, but it would tie the whole look together."

"Your drawn out *yes* means I don't have much of a choice," he grumbled.

"You do. I'm just telling you it works. It's a look."

Tony glanced down into the cart. "What look is that? Crap on the beach?"

Madison chuckled and placed the homely seagull in the cart. "It's beachy."

"Crappy beachy," he mumbled, but a smile tugged at the corners of his lips.

She crossed her arms. "And you can do so much better?"

"I didn't say that!"

"We're almost done. Then we'll decorate the house. I'm telling you, rich city folks love this kind of stuff. Ooh, a butter churn!"

"How is that nautical?" he questioned.

She picked it up. "It's Americana."

Tony gazed down at the butter churn in disgust. "You're a brilliant doctor, Madison, but you suck at home decorating. I'm just going to put that out there."

She stifled a laugh.

It was good to tease and have fun with him. Right now they were just two people having fun, not worrying about anything. It was kind of freeing. It also reminded her of the way her parents had been. The laugher and the teasing.

The love.

Heat spread through her veins and she tried to look away so Tony wouldn't see her blushing. She placed the churn in the cart.

"Okay, I'm done. Let's get this out of here and then I'll take you to lunch. My treat, since I'm forcing you to buy all this…what you call junk, but I call treasure."

"Deal." He spun the shopping cart around and they went to the cash register to pay for their items. The local girl at the till gave the items Madison had picked out a curious look. It seems she agreed with Tony. They carried their purchases out to the car and Tony took them out of Oak Bluffs to Edgartown, down to the water that overlooked to the Chappaquiddick Point.

There was a tiny restaurant nestled close to the beach. It was rainy and getting rainier by the moment. She pulled out her umbrella and they dashed from the car into the restaurant.

"See," she said, shaking off the umbrella and closing it. "Always prepared."

Tony shook out his coat and rolled his eyes. "Sure. Rub it in."

"The weather app is very useful." She grinned at him innocently.

The little restaurant was pretty bare of people. There weren't many tourists out and about today, not that Madison could blame them. It was a miserable day. Thankfully, she had taken outside shots of the house before the rain had gotten any worse.

"Two?" the waitress asked.

"Yes," Tony responded.

"You can sit anywhere by the window," the waitress replied. "It's a bit slow today."

"Thanks," Madison said.

She followed Tony as they wound their way through the tiny tavern. It was completely nautically themed, with dark wood, captain chairs and wall-mounted fish. Nets draped from the ceilings. It was a little over-the-top, but that's what she liked about places like this.

There was a little booth in the corner where they wouldn't bump hips in the middle. She slid in and he slid in on the other side.

Their waitress came over and handed them

menus and took their drink order before disappearing again.

"It's a shame it's so rainy," Tony remarked.

"Well, I'm just glad I got the outside photos done before the downpour."

"Me too. After lunch, we'll pick up our dinner at the market since our ferry doesn't leave until later tonight. I figure you'll need all that time horrifying my poor house."

She shook her head, laughing softly. "You mean improving it."

He chuckled. "Sure. We'll go with that."

"It's going to look good!"

"Okay…" he stated, grinning.

"You don't believe me, do you?" She was joking, but there was a part of her that was serious, because he just didn't seem to believe anything she said or did until she actually proved it to him.

"I do, I do."

Madison snorted. "You're *so* convincing."

"Okay, I'll trust you."

Her heart warmed when he said that and she reached across the table and took his hand.

"Thanks," she murmured.

"For what?" he asked softly.

"Trusting me."

"Trust is hard for me," he admitted.

"Why?" she asked.

"My childhood was a bit of an upheaval."

"I understand. Mine was as well. We have more in common than I thought."

Tony looked at her tenderly and he brought her hands up to his lips, brushing a light kiss across her knuckles, sending a rush of endorphins through her body.

*You can't, Madison*, a little voice reminded her.

Only she didn't pull her hand away. She ignored that little voice in her mind telling her that he was off limits, that he was just a friend. His kiss reminded her of all the times they had shared before. Not the arguing and not the work, but the moments she caught glimpses of the real Tony.

There was a time limit to all this though. She wasn't sticking around and she didn't want to hurt him again. She pulled her hand away, gripping the menu to keep her hands from trembling. She could feel the imprint of his lips on her skin and she longed for more.

"So," she said, clearing her throat and changing the subject. "Are you ready to decorate your house after lunch?"

"Just tell me how to make the weekend worthy of the silent auction. Should I put little mints on the pillows or...what?"

"You could offer up a gift basket full of things from the island. Other than that, they're getting a free weekend in a popular spot. Most people, I'm sure, dream of having a place overlooking Nantucket Sound in Martha's Vineyard."

"It is beautiful. I always loved my summers here as a kid."

She squinted and cocked her head.

"What?" he asked.

"I'm trying to picture you as a kid."

Tony rolled his eyes and the waitress came back to take their order. They both ordered the clam chowder and then spent the rest of their lunch talking about nothing in particular. It was nice just being herself with him.

*Why can't we have this?*

She would so love it if they could.

True to her word, she paid for lunch, which she was glad to do because he'd been right; it had been the best clam chowder she'd had in a long time. Rich and creamy, it just made her heart happy.

They dashed back out into the rain and got into his car, then headed to the market and grabbed some sandwich stuff for dinner, as well as cheese, crackers and wine. When they got back to his place, it seemed like the storm outside was getting worse and there was a niggling part of Madison that was wondering if they would be able to get back to the mainland tonight. How bad did it have to be before a ferry was canceled? To be honest, she was kind of nervous about traveling in choppy water.

"Shit," Tony groused glancing at his phone.

"What?"

"Ferry is canceled for tonight, maybe even into tomorrow. There are winds of sixty-five miles per hour gusting off of Cape Cod, causing high seas."

Her stomach knotted. "We're stuck here?"

Tony nodded. "Good thing we bought some bedding."

"Yeah," she agreed. "Speaking of that, maybe I'll throw a load of laundry on."

She had to put some distance between her and Tony right now. It was one thing to spend the day with him having fun, but she had an out. They had ferry reservations—there was an end.

Now, she was stuck here overnight with him.

It was too much temptation. She started the laundry machine, letting the whir of the wash and the hum of the dryer drown out the howling wind and lashing rain. Tony followed her into the laundry room. It was a tight squeeze and she could feel the heat of his body permeating through her clothes. She rubbed her hand absently thinking about the kiss.

"You okay?" he asked.

"A little freaked out about the storm and the fact we're trapped here." She spun around and faced him, gripping the dryer behind her, edging back as far as she could, but all she wanted to do was lean against him and have him hold her.

"Me too," he agreed. "Not the storm so much."

"Then what?"

"Being here with you," he said quietly.

She swallowed the lump in her throat. "Why is that?"

"I haven't stopped thinking about that kiss on the carousel at Frog Pond."

Her heart thumped, her body tingling with anticipation. "Well…try."

The truth was she hadn't been able to stop thinking about it either. Just being with him made her so happy. It broke up the monotonous loneliness of her life.

His dark brown eyes bore into her, searing her very soul, and her pulse thundered between her ears. The storm raging outside wasn't the only one—there was another howling in her heart. And she was trying to remember why she was holding back. When had she decided he was off-limits? She couldn't recall. Tony had changed and she was falling in love with him again.

He tore his gaze away and cleared his throat. "How long do you think the sheets will be?"

"A while yet," she responded, her voice trembling.

"Let's go have some dinner then. There's no use standing around here watching the laundry."

She laughed, the tension melting away. "You're right."

"Of course I am." There was a twinkle in his eyes.

"What happens when the ferry opens up? How will we know?"

"That eager to be rid of me?"

"No, just curious. Are we here a week? Do I have to reschedule appointments?"

"As soon as the ferry is running again we'll get a notification." He held up his phone. "I have an app and everything."

"Good."

They walked into the kitchen and worked together to pull out the groceries they had bought. She focused on helping get sandwiches put together while Tony worked on a small charcuterie board.

Her pulse was racing as she watched him. When he admitted to thinking about their kiss, it made her think back on it as well. She was sorely tempted to do it again, to just melt in his arms, even one more time.

"What?" he asked, catching her staring as he set meat and cheese on a wooden board.

"That's like a perfect picture," she exclaimed as he adjusted a bunch of grapes. She grabbed her camera to take a few shots and set up two wineglasses next to it. Tony watched her, his eyebrows arched.

"It's cheese and grapes," he stated.

"And it sells."

He laughed. "You're way too excited about this."

"Excited about the auction?"

He nodded. "It's not at Sotheby's or anything. It's a hospital fundraiser."

"And a gala," she corrected. "I want your place to look great and get the most bids."

"Then you shouldn't have bought that fugly seagull," he mumbled.

"Maybe I'll bid on this place myself," she replied, smiling.

"A romantic weekend for two?" he questioned.

"Sure. Why not?"

"Who's your plus-one?" he asked, his voice dropping lower as he leaned over the counter.

A shiver of anticipation ran down her spine. "Do I need a plus-one?"

"No."

"Then, no one. Just me enjoying your place on my own." She grinned wickedly. "My own romantic weekend."

"That's a shame."

"Why?"

"I was hoping you'd bring me."

"What? This is your place."

"You're right. Maybe you don't need to bid."

"Why? Are you going to bring me back?" She held her breath, regretting the question.

"I would."

Her heart caught in her throat as he moved around and touched her cheek. It caused tendrils of heat to unfurl in her belly. She was having a hard time telling herself to resist him again.

"Tony," she whispered. She wanted to tell him that they shouldn't. Every look, every touch just reminded her of what it had been like before.

When it was just the two of them and no work in the way.

This time they were older. Maybe it could work...? So she didn't push him away. She just wanted more, her body trembling with need, recalling every moment when no one else had ever made her feel the way Tony did.

She wanted to be in his arms again. Maybe that would chase away the ghosts that had haunted her for the last ten years. The lingering longing had been eating at her since she'd ended it all.

Would it hurt?

He pushed back a strand of hair from her face, gently tucking it behind her ear. "When I'm around you, Madison, I forget myself."

Madison closed her eyes and leaned into his hand, not wanting the connection to end. She'd missed this. All of it.

"I do too."

"Do you ever think of me?"

"Always," she whispered.

"What do we do?" he asked huskily.

"Kiss me, Tony," she said, breathlessly.

"Are you sure?"

"I am. Aren't you?"

He nodded. "Positive."

Tony kissed her again and she couldn't help but

melt into his arms like she had on the carousel. Only this time there was no one to stop them. His lips on hers seared her very soul.

Now was not the time to think. It was the time to feel. His tongue pushed past her lips, the kiss deepening, his hands in her hair as he cradled her head. He trailed his mouth down her neck.

Fire moved through her veins and all she wanted was him naked and between her legs. There was no stopping this moment. At least not for her. She wanted this again. Even if it was just for the night. Things had ended for them so quickly and she missed him after all this time.

Tony scooped her up in his arms and carried her into the living room as there were no sheets on the beds upstairs. She didn't care where this happened; she just needed it to happen now.

"What about protection?" he asked.

"It's okay. I'm on birth control."

They made quick work of their clothes so that nothing was between them. The only sound was their breath, her pulse racing with urgency, needing him.

Tony ran his hands over her skin and she trembled at the familiarity of his touch. How it made her feel safe.

"I've missed you," he said huskily against her ear as he explored her body.

Madison couldn't form coherent words. All she could feel was pleasure coursing through her as he touched her between her legs. She wanted to tell him that she missed him too, that she always thought of him, but couldn't.

"Oh, God," she gasped as he continued to kiss and lick her sensitive skin.

"I love touching you, Madison," he replied, his voice husky.

"I want…"

"What do you want?" He teased as he circled a nipple with his tongue.

"You," she responded, arching her back, begging him to take her.

Tony moved over her, his hardness pressing against her core. He slid into her and Madison cried out at the feeling of being completely possessed by him again. He thrust into her over and over. It felt so good. She was lost in the moment. It felt so right.

Tony moaned as he slid a hand under her bottom, lifting her leg up as he quickened his pace, sinking deep inside her. She closed her eyes, her body succumbing to the sensations of being lost in the arms of the only man she ever loved. The man who destroyed her heart and the one she'd had to leave behind.

Had anything changed? She wasn't sure, but she didn't care. All she cared about in this moment was him.

She came, tightening around him. She clutched

his back and rode through the wave of pleasure before he followed close behind her.

As she lay there in his arms, she realized she'd made a big mistake thinking they could just be friends and that nothing would happen between them. But at this moment, basking in all the heady pleasure she had just shared with him, she didn't care.

*What did I just do?*

Tony couldn't believe what had just happened. When Madison begged him to kiss her and touched him, he was a lost man. Making love to her again wasn't the best idea, but he didn't regret that it happened. He just had to be careful with his heart, because he wouldn't be able to handle losing her again.

He didn't want to hold her back, but he didn't want her to leave and he didn't want to ignore this or how he felt about her.

"I'm freezing," Madison said, smiling up at him from the floor. "Your area rug is not particularly cozy."

He grinned as he ran his fingers over her, reveling in her softness.

The dryer buzzed from the laundry room.

"Well, I bet those newly dried sheets will help." He got up and dashed into the laundry room. He pulled out the fresh sheets and then put the damp ones from the wash into the dryer. He took the warm sheets out to Madison. She wrapped herself up in one.

"So toasty," she sighed.

He grabbed two pillows from the couch and cuddled up next to her. "I guess we need to talk about this."

He was well aware she'd jumped around from job to job for the last ten years and his work was rooted here. He couldn't leave here.

*Why?*

Madison sighed. "We do need to talk. Tonight was wonderful."

"It was." He rolled on his side. "Why can't we have this?"

"What, sex?" She grinned.

"More. Why can't we try again? I've missed you."

She smiled and touched his face. "I've missed you too."

"We can take it slow. Get to know each other."

They couldn't go back as just friends now. Yes, there was an air of uncertainty, but it could be years before she moved on again. And maybe by then she'd change her mind.

"I would like to take things slow." She kissed him again. "I've missed you. So much."

He leaned over and took her into his arms, pulling her across his chest as he stroked her back. "Then we take it slow."

"One thing though," she said, resting her head on her chin.

"Now you're demanding things?" he teased.

"We keep it secret at work. For now."

He nodded. "Good idea."

"And..."

"Wait, you said one thing."

She giggled. "Fine. Two things. Can we make a bed up? I don't want to sleep on the floor all night."

"I think we can make that work."

# CHAPTER ELEVEN

*Two weeks later*

TONY MADE HIS way to the operating room board to see which room his procedure was assigned to. Today was the second stem cell transplant for little Gracie. The baby had been through a lot the past few weeks, but he was pleased with how she was responding. At first he'd been uncertain about the SCT because Dr. Santos hadn't recommended it, but Madison had been right.

He had a hard time focusing. He'd been having that problem since he came back to Boston from his place on the island, because he couldn't stop thinking about that night. It replayed over and over in his mind.

It was like a dream come true. They had spent all night and most of Sunday just curled up together, talking about everything and nothing. When the ferry opened back up, they headed back to Boston and at work they tried to keep their distance, but it was hard.

Every glance was heated with a promise. After their shift, they'd go out to dinner and end the night snuggled up in his bed.

Dr. Crespo remarked on Tony's exceptionally good mood. It was true. He was just living in the moment, instead of thinking about the looming deadline of the relationship, when he would have to let Madison go.

When they saw each other in passing since then, and every time he looked at her, his mind was flooded with images of their reconnection. He could still feel the silkiness of her skin, her breath in his ear, her nails on his back as she clung to him in the heat of the moment. It made him want her all the more. And every night he got to relive it. Their secrecy in the halls of GHH reminded him of the days they snuck around as residents.

Only this time there was no arguing, no hiding emotions. He could be himself with her.

He scrubbed a hand over his face and stared at the operating room schedule for the third time.

Since this was the final stem cell transplant for Gracie it meant that he'd be working closely with Madison today, on a day she was particularly lodged in his brain.

*You've got to get her out of your mind.*

"Morning," Madison said brightly, coming to stand next to him.

Her blond hair was pulled back tightly and covered by a scrub cap. Baggy scrubs hid her curves, but Tony knew every inch of her under those layers and his blood heated as he thought about it.

His body tensed. "You ready?"

"Yes." She nodded. "This will be good."

"What chemotherapy did you use this round?" he asked.

She cocked an eyebrow. "I used naxitamabgqgk."

His stomach knotted, but only for a moment. It wasn't what Dr. Santos would have used, but Madison knew what she was doing.

"I'm aware that Dr. Santos didn't okay it for patients under one," Madison continued, as though she read his thoughts, "but this medicine has good results. Even for Gracie's age group. Her mother consented when I gave her the facts."

Tony nodded. She'd dealt with the medicine side. If Gracie's mother was consenting, then that was all that mattered. It was a moot point.

Madison would not put a child's life at risk. She was talented and she was careful with her choices.

*She's not like your father. This is not a frivolous risk.*

"Let's get this done." He headed to the scrub room and Madison followed him.

Madison didn't say anything as they entered the operating room, but there was nothing much to say. In the operating room personal relationships were put to the side. He had to focus on the task at hand. She kept quiet during the procedure. He thought he'd prefer it that way, but instead he missed her talking to him.

The procedure with Gracie went off without a hitch and the baby was doing well. He was positive that this was a good move. After Gracie had the all-clear, Madison left the operating room. He knew she had some research to finish.

She was no longer putting in the tedious hours at her lab. Instead they spent their nights together, but he knew she had work to catch up on and he wouldn't interfere with that.

He scrubbed out. As he headed out of the operating room floor, he got a page from the emergency room, which was weird.

He was a surgeon, but a cancer surgeon. It was rare that he had anything to do with trauma, but sometimes some of his post-op patients came back with an infection or something. He made the call down to the ER from a nursing station.

"This is Dr. Rodriguez. I was paged."

"Yes. We have a patient who was brought in from Harbor Middle School for fainting," the nurse said through the receiver.

Tony paused, trying to remember all his current patients. "I don't currently have any pediatric patients that have been discharged…"

"Not a patient. You're on their emergency contact. Miguel Diaz. The school tried to get ahold of his mom but she's not responding."

Tony's heart skipped a beat. "I'll be right down."

He had to go make sure that Miguel was okay. He'd promised Jordan that he would be there for his son. Even though Jordan's widow was about to remarry and Miguel liked his new soon-to-be stepdad, even though Miguel was twelve and sometimes acted like he didn't need adults in his life anymore, Tony wanted to be there in the emergency room.

The nurses pointed him to the curtained bed where Miguel was lying under the blanket. He looked pale and was a bit sweaty. Tony was a bit taken aback, because the moment he walked past that curtain an image of Jordan flashed through his mind.

"Hey, pal," he said gently.

"Tony, what're you doing here?" Miguel asked.

"I work here. Remember?" Tony brushed back a few errant curls off Miguel's sweaty brow. "Tell me what happened."

"I don't know. I was playing basketball and then my legs were hurting a bit, I got dizzy and I woke up here," Miguel responded.

The trauma doctor, Dr. Carolyn Fox, came in. "Glad the nurses called you, Tony. You're his godfather?"

"I am," Tony responded. "What do you think, Dr. Fox?"

Carolyn frowned and motioned to step outside.

"I'll be right back, pal," Tony said, squeezing Miguel's shoulder.

Miguel nodded weakly.

Tony stepped on the other side of the curtain, crossing his arms. "Tell me."

"His blood pressure was low and he had a high fever. I am worried about the achy legs though and the petechiae. I've asked Dr. Sullivan to come down and have a look because of the history in his family."

Tony's stomach knotted. They'd paged Madison, which meant they were worried. "Okay."

Dr. Fox smiled briefly. "I'm sure it's nothing, but…"

"I get it," Tony responded quickly.

"Dr. Sullivan can order the tests she wants, but I will say that his platelets were a little high when I got back the results of a CBC just now."

Tony felt like the world was spinning out of control. This is how it all started with Jordan.

*Not Miguel.*

Usually, he could keep calm and collected, but right at this moment he was struggling. All these different scenarios were running through his head.

Madison entered the emergency room and made her way over. She took a step back when she saw Tony, and he was sure that his expression wasn't the most hopeful. All he wanted was to pull her in his arms and hold her, but they were keeping their relationship under wraps and that would not be very professional of him. Still, in this moment, he needed that physical connection to calm his jangled nerves. He held back but he hated it. He needed her.

"What's wrong?" Madison asked gently.

"It's my godson, Miguel. Jordan's son," Tony responded.

Madison's expression softened and she turned to Carolyn. "His chart?"

Carolyn nodded handing her the chart. "I ordered a CBC when he was first brought in. You'll have the report there."

Madison quickly scanned it. "I see. Well, let me examine him and we'll determine what to do next."

"Have the staff keep trying to call his mother," Tony responded. "I'll stay with him until Bertha can get here."

"Sure thing," Carolyn said before walking away.

Madison turned to face him. "It's probably nothing. It could be a lot of things, an infection or mono."

"His father had cancer."

"What kind?" Madison questioned.

"CLL—chronic lymphocytic leukemia," Tony responded. "By the time it was discovered, it had spread and metastasized."

*And then he refused all my suggestions of treat-*

*ment and I put him in the damn clinical trial he wanted anyways.*

"I see. Well, we don't know anything yet. How about you introduce me to Miguel?" Madison asked.

Tony nodded and they both headed back behind the curtain.

Miguel's color was improving, so that was positive, but Tony could see the petechiae clearly. He hadn't noticed it before when he came in.

"Miguel, this is Dr. Sullivan. She's one of my colleagues."

"I knew your dad," Madison said, brightly.

Miguel's face lit up a bit. "You did?"

She nodded. "He came out to visit Tony once, when we were students. We pestered Tony the entire time trying to make him do stuff like ride the roller coasters on the pier, let us bury him in the sand in California."

Miguel grinned. "That's funny! Dad always talked about getting Tony into trouble."

Tony frowned. "Yes. I'm sure he did."

Madison laughed softly. "You were playing basketball and fainted."

Miguel nodded. "I've been feeling a bit sick. Then I had this pain in my knees. It's been off and on for a couple of weeks. Mom said growing pains and a cold. Or the flu."

"It could very well be. Do you mind if I take

a look?" Madison asked, setting down the chart and pulling on some rubber gloves.

"Will it hurt?" Miguel asked.

"I don't think so, but if it does you tell me. Besides, you have Tony here," Madison responded.

"I'm right here, pal." Tony sat down next to Miguel and held his hand. "It's going to be okay."

Madison gently palpated Miguel's legs and he flinched a couple of times. Her gray eyes were focused on him and she was giving him words of encouragement, telling him to breathe.

"I'm just going to check your neck, for lumps, like if you have a sore throat or something. Is that okay?" she asked Miguel.

"Yes."

"Thank you." Madison gently checked his lymph nodes and then his eyes. Tony realized by her expression and the firm set of her mouth that she was seeing the petechiae too. It was hard to miss. Except Tony had missed it when he first saw him—he'd been too overwhelmed by panic and memories of Jordan. Madison was so calm, whereas he felt like a wreck. He loved that she was so gentle with Miguel.

Then again, she'd always had a great bedside manner when they were residents, whereas he'd struggled. As a surgeon he tried to be better, but he didn't have as much hands-on time with his pediatric patients. Usually they were with their parents.

Madison still had that easy rapport with her patients. It was something he admired about her.

"Miguel?" Bertha pushed back the curtain. Behind her was her fiancé, David.

"Here, Mom!" Miguel said, brightly.

Tony stood up so Bertha could step in and hug her son, and then David hugged Miguel.

"What's wrong, Tony?" Bertha asked, taking the seat he just vacated.

"He fainted. He has some joint pain." He was trying to be careful, because Bertha would jump to conclusions and they didn't want to get Miguel worried. David placed a hand on Bertha's shoulder, giving it a squeeze.

"I'm Dr. Sullivan," Madison said, picking up Miguel's file. "I'm going to be admitting Miguel for some observation and run some tests if that's okay."

"Tests?" Bertha asked.

"If you want to chat outside, we can," Madison responded.

"I'll stay with him, Bertha," David offered.

"You okay?" Tony asked.

Miguel nodded. "Yeah, if I'm staying, can you visit my room later? Maybe we can play a game...?"

Tony nodded gently. "Of course."

Bertha followed them out of Miguel's bed, and Madison led them to a small private room where they could chat further. She shut the door and Tony pulled out a chair for Bertha.

"What's wrong with him?" Bertha asked, her voice betraying a hint of terror.

"We're going to run some tests to find out. He was given a CBC when he was first brought to the emergency room and his platelets were elevated. I'm concerned about the joint pain and some bruising on his forearms. As well as the petechiae. His lymph nodes are also swollen."

"Oh, God," Bertha whispered, and she took Tony's hand. She was thinking about Jordan. It was hard not to.

"It could be an infection," Tony insisted, but he had a hard time saying it with confidence. Jordan's diagnosis was replaying on a loop in his mind.

"Tony is right," Madison agreed. "It could be an infection. I need to run some more tests, possibly a lumbar puncture, and for that, I need to admit Miguel. I'll find out the answer for you as soon as I can, but he'll be well taken care of here, Ms. Diaz. I promise."

Bertha nodded. "Thank you, Dr. Sullivan. And thank you, Tony, for being here."

"Well, I was in the neighborhood," he teased. "He'll be okay."

"I'm going to go back to see him." Bertha stood.

"I'll get him admitted. As soon as a room is ready, a porter will get you situated and I'll order some more tests," Madison finished as she opened the door.

"Thank you both." Bertha left the meeting room and Madison shut the door.

Tony just sat there. Jordan was in his mind and it was hard to contain all those emotions that he'd been bottling up for so long. His mother was gone, his father wasn't in his life and Jordan was dead. There wasn't much family around him.

All he had was Miguel and Bertha, but they were moving on too. He'd been happy for them, but now, the idea of Miguel being sick... It was too much to bear.

Then there was Madison. She was here now, but would she still be here in a year's time? Her track record spoke for itself.

"Tony?" Madison asked gently, squatting in front of him. "Are you okay?"

"No," he said stonily. "I'm not."

"Jordan?" she asked, softly.

He nodded. "CLL. Blood cancer—it's hereditary."

"It can be, but we can treat it. Tell me what happened to Jordan. All of it."

Tony nodded. There was no point in hiding it anymore. He kept his feelings locked up tight to protect himself, because he learned from an early age that feelings could be used against you. He watched his father use his mother's affection and feelings against her time and time again, but he was tired of holding this in.

He needed a release.

He needed to tell her.

Everything.

Madison's heart ached watching him slowly crumble in front of her. Seeing him so human and vulnerable with his godson made her soften even more. He was clearly hurting and she had never seen him like this before. Other than having met Jordan when he'd come out to California, she knew nothing about Tony's life, nothing about his history.

He was so closed up, but he was opening up to her.

She placed a hand on his knee, looking up at him.

"Tell me," she repeated softly.

"When Jordan was diagnosed with CLL, we found a small met on his lung and on his liver. The course of treatment is chemotherapy and radiation. Jordan refused."

"He did?" Madison asked. And then she remembered a previous conversation. "The naturopathic clinical trial?"

Tony nodded. "He wouldn't listen to me and, going against my gut, I got him on that clinical trial. He started a homeopathic treatment. Some new drug from another doctor that could clean the blood. I tried to convince him it wouldn't work, but he didn't care. I stood there and watched him die."

Madison rose to stand as Tony got up from where he was sitting and began to pace around the meeting room.

"So that's why you're so wary of clinical trials."

"If I said no, he'd find someone else to refer him. At least I could advocate for him. Maybe not treat him, but stand up for him during it. I know now it was all a mistake."

"You were trying to save him," she said gently.

"Chemo might've worked."

"There's no cure for CLL. You just live with it and maintain it," Madison stated.

"I know, but chemo would've prolonged his life. I shouldn't have agreed to the clinical trial, but I didn't want him going somewhere else. I took a risk. It failed." He shook his head sadly. "I failed him."

She realized that must've been incredibly hard for Tony, to even consider going against the grain of what he knew. He never did. He was steadfast and confident.

"You didn't fail Jordan," Madison responded.

"That's what Bertha says. We did both *try* to get him to see sense, but by the time he did, the cancer spread to his brain. There was no controlling the spread. It crossed that blood-brain barrier and he died. Slowly. Painfully."

Madison approached him deliberately and then put her arms around him. Tony resisted at first, but then his arms came around her, only for a moment before he stepped away, his back ramrod straight.

"It's not your fault. Jordan took the risk, not you."

"I should've pushed harder. I shouldn't have trusted his faith in something so foolish. I should know better. My father was always doing that. Chasing 'sure things' and squandering every last dime my mother had. He'd leave and only come back when he was out of money. Always taking a risk on our future." Tony's shoulders slumped. "It's hard to believe in anything, to try anything, when you've been constantly let down your whole life."

Madison swallowed the lump in her throat. She'd never known any of this. It explained so much about him. Her childhood was nothing like that, so she didn't understand what he went through, but she did understand the need for stability. For the first part of her formative years, she had two parents who loved each other and who loved her. She had this idyllic life.

Until cancer came.

Then she watched her own family get ripped apart. Her father shut her out. Madison had to step up to be that rock for him and for herself as her mother slowly and painfully lost her battle.

Surgery had been done, but that only made it worse.

After her mother passed, her father was heart-broken. She never wanted to feel that pain of loving someone so much and losing them. She couldn't even begin to process what Bertha and Miguel had gone through when Jordan died. What Tony was going through was something she just never wanted to feel, which was why she threw absolutely everything she could into researching and curing cancer.

Even at the risk of her own personal life. She flitted around the country and barely went home to Salt Lake City to see her father. The times she did manage to go home, it ached. The memories and the pain. The loneliness.

She had no real home.

Tony had stability here in Boston. He had a family in Jordan's family.

They had very different parents and child-hoods, but they both had come to the same cross-roads in life.

The only time she had felt somewhat safe and normal had been when she was with him, but it was hard to hold on to a love when Tony wanted to keep his roots and stay settled.

Maybe she had her own trust issues with regards to love…?

Right now, none of that mattered as she looked at Tony's back. All she could offer him was her expertise on Miguel's case, and herself. She could love him now and be his rock in this moment. And that was all. She was going to move on from Boston eventually to pursue her dreams and she was going to have to leave him behind again... There was no promise of forever.

*Why not?*

"You've got to believe in me though, Tony," she said carefully. "I'm going to do all I can for Miguel. Believe me."

He turned around slowly, his eyes laced with pain. "I know. And I do trust you."

He pulled her into his arms and kissed her deeply. She clung to him.

"It'll be okay."

"Just stay with me," he murmured against her ear.

A sob welled up in her throat. That was not something she could freely promise him right now, even if she wanted to.

# CHAPTER TWELVE

IT WAS TEN at night, way past the time she should've walked across the road and collapsed into bed, but she had ordered a whack-load of blood tests for Miguel and some of them were coming in.

Bertha had gone home to get some of Miguel's personal things and he'd been admitted to the pediatric floor. Tomorrow he would have to have a lumbar puncture and a bone marrow biopsy. Tony had gotten one of the other surgeons to do that, as being Miguel's guardian ruled him out.

She hadn't seen Tony since their talk in the meeting room outside the ER. After he opened up, he'd been paged back to the operating floor and Madison wanted to get started on Miguel's tests right away, but she couldn't stop thinking about what he'd revealed. He had let down his walls and she got to see a bit of what made him *him*.

It explained so much. And she was appreciative that he shared that with her.

What she was worrying about was the future.

Her plans hadn't changed, and it was hurting her heart to think about it all ending.

*Maybe he'll want to join you when the time comes...?*

She could only hope so, because while she didn't want to let go of her dreams, she didn't want to let go of him either. She wasn't sure if she was able to have both.

She stretched as the first couple of blood tests started to hit in her inbox. Dr. Fox had been right: there were issues with Miguel's platelet count and his white blood cell count was elevated. It could mean numerous things. Madison had also run some tests to check out his fibrinogen level, as well as prothrombin time and a partial thromboplastin time. These were used to check his blood-clotting levels, as sometimes leukemia caused issue with clotting.

There were no results about blasts in his bloodstream. Blasts were immature blood cells that were usually only found in bone marrow. The presence of blasts could mean leukemia. The BUN blood test showed that his kidneys were functioning normally, which was good.

She also ran a variety of checks for various infections and other diseases that could be genetic. She'd gotten a fairly extensive history from Bertha. There were autoimmune diseases in the family.

Tomorrow, Madison would feel a lot better. The

lumbar puncture and bone marrow test would be done and the analysis could be run. The results would let her know what she was working with. There was nothing she could do but wait for the tests to be performed tomorrow. She hated waiting.

She shut her laptop down and made her way up to the pediatric floor. She should go home and try to get some sleep, but she wanted to make sure that Miguel was resting comfortably. When she came to Miguel's room, she heard the murmur of voices and peeked in.

Miguel was still awake and there, sitting next to his bed with a table between them, was Tony. There was a deck of cards. Madison grinned and leaned against the doorframe, watching them.

It stung her to think that Tony blamed himself for Jordan's death when it wasn't his fault. If Jordan had gone to another doctor, it could've been worse. She couldn't understand Jordan's reasoning for not listening to Tony.

She felt bad for him. She knew he hated that loss of control.

*There are times I don't listen to him either.*

And she grimaced thinking about those moments, from when they were students and she didn't take his advice. She'd learned from those mistakes, but in hindsight those were the times Tony had been right in the first place.

It was why he was a brilliant surgeon.

She turned to leave.

"Madison?" Tony called out.

She turned around and walked into the room. "Hi, just doing a round."

"I thought you'd be back at your place," Tony said.

"I was catching up on work and I lost track of time. The auction gala is in a couple of days so I was getting stuff organized." She didn't want to say she was waiting for tests to get Miguel's hopes up. She understood he was scared about the tests tomorrow and she didn't blame him in the least.

"Why don't you come play crazy eights with us until Miguel's mom gets back," Tony suggested.

"Yeah," Miguel piped up. "It's more fun with more people."

"Sure." She shrugged. "Why not?"

Tony got up and pulled over another chair to the little rolling table that was over Miguel's bed. Madison sat down and Miguel dealt the cards. It had been a long time since she played crazy eights, but she remembered a bit.

"You knew my dad too?" Miguel asked, placing a card.

"I did," Madison replied, setting another down on the pile.

Miguel nodded and then frowned. "You're also a cancer doctor."

"I am," she replied.

"What if I have cancer like my dad did?" Miguel asked.

Madison glanced over at Tony. She wasn't sure what to say. Tony's lips were pursed in a firm line. She saw the idea that Miguel could have cancer was hurting him.

"I'll treat it," Madison said, confidently.

"She's good. You can trust her," Tony responded, his gaze meeting hers briefly. Her heart skittered and a warm flush crept up her neck. She was so in love with him. Still.

How could she walk away from this? She wasn't sure.

"Ooh, an eight. I'm changing the suit to diamonds," she announced.

Miguel groaned as he pulled a card from the deck. "Oh, no."

They played crazy eights for another half an hour before Bertha came with things for Miguel. Tony said he would be there tomorrow and with him through all the tests. They both slipped out of the room together to try to let Miguel sleep.

"He's a good kid," Madison remarked.

"He is. He was part of the reason I was so glad to come home to Boston."

"I bet," she remarked.

"Jordan thought I should've brought you," he said quietly.

"Oh, did he?" Madison smirked as they continued to walk the near-empty hospital hall.

"He liked you."

She nodded. "He was nice, but I go where the research takes me."

Tony frowned. "I know, but don't you ever miss home?"

"Salt Lake?" she asked.

He nodded. "Yes."

*Yes.*

Only she didn't say that out loud. When she went back to Salt Lake, things were different. The heartache and memories of her mother were too real, and how her father had been, how he'd emotionally shut down for a couple of years. Home wasn't the same, which was another reason why it was so important for her to keep moving forward and hopefully get to work with Dr. LeBret.

"No. I mean, sometimes I miss Salt Lake, but I want to help in the fight to cure cancer." She swallowed the hard lump in her throat. "My dad checked out, mentally and emotionally, after my mom passed. Salt Lake…is kind of a painful reminder of my lonely childhood."

"I'm sorry." He pulled her close and she held him again.

"I guess we both have father issues."

"Yeah, it sucks," he admitted.

She laughed quietly.

Tony didn't say anything more. "Well, I'm

going to head back to my place. I'll see you to-morrow?"

"Yes. Tomorrow. I'll be watching from the gal-lery and then waiting on the tests."

"Do you think it's cancer?" he asked.

She shrugged. "I hope not."

Tony nodded solemnly. "I hope not either."

The elevator dinged and he got on it with a quick wave. Madison sighed as the door shut. She did have a bit more work to do; she probably wouldn't be making it back to her lonely sublet tonight and that was fine by her.

Home was a lab.

And she was going to make sure she explored every avenue on the off chance that it was leuke-mia. She wanted to give Miguel a fighting chance.

For Jordan's sake.

For Tony's sake.

Tony was true to his word: he was there with his godson every step of the way through the lumbar puncture, the scans to check his lymph nodes and then the bone marrow transplant. It was all done while Miguel was under anesthesia, because it was a lot to put a young kid through. Even a kid at the age of twelve, who thought he was so big.

It was hard to stand off to the side and let an-other surgeon do the work. It was hard to let go of control as the head of the department, but he couldn't operate on his godson.

He glanced up in the gallery and saw Madison there. He understood her drive even more now. Both of them had fathers who'd left, in their own way. He hoped she'd come to his place last night, but he knew she was waiting on results for Miguel. The fact she was so invested endeared her to him all the more.

She was working on her laptop as she watched the procedure. Tony learned she'd put a rush on the diagnostics of the samples and approved it. Thankfully, GHH had a pathology lab that was second to none.

When Miguel was wheeled into the pediatric postanesthesia recovery room, Tony stepped back to let Bertha and David take over. As he was leaving the PACU he ran into Madison. She looked like she was moving in a hurry.

"The tests?" he asked, his heart slamming.

He knew the lab was good, but not that good.

"No. Not yet, but I got word from Jessica's fertility doctors that they're done with the egg retrieval. The mass has grown and there's concern about thickening in her uterine wall."

Tony cursed inwardly. It wasn't yet a month since they had first met with Jessica. The only way to properly stage her cancer was to do a biopsy laparoscopically so they could also check whether it spread.

"Is Jessica still here?" Tony asked.

"You're thinking of doing the biopsy today?"

"I am."

Madison crossed her arms. "You ready for the HIPEC?"

He groaned. He'd read all the stuff Madison had sent him. He was nervous about it, but he was ready to do it.

"If Jessica consented, then yes to HIPEC. If you are positive you can handle that, so can I."

She beamed. "We're going to have pathology hopping today."

"Indeed," he responded. "Shall we book it for today?"

Madison worried her bottom lip, which set him on edge a bit. "I'll get the medicines mixed. I'll be ready by the end of the day."

"Okay, I'll contact the fertility doctors and have them admit her. The last thing she needs is for it to start spreading to her other organs and making this whole retrieval a moot point. What about the paperwork for the clinical trials?"

"Already on your desk." She began to jog away, off to get the chemotherapy prepared.

Tony laughed to himself watching her scurry away. It seemed all the financial components and clinical trial details were squared away. There was no reason not to do it. With her by his side he had no doubt this would work. It would mean a longer time that Jessica would be under anesthesia, but if this gave her a chance to beat ovarian cancer, then it was something.

Tony got the operating room prepared and the staff all assigned. Jessica hadn't eaten anything to prepare for her retrieval, so they didn't have to wait a certain number of hours for her stomach to empty. Madison was already prepping her for the operation with all the preoperative antibiotics and fluids.

The other ovary, the nonviable one, was underdeveloped and it hadn't produced follicles during the retrieval procedure. Once Tony got in there, he was going to measure it under the care of the obstetrical team. If it had grown in size, then he would remove that too. He also planned to take a small biopsy of her uterus to make sure that the cancer hadn't spread.

He spent the rest of his morning reading to be prepared for the surgery. What he wanted to do was go and check on Miguel, but his godson was in good hands with Bertha and David. As much as Tony hated the idea of stepping back in his godson's life, Miguel was getting older and connecting with his soon-to-be stepdad more and more.

Tony would just be that fun uncle who came around sometimes. The prospect made him feel lonely. He'd come back to Boston because that was where he was from and he had Jordan, Bertha and Miguel waiting for him. Now Jordan was gone and soon Bertha and Miguel wouldn't need him as much.

Maybe Madison had the right idea. She didn't

have anyone holding her back or tying her down.
She had family back in Utah, but that didn't keep
her from pursuing her goals.

*What's keeping me here?*

Tony shook that thought away and headed to
the operating room when he was told that Jessica
was prepped and ready for the surgery.

He scrubbed in quickly and saw that Madison
was in there. She had the chemotherapy ready to
run through the perfusion machine as soon as he
was done removing Jessica's ovary. The porter
from the pathology team was waiting and they
were going to take the specimen to the lab right
away to determine if the mass on it was cancer.
Once that was confirmed, Tony would insert a
catheter and the chemo would be run through the
perfusion machine, which would heat the medicine, and they would start a wash of Jessica's abdomen.

When he entered the operating room he saw
that Dr. Crespo and a few others from the board
of directors were waiting in the gallery. A knot
formed in his stomach. They were being put on
display and an uneasiness settled over him at the
thought of doing this procedure in front of an audience—especially when he'd be doing it for the
very first time.

Part of him resented Madison for putting this
on his lap, but the other part was kind of excited

to try this procedure, to take the risk. And that was so unlike him.

His gaze locked with Madison's across the operating room as he took his place at the operating table. He glanced up at the colleagues in the gallery and nodded.

"Let's do this. This is Jessica Walters. Aged thirty-one. We're going to be doing a left laparoscopic ovary biopsy, as well as a uterine biopsy, to determine the presence of cancer. I will be making a small incision. If pathology determines the presence of cancer, I will remove the ovaries and any other diseased tissues. Once that is complete, I will be inserting a catheter for the hyperthermic intraperitoneal chemotherapy procedure with the assistance of Dr. Sullivan. Number four blade, please."

The scrub nurse handed him the scalpel and he made the necessary cuts. The abdomen was inflated with carbon dioxide. He dropped in the trocars to filter through the lights, cameras and laparoscope.

"Dim the lights, please," he stated over his shoulder.

The lights in the operating room were dimmed and he watched the video monitor. The ovary he was biopsying had a large mass, but it didn't look like a cyst. Measuring it, he could tell that it had increased in size since the last scan was done. He removed as much of the mass as he could and then biopsied some tissue from Jessica's uterus to see if it had spread, pulled it out and placed it in a specimen bag.

"Have pathology rush this, please," Tony stated to the porter who was in the room.

"Yes, Dr. Rodriguez." The porter quickly left.

Tony continued his examination and noticed the other ovary was indeed larger, which was not good. If the diagnosis came back as cancer, he would remove the rest of the diseased ovary, her fallopian tubes and the other ovary.

He just hoped the biopsy of the uterus was clean.

It felt like time was ticking by as he waited, but he knew that he was priority and pathology was working quickly.

The pathologist entered the operating room.

"Dr. Hilt?" Tony asked.

"Cancer in the ovary. It hasn't spread to the other tissue samples. Once you remove the ovaries and fallopian tubes, I can stage it, but since it hasn't spread to the lymph nodes or the uterus, I'm pretty confident it's an early stage."

"Thank you, Dr. Hilt." Tony glanced over at Madison and she nodded, but he could see the look of disappointment in her eyes. She might have been excited by the prospect of using HIPEC, but that didn't mean she wanted to hear her patient had cancer.

Neither did he.

His mind briefly wandered to Miguel. What if he had cancer? What if one day soon Dr. Hilt came in and told him that Miguel's labs were not good?

*Don't think like that.*

He had to put that out of his mind so that he could focus on the task at hand. Dr. Hilt remained in the operating room to take the ovaries and the fallopian tubes so he could do a frozen section and determine the stage of the cancer.

The biopsy of the mass had shown lesions and that was enough to have Tony remove the ovaries and other affected tissues. While he was in there, he checked other organs. Once he was done, he removed the laparoscope, camera and lights. The other incisions were closed and he fed a catheter into one of the trocars and out another one that remained, securing it. It would be a constant cycle through the machine.

Madison came to stand beside him. "I'm Dr. Madison Sullivan and I will be administering a dose of bevacizumab, carboplatin and paclitaxel which has been heated and will run through the perfusion machine to wash Ms. Walters's peritoneal cavity and hopefully kill any other cellular growth of cancer. This wash will take approximately ninety minutes. Once it is done, Dr. Rodriguez will close up and we'll be monitoring Ms. Walters's progress in the PACU. Please turn the perfusion machine on."

One of the nurses turned on the machine.

Tony could hear the whir and watched as the medicine moved through the catheter into Jessica. It would be a long time, standing here and waiting for the infusion to run its course, but they had already stood around while the pathologists ran their tests. They could wait for the chemotherapy wash to do its work.

Madison was now standing on the other side of the table, watching the machine. Their gazes met again and he smiled at her from behind the mask. She couldn't see the gesture, but he knew she understood when her own eyes crinkled. Madison was smiling back at him and it made his heart sing.

He had been scared about risking his heart again on her and he still was, but right now, sharing this moment where they were working together as an unstoppable team, he couldn't understand why he had pushed her away for so long.

Tony moved beside her and leaned over. "This is terrible timing, I get that."

"What is?" she asked, in a hushed undertone.

"Would you be my date to the silent auction?"

There were a few little twitters of laughter.

Madison's shoulders shook. "Poor timing, but yes. I suppose so."

There were a few more chuckles in the operating room.

"Great."

He knew the procedure was serious but he was sure patients could still feel emotions while they were under, and he wanted positivity in this place. What better way to get that than make a complete fool of himself and ask Madison out on a date?

"Well," she remarked. "So much for keeping it all secret."

# CHAPTER THIRTEEN

"How do I look?" Tony asked, spinning around in his tux.

Miguel frowned. "Weird."

Tony frowned. "How so?"

Miguel shrugged. "I don't know. You're too fancy."

"He looks good," Bertha chided.

"Why are you dressed up, Uncle Tony?" Miguel asked.

"The big hospital fundraiser is tonight. I'm auctioning off a romantic weekend at my place in Martha's Vineyard. I have to wear a tuxedo."

Not that he particularly liked wearing a tux. He was way more comfortable in his scrubs. He also loathed the schmoozing aspect of it all.

If he wasn't offering up an item in the auction, he wouldn't go. But then again he did ask Madison to be his date.

"Well?" he asked again.

Miguel shrugged and went back to the game on

his tablet. Bertha stood up and straightened his tie, tsking under her breath as she did.

"Tell me, Bertha…how bad?" he asked.

"You look good. Are you cleaning up nice for a certain doctor?" She winked and nudged him.

Tony rolled his eyes. "Maybe. Plus the board of directors will be there and it's a black-tie event."

Bertha snorted. "So romantic."

"What?" he asked.

"You can say it's for her. Weren't you two a thing before?"

"A long time ago," he answered gruffly. "And we are again."

"See, that's nice. A second chance."

Although, it wouldn't be much of a date. Madison was running the silent auction and she would be announcing the winners at the end of the night. She would be too busy to even look at him. Tony knew for a fact she was at the table with most of the wealthiest benefactors. He'd bought a plate at one of the other table before he asked her to be his date and before they got back together. A night of socializing wasn't his idea of a good time, but at least he'd be showing his support for her.

Usually, he'd purchase a plate but never show up. Work was more important. He could spend his night dictating or checking post-op patients.

*You have residents for that.*

Dr. Frank Crespo had mentioned to him that

several members of the board hoped he'd be there. It was a big old sign to Tony meaning he should go. Frank said that a lot of well-to-do financial backers and board members were impressed by the successful ovarian HIPEC surgery that he and Madison had completed on Jessica Walters. The fact that Madison had found Jessica through one of the funded free clinics was also a bonus. He'd been proud to stand there with Madison in the operating room. He could make nice to benefactors with her for just one night, as long as he got to take her home with him.

Bertha was chuckling to herself. "She's cute."

He hadn't gotten to speak much with Madison after Jessica's six-hour surgery. He had been absolutely exhausted. Once he made sure that Jessica was stable and recorded his operative notes, he went back to his place and crashed hard. Madison had kept him updated when Jessica came out of anesthesia, and she was doing as well as could be expected, but she was struggling with some pain and side effects from the wash.

When Tony had returned the next morning to check on Jessica, he found Madison curled up on a cot in her lab. A bunch of her research was lying on her desk, and he realized she had spent the night there.

He had woken her up and sent her home.

It wouldn't look good if the doctor in charge of

the fundraising gala was yawning and slugging back coffee the entire night.

Now, he was here for Miguel and Bertha's opinion on his designer tuxedo, which hhe bought a couple of years ago but hardly ever wore. He was glad it still fit him well.

"You should claim your happiness," Bertha said, running her hands down his lapels. "Jordan liked Madison and I do too."

"I know. Jordan lectured me about that," Tony grumbled.

Miguel wrinkled his nose. "Gross. Uncle Tony in love. It's bad enough you and David are always smooching."

"I thought you liked David?" Tony asked, chuckling as Bertha crossed her arms and raised an eyebrow.

"I do. He's awesome, but I don't need to see the smooching. Gross."

Tony and Bertha laughed.

Bertha sat back down in the chair by Miguel's bedside. "I'm waiting on the results of Miguel's tests," she sighed.

"Me too. I'm sure we'll hear soon. Take it as no news is good news." Tony straightened his tie. He was trying not to think about it. He didn't even want to entertain the notion that Miguel had leukemia.

Bertha cocked an eyebrow. "You forget. I've been here before. Waiting."

"I know," he replied. "Try not to worry."

But it was hard not to. When he looked at Miguel all he saw was Jordan and how he couldn't save his best friend's life.

There was a fast click of heels coming up the hallway. He turned just as Madison came swishing into the room, decked out in a tight-fighting, gray sparkly dress and with her makeup done. Her blond hair framed her face in big wavy curls. He had to do a double take to make sure that it was really Madison. He was so used to seeing her in scrubs or business suits, her hair always pulled back tight. Now it hung down just past her slender shoulders, like a golden waterfall that he wanted to push aside so he could press kisses to her neck.

She blinked a couple of times as her gaze traveled the length of him. "You look great, Tony."

"As do you," he said, clearing his throat. He couldn't tear his eyes from her. She was stunning. And she was his.

*For now.*

It suited her, but then he liked her in whatever she wore. It was all just a fancy dressing for the woman he cherished underneath.

Then he noticed the paper in her hand and his pulse began to race.

"Results?" he asked, pulling out his phone because he hadn't gotten a notification.

"Yes!" She handed him the paper to save him from logging into his GHH email. His hands were shaking, trying to hold back all the emotions that were threatening to spill out of him as he scanned the results.

He beamed with happiness and took a deep breath. "You're the oncologist, Madison. You tell them."

"You're sure?" Madison asked.

"Yes. You ordered the tests. You're Miguel's doctor."

Bertha was sitting on the edge of her seat. Madison turned to her.

"Not cancer," Madison exclaimed.

Bertha covered her mouth and strangled back a cry of happiness. Miguel was so happy, he had set down his tablet.

"What is it then?" Miguel asked.

"Thrombocytopenia, or rather immune thrombocytopenia caused from a mono infection. We also suspect you may have an autoimmune disease, so we're going to refer you to a geneticist and immunologist. The thrombocytopenia and mono can be cleared up with antibiotics and steroids. I'm going to discharge you in the morning. Does that sound like a plan?" Madison asked.

Bertha sobbed. "I would hug you both, but I don't want to wrinkle your nice outfits."

"Oh, you can hug me. I don't care," Madison said. Bertha flew into Madison's arms. Tony hugged Miguel as he bounced up and down.

Tony was thrilled with this news.

Not cancer.

Immune thrombocytopenia and mono was still serious, but mono could be cleared up and IT could be managed.

"I can't wait to go home!" Miguel said excitedly.

"I know, buddy." Tony rubbed Miguel's head. "It's great."

"Well, I have to go as I have to start the auction," Madison announced. "But I couldn't leave without giving you the results."

"I'm so glad you did," Bertha responded, wiping a tear from her eye. "Thank you."

"Yes. I better go as well. I'll come by tomorrow before you leave," Tony stated. He turned to Madison. "Shall we go?"

Madison nodded, her gray eyes twinkling. "I thought you'd never ask."

Tony held out his arm and she slipped hers under his. It was nice to escort her to the auction especially after it felt like a huge weight was lifted off his shoulders.

Miguel didn't have cancer like his father.

He wasn't in danger and Madison was on his

arm. It was time to celebrate. Tonight was going to be a good night.

He was sure of it.

Tony couldn't tear his eyes off her all night. Every time she looked over at his table, she could see his dark brown eyes locked on to her and she didn't mind in the least.

It made her weak in the knees. It made her heart race.

And damn if he didn't look good in his tailored tux. It had been so impulsive of him to ask her out in the operating room. They had both agreed to keep their romance secret, but she'd loved that moment.

Everyone else in the OR had too. She had several young interns gushing about how romantic it was. And they weren't wrong. It was so out of the ordinary for him.

Every time their gazes met, she could feel the warmth, the flush of heat creep up her neck. A curl of desire was fluttering deep in her belly. There were people talking all around her, but she couldn't hear a word that was being said. All she could think about was Tony and how she wanted to tear that tux off his body.

She was so glad the results came in tonight before the gala and she was so relieved that Miguel did not have cancer.

For a moment when she'd seen Tony there with

Bertha and Miguel, she'd been a bit envious. He was real around them. He had family and friends to support him here.

She had no one and that was her fault because she never settled. There was no time to do that when you were out fighting a silent killer every day.

She was honored to deliver the news and share that happiness with them. She'd forgotten, until that moment, what it meant to belong and to be surrounded by people who cared about you.

It had a been a good couple of days. The HIPEC surgery was a complete success and pathology had gotten back to her today determining that Jessica's cancer was a stage zero with the removal of ovaries. With the wash of chemotherapy, she would be pleased to let Jessica know she could ring the bell next week.

She was also able to fully discharge Gracie on Monday and now Miguel tomorrow. Miguel wouldn't be ringing the bell like Jessica or Gracie's mom would on her behalf, but that was more than okay. Thrombocytopenia and mono could be cured or at least managed, which was far better than cancer.

"Dr. Sullivan?"

She glanced up to see one of the wealthy benefactors looking in her direction from across the table.

"Mr. Morrison, sorry I was bit lost in thought. Thinking about some patients," she replied.

There was a subtle twitter of laughter at the table.

*Oh, doctors, lost in their own world.*

That was fine. She'd rather be in her lab or with Tony. This sucking up to people with money wasn't her idea of a good time. It was just all part of the job.

"It's okay, Dr. Sullivan. I was just saying how impressed we were with the gala you helped put together and the HIPEC surgery you and Dr. Rodriguez preformed yesterday. I understand from Dr. Crespo that it was a first for GHH," Mr. Morrison stated.

Dr. Crespo had a wide grin on his face and was nodding vehemently.

Madison swallowed the lump in her throat. "I will not disparage my predecessors, as HIPEC can be tricky. It's a long operation and it all depends on the health of the patient. We were fortunate to be able to perform it with our patient yesterday. I'm also thankful GHH has the amazing facilities to do so."

*There. That should make them happy.*

"And that patient came from one of our free clinics," Dr. Crespo piped up.

There was a mumble of excitement and nods.

"She did, and I worked to get her on a couple

of clinical trials, not only for her cancer, but fertility," Madison confirmed.

"Excellent. Well, I can't wait for you to announce the winners of the silent auction. I'm sure I've won that weekend at Dr. Rodriguez's Martha's Vineyard house," Mr. Morrison said.

Madison glanced at the clock. "I think it's almost time to do just that. Excuse me, ladies and gentlemen."

She got up from the table and made her way to the private room with Dr. Crespo and a couple of other volunteers who were going to hold up cards with photographs on them. She had someone who was going to collect the checks from the winning bids.

After the auction was over there would be some dancing and cocktails, but really after the auction part was over, she was off the hook and she planned to take the complimentary hotel room she was given, order some room service and have her way with Tony for the rest of the night.

The butterflies in her stomach did a little flip as she thought of him and her in that king-size bed together. It was definitely better than the floor.

She made her way to the little stage in the banquet hall and turned on the microphone.

"Good evening, everyone," she said brightly. "I'm Dr. Sullivan and I want to thank you all for being here to support the GHH's free clinic initiative."

There was a round of applause.

"Now that we've had our delicious dinner and the auction has been closed, we're going to announce our lucky winners. We have some great items that were donated by fellow staff members and generous benefactors. So let's get started!"

As she gazed out into the crowd, her gaze latched on to Tony, sitting a couple of tables away. There were a few younger women at his table and for a moment she had a brief flicker of jealously course through her because she saw the way they were looking at him.

They wanted him.

Not that she was shocked, but she was a little green eyed. Then she saw that he wasn't even paying attention to them. His eyes were locked on her. Warmth spread through her as her body trembled, and she could feel the heated blush creeping into her cheeks.

Images of Martha's Vineyard and their frantic night on the floor of his living room flashed through her mind.

*Get it together. Auction. Remember?*

She tore her gaze from him and focused on the list of silent auction items. It was tedious going through each bid and congratulating winners. Her face hurt from smiling all night. Finally, they were at the end. Soon this would all be over. Tony's place was the last on the auction block and it had the most bids.

"The final item of the night is the one we've all been waiting for. A summer weekend at a glorious three-bedroom farmhouse-style home outside of Oak Bluffs, Martha's Vineyard. The house overlooks Nantucket Sound. It was generously donated by Dr. Tony Rodriguez."

There was applause and Tony stood hesitantly to nod his head quickly before sitting down. He was embarrassed about being called out.

"I got to tour the house myself and took pictures for the auction. Dr. Rodriguez's family originally built it and he just recently repurchased it. A weekend like this, in a private home, doesn't come up very often. It's a century home on the exclusive Martha's Vineyard. You're a short walk from a glorious white sand beach, or you have a heated saltwater swimming pool and hot tub at your disposal. Dr. Rodriguez also kindly offered a round-trip ferry crossing, and a romantic gift basket containing champagne and charcuterie for two. This was definitely our most popular item tonight. And the winner of this glorious weekend is Mr. Chad Morrison, with a generous winning bid of ten thousand dollars."

There were some gasps and a huge round of applause. Even Tony looked shocked. Mr. Morrison climbed the stairs of the stage and she shook his hand, giving him a quick peck on the cheek. Dr. Crespo shook his hand.

"Could Dr. Rodriguez could come up here?" Mr. Morrison asked. "I'd like a picture with him,"

"Of course." Madison waved. "Dr. Rodriguez, a picture, please?"

Tony nodded and climbed the stage. They all huddled together and Mr. Morrison handed the check over to Dr. Crespo, posing for the camera. Tony sneaked in behind Madison. She could feel the heat of his body against her bare shoulders. Then his hand brushed gently over the small of her back, just like it used to do when they were residents.

A secret touch.

That curl of desire was now a full-blown inferno raging through her. Her body was reacting intensely to that simple touch, her nipples hardening under her dress, her blood heating. But she plastered on her best fake grin as several photos were taken.

After the photos were done, Mr. Morrison, Dr. Crespo and Tony walked off the stage. She could see Tony was deep in conversation with them. Her job as emcee was almost done and she could escape.

"Thank you for your generous donations for our free clinics. The gala tonight has raised seven hundred thousand dollars," she announced.

There were more cheers and applause.

"The bar is now open—again all money is going to the free clinic—and there will be some dancing. Thank you again and enjoy the rest of your evening." She set the microphone down and Dr. Crespo came up to say a few words.

As she came down the stage stairs Tony was waiting. Her heart hammered against her chest and he held out his hand, taking hers and helping her down the rest of the steps.

"Thanks," she whispered, her voice catching in her throat.

"I didn't want you to trip."

"I appreciate that." She was pretty sure her palms were sweating.

He didn't let go of her hand either, just held it, and she didn't pull away. A rush of adrenaline was running through her and all she could think about was him and her naked.

*Oh, my God. I need to chillax.*

"Dr. Sullivan and Dr. Rodriguez?"

Madison pulled her hand away quickly and turned around as Mr. Morrison came over to both of them with another man.

"This is Dr. LeBret. He's a colleague of mine from France," Mr. Morrison explained.

Madison's heart stuttered and she looked at the man. She knew exactly who he was. This was the physician she wanted to learn from, the man she wanted to be her mentor and someone she admired so much. She was trying to find all the words, but couldn't seem to.

"Pleasure." Dr. LeBret shook Tony's hand, but then took hers and kissed her knuckles.

"It's an honor to meet you, Dr. LeBret," Madison gushed.

"*Non*, the pleasure is all mine. I was visiting and Chad said I simply had to come and see some of GHH's work. I was there when the HIPEC was performed. Masterfully done, by both of you."

"Thank you, Dr. LeBret," Tony said stiffly.

*He was there?*

Madison's head was spinning. "I'm so glad you got to see it."

"I expect some great things from you both. Good evening." Dr. LeBret walked away with Mr. Morrison to greet some other people.

Madison grasped Tony's arm. "Can you believe that?"

"Your nails are digging into my flesh," Tony teased.

"Sorry. He's kind of an idol of mine. I've been following his research since my Bachelor of Science days."

Tony chuckled. "You told me. I had no idea he was in the gallery. Maybe he'll offer you a job…?"

There was a hint of reproach in Tony's voice and her stomach sank.

"I'm years off. I was told I need to publish more."

"Well, it's apparent he's watching."

"Not just me. The both of us," she offered.

"There's no point in watching me. I'm not leaving," he said quietly.

The little bit of excitement she was feeling fizzled away at Tony's admittance. Yeah, he wasn't leaving. He'd made that clear. Her plans were unchanged too: she would move on to Paris to continue her research if she got the chance. Tony was rooted in Boston and she wasn't.

The string quartet started up and couples were gliding onto the dance floor.

"Would you like to dance?" Tony asked.

"Okay," she responded.

She didn't really want to, but there were benefactors and colleagues watching, and she had to put on a good show, a brave face.

While inside her, a battle raged between the career she'd always dreamed of and the man she was once again falling in love with. The man she'd never stopped loving.

Tony was very well aware of who Dr. LeBret was. Everyone knew Dr. Mathieu LeBret was at the forefront of cancer research and a Nobel winner. If you were a cancer doctor and didn't know him, then you were living under a rock.

He was quite shocked to learn that not only was Mr. Morrison a friend of Dr. LeBret but also that Mathieu had been at the HIPEC surgery on Jessica. He'd been watching them, which caused Tony a little bit of uneasiness.

Madison thought she had to publish more before she'd get offered a job in France, but Tony had a sinking feeling that that offer was going to come sooner rather than later. Honestly, when he saw the gallery full of other doctors that Dr. Crespo knew, he was sure that someone in that crowd would put in a word about it. What he hadn't known was that the Dr. LeBret was in that gallery as well.

*I'm going to lose her again.*

That's all he could think about as they swayed slowly on the dance floor. She was in his arms right now, but he felt like it was fleeting and soon she'd fly away. Just like before.

It was a selfish thought and he knew that. This was always her dream and he wouldn't hold her back. So Tony just tried to focus on her in his arms—on her body pressed close to his, on the coconut summery scent that he loved to get wrapped up in. He gently ran his fingers over the exposed skin of her back.

She was so beautiful. He hadn't been able to take his eyes off her all night and he didn't want to now.

As they danced, he realized something had shifted between them. She seemed unhappy.

"Are you all right?" he asked.

"Fine," she responded, mustering a smile.

"You're not."

"Just tired. It was a lot."

"I understand. You ran it well."

She nodded. "To be honest, you didn't seem too excited about Dr. LeBret."

"Oh, I am. It's just…"

"Just what?" she asked.

He wanted to tell her he was falling in love with her, that he never had stopped loving her because no one held a candle to her. Only, he couldn't say those things out loud. She had a dream and he wouldn't give her a reason to stay behind.

He wouldn't keep her here because he wanted her to stay with him. Just like she shouldn't expect him to follow her. With her in his arms it was hard to think of the end, but with Dr. LeBret now aware of Madison's accomplishments it was difficult not to focus on the likelihood that Madison would have a job offer sooner rather than later.

This could very well be the last time he held her.

It saddened him, but he wanted good memories if the end was coming. If there was no future for them, then he only wanted her to look back on this moment with happiness rather than regret.

"We make a good team," he said. "A powerhouse."

Her eyes twinkled and she smirked. "I never thought I'd hear you say that."

"Honestly, I never thought I would. Can you imagine if Dr. Pammi saw us now?" he teased.

Madison giggled. "She'd have a stroke. I'm sure."

Tony chuckled. "Indeed."

"We do make a good team. I'm so pleased about Miguel's results."

He nodded. "Me too."

Tony spun her around and then pulled her close against him. His pulse was thundering between his ears and he could feel her trembling in his arms.

"Tony," she whispered.

"Yes?"

"I'm so tired of mingling."

Heat unfurled in his belly. "What're you suggesting?"

"Well, I've wanted to rip that tuxedo off you the moment I saw it. What I'm saying is I have a complimentary room upstairs."

The dance ended. There was a pink flush in her cheeks. He was so in love with her and it pained him to think that this might all end soon, but there was nothing to be done. Nothing had changed.

He held out his hand and she grinned, taking it and pulling him off the dance floor and out of the banquet hall. They jogged to the elevators and Madison swiped her keycard.

The elevator door opened and they stepped in. She pushed the button for the top floor, the doors closed and the elevator began to rise.

Madison pushed him against the back mirrored

wall and kissed him. She claimed his mouth fervently and his body hardened under her touch. Her tongue pressed against his lips as the kiss deepened. He burned for her. He wanted to claim her again, like some primeval urge was overtaking him, and he wished there was nothing between them.

Tony crowded her against the opposite wall and began to hike up the layers of fabric of her dress until he found her skin, running his hands over her thighs, touching her and making her moan and grind against his hand.

"Oh, God," she gasped breathlessly against his neck, clinging to him. She wrapped a leg around his hips and he ground his erection against her, letting her know how much he wanted her.

It was taking all he had in him not press the emergency stop button and take her right there.

Tony nibbled her neck, cursing the longest elevator ride of his life.

When it came to a stop, they reluctantly pulled apart. Madison adjusted her dress and they got off, walking quickly down the hall to her suite.

She unlocked the door with a swipe of her keycard and then grabbed him by the lapels, pulling him into the darkened room, the door slowly shutting behind him.

Her arms wrapped around his neck as she drew him closer. A tingle of anticipation ran through him as he touched her in the dark. There were so many things he wanted to say, but couldn't right now. He just wanted to savor this moment.

He kissed her again, at first light and feathery, lingering in the sweet taste of her. He cupped her face, deepening the kiss again, and undid the clasp at the neck of her gown before trailing his fingers down her bare back to the second clasp and undoing the small zipper. She slid her arms out of the sheer part of the dress and he tugged it down over her hips where it pooled at her feet.

The thin sliver of streetlight cast shadows, but it allowed him to catch a glimpse of her. She hadn't worn a bra, just a lace thong. The dancing of the minimal light and darkness played across her skin and he ran his hand over the curve of her hip.

"So beautiful," he murmured, kissing her neck and shoulders. He ran his hand down her back, reveling in the silkiness of her skin.

Madison turned around and he cupped her breasts, dragging his thumbs over her nipples. She let out a small mewl of pleasure that sent a bolt of heated desire straight to his groin. She began to undress him, peeling off his jacket. Her fingers moved quickly over the small buttons of his shirt, thrusting it aside to run her hands over his chest.

Her simple touch fired his senses all the more. When her hands slipped below the waist of his trousers, he almost lost control as she stroked him and touched him.

"Madison," he groaned softly.

"I know. I want you too." She kissed him again. "I'm so ready for you."

They finished undressing and she pulled him down, spreading her legs so he could rest against her. His length pressed against her soft, wet core. She was arching her hips, making it hard for him not to thrust into her and take her like he desperately wanted.

He pinned her wrists over her head.

"Be good," he teased as he trailed his kisses over her body until he kissed her intimately, dragging his tongue achingly slow over her slit.

She cried out, her hands gripping his head as he held her hips down, controlling her movements and taking his time tasting her.

"Tony, please," she begged.

He chuckled huskily and moved over her. His arms were braced on either side of her head as their gazes locked. He kissed her and she clung to him as he thrust into her, finally claiming her. Except she wasn't his. Not as much as he wanted, but all he could focus on was the pleasure as he moved inside her.

Slowly.

He was in no rush, holding the only woman he ever wanted close as he made love to her. She wrapped her legs around his waist and he quickened his pace, each movement firing his blood and making him want to forget how scared he was to even contemplate being with her again.

To forget his broken heart.

Madison came, crying out, her nails digging into his back, and he soon followed, giving in to the feelings he was trying to hold back and collapsing beside her.

She curled up against him and he held her. He didn't want this moment to end, but what future did they truly have together? Boston was his home.

*Why?* a little voice asked.

What was he waiting here for? His father to come home?

No.

He wasn't sure.

"Should I go?" he asked as he held her. "You look so tired."

"No. Stay," she whispered, touching his face.

He kissed her wrist and then her lips, pulling her close. He might not have forever, but he had this moment. He had tonight and every night until she left.

# CHAPTER FOURTEEN

*Three days later*

A BELL SOUNDED out across the atrium, signifying the end of a patient's treatment. Madison stood next to Tony, smiling proudly and clapping her hands. Even though the patient herself was too young to pull the bell, she was cradled in her mother's arms, her eyes open and looking highly confused. Her mother was crying and laughing as she yanked the pull cord with all her might.

Gracie tried to reach for the shiny bell, but then startled a bit as it rang out. Her mother comforted her and rocked her back and forth.

"Congratulations," Madison said, before turning to Gracie. "I'm going to miss you. Even though you have no idea who I am."

Tony snickered and shook Gracie's dad's hand.

"We're here if you need us," Tony said.

"I sincerely hope you don't," Madison added. "But I'll see you in a month for a checkup and then we'll space them out from there."

"Thank you both so much." Gracie's mom handed her daughter over to her husband, then stepped forward and shook their hands.

"Best of luck," Tony remarked.

This was the best part of the job as far as Madison was concerned. Her mother had never gotten to ring the bell and she got so emotional when she was able to celebrate that moment with her patients. Today it was Gracie and in a few days Jessica could ring that bell with all her heart.

Madison walked away slowly from the atrium, Tony by her side. Ever since they'd gotten back together it had been wonderful. It was like old times, but better. Now, she felt more like a partner to him. They were a team and yeah, they did work well together. They hadn't made any promises, and there was no need for long-term promises. She had no doubt they had time to figure it all out. She was planning on being in Boston for the next couple of years, at minimum.

Her plans hadn't changed, so while she was here, the two of them could figure out what to do and what their next move would be when the time came. For now, she was just going to relish this time together. She was hopeful he would come with her when she moved on, but she wasn't sure.

"You're very happy today," Tony remarked as they took the long way through the gardens. "I thought you had a bunch of grant proposals to write. I wouldn't be that upbeat if I had to do that."

She leaned into him, giving him a little shove with her shoulders. "I do, but I like when the patients ring the bell. I was just thinking of my mom and how she didn't get to do that."

Tony's arm slipped around her. "I understand."

They stopped for a moment and he sneaked a quick kiss.

"What're you doing, Dr. Rodriguez? We said we wouldn't do that here."

He grinned, his brown eyes sparkling. "I can't help it. Besides, everyone knows. Still, it's kind of illicit to make out with you at work."

"Well, I can't argue with that."

"No. You can't." He leaned in and stole another kiss. She loved it, but they hadn't really decided on the next step.

Madison wasn't sure what the future held; their paths were so different professionally. There was part of her that wanted to talk about it, hash it all out, but there was another part of her, a naughty side to her brain, that just wanted to enjoy the ride while it lasted.

"Paging Dr. Rodriguez and Dr. Sullivan to meeting room three. Dr. Rodriguez and Dr. Sullivan to meeting room three."

She cocked an eyebrow. "Meeting?"

Tony shrugged. "No idea."

"I guess we better find out."

They left the privacy of the atrium and headed to the meeting rooms. Meeting room three was one of the larger ones. Madison could see through the etched glass there were other people present already. She glanced back and Tony and he just shrugged again.

Madison knocked and heard a muffled "come in" from Dr. Crespo. She stepped in the room, followed by Tony, to see a few members of the board of directors sitting around the table, Mr. Morrison included. And then her gaze landed on Dr. Mathieu LeBret. His hands were folded neatly in front of him.

"Shut the door, Dr. Rodriguez," Dr. Crespo said.

Tony nodded and closed the door.

"Have a seat." Dr. Crespo motioned.

Tony pulled out a chair for Madison and then took the seat next to her.

"Dr. LeBret, you're the one who wanted to speak to them," Dr. Crespo said. "The floor is yours."

A faint smile hovered on Dr. LeBret's thin mouth. "*Merci*, Dr. Crespo. I've asked you both specifically, because I'm impressed by your teamwork. It's not often I see such a balanced yin and yang team of surgeon and oncologist. It was like watching a duet."

Madison glanced quickly at Tony. Her pulse had started racing and her stomach was in knots.

*Oh, my God.* Was this it? Was this the moment she'd been dreaming of?

"I've read what you've both accomplished over the years and that HIPEC was impressive. I know your old teacher Dr. Pammi well. Dr. Rodriguez, you're a skilled surgeon that everyone seeks out."

"I'm flattered," Tony stated. "I'm not the best…"

"No. I am," Dr. LeBret teased. "But I do recognize talent."

"Th-thank you," Tony stammered.

Dr. LeBret smiled. "Dr. Sullivan, you are a brilliant oncologist and you're willing to take risks on new treatments. You have proven yourself. I want you both working with me, before I retire."

"I…" she trailed off, at a loss for words.

It was everything she ever wanted and more because Tony was offered a position too.

Except Tony might not think that this was an amazing chance and she had the distinct inkling he could say no. How could she leave him behind?

She thought she'd have more time with him. This was happening faster than she expected.

If Tony did say yes, it would be amazing, but if he said no she'd have to leave him again, which was hard to contemplate.

Dr. LeBret looked at them both expectantly. "Well?"

"I'm at a loss for words," she managed to finally say, finding her voice.

"Think about it, but this is a once-in-a-lifetime

opportunity. I wouldn't pass it up if I were you. I've already told the press that I'm here and retiring after I train you both," Dr. LeBret said.

"You've painted us into a bit of a corner," Tony snapped.

Dr. LeBret shrugged. "You two are the best. You'll make the right decision."

Tony glanced at her and she could tell by his stormy expression that he was not pleased with Dr. LeBret just assuming he would take the job offer.

Dr. LeBret and the other board members stood.

"The world is watching, Doctors." Dr. LeBret left the boardroom with Mr. Morrison, Dr. Crespo and the others trailing out. The message was clear. Dr. LeBret and the board weren't going to take no for an answer.

It was the opportunity of a lifetime.

Silence descended between them. The tension was absolutely palpable.

"Well," Madison said, letting out a huff. "I don't even know where to begin."

Tony snorted. "Same. It's quite the offer, but he's kind of egotistical."

"What?" she asked. "He's a Nobel laureate."

"So?" Tony shrugged.

*"So?"* she repeated, stunned.

He scrubbed a hand over his face. "I don't know. This is complicated. I don't even know what to think."

This was Madison's dream, but she knew it wasn't Tony's. She couldn't turn it down. Why couldn't he go too? It would make everything so much easier. There was a part of her that didn't want to leave him behind, but if he didn't want to go she would have no choice and it was tearing her to pieces. She worried her bottom lip and he was watching her.

"What're you thinking?" he asked.

"I want to go. You know I do. It was always the endgame," she said, trying to keep her voice from breaking and holding her emotions in check, just like she always did. "What about you?"

"I have a job. A good steady job here. Leaving is a risk—it's giving up so much."

She sighed. "Good doctors take risks. It's how we improve."

"Not all risks are worth improvement. Sometimes reliability and staying in one place to build a reputation is just as good."

"Is this about me following my dreams by moving around?" she asked, choking back the tears. "I don't regret any of my choices."

Tony frowned and didn't look at her, which gave her the answer that she needed. Nothing was going to change. He was staying here.

"Running from place to place won't bring you happiness," he stated roughly.

"I'm not running. I'm pursuing my dream. Why won't you join me and take this chance?"

"Why won't you remain here and finish out your contract?"

"I don't think there will be an argument about my contract from the board of directors. It's a feather in the hospital's cap for us to be offered this honor."

"And it's so much better moving from one job to the next and never settling down. Always looking for the next good thing. How can anyone rely on that? You're running from something, Madison. You always have been."

"You have so many walls," she said quietly. "And you've never let me in."

"You have your own walls too. You put on a brave face, but you're pushing me away just as much as I'm pushing you away."

"How? I'm telling you that you should come to Paris—with me."

Tony's lips pursed in a firm line. "It's only about your career. That's all it's ever been."

"What do you mean by that?" she asked, angry now.

"I never knew how you felt. Ever. How can I take a chance with someone who is always moving on to the next big thing? Someone who always holds their emotions in check?"

"I loved you," she said as she choked back a sob. Tears were running down her face. "I love you."

The words came tumbling out before she could

stop them. Yes, he was right: she locked her emotions away. She'd learned to do that so she could function and take care of her father. She had given up so much to keep her father alive in those dark years.

Emotions held you back and left you open to pain.

Keeping everything locked up tight had allowed her to pursue her dreams and get to this point. Except now, it didn't feel so much like an accomplishment. Her plans were still the same in spite of her declarations, just as he apparently planned to stay in Boston. How much of herself did she have to give up to be with him?

She thought things were different, but they weren't. How could she trust him with her heart? She didn't want that pain again; the heartache wasn't worth it. She didn't want to retreat into herself like her father had done.

She'd been pushed aside back then too. With no one to lean on, no one she could rely on, she had to be strong for herself. What pained her was she thought she could rely on Tony, but she was fooling herself.

She knew better.

Madison blinked back a few tears. She held her breath waiting for him to say something. Anything. Only he didn't respond to her and it stung.

"How can we be together when we're clearly on different paths?" he asked stiffly.

"You mean because I want to go with Dr. Le-Bret and you're staying here?"

He nodded. "Boston is my home."

"Why? You have no ties here."

"I have Miguel. I made a promise to Jordan."

"Bertha is moving on with David," she said softly. "Miguel is well taken care of. So the question is, why do you want to push me away? Why are you so scared of taking a chance?"

Tony scrubbed a hand over his face. He was still in shock that she'd admitted she loved him. There was never a moment in the past when she had told him that before. He didn't know how to really answer that.

He wanted to go with her. In theory it was a good idea, but his mind kept going back to his father. He wanted to tell her that he loved her too, that he'd always loved her. But at the back of his mind he wondered if Madison confessing her love was just a ruse to get him to agree to go to Paris. His father would always manipulate and gaslight his mother. Then Tony would have to go in and pick up the pieces of her life and shattered heart. Could he really follow Madison around the world?

What if her declaration was doing the same, using how he felt to go against his instincts, to go against the grain of what he'd always done, which was always the safe thing?

There was no one to help him when his heart was broken.

Bertha had told him to seek out his own happiness.

He didn't know what to do.

*She said she loved me.*

He was so confused. He didn't know which way he was going. Why couldn't she stay here? It would be easier here.

*Would it?*

Tony sighed. Could he really take this risk?

Their gazes locked. Her gray eyes were filled with tears. Madison may chase after the next big thing, but she was steadfast and sure. She was educated and made good decisions. She owned up to her mistakes and never shirked her duties. She'd been right about the tandem SCT and the HIPEC. And maybe she was right about Dr. LeBret, who was willing to take a chance on them.

Tony swallowed the lump in his throat. "I love you."

A tear slipped out of the corner of her eye and she brushed it away. "Pardon?"

"I love you."

And he did. He'd always been in love with her. He just wasn't sure he could trust her and he wasn't sure he could follow her halfway across the world.

"I'm not sure I trust—"

"What?" she asked. "Me?"

"I'm just not sure." Tony stood up and walked away from her. His heart was aching. He needed to clear his head, because it felt like all his carefully planted ties were being uprooted, and he was terrified at the prospect.

He wandered the halls trying to figure out what to do. He knew Dr. LeBret had told the whole world about the job offer. It should be so easy to make the decisions, but he was so scared. He went to his office and just buried his head in his hands.

There was a ding and he glanced at his phone to see the offer from Dr. LeBret's hospital pop up. It was very generous, but could he give up everything here for that?

"Knock-knock!"

Tony glanced up to see Dr. Crespo standing in his doorway.

He groaned. "Frank, I'm so tired."

"I know. I'm sure you're mulling over that decision. Although, I think it's a pretty much done deal."

"How do you mean?" Tony asked.

"Mathieu announced it to the world. His hospital is doing many amazing things!"

"I know he's well respected, brilliant and I'm sure he's at the forefront of it all, but I haven't made a decision yet. It's not a done deal."

Dr. Crespo raised his eyebrows. "What's keeping you here?"

"Oh, thanks a lot, Frank," Tony chided.

Dr. Crespo shook his head. "That's not what I meant. Of course I'd rather have my head of oncology stay, but if I was your age and in your position I would jump at the chance to learn from Dr. LeBret. Besides, you'll be back and GHH will only benefit from you and Dr. Sullivan having studied in Paris. It would be such an amazing thing."

"Thanks, Frank."

He did have a point, but it wasn't helping him any and he was annoyed that Dr. Mathieu LeBret just assumed he was going to take him up on the offer.

Dr. Crespo clapped him on the back. "Try and rest."

Tony watched him scurry away, no doubt to speak to the press and gush to the benefactors about how he and Madison were stars. He could no longer just sit in his office. He was feeling a bit caged in. He wandered into the atrium and stood there, under the tree he had planted in Jordan's honor and at the bell Jordan never got to ring.

*What is keeping you here?*

Frank's question was playing over in his mind. Condos and property could be rented. Bertha and Miguel were moving on. He had no family here.

All he had was Madison, so what was holding him back?

He glanced up at Jordan's tree and he thought about Miguel and his close call. Madison had stood by him through that whole thing. She had put him first in that moment. His father had never done that for his mother, or for him.

"I wish you were here, Jordan," Tony murmured.

He needed to talk through all these conflicting emotions. Yeah, maybe it would be easier if Madison stayed here in Boston, but it would only be easier for him in the long run. She wasn't like his father and he was foolish to think that.

Madison had had to be independent to survive since her mother died. She only had herself to rely on. If she didn't really love him she would just go to Paris, but she wanted him there, with her. It wasn't manipulation. She wasn't like that.

He scrolled through his contacts and hit Bertha's name.

"Tony?" Bertha asked. "Is everything okay?"

"Just checking in," he said, taking a seat on a nearby bench. "I know it's late…"

"No, it's fine. Miguel's in bed."

"I actually want to talk to you."

"Oh?" Bertha asked.

Tony sighed. "I would usually talk to Jordan about this."

"Lay it on me."

Tony sucked in a deep breath. "I promised Jordan I'd be there for Miguel, but I've been offered a job overseas."

"I heard about that on the news," she said. "It's amazing. A huge congratulations. So what's stopping you? It's with Madison, right?"

"Yes."

"I told you to seek out your happiness."

"The thing is, I promised Jordan…"

"Tony, you've been amazing to us since Jordan died, but we're good. David is here and you need to live your own life now. Of course, I expect to be able to crash at your Paris pad whenever I want."

Tony chuckled. "Of course."

"Take a risk on something, Tony. You deserve a chance."

Tony steadied the emotions welling up inside him. "Thanks, Bertha."

"Anytime. We love you and you're always a member of our family."

"I love you all too."

"Bye."

Tony ended the call and took a deep breath. It was like a huge burden was off his shoulders. His dad never kept promises, but Tony had kept his. Maybe for too long—the only promise he broke was to himself and his heart by pushing Madison away. Bertha was right: they could always come home to Boston.

The job was for two years of studying and research. It was worth the risk.

And it was worth the risk to take on Madison, because he loved her and to move forward he had to learn to let go of the hurt and trust her with his heart.

Madison's stomach knotted when Tony walked away after she told him she loved him. He claimed she didn't open up, but it was hard to do that especially when she always had to take care of herself.

She'd spent a life swallowing back all her fears, her grief, her love, and instead just focused on her work. This was all to help others from living like she had, a life where a child had to become a parent to a father who mentally checked out. This offer was everything she wanted. Or so she thought. She never thought it would happen this soon.

All of her dreams were coming true, except it didn't feel like that much of a fairy tale, because Tony wouldn't go with her. Part of her wanted to turn the offer down, but it was hard to do that. This was her goal. The research she'd conduct at Dr. LeBret's hospital would be priceless. This was what she'd been striving for, for so long. She'd be able to really focus on her work with the CRISPR-

Cas9 gene and explore other research proposals she had in the works.

It was only for two years; maybe Tony would wait for her?

*You can't expect that.*

It stung. She was fighting back tears. Just when they were back together, she was going to have to leave, but she'd spent most of her formative years being strong for her dad. She was strong for her patients and other colleagues.

She had to make her dreams come true. She was pushing Tony away again, but expecting him to wait for her wasn't fair. And she was scared about entering into a long-term relationship with him. The idea that she could lose him again was too overwhelming.

Losing anyone she cared about was difficult, which was why she kept moving and didn't make connections. As much as he pushed her away, she did the same to him. What if she stayed here? Would it be so bad? She'd have Tony.

Her heart ached.

*Tony doesn't trust me though.*

And she understood it was hard for him to trust in someone after his childhood, but it was hard for her to stay for someone who didn't have faith in her.

She wandered down to the atrium because she had heard that was where he was. Sure enough

Tony was sitting on a bench staring up at the night sky through the glass dome.

"Hi," she said tentatively.

"Hi," he responded. "Come sit with me."

She nodded and sat next to him, his arm resting on the back of the bench and then on her shoulders, and she laid her head against his shoulder.

"I'm sorry I walked away. I just needed to clear my head."

"It's okay. I understand."

"I needed some time."

Her stomach wrenched, because she had no doubt that he was going to tell her that he wasn't going to Paris. It hurt so much, but she couldn't let it hold her back. She sat up straight. "I'm going. I need to go."

"I know," he said softly.

"I love you, Tony. I don't want to go without you but…since my mother died this has been a dream of mine."

"I know. I remember."

"I love you. This is killing me to leave you, but I can't let this opportunity slip by. I'm not running from you or pushing you away." She swallowed, and her throat felt tight. "I don't know how you feel about long distance…"

"What?" he asked.

"What do mean *what*?" she retorted, her voice shaking.

"Why are you talking about long-distance relationships?"

"Because I love you."

He cocked an eyebrow. "I'm aware, but here's the thing—I do love you."

She shook her head. "You're a butthole."

He grinned and pulled her close and she pushed back at him.

"Madison, I don't want a long-distance relationship."

She crossed her arms. "So you want me to just stay here?"

"No."

She gave him a side-eye. "Then what, Tony? I'm not like your father."

"I'm very well aware of that."

"Then what?" she asked, exasperated.

"I trust you," he said.

Her heart skipped a beat. "You…you trust me?"

He nodded. "I do."

She brushed a stray tear away. "So what do we do? I mean, if you want to stay…"

Tony grabbed her hand. "I'm going with you."

Her heart stuttered and she widened her eyes in disbelief.

*Did he just say what I think he said?*

She turned. "What?"

"What do you mean *what*?" he teased.

Madison slugged him in the arm. "Butthole, remember?"

Tony laughed and then stood up, tilting her chin back. "I love you and I know that we bicker a lot, butt heads, but I trust you. No, you're not like my father and I had to be a rock for my mother so long that I kind of became rooted, like a statue. Even though Boston is home, it's not saying we can never come back. I'm going to take a risk that's actually a sure thing and risk it on a rebel doctor—you. I'm going to Paris."

Madison stomach breathing, her pulse thundering in her ears. "You are?"

He nodded. "It's your dream. I won't hold you back. You don't need to be the adult for me to protect me, like you protected your father. I'm not leaving. I'm here and I love you. I want to marry you and I should've asked you that ten years ago."

A sob caught in her throat. "Marry?"

*As in family?*

Tony nodded and got down on one knee. "I don't have a ring, but I want to marry you and go to Paris with you. It's time to take a risk and follow my heart."

"I love you too," she whispered.

"So is that a yes?"

She nodded and he stood up, pulling her close. For so long she'd been alone and she thought it was for the best, thought that it was easier. But this was so much better. With Tony she really did have all her dreams.

She could finally have a family and another reason to keep fighting.

Fighting for forever.

# EPILOGUE

*Two years later*

MADISON WATCHED A storm rolling in off Nantucket Sound as she walked along the beach. She'd left Tony in their house on Martha's Vineyard, still sleeping off the jet lag. They had spent two glorious years in Paris, but it was nice to be back.

After quickly getting married at city hall in Boston, they'd packed up and headed to Paris. It was amazing and everything she hoped for. Her first award-winning paper was being published, and Tony was now one of the lead experts on the NIR surgeries, as well as HIPEC. Under Dr. Le-Bret's tutelage they learned so much and had everything they needed at their disposal, but it was time to go back home.

Their visa had run out and GHH was excited to welcome back the award-winning superstar oncology team. The expert surgeon and the rebel doctor.

Though Madison didn't quite understand what

she'd done to earn that label, Tony always got a kick out of telling people his wife was a rebel. All she could do was just roll her eyes and go with the flow.

"There you are," Tony said, walking up the beach.

"I like watching the storm," she remarked. "I've missed this place."

"Well, before I fell asleep and before you woke up, I made up the guest rooms for your father and stepmom."

Madison glanced at her watch. "Their plane should land soon."

"You told them how they have to make their ferry connection, right?" Tony asked.

Madison nodded. "I did."

"I put that fugly seagull in his room."

Madison giggled. "You're hoping he'll break it, aren't you? Because he had that long conversation with you about how he's a butterfingers. You think he's kidding, but he's not."

Tony shrugged. "Hey, it survived two years of being in a vacation rental while we were gone. It'll survive your dad. Maybe he'll like it and take it with him as a memento."

Madison laughed. "You know if it gets damaged or disappears we have to get another one."

Tony frowned. "Why?"

"It's a thing. Didn't you read reviews from

people who stayed here? They all love my fugly seagull."

Tony groaned. "Maybe I'll just move it, so we don't get another one."

Madison grinned. "Maybe I'll get more of them and have a little family of them."

"No."

She loved teasing him. She was looking forward to this weekend. Her dad and stepmother were arriving from Utah and they were having a bit of a family reunion. It had been so long since she last saw him and her dad was so excited to meet Tony face-to-face. There had been many video calls, but her dad insisted he was going to walk her down an aisle of some sort since he couldn't be at their quick city hall wedding before they went off to France.

She'd had a heart-to-heart with her father about those years where he checked out. She forgave him and she was just glad that she wasn't running away from the sadness. She and Tony would fly out to Utah at the end of the summer so she could show him where she grew up.

"Miguel, Bertha and David are coming out tomorrow for the barbecue?" Madison asked absently.

Tony nodded. "I can't wait to see Miguel. Bertha says he's almost six foot."

"They grow fast. Speaking of which…" She trailed off. "There's something I need to tell you."

He frowned. "You got a job offer. Again?"

She snorted. "Always, but I want to return to my lab at GHH. I promised Dr. Crespo and signed the deal."

"Then what?" Tony asked.

"Well, our little duo might have to be put on hiatus in six months. You might need a new partner or lead oncologist."

Tony looked puzzled and then his eyes widened. "What?"

She nodded. "Yep. I'm about twelve weeks along. I just thought it was all that French food. Are you happy?"

"Am I happy?" Tony asked as he pulled her into his arms and kissed the top of her head. "I'm thrilled."

"There's more," she teased.

His body stiffened. "What?"

"Remember that hospital appointment in Paris before we left? I was violently ill and we thought I had a gallstone. Again, all the French food."

"Yes," he said cautiously.

"I had an ultrasound. That's how I found out I was pregnant, and that's how I know it's twins. Scans confirmed it. Surprise!" She ended with a shout, throwing up her hands.

Tony's eyes widened and then he laughed. "So a quartet?"

"Yes. We might need a bigger condo in Boston."

"I think so." He touched her face gently. "I love you, Madison. So much. I was a fool all those years ago."

"You mean a butthole, don't you?" She winked.

He chuckled again and kissed her gently. "Right. That."

"I love you too. Always."

And then they walked back to their home before the storm got closer, thinking about their future and their happily-ever-after.

\* \* \* \* \*

# A NOTE TO ALL READERS

From October releases Mills & Boon will be making some changes to the series formats and pricing.

## What will be different about the series books?

In response to recent reader feedback, we are increasing the size of our paperbacks to bigger books with better quality paper, making for a better reading experience.

## What will be the new price of Mills & Boon?

Over the past four years we have seen significant increases in the cost of producing our books. As a result, in order to continue to provide customers with a quality reading experience, the price of our books will increase to RRP $10.99 for Modern singles and RRP $19.99 for 2-in-1s from Medical, Intrigue, Romantic Suspense, Historical and Western.

For futher information regarding format changes and pricing, please visit our website millsandboon.com.au.

# MEDICAL

## Life and love in the world of modern medicine.

## Available Next Month

All titles available in Larger Print

**Festive Fling With The Surgeon**  Karin Baine
**A Mistletoe Marriage Reunion**  Louisa Heaton

........................................................................................

**Forbidden Fiji Nights With Her Rival**  JC Harroway
**The Rebel Doctor's Secret Child**  Deanne Anders

........................................................................................

**City Vet, Country Temptaion**  Alison Roberts
**Fake Dating The Vet**  Juliette Hyland